Running the Whale's Back

Running the Whale's Back

Stories of Faith and Doubt from Atlantic Canada

Edited by Andrew Atkinson and Mark Harris

GOOSE LANE

Edited by Bethany Gibson
Cover and page design by Chris Tompkins
Cover artwork by David Blackwood
Sick Captain Returning (detail), 1973
etching, aquatint and drypoint on wove paper
Image: 81 x 50.5 cm (31 7/8 x 19 7/8 in.)
Overall: 92.2 x 61.9 cm (36 5/16 x 24 3/8 in.)
Art Gallery of Ontario
Gift of David and Anita Blackwood, Port Hope, Ontario, 1999
99/933
Canadian, born 1941

Printed in Canada.
10 9 8 7 6 5 4 3 2 1

Library and Archives Canada Cataloguing in Publication.

Running the whale's back: stories of faith and doubt from Atlantic Canada / edited by Andrew Atkinson and Mark Harris.

Issued in print and electronic formats.
ISBN 978-0-86492-913-6 (bound). — ISBN 978-0-86492-782-8 (epub)

1. Short stories, Canadian (English) — Atlantic Provinces. 2. Faith —
Fiction. 3. Belief and doubt — Fiction. I. Atkinson, Andrew, editor of
compilation II. Harris, Mark, 1958-, editor of compilation

PS8329.5.A85R85 2013   C813'.01089715   C2013-903042-5   C2013-903043-3

Goose Lane Editions acknowledges the generous support of the Canada Council for the Arts, the Government of Canada through the Canada Book Fund (CBF), and the Government of New Brunswick through the Department of Tourism, Heritage, and Culture.

Goose Lane Editions
500 Beaverbrook Court, Suite 330
Fredericton, New Brunswick
CANADA E3B 5X4
www.gooselane.com

To Amanda, Gavin and Josie.

In memory of Stuart and Rita Macpherson and George Harris.
For Violet, with love.

Contents

Andrew Atkinson

Fish Stories or
Some Likeness Thereof

"Then why the hell do you believe in it?"

"In what?"

"I don't know, I don't know, I don't know," Denis said, shaking his head abruptly while Steven lit one cigarette off the other, and the room was stale with the smell of their heat and sweat. "In fish..."

— Richards, "We, Who Have Never Suffered"

More often than not, when Atlantic Canada comes up in conversation, the subject turns to fishing. I've been in countless conversations where the fisherman looms large, and yet, as a diasporic Atlantic Canadian, I've done more fishing in Ontario. The fish has been a tricky symbol for ages. You are never certain whether you are talking about the real, scaly and pungent variety, or whether you are listening to a fish story. And when you are listening to a fish story there are all sorts of footnotes and addenda about the gear, the quality of conversation, the nets, the cold shack the fisherman sat in, the rituals, the goof, the lures... but what you hear most is the remembrance of *desire*—the heart of the fisherman projected into the pumping flesh of the fish who jumped, shook the line and evaded the eager net of someone in the boat. The excitement and the imagination, the pathos and the pride, these dimensions shape the geography of the story, but the dynamo is the desire, natural or cultured, to hook that hidden fish and bring him into the boat.

Think back, way back, and if you're thinking long term, you're thinking crossword, you're thinking like a Dan Brown sleuth, chances are you'll find the Greek word for fish, *ichthys* (ΙΧΘΥΣ), lurking below the choppy surface of your consciousness. It's a symbol from an age of rhetorical thinking, where numerology, acronyms and secrecy were the order of the day. *Ichthys* was a hidden brand. If you saw it in a floor mosaic or scraped into stucco you knew you were in the presence of a hidden church. If you met a wanderer on the road and he drew an arc in the dirt, you might finish that off with a second arc, signalling your stealth allegiance to Jesus Christ, whose initials correspond to the first two letters of the acronym, followed by "Theos" (God), "Ypsilon" (Son), "Soter" (Saviour). This *fish* was also a teller of fish stories, where would-be disciples were filling their nets, only to be converted to the figurative task of fishing for men. Like the two fishes of the generous young boy, these fish symbols multiplied, gained power, influenced multiple lineages of literary culture and crossed the Atlantic—all to find their place on the back of a late-model sedan, growing legs, with the equally symbolic name of Darwin filling the belly.

Truth be told, Atlantic Canada is home to these two varieties of fish stories: the folk narrative and the broader network of religious figuration. Often the two are braided together, as they are in Alistair MacLeod's mesmerizing story, "Vision," which has, for years, frustrated students of Canadian literature with its complex, twisting narratives. The story moves from Cape Breton lobster boats to the mythical coast of Scotland, full of second sight and Celtic Christianity, to the raucous Legion Hall, all without ever arriving at a conclusive point. The effect draws us into the twirling story arcs of love, violence, shame, passion, blindness and revelation. A central symbol in the story is the young mackerel, who like the Apostle Paul, has scales on his eyes. Readers of "Vision," like the apostle and the mackerel, gradually have their scales removed.

Near the end of "Vision," MacLeod takes us to the back of a lobster boat to gaze on the sublime trapline emerging from the water. Anyone who has been lobster fishing will know that the line is as deadly as a cobra—it can catch a seasoned lobsterman by the foot and drag him helplessly to the ocean floor—but also life giving and strong, drawing treasure from the depths. MacLeod connects these oppositional tensions to long-standing antagonisms in Maritime communities, and, more specifically, the mysterious power of narrative to relieve these tensions: "And when the wet ropes of the lobster traps came out of the sea, we would pick out a single strand and then try and identify it some few feet farther on. It was difficult to do because of the twisting and turning of the different strands within the rope. Difficult ever to be certain in our judgements or to fully see or understand. Difficult then to see and understand the twisted strands within the rope. And forever difficult to see and understand the tangled twisted strands of love." As MacLeod intimates, the strands of these twisting stories are stretched taut with the weight of love, of desire; and often that desire is for something sensual and immanent — as with the mysterious grandfather of the narrative — but as the rewards of the immanent wane, the desire arises for resolution, fullness, for a sense of permanence. Over the long view, the difficulties of MacLeod's rival fishing families seem trivial. They both share a mystical origin in a promiscuous ancestor and they both have similar material needs, yet their awareness of their layers of feuds awakens them to a different way of being. This fresh perception heals an age-old rift in the community, and in doing so lifts the gaze, so focused on the finite economy of the fisheries, toward the seemingly infinite horizon of love.

MacLeod, like many of the short story writers who have followed him, interweaves spirituality and religious symbolism with a tough-headed view of the world. His spiritual musings are communicated through men with calloused hands and big hearts. These men are not so different from the characters that populate David Adams Richards's "Miramichi." After you read Richards's early story "We, Who Have Never Suffered," you'll feel like you have grit in your mouth — it's that real. Like a creation of Flannery O'Connor, his character, Hilda, leans against the door of her slummy apartment in downtown Newcastle with her grotesque "fifty-year-old paunch hanging out of her slacks." After just a glimpse of Hilda, Steven "feel[s] heaviness coming over him," and yet amid the sight of her "withering double chin" he hears the "almost silent gonging of the Presbyterian church in the quiet afternoon." Richards's characters are always doing something around churches — whether, like Sydney Henderson (*Mercy Among the Children*), they are pushing a nemesis off the roof, or like Nevin White (*For Those Who Hunt the Wounded Down*), a recovering alcoholic, they are pitching in to build the steeple of the local Pentecostal sanctuary. His fictions require a place where transcendent peace has at least a physical presence. Yet, as the first stories of this collection remind us, this desire for peace, for fullness, is as often unsatisfied as is the fisherman telling a fish story—the transcendent desire is vouchsafed by our perpetual loss.

This is to say that Atlantic Canadian writers do not hastily overlook the thorny bits of human experience, of living in small communities, nor do they portray religion as a quick fix for existential ills. Many of the stories you'll read in this collection explore the precarious terrain between faith and doubt. Samuel Martin, a protégé of Richards's, holds the "title track" of this collection—"Running the Whale's Back." The image is not one that refers to Jonah's "fish," which has so captivated Michael Crummey in recent years (*Galore*), but rather the risky act of jumping between ice pans during the spring breakup. The image is one where nature, that perennial theme of Canadian literature, is not enough. In the spring breakup, the solid ice cracks and moves with a degree of unpredictability that we associate with the stock market and the medieval wheel of fortune. To use a pithy truism, the only constant is change. The fool who chooses to run the whale's back must supplement the erratic movements of the ice floe with gumption, faith, quick judgement and a great deal of hope. And who hasn't been in this fool's shoes?

Larry, from Kathleen Winter's "French Doors," is a version of a character type that so fascinated the Russian writer Fyodor Dostoyevsky—the holy fool. In a sense, the "holy fool" is the figure who "goes long" on Pascal's wager—he trades the wisdom of this world for the foolishness of God—the great fish story. Tired of living at home in a Newfoundland outport, Larry builds a shack from scraps around town. He traces the edge of the townsfolk's respectability, save one admirer, Marianne, who narrates the story. Unlike the local women, Marianne is drawn to masculine-coded activities. Like so many women of her generation, she rejects traditional domesticity from the gut level and charts some other settlement. The oddball, Larry, is a fellow traveller down this path of unconventional gender roles. His quirky, slightly discomforting habits are, from Marianne's eccentric perspective, a sign of wisdom. She seems almost to be quoting from 1 Corinthians when she ruminates on the subject: "Wisdom, thought Marianne. Wisdom kept eluding her. Foolishness seemed like wisdom to her in so many places." In a scene reminiscent of the climax of Patrick Kavanagh's Newfoundland epic *Gaff Topsails*, Larry and Marianne sit in his truck, drinking beer and gazing on the water. The moon is high and it lights the dark water, broken by cresting waves, with a gold path—a typical nightly scene, except this time Larry notices that the moonbeam is enchanted. The average viewer might not see it, but "sparks" are "flying off the main path" riding up and down the moonlight like some vision in a song by Van Morrison (who could be playing on the radio). We might call this night "fantabulous," the sort of night that stirs the coals of myth and ignites the sparks of mystery. Who knows what lurks below the surface or lies beyond the dark side of the moon?

Many of the stories feature characters that the British might call "queer fish." In Jessica Grant's Kafkaesque short story "My Husband's Jump," the protagonist is married to an Olympic ski jumper who, during an internationally broadcasted competition, launches off his intimidating ramp and just keeps going "Up. Over the crowd, slicing the sky." His absurd ascent is interrogated by those left in the mundane world where nothing *exceptional* happens, or so they believe. For Sister Perpetua, the event disproves the existence of God,

> When he failed to land, she said, they felt something
> yanked from them, something sucked from the room, from
> the world entire—something irrevocably lost.
>   God?

Yet for Grant's protagonist the missing husband has the opposite effect: "I was sure of God's existence now, as sure as if he were tied up in my backyard." We sense, while reading Grant, that this unlikely event symbolizes the absurdity of religious experience, or for the more intellectually inclined, the stubborn persistence of *transcendence* in our otherwise secular, empirical, grounded forms of thought.

While Grant's protagonist celebrates absurdity, Lynn Coady's characters are anxious about being thrown into a world of oddballs. Coady tightens the screws of her fictional apparatus, twist by torturous twist, until the awkwardness of her protagonist's situation is unbearable—whether Bridget Murphy (*Strange Heaven*), Larry Campbell (*Mean Boy*), Murdeena ("Jesus Christ, Murdeena") or the uncommon second-person "you" of "Batter My Heart"—the reader always sides with the rational protagonist against the crazy yet powerful forces of her family and community. Religion often ends up on both sides of the equation.

The title of her story, "Batter My Heart" is drawn from John Donne's "Holy Sonnet 14" in which the poet compares his interior resistance to God to a wall that he can't tear down. In Coady's story, "you" are taken into the walled fortress of a monastery, a sanctuary for monks and drunks (it functions as a detox centre); it's a location devoted to the sort of inner transformation that Donne seeks but can't attain. She situates us beside Donne "There you were in the monastery, once upon a time, a walking sin." What an odd situation to be in…who put "you" there in the first place? When you're not in the monastery you're watching your beat-down erratic father, who seems to be holding the town together with the long-lost sacred dew of his baptism, a bit of ear wax and a plethora of vulgarities. This father, just a regular man, seems yet to be endowed with divine power—capable of terrible faces and ferocious dressing-downs, he's also compassionate and kind. The last scene has him coaching Little League, because none of the other "[s]elfish whores" (his words not mine) wanted to do it. Frustrated with the ineptitude of the young boys, the arthritic father hobbles to the plate to show them how it's done: "[an] overweight, balding man clutching a child's tool in his large, pink hands. When he swings the bat, it makes a sound that frightens you and you look up from picking at your nails and see all the little round faces are turned upward in awe." What do we make of this Zeus-like monstrosity so loved, and yet in a certain way feared, by the protagonist—you? Is he not similar to the Catholic mass "you" resent, and yet unconsciously perpetuate, repeating the words by rote as though they must be said? As Donne has written, "Batter my heart, three person'd God…overthrow me, and bend / Your force to break, blow, burn, and make me new."

In the last story of the collection, Anne Copeland's "Rupture," the monastic setting is inverted. Like Copeland herself, Claire Richardson is a former nun who entered the monastic movement in pursuit of the ideal of Catholic femininity; midway on life's journey she finds herself caught in the aftershocks of Vatican II, and sees no hope in the strict practices of medieval discipline. Instead, she leaves her order, marries and has a family. Yet the monastic life remains with her. When asked to appear on a Canadian afternoon talk show to speak about the cloistered life, Claire can hardly refuse, even while she dreads the thought of airing her dirty laundry in front of a skeptical public. Questioning the discipline of celibacy, the fictional talk show host puts

Claire on the defensive: "How could you...It just isn't NATURAL to live without...sex. Is it?" On the airplane back to the Maritimes, Claire fantasizes her response, "Is it natural to live without God? Or without belief in something larger than oneself?" Where Grant and Kathleen Winter delight in the stigma of the "queer fish," Copeland seems less impressed; she identifies the uncomfortable social antagonisms that trace the divide between faith and skepticism, belief and agnosticism, religious traditions and the intolerant forces of contemporary conformity. Claire, probably like many readers of this anthology, finds herself caught in the gap between many of these positions.

Questions of faith, questions of doubt, of hope, depravity, dignity, death, respect, the stigma of religion, the enchantment of the land—these and many others are queries that live and move under the sacred canopy of Atlantic Canadian literature. With great ambition we set out to represent the depth of engagement that Atlantic authors embrace when writing about religion and spirituality. The short stories in *Running the Whale's Back* are just the tip of the iceberg. Many of the authors featured here, and other major Atlantic Canadian writers like Wayne Johnston, Patrick Kavanagh, Lisa Moore, George Elliott Clarke and Linden MacIntyre, take up similar questions in the novel form. So, while the offering we have for you should whet your appetite, there is something akin to a lobster smorgasbord available beyond the covers of this text. But between these covers, ah...there is something special for you here.

Michael Crummey

Miracles

For convenience sake, let's say this story begins on a clear night in October. The moon is full, it stands out against the darkness like a single Braille dot perforated on a black page. If you could reach your hand up to touch the sky, you would feel it raised beneath your skin like the improbable beginning of a letter, a word, another story. The air is cool, the leaves on all the trees have turned and started falling; they make an ambiguous rustle as you walk through their brittle brilliance, rich and melancholy all at once.

My brother and his wife are celebrating their tenth anniversary. I've been invited to join them for dinner, and after repeated attempts to shirk the obligation, I have relented. I don't enjoy the walk across town. I don't notice the moon, or the cool air except to pull my coat tight at the collar. I have a small package of fresh mussels under my arm—a surprise—my contribution to the evening meal. When I reach their house I stand at the front door for a moment, as if even now I might change my mind. It's been so long since I've visited that I feel compelled to knock and wait for permission to enter.

My younger brother answers the door and takes my coat; his wife, Jade, offers me a drink. We make stilted small talk about the weather, the state of things at the mine while Jade steams the mussels and then we sit at the table to eat. My brother stabs a mussel with his fork, eats it, reaches for another.

"Are you sure you should do that, Kim?" Jade asks him.

That's my brother's name, Kim. A peculiar name for a boy, and even more peculiar at the time he was born, in a small community in Newfoundland.

If I want to be honest, I'd have to say that's where our problems began, his name. And now that I think about it, maybe that's where I should have begun.

Mother had always warned us about the danger of putting convenience ahead of other things, like truth for instance, or thoroughness, which in her mind were almost synonymous. She was a strict Salvation Army woman, our mother, and though Father attended church only for baptisms, weddings and funerals, Mother marched into her uniform every Sunday. Morning and evening she took her black leather Bible and silver trumpet from a shelf in the back porch and headed off to the Salvation Army Hall without him.

She had a no-nonsense approach to her religion that some servants of the obvious would label "military," but might more properly be called rigorous. Practical. She was always raising money for an overseas mission, or an alcohol treatment program, or a Christmas soup kitchen. Mother was also a member of the infamous Salvation Army band that commandeered the busiest corner of Black Rock's Main Street every Saturday in December and honked out metallic renditions of Christmas carols for most of the afternoon.

She loved to sing old hymns as she worked around the house as well, "Onward, Christian Soldiers" being her favourite. It was a kind of battle cry against "domestic ungodliness." When she was called upon to break up a wrestling match between myself and Kim, twisting an ear on each head to keep us apart, you could sometimes hear her humming the refrain under her breath. One Sunday afternoon she brought out the trumpet and played it for fifteen minutes in the kitchen because Father had the unmitigated gall to sit down to a game of cards on the Seventh Day. He gave up on it finally, knowing Mother would go on till her lips fell off if he persisted.

But I was speaking about my brother's name. I was only a year old when Kim was born and it was a long time before I realized how strange a name it was and began asking questions. The story goes that in the third month of her second pregnancy my mother had a dream. And in the dream an angel of the Lord appeared unto her and announced she was going to give birth to a girl-child whose name was to be Kimberly. Mother put little stock in dreams and not much more in angels, and the anointed name was so ridiculous that she put the whole episode down to the pickled eggs she'd been eating by the dozen. But such a visitation was so alien to her tradition, so foreign and unexpected, that she was unable to dismiss it completely. Days before she delivered she had the dream a second time and Mother resolved to act in accordance with

what she saw as the Will of God.

"But he wasn't a girl," I pointed out.

"Yes, well," Mother said. "There was some kind of mix up I suppose."

Father expressed his misgivings about the name after the birth and even Mother was perplexed by this turn of events. Still, she decided to shorten the name from Kimberly to "Kim" and go ahead with the christening. My father, having voiced his objections, wouldn't stand in the way of what he called her "religious convictions."

As far as I know nothing came of it. No descending doves, no parted waters, no speaking in tongues. I was the one who attended church regularly with Mother, and kept her company outside the Imperial General Store on bitter winter evenings before Christmas with a bell and the Salvation Army donation bubble. I was the one who wanted my own uniform and black leather Bible, who joined the junior band and tried desperately to learn how to play something, descending inexorably from trumpet to tuba to bass drum to the lowly tambourine.

"Mother," I said to her during the walk home from church one Sunday morning, "did you ever have any dreams about me?"

She looked sideways in my direction. It was a hot August morning, there were lines of perspiration trickling from beneath the band of her officer's cap. I felt embarrassed to have asked, but plowed stubbornly ahead. "Before I was born, I mean," I clarified.

"Why yes, of course," she said. Her tone was cheerful but she looked uncertain, as if God was late with a sign she'd been promised. "Haven't I ever told you? Well," she said, "I had this dream three times before you were born. I was asleep in my bed and the angel of the Lord appeared unto me. It was so bright, Stuart, that it hurt my eyes. It was as if the room was on fire. And then the angel spoke without moving its mouth. This voice seemed to come from all around me, from the air. 'You are going to have a son' the voice said...."

"Didn't the angel say 'boy-child'?" I interrupted.

"Yes, you're quite right, now that I think about it, that was what the angel said. 'You are going to have a boy-child,' it said, 'and you shall name him Stuart.'"

"But I thought I was named after Poppy Ellsworth," I said suspiciously.

"Why yes," Mother said, hesitating a little. She took a tissue from her purse and mopped her brow. "That too," she said.

～✑

Our house on Pine Street was identical to the other Company houses in design, but the details reflected my parents: family pictures, sturdy furniture, basic colours, nothing garish or flashy or outrageous. They even managed to avoid the sparkled stucco craze that gripped the town during the early seventies, sticking resolutely to flat white ceilings. In many ways, Mother and Father were remarkably similar people: serious, stubborn, straightforward.

There was a lot of talk about Saving in that house. Father grew up during the Depression and never fully recovered from the experience. His next meal wasn't something he ever learned to take for granted. He was happiest sitting down with his blue bank book to go through each entry, adding and subtracting meticulously on a piece of scrap paper. The result was never in question, he just enjoyed the confirmation, the sense of security it gave him, however brief.

My mother *tch tched* over this obsession of his. "You can't take it with you, Father," she'd tell him. Mother was more concerned with saving souls than money. Though that's too strong a word, I think. "Soul" was too airy-fairy for Mother, not concrete enough, not at all practical. She preferred to use "person" or "individual"; to her mind they were more inclusive, they didn't oversimplify.

"Father," she might announce as she came through the front door after a Sunday service, "an individual was saved this morning!"

"Praise be," Father would say over the potatoes and carrots he was peeling for Sunday dinner, and he said it without a trace of irony. He was never fierce in his disbelief, or evangelical about it, he simply hadn't managed to settle anything to his own satisfaction.

Throughout our childhood and adolescence Kim and I fell on either side of that issue like opposite sides of a coin. Our parents never pressured us either way, but being young and being brothers, we weren't as kind to each other. He ridiculed my earnest fundamentalism. I badgered him to come out to church, to the youth group. These encounters usually ended in physical confrontations that Mother was forced to break up with our ears twisted in her fingers and a hymn barely audible on her breath.

By the age of fourteen I had become passionately interested in miracles. Having read through the entire Bible, and the Gospels twice, I was struck by the kinds of stories that were rarely mentioned at the Salvation Army Hall, or were glossed over briefly at best. Sermons and studies tended to focus on the Good Samaritan approach, the Boy Scoutish good-deed-a-day variety of religion. I was fascinated by the inexplicable, by the way Spirit transformed the physical, imbued it with properties it had lost or never possessed: the voice in the burning bush, the feeding of the five thousand, the healing of the blind and the cleansing of lepers. That spark lurked in the cells of all things like a dormant seed, a knot of latent potential.

This passion caused my mother some concern. She'd been brought up to think of miracles as a *Catholic thing*, a questionable devotion to pictures of the Madonna that wept real tears, and her own ambiguous experience with the "angel of the Lord" made her wary. She *tch tched* over it in the same resigned tone that she used for Father and his bank book.

It was Kim who was most offended by my obsession. His doubts about spiritual matters were confirmed in his grade seven science class where they were studying evolution. He began tracing caricatures of apes and tacking them to my door, leaving them on my desk, taping them to the bathroom mirror when I showered. *Stuart*, he scribbled across the top of each drawing, *the one that got left behind*.

I suppose I was an embarrassment to him. He was one of the best players on the local bantam hockey team. He pursued his burgeoning interest in girls with the same adolescent fervour I brought to my faith. He wanted an older brother he could look up to publicly, someone who could fight or smoked cigarettes behind the school. All I offered were lectures on "healing prayer" and "life after death" and inept tambourine lessons. It was Kim's popularity that protected me from the worst of the persecution I might have received from other kids and he probably resented that fact. Even if he had wanted to love me then, I made it impossible.

❧

One Saturday morning the summer I turned sixteen, I was pulled out of sleep by the Company siren. ASAMCo provided firefighting services for the community and everyone knew the sector codes — one blast meant fire on Company property; two was the north end, from Main Street across to the post office; three was our side of town, from Main Street to Pine; and four meant the townsite to the north of Company housing. As I scrambled downstairs in my underwear that morning the prospect of disaster set my body vibrating like a struck bell. I'd never heard anything like this before, the siren went on and on in the grey dawn light.

Mother was standing at the window in her housecoat. Father was already dressed and pulling on his work boots, tying the laces with methodical fierceness.

"What is it?" I asked.

Father didn't look up. Mother held her hand to her mouth as if she were about to cry. Kim came into the kitchen behind me, still half asleep. "What is it?" he said.

We hardly saw Father over the next three days. He'd come home at odd hours, sleep for an hour or two and then head back to the mine. No one in town slept much more than that. The rock had fallen in the Number 7 shaft of the old Lucky Strike mine and seven men were under.

The churches organized a constant prayer vigil, and there was an ecumenical service at the Roman Catholic church, the largest in Black Rock. I spent a lot of time in those three days on my knees. It was the first time I had a concern I felt was worthy of the grand gesture. I don't know what I wanted exactly. Proof I guess, a sign that God was acting in our lives in some tangible, quantifiable way. Something that Kim couldn't refute.

They made it through late on the third day, and six of the men were found alive. The seventh, Clay Keough, had been killed under the fall of stone. He was only a year away from retirement.

"Well," Mother said, "thank God the other six came out alive."

"Not much consolation to old Clay probably," Father said, and that's where they left it.

Kim had dismissed my requests for divine intervention from the start, and he taunted me with the dead man, held up the corpse the way some preachers hold up the Gospel, as if it were ultimate and indisputable truth. There were a thousand things I could have said to him, I could have talked about the unfathomable Will of God, I could have said something about faith and the lack of it. *Where wast thou*, I could have quoted, *when I laid the foundations of the earth?* But Clayton was dead for all that.

"It could've been Father down there," Kim shouted at me. The slight, almost pretty features of his face had the ruthless focus of a predator on the scent of blood. "They could both die tomorrow," he said.

⁓

Things seem completely inevitable in retrospect. Even though it took place two years later after countless ordinary events, after thousands of inconsequential moments, it seemed to me that the next piece of this story — the hardest part — was set in motion and followed inexorably from that time, from those arguments.

It was a clear night in October. I was supervising a youth group sleepover at the Army Hall, Kim was away at a weekend hockey tournament in Corner Brook. I'd managed to settle everyone into their sleeping bags with the usual combination of empty threats and pleading, and had just begun drifting off when the siren began wailing. One. Two. Three. "Stuart," one of the kids whispered in the darkness, "that's your side of town."

They tell me my parents died in their beds, of smoke inhalation, before the flames touched them. An investigation placed the blame on faulty wiring and speculated that the fire may have smouldered behind the wall for days before erupting into the living room. By the time I reached the house that night the entire quad was burning. A helpless audience of neighbours stood about in nightgowns and undershirts. The light of the fire gave the street an intense, subterranean glow that made it seem as if the event was taking place underground. As if the entire town had been swallowed by grief.

The next September Kim left for university in St. John's. I was hired on as a clerk at the Company office and eventually worked my way up to accountant, taking night courses at the public school. I lived alone in a Company apartment and kept to myself. I stopped attending church, and as much as possible in a town the size of Black Rock, I avoided the people I'd grown up with at the Salvation Army Hall. My days were devoted to the artless certainties of arithmetic, my evenings to the television's bland menu of black and white movies and hokey Hollywood biblical epics.

In St. John's, Kim fell in love with Jade, a Fine Arts student who had come to Newfoundland from New York to study after she'd read *Death on the Ice*. She thought it would bring her closer to a world where nature still reigned, like Job's God, both provident and pitiless. She was disappointed to find herself in a real city, a small one granted, but a city nonetheless, with cinemas, theatres, public transit. Her only real consolation, she claims, was meeting Kim.

At their wedding Kim wore a traditional tuxedo, while Jade was adorned in a paper gown hand-sewn from the love letters she and Kim had written one another in the previous two years. "I know he doesn't seem like my type," I overheard her explaining to a friend from New York. "If it hadn't been for his name, I wouldn't have looked at him twice."

After he completed his engineering degree, Kim moved back to Black Rock where he worked with a team of prospectors, searching for a new mineral strike that would save the local industry from collapse. He made periodic attempts to establish a relationship with me but I kept him at a distance. Kim had never meant his ape caricatures as prophecy, I'm sure, but there I sat in the grey television light night after night: sullen, hopeless, deficient in some significant way. The One That Got Left Behind.

"Are you sure you should do that, Kim?" Jade asked my brother.

I looked at her quickly, then turned to Kim. "Is there something wrong with the mussels?"

"No no," Kim said. "It's me."

"The last time he ate mussels," Jade explained, "he had an allergic reaction."

"Don't make it sound so dramatic. I got a tickle in my throat, that's all. And it's worth it. These are great Stuart." He stabbed another one with his fork, knowing I would have been uncomfortable if he didn't touch them at all.

"I don't think it would be a good idea to eat any more," Jade said. There was an abrasive note of warning in her voice, like grains of broken glass in the fibres of a carpet, and Kim held up his hands in mock-surrender. "All right," he managed as he chewed.

After the meal, we moved into the living room and sat with liqueurs. The conversation lurched uncomfortably as it had for most of the evening. Jade began presenting some of her latest sculptures and paintings and I tried to humour them both by paying attention.

"I'm trying to connect with something here," she said, holding a canvas upright on the floor. "Something at the core of things. I don't know if I've got it yet." There was a gnarled leafless tree against a background that might have been the barrens around Black Rock. The tree was in the approximate form of a cross. The piece was called *Salvation Landscape III*.

Kim cleared his throat loudly and sipped his liqueur. "That's one of my favourites," he said to Jade. "I think you've really hit something there."

I stared at him in surprise. "That sounds a bit too flakey to come from you," I said, a little unkindly.

Kim shrugged, as if the abuse wasn't out of order. "Who knows, maybe she'll make a religious man out of me yet." He cleared his throat again. "There's that tickle," he said.

Jade scowled at him. "You know better," she said and got up to start clearing dishes from the table. Both Kim and I moved to help her but she waved us back into our chairs. Kim smiled at me through his obvious discomfort. "She's as stubborn as Mother," he said.

We sat in almost complete silence then, except for the clatter of Jade stacking dishes and the frequent sound of Kim clearing his throat. And as I stared at his reddening face, at his helplessly watering eyes, my grey, abysmal life unexpectedly erupted. It came to me like a vision, I saw it happening this way: the muscles at the back of Kim's throat swelling so severely that his windpipe was blocked, his body going into shock, convulsions. My brother, who had been right about the world all along, dead on the floor of his living room, a glass of crème de menthe spilled on the carpet.

It was as if a fire smouldering in the walls of a home had finally surfaced. "Jade," I shouted, my voice constricted to an octave above its natural range. "Jade, come in here."

Kim waved at me in annoyance, as if he was trying to quiet a child. "I'm all right," he said. "I'll be fine."

This story ends with the dream I had the night my brother and his wife celebrated their tenth anniversary, the night my brother said he would be fine and it was so, a clear night in October. There was a full moon, it stood out against the darkness like a single Braille dot perforated on a black page. The leaves on all the trees had turned a brilliant red and were falling. All the way home I was shaking, pricked by this revelation, aware for the first time that what I wanted more than anything in the world was my brother to go on living. And to be there with him. Living.

I woke up in the old house on Pine Street. The rooms were full of light, luminous, as if the sun was out on all sides of the house at once. Downstairs I found Father in the kitchen, peeling a sinkful of potatoes and carrots for dinner. Sunday morning. I could hear the knife shearing the wet brown skins from the potatoes and the serene tick of the stove clock. I don't think I was there as myself, in this body. Father took no notice of me and I didn't try to speak. I felt transparent and dispersed, like the air. There was a loud tramping on the step, and Mother marched in through the front door in her uniform, holding the gleam of her silver trumpet.

"Father," she said triumphantly, "an individual was saved today!"

And my father looked up from the vegetables with a smile.

"Praise be," he said.

Sheldon Currie

The Accident

He could still remember the cards in his hand when the phone rang. The seven, three, queen and five of spades, the three of hearts turned up. Fifteen-two, fifteen-four, fifteen-six and pair of threes for eight and the flush for twelve.

Afterwards he told people that when Christie went to answer it, he sat there and knew the message was for him. He knew what it was. He looked at the four spades and thought, I hope he's not killed.

His friend Archie, on his right at the square dining-room table, was humming the Kyrie Eleison. Any other time, Christie, Archie's mother, when she came back would say, "Archie, for God's sake stop that mournful noise." But this time, Ian knew, she would not. Across the table Archie's father drummed his fingers on the table and said, "You fellahs better have good pegging cards if you don't want to be skunked." Another time Ian would have said, "You said it partner." But this time he stared at his spades.

There was no telephone in his own house and the ring always sounded to him like an explosion, and every time he heard it, he expected it would bring bad news. When he heard Christie's voice diminish, and say to the telephone, "Ian's here now, mumble, mumble, mumble," he thought, I knew it, I knew it when it rang.

"An accident in 25," Christie said. She put her hand on Ian's shoulder. He stared at his spades and waited. "Two men are killed and two men are hurt."

"My father is one of them?"

"Yes."

"Are they up?"

"Mrs. McLeod it was that called. She didn't know if they were up yet."

"Okay, I better go."

"You want me to drive you?" Archie said.

"No, I'll run home. My cousin is visiting. Johnny will take me out."

"Good luck," Christie said.

"Thanks" he said, and ran off in the dark.

There was a good chance his mother didn't know yet. Someone would have to call a neighbour. The neighbour would have to run over. They'd want to wait until they had definite news. He started to run faster. He was glad they didn't have a telephone. What a way to find out, especially if Johnny and Daisy were gone. If they were gone he'd have to get someone else to drive him. He slowed down to a walk. He didn't have far to go but it was pitch black. The road was rocky. He had been playing cards at his friends the MacNeils, who lived across the highway in the newest of the co-op housing groups. Once across the highway there were lights and the road was graded and he started running, but he was soon near his driveway, the first one, in the oldest of the co-op housing groups. He walked the short driveway slowly, so he wouldn't be huffing and puffing going into the house.

His mother stood at the stove when he opened the door. In one hand she held the lifter with the cover hooked onto it; in the other hand she held the poker, thrusting it into the burning coal.

"Well, you're back early," she said. "Want a cup of tea? I'm just about to put some on."

"You didn't hear the news?"

"News. What news? Oh my God. Your father."

"They called the MacNeils. I came right up."

"He's dead?"

"I don't think so."

"I think he's dead."

"There were four in it. Two are dead. But two are just hurt. I think Dad's just hurt."

"Oh God. I can't believe it."

"I better go and find out," he said. Johnny came out and offered to take him in his truck.

"Thanks," Ian said.

"Where'll we go?" Johnny asked. "The pit or the hospital?"

"The pit first. They mightn't have them up yet. And even so we don't know what hospital. If they were bad off they might just go to the closest."

Ian expected a big crowd milling around the pithead, but there was nobody. It started to drizzle. Johnny stopped the truck in the middle of the yard near the wash house. The lights on the poles seemed able to light up only themselves; the buildings were soft shadows and in the wet dark seemed larger than they were. The door opened, a miner, his lunch can under his arm, emerged through the light and disappeared into the dark around the corner. "We might as well go in there," Ian said.

Ian pulled open the door and stepped in. The room was steamy and crowded. A few men still in their pit clothes, a few in their street clothes. Most were naked, half of them black-faced with coal dust, half finished showering and pulling their street clothes down on the ropes and pulleys that kept them near the roof-beams while the men were in the pit. Ian wound his way through the crowd of men until he found a familiar face. "What happened, Frankie, where's Dad?"

"He's at St. Joseph's. They just left."

"We didn't pass them."

"They probably went the Sydney Road way. You must've come through Rabbit Town."

"Is he all right?"

"I don't know. He's hurt pretty bad. Likely he'll be all right. He was hunched down next to the machine. He got squeezed in the wedge but I think it saved him. Peter got killed."

"Peter?"

"Peter, your cousin. He just started workin' with your father."

"Oh, God."

"Roddie got killed."

"MacEachern?"

"Yeah. And Joe got hurt, don't know how bad. They took him off in the same truck with your father. They had the priest out for the other two. I heard him say St. Joseph's."

"Okay. I better get down there."

"Tell your father I'll be down."

Inside the hospital front door the receptionist told him, "Down them steps straight ahead, right at the bottom is the room." At the bottom step he saw the family doctor come out a doorway facing the stair.

"How is he?"

"Touch and go," he said, and fled down the hall. "So far so good," he said over his shoulder and went through a doorway.

Ian went in. There was nothing in it but his father on his back, knees up, and a bed with steel legs and big rubber wheels. He was just as they pulled him out. The right leg of his pants was ripped to the knee. A gash like a long mouth full of blood and coal dust ran from his knee to his ankle. The ankle looked like a bone sticking out of a roast. The right arm of his shirt was missing. The arm was black where it wasn't blue. His hands were on his belly, palms down, the tips of his fingers clutching his skin. His face was black where it wasn't red. His hair was full of blood.

"Hello, Dada," Ian said. His father raised his black middle fingers and his blue eyes.

"How bad is it?" His father beckoned him down with his black index finger. Ian put his ear close to his father's mouth. "The son of a whore got me by the throat," he said. "Say a prayer, eh."

"I will."

"Put your head up now. I can talk loud enough. I didn't think I could." The voice was strong but whispery and gurgly. Ian straightened up.

"Does your mother know?"

"Yes, but she doesn't know yet if you're hurt or dead."

"Tell her I'll be okay. I think I can beat the son of a whore."

"Okay, just a minute. Johnny's out there. He drove me down. I'll go tell him to go up and tell them. I'll stay here." He went to the door and found Johnny sitting on the steps.

"How is he?"

"Don't know. Hurt bad but he'll be okay I think. I'm gonna stay. Would you go and tell Mother? Tell her he's gonna be okay. He'll be in for a while, but he'll be okay."

Back in the room, Ian found his father unconscious. His eyes were closed but his mouth was open, the teeth clenched and the lips pulled back in a

grimace. There must be another way a person could make a living, Ian thought.
His father's eyes opened.

"You're back," he said.

"Yes."

"Was I out long?"

"No. Just a minute."

"Ian."

"Yeah."

"My feet are awful sore. Would you take off the boots?"

"Okay," Ian said and went to the foot of the bed and started to unlace the boots when he was startled by a harsh female voice.

"What are you doing?"

"Takin' off his boots."

"Who are you?"

"I'm Ian. His son."

"Oh, okay. Take out the laces. But don't move the feet. I see he's unconscious again." She was only a few years older than Ian but she talked as if she owned the hospital. "I'm Sister Magdalene of the Holy Eucharist," she said, and pulled a foot-long pair of scissors out of a holster at her hip and took a few snips at the air over her shoulder.

"What's wrong with him?"

"Nothing much," she said. "His back is broke. Four broken ribs. He might have a rib stickin' a lung. His head is split, his spinal cord might be injured. Broken ankle, twisted knee plus a million cuts and bruises. My guess is he'll live. But x-rays will tell the tale. Have you got the laces out?"

"One."

"Okay, do the other," she said and she took the scissors and cut all the buttons off the shirt, then snipped it across the chest. She opened his belt, cut open his fly, snipped the pants across, then down the legs, folded everything back, slashed both legs of his father's boxer shorts until finally everything but the shoes were in rags, hanging down from the sides of the bed and his father lay stark naked, his penis hard and sticking straight up in the air.

"See that," she said, "I told you he'd live. They're often like that after an accident. It's because they think they're going to Heaven. Did you finish the laces?"

Ian stared between his father's knees. He couldn't get his mouth going to say yes.

"Don't be embarrassed," she said. "I'm used to it. I used to be a whore before I entered the convent. I guess that's why they put me down here." She came to the end of the bed and went to work with the scissors on the shoes. "You go to the next room. Bring in the pan of water by the sink and start washing him. Once we get him clean we can cover him and up he goes. Go now, this kind of thing is easier if you keep busy and keep talking so you don't get mopey."

When they finished they put him, bed and all, covered with a sheet, on the elevator. "Sister Mary'll look after him now," she said to Ian, "won't you, Sister Mary?"

"Yes," Sister Mary said through the open elevator door. She smiled.

"They won't let me up there," Sister Magdalene of the Holy Eucharist said. "They're scared I'll say something dirty and disgrace the Order. Isn't that it, Sister Mary?"

"Yes," said Sister Mary. She smiled.

"How about you stay here and help me with the other one," she said to Ian. "You might as well while you wait. C'mon, his two legs are broke — he might be cranky."

The other one was Joe the Pig Two MacDonald. The name he inherited from his father, also Joe MacDonald, nicknamed to distinguish him from the dozen or so other Joseph MacDonalds, most of whom had somewhat weaker distinctions such as D.P., Joe D., ABCD and so on, and because he once pronounced to his buddies, during a tea break in the pit, one of the few general conclusions he had distilled from forty years of living, "You know," he said, "a man had a good pig, he wouldn't be in the need of a wife."

It turned out Joe the Pig Two was not cranky. He was sore, exhausted and astonished at his good luck, having once again escaped death. His mind shifted between sorrow when he thought of his two dead buddies and happiness when he thought of himself and Angus and their wives and all their kids.

"Watch them scissors, Maggie," he said to Sister Magdalene. "My wife'll be down to inspect and if she finds anything missing she'll be fit to be tied."

"Don't worry b'y, it's only your legs'll be shorter. The rest of you'll be all right."

"You don't mean that. My legs?"

"No, no, no. Just kiddin', they won't need to cut them off."

"How is Angus makin' out?"

"Gone for x-rays. I think he'll be good."

"Thank Christ. Them other two didn't have a fuckin' hope. Excuse me, Sister."

"It's okay."

"What happened anyway, Joe?" Ian asked.

"Whole goddamn roof came down on us. I heard 'er crack and jumped for the door. Got everything out but the last of my legs. Broke both, crushed a foot. Your father was hunched down by the machine. Saved him. Held up one side of the stone enough. He was crushed in there but it was enough room. Peter and Roddie were in deeper. Flattened like pancakes. Your father said that roof was no good before we started. Too late now."

"Now turn over on your belly," Sister Magdalene of the Holy Eucharist said and Joe the Pig Two turned over and she began to wash his back.

"Could I ask you a question, Sister?"

"Ask away."

"Well, I got two questions," he said. "One is, how much would you charge a week to do this every day? And the other is, would you make house calls?"

"You don't shut up," she said, "I'm goin' for the scissors again. Ian, would you go and change the water? I think it's makin' him worse."

The coffins at both funerals were closed. At Roddie the Log MacEachern's wake the children were all grown, the widow sedate and the wake calm, sombre and formal. It was Ian's first Protestant funeral, and once in the little front room where the mourners were gathered he discovered there was no kneeling-bench, and since the coffin was closed, he felt silly standing there looking at its brown curved top. So he knelt anyway, thinking that no one could object to a prayer, even a Catholic prayer. But with all the Protestant eyes arrayed around the room he couldn't bring himself to make the sign of the cross and finally in his confusion he didn't even pray; he held his hands together on his belt buckle and studied the curlicues on the burnished brass handles of the box.

Before getting to his feet he tried to figure out where he could go next. Most times he simply said a prayer and left unless it was a wake of a close relative. But this time he felt he was a representative of the family, for his father who was still in the hospital, for his mother who was still reeling and for his brothers and sister who would come too but who were younger than himself and still officially children. He noticed that the regular living-room furniture had been removed and replaced by kitchen chairs and card-table chairs arranged around the walls. The people in chairs were not looking at him at all, but quietly talking or looking at their hands, knees or feet. He spotted some empty spaces and walked over and sat. The widow, Mrs. MacEachern, came and sat beside him.

"Thank you for coming, Ian," she said.

"That's okay," he said. "I'm sorry it happened." It was what his mother told him to say.

She wore a black dress with a black belt and silver buckle, and black shoes and a small, black hat with a black veil hanging from it over her eyes. It was the first time he had seen a veil on a grown woman. Behind the veil her eyes were quiet and black as if concentrating intently on some unimportant distraction.

"I'm fine for now," she said. "How is your father?"

"Well, he's very sore, but they're saying he'll be okay."

"And Joseph, too, will recover?"

"Yes."

"He'll be better soon."

"Yes."

"How long will your father be in the hospital?"

"I don't know. At least a month, I guess."

"Does he get up?"

"No, not yet."

"How is your mother?"

"She hasn't gotten over it yet. She's still not sure he's going to get better."

"Poor thing," she said. "Well, at least in the end, she'll have him back."

"Yes, that's true."

"Have you been to Peter's wake?"

"No, I'm going after."

"I was over before," she said. "Poor Gloria is taking it awful hard."

"I heard that, but I haven't seen her yet."

"You can't talk to her."

"I heard she can't stop crying."

"She can't. She can't help it. She does stop sometimes, but the minute you start to talk to her, or she tries to talk to you, she starts to sob."

"They say she doesn't sleep," he said.

"She'll doze off. But she hasn't left the room to sleep or eat. She won't leave the room. She sits there and every now and again she gets up and goes over and puts her hand on the coffin. It's closed, you know, same as Roddie's. She goes back and sits. She just won't leave the room."

"Yes, I heard that."

"She's young enough," Mrs. MacEachern said. "She'll get over it. Next week she'll stop."

"Yes," Ian said. "She's young. She has two babies."

"Yes. Next week she'll stop," Mrs. MacEachern said. "And when she stops, then I'll start."

Ian felt he should say something reassuring, but he couldn't think of anything. He looked through the veil at her fearful eyes. "This week," she said, "I'm talking to people. I hope they don't mind."

"I'm sure no one minds," Ian said. "Everyone knows how hard it is."

"Yes. We're all used to it. We know how hard it is. I always see you going back and forth to school ever since you moved up Sydney Road. But this is the first chance I had to talk to you."

"That's right," Ian said. "I still don't know many people up this way."

"Do you know Roddie's nickname?"

"Yes."

"Do you know how he got it?"

"No. I never heard," Ian said, although he had. He wanted to hear her version.

"When the kids were little, we had a fire. We were in the company house then, up in Reserve Rows. I was right there when it happened, in the kitchen, having a cup of tea with my sister, Marie, but I don't know yet how it got started. The wall behind the stove broke into flames. It was hot, I guess. The middle of July. I was baking bread. Three of the kids were sick upstairs having a nap. The baby was in the front room. Marie ran for the fire department. This was just after they got their truck. I got all the kids out and the men came and put out the fire. The place was a mess. Water all over the kitchen. When the smoke cleared we cleaned it up and sat down to our tea again. The kids were all excited, the baby crying. It started again. They had to come again and put it out. This time they had to rip open the wall. This time we took the kids over to Marie's. We had our tea there. An hour later there's a knock at the door and who comes in but Roddie. 'Flora,' he said, 'what's goin' on? There's water all over the kitchen floor.' Well we laughed to kill ourselves. I forgot what shift he was on. I thought he was at work. He slept through the two fires. Never even knew they happened. But I thought afterwards, he could have been burned alive, and I wouldn't have known, thinking he was all the time at work. Of course when your father heard that, he said now that's what I call sleeping like a log. I felt guilty for years thinking I could have as good as killed him. Now he's dead anyway. He was an awful good man. Thank God it wasn't me that killed him. Come on out to the kitchen, Ian, and have a cup of tea and a bite. They called him the Log ever since, Roddie the Log MacEachern."

"Thanks," Ian said. "I might have a cup."

Fortified with tea and pieces of ham, Ian walked down the Sydney Road past the corner where it met Main Street to the rows of Company houses in the Lorway. He didn't know the house but he kept on until he saw the wreath beside the front door. He knew both Peter and Gloria. They were in the same grade. He walked with her the mile or so to school every day when they lived in Reserve Rows. Peter, who lived in Rabbit Town, walked down the tramcar tracks and joined them every day where the tracks and Main Street came together. Ian courted her as far as there, in his indirect fashion, every day. He stopped there because she was Peter's girl. She knew he was courting her but he did it so she could know yet not acknowledge it. She never acknowledged it. "I'm telling you this," she said, "as if you were my brother, because you won't breathe a word. I'm going to marry Peter or I'm going to be a nun."

"*Gloria in excelsis Deo*," he said.

"Yes," she said, "or Peter."

"What about *Gloria in excelsis* Ian?"

"Nope," she said. "It's God or Peter."

"I'm pulling for God," Ian said.

"Well, I'm pulling for Peter, tell you the truth," she said.

When she became pregnant, God dropped out of the competition. "I'm glad," she told Ian. "I'm not cut out for a nun. I just love Sister Immaculata and her *servabo me servato te*. I'd like to be able to talk like that, but I know I'm not cut out for it. You, maybe. Not me. I'll be sorry to quit school though. Peter'll quit too. He doesn't like school a lot, but he's doing okay."

"Will you finish the year?"

"I think so, if I don't get too big. Peter thinks they'll hire him right away. He'll quit school."

"Will you tell Sister Immaculata?"

"I think I'll just let her find out. I wonder what she'll say."

"I know what she'll say," Ian said.

"What?"

"She'll say *passer mortuus est meae puellae*."

"What does that mean?"

"It means you better get ready to do your own flying."

When Ian arrived at Peter's wake the priest and the nuns were all kneeling in front of chairs around the wall saying the rosary. Gloria was sitting in a corner in a stuffed chesterfield chair her mother brought back into the front room, hoping the comfort would seduce her to sleep. She perched at the front edge of it, her elbows on her knees, her face in her hands. Her sobs dry.

They began the first Sorrowful Mystery, "The Agony in the Garden."

Ian bent to the kneeling-bench in front of the coffin and studied the brown polished wood. After he said a few prayers he saw no convenient place to go in the small room; people were kneeling out in the middle of the floor as well as in the front of chairs at the wall, so he stayed on the bench in front of the coffin and joined in the prayers, led by the priest. "Hail Mary, full of Grace, the Lord is with thee, blessed art thou among women and blessed is the fruit of thy womb..."

Because he couldn't see Peter's face in the coffin, his head filled with images of Peter in their common past. He and Peter hunting squirrels with their slingshots; digging a bootleg pit, thinking they would make a fortune selling coal and take a trip to Boston to see their cousins; swimming naked in the icy May water in the So'West Brook; walking out to Dominion Beach in the hot summer to dash into the icy ocean, three miles of walking with the gang and telling dirty jokes, and after swimming, sitting around the beach, talking to the girls, and trying to be mature; Peter sliding into second base and standing up in one motion; Peter scoring a goal with a backhand shot over the goalie's shoulder after he thought Peter had made the turn around the net; Peter racking up fifty-six points off the break to start a winning streak; playing snooker for three months with the same quarter in his pocket. He had it so long, he said, that he rubbed the king off one side and the moose off the other, so when he finally lost a game, Joe thought it was a slug and wouldn't take it, so he had to owe him for the time. Peter pulling out an unexpected pint of rum when they were taking the shortcut home after the dance, saying, "Have a slugga black death," and passing it back and forth, and throwing the empty in a high arc over the trees, and standing there, his penis gleaming in the moonlight, saying, "Have a slugga white death," and Ian saying, "No thanks, I just had an orange." And laughing.

Ian, without thinking, lifted his hands from his belt buckle and put them on the edge of the brown coffin. I was always a little jealous, he thought. I have to admit it. He always had been, a little, because although Ian made the slingshots and invented the use of marbles instead of rocks, which tended to veer off target, it was Peter who dared to make a present of the squirrels' tails to the girls they lusted after and to tell them, "You wear them where we'll have to look for them." It was Ian who'd say, "The So'West must be pretty good by now," but it was Peter who knifed into it from a tree without even testing the water with his toes, scattering the surprised trout, taking a long slow swim under water, and climbing out, red-skinned from head to toe. "Warm as toast," he'd say. You had to admire that. He envied him. But not much or for long because he thought of him as a brother. More than a brother because sometimes you could hate your brother. "Holy Mary, Mother of God, pray for us sinners, now and at the hour of our death. Amen. Glory be to the Father, and to the Son, and to the Holy Ghost."

"Amen."

"De profundis clamo ad te, Domine."

"Domine audi vocem meam."

Everyone got off their knees and stood or sat in the chairs around the wall and prayed in silence, or chatted. Some went out to the kitchen for a cup of tea and talk. At a wake, there are always people you never see any other time.

Ian left the kneeling-bench in front of the coffin and walked over to Gloria's chair and sat on the arm. She was leaning over the front edge of it as she was when he came in, her face in her hands. He put his finger on her shoulder.

"Hello, Gloria," he said. She took her face out of her hands and put her thumbs under her chin and turned her head.

"Ian. I'm so glad you came."

"How are you doing?"

"Terrible. Just terrible. My mother has to do everything! I should be doing things but every time I try to talk, I start to cry."

"You seem better now."

"Yes. This is the first time. The first dry words since they brought him home in that box. I didn't cry till then. I didn't believe it till then. But look, my eyes are dry now." They were dry, and brown, and large and round. Her ordeal did not harm her beauty. If anything, she was better looking than he remembered. She was still small, but seemed more substantial, and dressed in black, she seemed older. Ian remembered her ambition to become a nun. All she needs now, he thought, is a cowl and a longer dress and she'd be one of the nuns who came to pray at her husband's wake.

"You look awful tired," he said.

"I am tired. I haven't slept since they brought him home."

"Why don't you go up and lie down for a while now?"

"Will you take me up?"

"Sure," he said, and they stood up as if he had asked her to dance, and they faced each other for a moment. Sister Immaculata came over and put her gentle hands on their arms.

"I'm terribly sorry, Gloria, you've had such trouble."

"Thank you Sister. It's awful, but I'll get over it, at least they tell me that."

"That's right, you know. You'll never forget it but you'll feel better as time goes by."

"She's going to go up and lie down for a while," Ian said.

"Oh that's good, Gloria, have a good rest. You'll need it."

Upstairs, lying on her back, her long brown hair splayed on the white pillow, she started to cry again as Ian looked down at her and tried to smile reassurance.

"Would you sit down beside me for a minute, Ian?"

He sat.

"Would you hold my hand?" He took her hand and held it on his thigh. Her eyes watered. "Can I tell you something?" she said.

"Yes."

"The last thing I said to him, I said, 'If you never come back, I don't give a shit.'"

"How come?"

"Oh we were having an argument. About nothing, of course."

"Well, you didn't mean it."

"No. But my God I said it."

"He'd know you didn't mean it."

"I feel guilty."

"You know you didn't mean it."

"I loved him."

"He'd have known that. He'd know you didn't mean it."

"Can I tell you something else, Ian?"

"Yes."

"I loved you a little too. Did you know that?"

"Yes."

"I couldn't tell you."

"I know."

"I feel guilty about that too."

"It doesn't matter if you feel it. You didn't do anything wrong. The feeling will go away."

"I hope so," she said. "I loved the both of you."

She lifted her black dress and black slip and lifted Ian's hand and placed it on the round of her belly, above the tops of her black stockings. His hand jerked in panic.

She said, "Don't worry, Ian. I wouldn't hurt you. I just want your hand to breathe against." She closed her eyes and almost at once began to breathe deeply, her bosom rising and falling rhythmically, and her fingers curled over his hands.

Ian watched his hand slowly rise and fall. Then her hands lay beside her on the brown, brocaded bedspread, palms up, as if in supplication. He became aware of the silence, and then he could hear that the prayers had started up again downstairs. "...blessed is the fruit of thy womb..." He wondered how anyone could wear garters tight around the legs; he couldn't stand even the elastics of stockings. "...pray for us sinners, now, and at the hour of our death..." He waited until he heard the final words: *"Requiem aeternam dona ei, Domine: Et lux perpetua luceat ei,"* then he pulled his hand free, pulled Gloria's slip and dress over her knees, covered her with a quilt from the foot of the bed, walked downstairs, smiled and nodded at Sister Immaculata when she asked in a whisper if she was asleep.

He went home.

Joan Clark

Salvation

Mary Anne stood at the kitchen sink holding the comb under the water so she could flatten her hair with it. She could feel her mother's eyes on her. Lou sat bunched into a terry cloth bathrobe, tracing around flecks on the arborite table and drinking tea. The tea, Mary Anne knew very well, was to cure a hangover and to keep her mother awake. Her mother thought she didn't know about the hangover or why she was so tired. But Mary Anne knew all right. She also knew why her mother kept getting up every Sunday to make breakfast when Mary Anne was quite capable of making it herself and did every other day of the week. Her mother was a fallen woman was why. She was having an affair with Corporal Simpson. It was true the Corporal's wife was in the insane asylum for the rest of her life, but he was still married to her so it was wrong.

He was the third man her mother had taken up with since Mary Anne's father had died of a brain tumour ten years ago. Her mother had been brought up in the church; she knew she shouldn't be carrying on like this but she wouldn't come to church and confess her sins. She figured that by getting Mary Anne's breakfast it was enough.

"Why don't you come with me?" Mary Anne said.

"Now don't start that again," Lou said grumpily. "If you want to go, fine and dandy, but I have no intention of going to church. All they do is make you feel guilty about having fun. I work hard. I deserve what little fun I have." She stuck her worn mules out from beneath the table and rubbed her swollen ankles, a reminder that she'd been standing on them all day Saturday.

Mary Anne had heard all this before: how after Rudy died she had to go to work to support them. He had left the house, but that was all, so Lou had borrowed some money to take a hairdressing course. While she was gone, Mary Anne's grandmother kept house. That was when Mary Anne started going to church—with her grandmother who never missed a Sunday. Her mother never went to church, not even after Mary Anne's grandmother had a stroke and couldn't take Mary Anne anymore.

After hairdressing school Lou came back and opened up her own business—nothing fancy, but she had three operators working for her. It was true her mother worked hard but that didn't excuse the other. Once Mary Anne had overheard her grandmother and her mother having an argument. Lou was saying how worried she was about Mary Anne never going out with boys or being interested in clothes or movies. All she cared about was going to church and reading the Bible. It wasn't normal. At her age Lou would have been crying her eyes out if she'd missed a dance. Mary Anne had been mad at her mother for saying that. But her grandmother had put her in her place. She told Lou she'd be a lot better off if she mended her ways and took her daughter to church herself.

When Mary Anne's hair was wet enough to suit her, she pulled it back so tight it hurt the temples and secured it with an elastic.

"You keep watering it like that and it'll grow darker," Lou warned. Mary Anne ignored the remark.

"I can't figure it out," Lou went on. "Every week I've got customers coming into the shop asking me to dye their hair the same colour yours is and what do you do? Darken it."

"I'm sure God doesn't care what colour my hair is," Mary Anne said primly.

"Did you ask him?" Lou said sarcastically. "Now there's an idea. I'm thinking of opening up a shop in Sheffield. Maybe I should ask God first."

Mary Anne glared at her mother. How dare she blaspheme the Lord? It was because her mother thought she had a sense of humour. She was always telling Mary Anne she should develop a sense of humour; it could get you through some rough times in your life. If having a sense of humour meant you mocked God, Mary Anne didn't want one.

"At least you get to wear that dress someplace," Lou was saying, "I had a lot of trouble with the pleats, you know. Are you wearing a bra?"

"I don't need a bra."

"True," Lou agreed, "you've got nothing to hold up. Still, a fourteen-year-old girl should wear one just to be feminine."

"Well, I'm not."

"When you get your periods," Lou said knowingly, "you'll develop breasts."

Really, her mother required so much patience. She was forever nagging her about menstruation. Did she have any questions? Did she want to talk about it? Mary Anne had known about menstruation since she was ten years old. She had read the booklet on it in the library from cover to cover. She didn't see what all the fuss was about. The subject was boring. All this stuff about developing breasts, having babies and bleeding, as if there was nothing else to think about.

Mary Anne took the two dollars she had earned babysitting at Foleys Friday night from the windowsill and put it in her purse deliberately in front of her mother so it would be an example. "Do you want to give something?" she said. "There's a special collection today."

Lou took this in her stride. "Look. The wealthiest people in town go to that church. They don't need my hard-earned money."

Mary Anne was tempted to remind her mother of the widow's mite, but what good would it do if her mother didn't care? Instead she said, "It would have been better spent in church than on liquor."

Every weekend her mother bought a bottle of rum to have here when Corporal Simpson, Al she called him, came over. Usually he came on Fridays when Mary Anne babysat for the Foleys but if he was on duty Fridays, he came on Saturday night instead. They had a couple of drinks sitting in the front room with the TV turned up loud trying to fool Mary Anne into thinking they were watching it. They weren't. What they were doing was gossiping. Bearing false witness, Reverend Notley called it. Being head of the RCMP detachment, Al knew all the dirty business in town and her mother being a hairdresser was told all kinds of gossip. She once said that people must think she was a priest; they always treated an appointment like a confession. That was the way her mother talked about religion, always mocking it. That was why Mary Anne would never trust her with anything important. She knew her mother didn't know this was the reason she didn't confide in her; she thought it was because Mary Anne was quiet like her father had been.

Mary Anne didn't remember her father as being quiet. Maybe that was because what she mostly remembered was sitting on his knee and bouncing her up and down until she laughed and then he laughed too. He used to carry her around on his shoulders. His photograph on her bureau showed a young man, a boy almost, serious and sad. Mary Anne didn't know if he really had been serious and sad or whether it was because she wanted him to be. Once she'd asked Lou if he'd been a churchgoer wanting her to say yes and Lou laughed unpleasantly and said, "Him? Only time he ever was in church was when we got married."

After Lou and Al figured Mary Anne had gone to sleep, they turned off the TV and went into Lou's bedroom. Mary Anne heard the door close and the bed thud against the wall. They thought that because she was upstairs and Lou downstairs in what used to be the dining room Mary Anne didn't know what was going on. She knew all right. And she couldn't get to sleep until she heard the toilet flush and the back door close, which was the signal that Corporal Simpson had gone home. Until he left, she had to lie there in her own bed and be punished for the sins being done on her mother's bed. It wasn't right. And if it made her mother mad to hear the truth, well, it was just too bad.

"Listen, Miss High and Mighty," Lou had got up now and was balancing herself against the table with one hand and holding her bathrobe closed over her cleavage with the other, a pretty woman without softness, "don't you start telling me how to spend my money. I work hard to keep food in your mouth and decent clothes on your back. Do you have any idea why I'm staying in this dump? Do you think I want to slave away like this forever? I'm thirty-two years old and if I don't want to spend Sundays on my knees, that's my business not yours. Don't they teach you respect for your elders in that church?" She stumbled toward the door, "That's one of the Ten Commandments," she flung over her shoulder and went back to bed.

Mary Anne sat at the back of the church in the last pew, hard against the wood panelling. She always came to church half an hour early so she could look up the hymns ahead of time. It appealed to her sense of order and rightness, like making her bed as soon as she got out of it or returning a book to its shelf each night after she'd read it even though it meant padding across the cold floor in her bare feet. She couldn't get to sleep if she left it on the night table.

After she had marked the hymns with Kleenex, she leaned back and looked around the church, composing herself, waiting, allowing the church's interior to seep into her own. The church was dimly lit with dark hidden corners and tattered flags swaying over the heat register like ghost banners being marched into a battle by an army of Christian saints. Mary Anne liked the smell of the church. The air was little changed, smelling mustily of all those who had breathed into it during years of Sunday services, Wednesday prayer meetings, weddings and funerals.

She sat alone. When her grandmother used to bring her she marched Mary Anne right down to the front row, which embarrassed Mary Anne because everyone stared at them. This didn't bother her grandmother who before her stroke had been as solid as a chunk of granite. When Mary Anne whispered couldn't they sit at the back, her grandmother scoffed, "Nonsense, we've got nothing to hide. Good Christians must stand up and be counted."

People were moving erratically down the aisles now to the front pews. These were the born Baptists secure in their churchgoing, in what Reverend Notley called Christian fellowship. They smiled at one another, their broad smiles bolstered by gripping handshakes. They whispered sideways to one another, leaning their heads together. None of them acknowledged Mary Anne or even looked at her. Although she wanted to be alone, she didn't want to stand out in her aloneness as one scraggly tree on an island. To her relief an old man she knew as Mr. Thomas came through the doorway and with the intense concentration of the severely arthritic lowered himself slowly onto the other end of the padded seat. He hooked his cane over the pew in front and groped in the rack for a hymnal. It fell to the floor. He left it there and picked up another. Mary Anne wondered if she should slide over and pick it up for him. If she did, he was sure to say something to her. She knew he was hard of hearing and spoke too loudly. Everyone would turn around and look at her. It occurred to her that God might be testing her, that she should pick it up. But she wasn't ready to risk the embarrassment and remained sitting where she was, her own hymnal in her lap.

The choir filed in, dressed in wine-coloured gowns that matched the pew cushions. When they were in place, Reverend Notley opened the door of the side wall of the choir loft, the door of the inner sanctum, a secret hollow near God's heart and out stepped a second minister, one Mary Anne had never seen before. Reverend Notley looked stern and serious, very different from the way he looked outside the church. Whenever Mary Anne saw him downtown, he was smiling. He smiled at everyone whether or not they were Baptists. Though he was a short, wiry man, he had a tall, thin wife who had five daughters and another baby on the way. She always looked ill, washed out. Mary Anne had overheard a lady say after last Sunday's service that she was one of those poor souls who was sick every day of her pregnancy. Maybe that was God's way of punishing her for fornicating, which you had to do to get babies. Mary Anne had no intention of ever fornicating or having babies. She was going to be a missionary. Often she put herself to sleep at nights by imagining herself in white, ministering to the halt, the sick and the black far off from civilization.

Mary Anne could see Mrs. Notley in the front pew but Reverend Notley didn't seem to notice her. He never looked at anyone in church. The minister with Reverend Notley was older with grey hair and metal-rimmed glasses. He was beak-nosed and frightening. After the first hymn, Reverend Notley introduced this man — he was Dr. Richard Wallis from a big church in Halifax. Right after he was introduced Dr. Wallis read the scripture. It was Luke 18, verses 18-30, the story of a certain ruler who asked Jesus what he must do to inherit eternal life. Jesus told him to sell everything he owned for he was exceedingly rich and give the money to the poor. The rich man could not do this and went away sad. The disciples asked Jesus, "Who then can be saved?" and Jesus said, "The things which are impossible with men are possible with God."

After the scripture there were announcements, collection, another hymn and an anthem. Then Dr. Wallis stood up to give the sermon. He gripped the sides of the pulpit and leaned forward, staring at the congregation like a mighty eagle surveying the forest kingdom from his lofty nest.

"Today," he began, "I am going to bring you the message of joy, the joy of giving. The joy of giving oneself to God totally, completely, holding nothing back. Take the story of the rich man who came to Jesus. He wanted to be like Jesus. He wanted to lead a Christian life but he couldn't pay the price. It cost too much. The price," here Dr. Wallis paused emphatically, "the price my friends was *too high*! But it isn't money we use to become good Christians. That is why Jesus told the rich man to get rid of his money. The currency we use is ourselves. Our souls, my friends, these are what Jesus wants." Dr. Wallis's voice was strong and resonant. Mary Anne could feel it echoing inside her head.

"To give ourselves to Jesus we must first be cleansed by acknowledging our sin, our own personal sin, for we are *all* born in sin and without Jesus's help, we die in sin. But," Dr. Wallis paused again and pointed one finger in the air, slightly backwards and to one side like a teacher chalking GOD on the blackboard for his pupils to see, "God knows this. He understands. He loves us. Loves *us*. Isn't that wonderful? So he sent his only begotten Son into the world to *save* us. Save each and every one of us. That is the miracle of Jesus. To save sinners like ourselves from ourselves!"

Mary Anne heard someone up front say, "Yes. Yes." No one in Reverend Notley's sermons had ever done that. His sermons were quiet. Sometimes they were hard to understand. Never were they as strong and clear as this. Mr. Thomas was moving around at the end of the pew. He was nodding his head up and down, agreeing with the minister.

Dr. Wallis's voice rose. His face was red. He raised himself onto the balls of his feet. When he spoke now it was as if he were angry at everyone and at Mary Anne personally. Was he angry because he knew she hadn't been saved?

"God is not asking us to take on the guilt of mankind. We cannot take on the sins of others. All he is asking is for each one of us to confess his own sins. Here. Today. The miracle is that each of us is a gift, a unique gift, a gift no one else can duplicate. Now we don't give each other gifts wrapped in soiled paper, do we? We use new paper. It's the same thing when we give ourselves to God. Before we make our gift, we must confess our sins, purify ourselves, make ourselves new. Then we are ready to be saved!"

Dr. Wallis pounded the pulpit with his fist.

"What we are going to do right now is to bow our heads and pray to God for our forgiveness. After we pray, we will wait in silence for the healing power of His love to flow through us. Those who want to throw off their yokes of sin, those who want to give themselves to Jesus can step forward. Then we can rejoice in their salvation. Let us pray."

Mary Anne bowed her head, released from Dr. Wallis's fierce stare: his eagle eyes pierced through her seeing what she hadn't been able to see herself. She knew her mother's sins had made her feel unworthy. But hadn't Dr. Wallis plainly said you couldn't take on the sins of others? All this time she had been weighed down by her mother's sins. She felt guilty for the two of them. That was why she hadn't been saved. And she couldn't be baptized until she'd been saved. Sometimes during services Reverend Notley asked those people who'd been saved to get up in front of the congregation and tell about it. Witnessing, he called it. Mary Anne envied these people. They sang, they shouted, they praised the Lord in their joyousness. She wanted to have that feeling. She never understood until now why it had been denied her. She had never thought of herself as a gift before. All she had to do was to confess her own sins and give herself to Jesus. Once she was purified, *He* would take her. What had once been beyond her understanding was now so simple and clear. As Dr. Wallis said, the things that are impossible with men are possible with God.

She closed her eyes and concentrated on her own sins. She was in the habit of stealing Mrs. Foley's baking goods when she was babysitting. She didn't know why she did this. Her mother kept the same supplies at home but she never touched them. But always on Friday nights after the Foleys had gone out and she had read the twins a story, she'd sneak into the kitchen, going directly to the cupboard over the stove where the baking supplies were. One by one she opened up the bags of walnuts, raisins, currants and chocolate chips. She never took many, only a few from each bag, putting them back exactly where they had been so that Mrs. Foley wouldn't be able to tell. She never drank the bottle of Coke Mrs. Foley left for her as if by not taking it, it was all right to take the baking goods. But it wasn't right. It was stealing. She pressed her hands together tightly and asked God for His forgiveness. And for the time she'd taken the book on Albert Schweitzer from the school library, deliberately taken it and not signed it out. Monica wanted it for a report she was writing. Had to have it, she said, and nearly cried when she couldn't find it. Mary Anne had slipped it inside her binder. She returned it next week after she'd read it and the reports had been passed in. Mary Anne wasn't assigned a report but why shouldn't she have the book? After all, she was the one planning to become a missionary, not Monica. Monica was one of those who smoked in the washroom, swore and went out with boys. Now Mary Anne understood that by keeping the book she had been guilty of selfishness. Fidgeting blindly with her Kleenex, she prayed she'd be forgiven so she could be saved. She remembered Mr. Thomas's hymnal.

Opening her eyes, she quickly slid across the pew, picked up the hymnal from the floor and returned it to the rack. As she eased back to her place, she felt a stab of pain in her stomach, then a slight wetness between her legs. She felt strangely heavy, almost too tired to sit up. She closed her eyes, swaying in an effort to stay upright. She couldn't hear Dr. Wallis's voice anymore, which meant the prayer had stopped. The moment of silence had begun: the time for being forgiven.

There was a clumsy shuffling at the end of the pew. Mr. Thomas was moving around. His cane clattered to the floor. She thought she could hear him going down the aisle. Still she dared not open her eyes, afraid that if she did too soon, before she was ready, she might be denied her salvation. There was one more sin to confess and that was the picture of her mother and Al lying naked in bed fornicating. When they were doing it, the picture of them was so real she had to pull the sheets up over her head and still she couldn't blot it out. Reverend Notley had once said that people can commit adultery in their minds, which is as bad as doing it. She prayed to God to forgive her for imagining it. With God's help she would push that picture out of her mind. Her mother's sin had nothing to do with her even if she got a baby out of it. Her mother would have to look after her own salvation.

There was a shout from the front of the church, then another. Mary Anne recognized Dr. Wallis's voice. "God be praised!" he was saying.

Mary Anne opened her eyes and looked to the front. Mr. Thomas was walking back and forth in front of the pulpit without his cane. He was smiling at the congregation, lifting his legs high like a soldier proud of his new uniform.

"I'm saved! I'm saved!" he shouted over and over and some of the people replied, "God be praised!"

Dr. Wallis was smiling now and shouting above the din. "Is there anyone else who wants to feel God's power by giving herself to Jesus?"

He scanned the congregation and his eyes fell on Mary Anne. As she sat under his brutal stare, two bright spots appeared on her cheeks. Her eyes were riveted to his. Her time had come. She had confessed her sins. She was ready. She forgot the pain, the wetness, the heaviness; she forgot her shyness, she forgot her guilt. All of it came up out of her, thrusting upward, lifting her heart up until she found herself on her feet with her arms over her head.

"I want to give myself to Jesus!" she shouted, "I want to give myself to Jesus!"

"God be praised!" Dr. Wallis shouted back. He held out his arms. "Come forward, my child. Come forward. God's arms will protect you."

Mary Anne stumbled out of the pew and down the aisle to the front. Dr. Wallis came down from the platform and caught her as she reached the pulpit. Her chest was tight with the pressure of joy inside it. Now she really belonged to Jesus. She began to cry for the freedom she felt and for the joyousness flowing through her, knowing at last that Jesus loved her, that his gentle eyes were on her soul, which was as cleansed and unblemished as a newborn baby's. Now she was ready to be baptized.

Dr. Wallis put the hymnal in her hand, open at the right page, but she could scarcely see the words through the happy tears. She heard Dr. Wallis's strong voice beside her and the congregation singing full out, racing ahead of the organ's slow thundering. As the people sang she felt her heart would burst with gladness. She soared uplifted, up to the heights of glory where saints and angels sang.

When the benediction had been given, Dr. Wallis embraced her and Reverend Notley came down to shake her hand. Old folk from the front pew came forward to pat her on the back. Mary Anne wiped her eyes and blew her nose. She felt drained, weak, now that it was all over and full of what she took to be God's peace. There was nothing more to do so she drifted up the aisle, allowing the congregation to move her along like the Virgin being borne on the shoulders of pilgrims.

Outside, people stood in knots of conversation on the pavement. As always they ignored Mary Anne. She drifted past them across the road to the sidewalk and started in the direction of home. It wasn't until she was within a block of the house that she became completely aware of the dampness between her legs. Still she didn't quicken her pace.

Once she got inside the back door she went straight for the bathroom. With the same disinterest she had once given to undressing her doll, she took off her pants. There was a red stain in the crotch. She twisted around and saw two pleats of her white dress were red.

She knocked on Lou's bedroom door. Her mother was still groggy.

"There's blood in my pants," Mary Anne announced.

Lou sat upright. "Well, well," she grinned and swung her legs energetically over the side of the bed. "Your period at last. It's about time. Go to the
bathroom and wait for me."

Obediently Mary Anne went into the bathroom. While Lou rummaged
in her lingerie drawer for a belt and pads, she saw the book. She picked it up
and took it with her. It was now or never. You couldn't have your daughter
menstruating and not knowing what was what.

After Mary Anne was fixed up and the white dress put to soak in the
bathtub, her mother sat her down on the bed and went over the book with
her. She even got a piece of paper and a pencil and drew pictures to make it
clearer. Throughout all this Mary Anne sat quietly on the edge of the bed.
She didn't ask questions. She didn't say she already knew about menstruation.
She let her mother explain it. It didn't occur to Mary Anne that her mother
might interpret this acquiescence as a need for motherly support.

"Some girls are frightened at first by the idea of blood coming out of them."
Lou said warmly, "But it's perfectly normal. You mustn't be frightened." She
reached over and pulled Mary Anne closer.

Mary Anne allowed this embrace but she didn't tell her mother that she
wasn't frightened. Nor did she tell her the real reason for beginning to menstru-
ate on this special day, the day she had given herself to Jesus. Her mother would
never know that the blood was a sign from God, a symbol of her salvation.

David Adams Richards

We, Who Have
Never Suffered

"It wasn't your fault," Denis said, and as he did he smiled slightly—his smile vague, so that Steven shifted his eyes to the dust filtering in the sunlight, and on the floor; and so Denis spoke again, clearing his throat somewhat, and balancing the tips of his fingers on the edge of the table. "We're all human anyways," he said, and Steven Boyd looked at him and smiled back.

They were sitting at the table near the window and their beer had gone flat with the sun in it, and flies crawled along the ashtray and up the side of their glasses, so that Denis continually waved his hands to shoo them away.

People had come out in the warm afternoon to sit on the cement steps across the street, and Emmerson Morrison's sister Hilda leaned against the door of her apartment with her legs wide apart and her fifty-year-old paunch hanging out of her slacks, and it was seeing her that made Steven Boyd feel heaviness coming over him—remorse for the dusty streets where she sunned her withering double chin and the almost silent gonging of the Presbyterian church in the quiet afternoon. Looking at her he thought of Emmerson falling, as if it were in slow motion now, falling onto the pavement in front of the liquor store—and Steven and everyone laughing.

"Anyway—it's over and done with now," Denis said. He laughed and drank his draft beer and shook his head, and in the dark corner at the other side of the tavern old men began to sing "Goodnight Irene" drunkenly and out of tune. Steven nodded again and Denis laughed loudly and patted him on the shoulder.

"Mayswell get drunk," Denis said, signalling the waiter who was leaning against the counter. He nodded, put his hands in the money pouch and jiggled the coins together. The faint gonging of the bell tapered off.

Hilda stood and moved slowly in the direction of the square, her shoulders like a man's in the blue sunlight, her orange slacks bulging, frayed and dirty, and in her movement Steven saw, with every stride she took, an old and scowling self-possession, a commanding ignorance and anger.

The waiter stood beside them a moment talking and then went back to the counter, and the old men stopped singing, cursed and mumbled to one another and then started again, the same song, the same voices. There were shouts from the taxi stand across the street.

"Hey Hilda come up the bank with me?"

"Awhooo—Hilda honey."

"Ahhh—Haaa Horny Hilda."

Denis laughed. His face, flushed by the sunlight, looked confused, trying to utter something to make Steven understand him, and Steven seeing this, in an instant before the look faded, hated himself again.

"Yes, well we're still the very best a buds as far as I'm concerned," Steven said.

"Same here," Denis said, his face once again expressionless and quiet.

"Christ yes."

"Anyway she says to say hello," Denis muttered.

Steven nodded quickly and picked up his glass, looking at the floor again. Because the face reminded him of the endless arteries of the city, with the houses shuddering in the winter afternoon, the trees faded, or of the feeling he'd had at the moment they passed the provincial hospital, and the mindless jokes told about it.

Denis laughed again, and solemnly drank his draft off.

"Are they going to sing all day—is that all the old fuckers do around here? Sit and drink and sing to one another—ha shit."

"Yes," Steven answered. "What else to do when you're seventy?"

"Lots—hell."

Hilda turned around and standing in the middle of the street swore at the boys who'd insulted her and then continued on, out of sight—and the boys, young mostly, yelled back at her without heart or voice, and then went silent. And Denis hearing this became fidgety and slapped roughly at the flies that buzzed frantically and were suddenly still. He laughed and rubbed at his cheeks which were an inexplicable white where innumerable small reddish veins showed themselves.

"There's no need for people to do this," he said suddenly, "not with the advances we've made this century—my God the most affluent country in the world almost and still they do it."

"Do what?" Steven said.

"Everything—hear them—" The drunken voices of the men at the other end of the tavern singing in rhymeless, almost comical sequence and the hissing of the cauldron on the giant hot plate at the end of the counter.

"Yes," Steven said.

"Yes nothin," Denis answered, his voice not loud but charged, "ha shit you said this was a great river."

"It is," Steven said.

"Ha shit—a mud puddle filled with shit," Denis laughed.

"Perhaps," Steven said.

"Don't start that again."

"What again?"

"Nothin, nothin." His face seemed to twitch somewhat, the sun entered cold upon it, children ran in bare feet over the broken pavement on their way to the wharf. An ore boat anchored in mid-channel was a black hulk against the quiet soundless waves.

And Denis said, "Anyways here we are, after all these months and months—the situation changed somewhat—ha you didn't think I'd find out or somethin—"

"I never thought about it," Steven said, "I guess I musta been crazy—"

"You weren't crazy," Denis said, "Lorna—" he broke off, finished his beer, "says to say hello."

Across the street a group of boys on downers drank wine and hid behind the cement siding and girls came by and sat with them and said, "Hey can we score here?"

"Yer too young," the boys laughed.

"Ah fuck off man ya got any more downers eh?"

"What's downers?" the boys said, their laughter inflected and drowsy and numb.

"Ah fuck off man come on man Jesus."

"Come on man Jesus," the boys said. And Steven watched them for a time without hearing them, until the boys moved from the shelter and walked toward the water, and the girls turned back toward the park, and he wondered why Denis had driven all this way to see him, and then forgot about it again. It was over five months ago he'd last seen her, the morning he'd left the house smelling her sweat on his hands, and passed the snow-driven houses, the great Cathedral where the wind blew snow, smoke-like, against the golden windows etched over a century before. Against the stone steps snow scattered, his ears became red and burning and then numb, his eyes watered—and filled with ice and wind, he remembered the reverberations of the mass in its timeless entity and the songs lifting, smelled ice from the wire fence beside the convent; and the drowsy lights from the great empty hallways behind the convent's bared doors were seen as something murmuring. The sound of dull machinery, the early morning haze scattered on the cold sludge.

"I can't understand people anymore," Denis said. "With the advances we've made—you know we'll probably live forever."

"I doubt that," Steven said not looking at him, "but perhaps *longer*."

"At least *longer*," Denis said, "and yet no one understands it—do you understand it?—the principle of any discovery in the last seventy years."

"A few maybe," Steven said, and the waiter set more beer down beside them.

"None," Denis said, "none—I do."

"I know," Steven said.

"Yes you're fuckin right I do—and you with all the talk about art and humanities understand nothing, do you?"

"Not too much about what you're talking about," Steven said, putting his hand up and hauling the lanky hair that fell about his cheeks and looking at the old men, the giant cauldron, the floor.

"Ha what has anything you know got to *do* with anything? Fuckin tell me that—you're a myth lover, that's why you think this is a great river—"

Denis slapped him on the shoulder and lifting a beer clinked his glass, his eyes blank and penetrating. Outside, children were at the wharf now, diving into the brown water, their shouts absurd and joyous under the sun.

"I had to destroy myths," Denis said, and it seemed he was talking to no one in particular, while more people entered the dark drinking place, "when I first started goin out with her—my God she knew nothin at all about anything—you know that?"

"Yes," Steven said.

"I had to tell her not to listen to her old man anymore."

"Yes," Steven said.

"She never even knew what a pack of cards looked like—that's what kind of religious joker her ole man was—she couldn't even play fish for fuck's sake."

"I know," Steven said.

"I had to teach her just about everything—now when she goes ta visit them at Christmas she breaks out in a rash, Christ." He laughed, beer dribbling against his chin. "Oh yah, all this about religion and humanity—and she couldn't even play fish, ya know what I'm sayin?"

"Yes," Steven said.

"Then why the hell do you believe in it?"

"In what?"

"I don't know, I don't know, I don't know," Denis said, shaking his head abruptly while Steven lit one cigarette off the other, and the room was stale with the smell of their heat and sweat. "In fish," he laughed trying to slap a fly on the table. A warring whoop from the boys outside who came back from the direction of the wharf with a bottle of wine, and a light wind blowing the light-coloured dust across the gutters. "It must be great to be in love," Denis sang under his breath, "It must be great to give it a shove." Then his face turned red, as if the innumerable small veins in his white cheeks had burst and he moved his hands back and forth against his pant-leg, and drank again without looking up.

They were silent for a long time, while across from them Hilda Morrison leaned against the faded cement fountain, her large thighs splitting the seams of her orange slacks, her tongue licking the drying flecks of skin on her curved lips, as the sun bothered her greying head. It was she the boys centred their insults around, as if she were the nucleus of all that was disgusting and bad. And they'd say, "Heard ya were gettin inta Hilda real regular."

"Heard ya were bud—heard ya were down on her last night."

"Ah, he didn't go down on her."

"Not even Emmerson himself'd go down on her."

"I'd go down on her."

"You'd go down on a fuckin cat."

"I've been known to—ahhwoo."

And their eyes were brighter and better and wine-glazed, dancing behind the brick buildings, the pale moon shining on their drunken faces, along the streets at the fringe of empty pulp fields where under the starlit sky the river was soft.

Steven coughed and inhaled, and the smoke burned in his lungs, and then he was calm—a calmness where what he'd done was not sordid any longer, or evil or deceitful. He drank his beer feeling the sun through the window, while the cauldron still hissed on the giant hot plate, the voices from across the street stirred and relaxed.

"All those fools across the street there," Denis said pointing his finger, his hand rising slowly from its grip on the glass, his face an improbable white again, "what do they do anyways, think—I doubt it—ha, so this is your town—"

"Oh they think—" Steven said straightening in his chair and grabbing a strand of lanky hair that fell across his cheeks, "they know—they think as much as anybody else; you can't tell me that no one else does what they're doing right now—that only they do it." He stopped speaking; there was a sound a long way off from a train.

"Mindless idiots," Denis said. "Forget I mentioned it." He crossed his legs, leaned back in his chair and drank, and then laughed loudly to himself and cast a glance out the window again where girls chased each other about the parking lot, their bodies glistening with the oily water off the wharf.

Here Steven thought *there once was salmon forever, and in the spring my grandfather was kept awake at night hearing the June run.*

"I taught her everything," Denis said. "She didn't even know the universe existed before I explained it to her—she was like those people—" He pointed to the girls who were laughing and giggling and running across the street toward the fountain, "except she didn't have hardly as much fun—and now—yes," he continued, smiling a little, "her old man was a fuckin religious fanatic; you know when I met her she wore those brown cotton stockings, her hair in a ponytail—I had to explain to her—I had to explain to her. Now when she goes home she breaks into a rash."

"You probably saved her," Steven said quickly.

The old men who'd left the tavern returned and sat at the end table again whispering to each other until their beer was served.

"I saved her from nothin," Denis yelled.

Then his voice became calm once more.

"I didn't *save* her Steven," he said. "No one in this country has to be *saved* from anything—God knows we've never suffered anything here in this mindless country—half the population doesn't even need to work any longer—God knows, God knows—just look at them!"

He broke off. Steven didn't answer while the whistle from the mill came sharp and clear across the water, and the black hulk of the ore boat remained stirless and quiet.

There was singing once more—this time one man, the lost ballad of the woods plaintive and mournful, and yet somehow a feeling swept over those who listened to it of finding dark unconquered places in the earth, a smell of water on the soil.

"Save 'er up for the festival boys," the waiter said, going over to the table and clearing their ashtray. "We don't have money for entertainment."

The man was mute again while the rest laughed loudly, and Steven could see an old and toothless grin breaking from him and his large brown hand wiping spittle from his mouth.

"*There is none so happy as I.*" He turned his head and it sank on his chest, and the other men laughed again.

Hilda left the fountain, her movement sluggish as the sun's brightness diminished and traces of shadows formed on the building fronts, and sat at her apartment steps across the street, her face a withering reminder of Emmerson himself, falling, almost in slow motion—and Steven and everyone laughing. Emmerson sighed and was still and the breeze blew across the naked sores on his neck. "Drive 'er Emmerson you ole cocksucker," Bruce yelled. "Ahhwoo," Terry said.

It was gone now—the laughter of the children from the wharf, the girls in the parking lot laughing. The boys also had finished drinking and stumbled toward the bank.

"No, no it wasn't your fault," Denis said, taking a deep breath, the beer glass loose in his hand. "It musta been my fault—her doing that."

"It was no one's *fault*," Steven said quietly. "No one—we're all human and people get hurt because of what we do—I'm sorry."

"Will you shut up," Denis said. "Just shut up." He lifted the glass quickly and it seemed for one instant as if he wanted to fling it somewhere but he laughed slightly and drank. "Mindless idiots—live like sheep," he said suddenly.

"Who?"

"Everyone a ya ta tell the truth—but she loves me and I'm quite content."
Steven said nothing.

"Quite content," Denis said again, "ha Jesus man quite content to know
what's going on—you know you're just like her, that's why—"

"That's a stupid thing to say—"

"It's true."

"It's stupid."

"Yes it's stupid, but it's true," and he laughed again and his face reddened
considerably while outside the afternoon sun was red upon the water, and
the great ore boat cast a murky shadow and men from the mill, their clothes
covered with lime and dirt, came in and filled the tables to the left.

And the old man that had been singing rose and stumbled to the entranceway and then into the sun where the heat hit him so suddenly he staggered
against the side of the wall and laughed.

"Can't ya walk no more Hyrum?" Hilda yelled across to him, and he raised
his hands in a pleading gesture and pressed his face against the hot cement
wall, smelling, in its crevices and his own sweat, the years.

"Can'tcha buy wine no more?" Hilda yelled across to him, scratching her
loose scarred belly above her slacks, and looking this way and that and laughing
again—as if she expected and wanted everyone to laugh with her. The smell
of the chicken shop next to her and the giant clanging of the ore boat lifting
anchor, the tarps covering the ore at waterfront.

"I can get wine ya know," Hyrum whispered, "I can get—" He pushed
away from the wall and continued across the street.

"*Anyways,*" Denis said and Steven turned once again in his chair to face
him, "I believe in nothin anymore—ya understand that, especially kindness
or whatever I believe in nothing—I bet ya'd thought it would just pass over
or somethin, but I believe in fuck all now—I'm not jealous of ya so don't
think that ya fucker."

"I know that," Steven said.

"Yes ya fucker, you know a lot don'tcha—ya keep preachin about how
much ya know, but ya don't." He tossed his head drunkenly and lifted his
hand to rub his forehead and Steven could see that he was sweating about
the temples and that his eyes had become exhausted and red. "So don't go

thinking that I'm jealous of ya or that I cry over it—Jesus Christ she went
back to church—ha; 'I'm going to be a good Christian from now on,' she
said—Christ—"

*Between the ribs of a beached and broken boat they'd lie never speaking while
the bay wind moved the sand into concise and frozen rivulets and once she told
him her brother rode the gelding about the lane shouting to everyone about God
and the devil.*

"There's nothing wrong with her going to church if she wants," Steven
said, remembering her finally, and the night when he moved with her on the
couch, her bitter laughter.

"Who are you, her husband?" Denis said. "Or what—she'll get back into
that now—who the hell are you?"

"Nobody."

"Nobody is goddamn right—I taught her everything she knows taday
about life and that's a fact, and then you come along and tell her to go back
to church."

"I didn't say that," Steven said laughing. "I don't believe in church."

"Christ."

"Christ yourself," Steven said.

And again in an instant Steven saw the look as if he wished to expiate
something, be rid of it.

"You know," Denis said, "I liked you and you—" He stopped, puzzled, and
breathed deeply and beer spilled across the table when he lifted his glass, and
then suddenly he turned the glass completely over and the beer foamed and ran.

"You'll be kicked out now," Steven said.

"I don't give a fuck," Denis said. "Ya think I give a fuck?" And the waiter
jiggled the coins together in his pouch and men looked up quietly from their
glasses.

"Well you will."

"Did you ever see her old man, did you?"

"No—you know that."

"Well, ya just take a look at him sometime and then ya'd know; ya'd know
what I'm talkin about then for Christ sake—the ignorance—the fuckin blind
ignorance he has about God, and she breaks out into boils everytime she goes
home—you'd know her a bit better than if ya just fucked her," he yelled.

Steven said nothing and the waiter moved forward and then stopped, and Denis's face charged and white as the sunlight that streaked across it, while the ore boat maneuvered to dock upon the listless dirty water.

"Listen tell me what it was like," Denis said, a twisted smile on his lips.

"Shut up," Steven said.

"No, now I want to know—you've been reading books all the time, you should be good at description; come on what was it like—fuckin her when I wasn't around?"

"It only happened once," Steven said, and he felt his throat swell.

"Was it good?" Denis yelled. "Fuckin my wife."

And the waiter moved in the sunlight and pointed to the door.

They left the tavern, the sun upon them. Across the street Hilda leaned against her apartment door, her withering double chin contorted by the shadows and Hyrum, with his hand stroking her leg, swayed in an almost deliberate fashion.

"I'm all right," Denis said and Steven looked at him and looked away.

"I'm all right now," Denis said spitting ineffectively into the loose gravel. "Listen let's—" He stopped speaking, his voice having failed him.

"I hafta be off," Steven said. "Take care."

"No, now wait," Denis said. "Let's go somewheres—find some women or something."

Steven didn't speak, the bells churned quietly and it was six o'clock.

"Do ya think yer that fuckin good I can't be your friend?" Denis said.

Steven shook his head and then said, "I hafta go—take care," and he turned away from the white and heavy face.

"Go on then, go on you mindless hypocrite," Denis yelled after him. "You mindless hypocrite."

Hilda laughed. The boys lay in the park on downers and wine.

"You lifeless son of a whore," Denis yelled. "All of ya."

Hilda's laughter was perfect and uncontained.

Then in twilight and later in darkness he walked, away from his friend whose last look was something leaden, and, too, at length Steven heard the boys again crossing the road below him yelling and swinging at one another playfully. In the dull heat of after dark he could see the thousands of lights of the river cut a sheen across it, and the moon over the trees came upon his face and hands. Here he remembered her again and felt repelled because of his white skin and the so many patterns of veins bursting out upon it.

"Ahhwoo," the boys yelled below him. "Drive 'er Francis," they yelled. "Fuckin dance 'er Timmy." The roadway was like that also — was like their calling out over the dried summer night.

He left the roadway and went onto the lawn of the churchyard and sat in the cool grasses beyond the church steps. She could tell him no more — that night when he ran from her into the snowy deadened city he'd heard her laughter following him.

"Yes you know," she said, "Denis is the same — he's the same as my father, he's the very same isn't it good to know we're all the same, everyone my brother too and Denis we're the same and you Steven don't forget you —"

don't forget you Steven don't forget you

And marijuana made him laugh until, weak, he leaned against the great warm steps for support.

Kenneth J. Harvey

Two Crosses

I've seen plenty of things die. Animals. Mostly animals. First thing, I see them sick: hobbling or falling over, then struggling up. I take care of them. I give them food and do my best to nurse them because there's something about saving things that just seems right.

Then they get a little better. They get real active, like everything's coming back to them, but then I find them on the floor or in the grass, dead.

I got used to it after a while. Living alone out here with no one but the animals, I got used to things like that. Dying. They're just empty. Animals are empty when they die. But people, people are a different story. I saw a couple of them dead myself. They were out on the lake and they didn't look empty at all. I think it's because of the flesh. Us being the same, being made of the same thing and not understanding how we'd be empty ourselves. Animals can be empty. Sure. But us, I don't think so. Empty doesn't seem right. Flesh just doesn't go that way.

The two dead people I saw were frozen on the lake. They were lost in a blizzard. I know it. Those blizzards close in around you and you see nothing but the white stinging and freezing your face from all directions. I've been trapped myself. I know how you've got to push to make it home, how you've got to cling onto something and move away from sleep that's like warm wind wanting to take you. I know about that and how I could've been dead too.

One of those dead men was frozen sitting up, staring, like a kid. The other one was on his knees with his head tucked down. They were men, full-grown and heavy. Tough and dead like that.

The one sitting was staring toward the sky, his eyes still open when I found him. His beard was white and hard and I touched it and grabbed his arm to lift him but he was heavy and the arm felt like it'd snap in two if I pulled harder, so I stopped. I imagined the sound that the arm would make snapping. I imagined the sound like nothing else. His fingers were the coldest, smoothest things I ever felt. But they were thick and numb like when your arm falls asleep under you. He had no mitts on. I couldn't figure that. But then I could. The other guy on his knees had two sets on his hands. What did that mean? I thought of things like love. I don't know why I thought love, but I did. I thought of that, but where was love here? Maybe they were brothers. Maybe just friends. Either way, they weren't much of anything now, mitts or no mitts.

They were on the edge of the lake and they looked alive when I first saw them. People always look alive. Just sleeping they say.

I saw them from the window of my cabin. I stood there with a cup of tea. It was early and the sun was red coming up. I watched the colour leak across the lake and then I saw the two of them on the edge of the ice. They were facing my cabin. The one who was sitting was staring as if he could see me. I waited for them to move but they never did. I remember laughing kind of soft at first and shaking my head. I sipped some tea and it was warm. I shook my head again.

I laid the cup down and pulled on a sweater, my parka and boots, and pushed the door open. I had to put my shoulder into it to get the door through the snow outside. It opened a crack and then further until I could get my foot out. I kicked at the snow, and the door gave a little more. I squeezed out, sucking my breath to get through.

The sun was up now and it wasn't red anymore. I struggled like a new colt, knee-deep in snow, until I got to the edge of the lake. The ice was smooth and pale blue like old worn glass. The snow had blown off and there were huge banks around the edge of the lake by the dark green trees. I walked to the two men with my boots giving good traction. They were there, just the way I'd seen them first. The closer I got to the sitting one, the more I figured he was going to say something. He was staring like he was going to ask me a question. It was like that. But I knew he wasn't going to say anything. That's what frightened me the most: knowing how his tongue was hard and frozen in his mouth, how he was never going to say anything again, ever.

I stood there considering them with the winter sun on my face and my breath puffing. I watched them like that for more than an hour. They didn't seem empty. I shook my head and looked at my bare hands and at the kneeling one with his head tucked down and his woolen cap covered with frozen snow. I studied my fingers and slowly moved them back and forth, then looked at the sitting one again. The more I watched his eyes, the more I wanted to keep moving my fingers. I had to keep them going. Otherwise, I feared they'd stop. He was staring at me and his eyes were filled with something that emptied everything out of the woods around us.

I left the bodies the way they were. Snow fell on them.

The wind came up and blew it off. A hard snow crusted over their bodies, then a white ice covered them. They were in the middle of nowhere. What could I do? I could bury them in the snow, but the snow would melt and they'd be there just the same as always. There was no way of cutting through the hard frozen earth with my shovel blade; it would easily snap. And what good would that do anyone? So I left them on the lake and wondered how they'd gotten there in the first place. I watched them every day, wondering.

They must have come a long way.

When spring finally came round, I buried their thawed carcasses next to the animals I'd tried to save. I hammered two crosses into the ground with the back of my shovel. It took me some time to summon the words. I began reciting what I recalled of a prayer, but it was filled with holes and my whispering voice soon trailed off. I was thinking of how I didn't know what to write on the crosses. I tried to form something, but nothing offered itself. Not knowing what to do, I left the crosses blank and went back to my cabin.

No one showed up looking or asking questions.

I planted a few flowers on the graves and watched them grow; the colours were bright and healthy. When winter came again, the flowers died and snow covered the earth. I could see the two crosses there for a while, but after the third bad storm they were buried. No sign of nothing. Whiteness blanketing everything, as far as the eye could see, but I couldn't forget that those two were down there in the ground, bundled up for winter and staring straight into my head.

Clive Doucet

Miracle Potatoes

Father Aucoin was not happy with Daniel eating Sunday dinner *chez la famille* Cormier. Théophile Cormier was not from the improving side of the parish. He was one of those eternal talkers who ran everyone's business better than his own, including Father Aucoin's. Fortunately, while Théophile was busy saving the world from ineptitude, his wife was busy feeding his children.

When Théo rolled his cigarettes and considered the state of the universe his wife tended an enormous garden. When Théo walked down to the harbour to cadge a few cod from the fishermen, his wife was churning butter or knitting or preserving. Madame Cormier kept her girls fed and clothed through dint of hard work and reused wool. The only thing that Théophile did with any efficiency was make children. He had seven girls, all of them beautiful, which was the reason Father Aucoin suspected Daniel wanted to have dinner there.

Before Daniel left, the priest went over his list of chores: the barn, the church, homework, piano practice. But they had all been done, and it was Sunday. There was no reason the boy could not go. Mrs. Cross gave him a large hamper of food to take to Mrs. Cormier's, and the boy set out down the lane towards the Cormiers.

Madame Cormier opened the door when Daniel arrived. Théophile was already preaching to a large assembly at the Sunday table. She picked up the basket and began to lay out the food Mrs. Cross had packed, strawberry preserves, scones, buns, cream, butter and jars of soup ready to serve. Madame Cormier shook her head admiringly.

"And this, she told me to make sure you got this," and the boy reached into the basket and took out a large bar of chocolate. "It's chocolate," said Daniel, unsure of what to make of Mrs. Cormier's astonished expression. "It comes from the Boston States. Father Aucoin's sister sent it."

"It's pretty," said Mrs. Cormier, turning the sleek tablet over in her hands. The girls got up from the table and gathered around their mother each anxious to touch and see the Boston chocolate. The wrapping was dark brown and it had CADBURY'S MILK CHOCOLATE written in yellow-gold.

"Bah, sit down at the table," called Théophile, annoyed at his family. "A bar of chocolate is not a miracle. Come, the food is getting cold."

The girls went back to the table, and Mrs. Cormier set the chocolate down on its side in the middle of the table so that everyone could see it.

"Daniel, will you say grace?" asked Mrs. Cormier. The boy crossed himself and said grace, the words coming out with practised ease. When he looked up, Elodie was staring at him and he felt his face flush to the roots of his hair.

"So Daniel, are you going to be a priest like Father Aucoin?" asked Théophile, watching the boy blush.

"No," said the boy.

"Why not? You'll get chocolate from the Boston States. A nice, big Presbytery to live in, and someone to cook your meals and all you have to do is look prayerful. You do a pretty good job already."

"Don't tease the boy, Théo. It's not fair."

"I'm not teasing him, Jeanine. I'm delighted to hear Daniel doesn't intend to become a priest, there are entirely too many priests in the world already."

"What should he become?" asked Elodie, curious.

"A millionaire."

"But he has to do something to become a millionaire."

"Absolutely, and that's for Daniel to decide. All I'm saying is that if Daniel wishes to marry one of my daughters, he will have to be a millionaire first. One poor man in the family is enough."

"Théo, I asked you not to tease the boy."

"I'm not teasing, I'm stating a fact. Each one of my daughters is worth a million dollars. They're not going to marry for anything less, right Daniel?"

The boy's face went a deeper scarlet.

"How do you like working at the Presbytery, Daniel? I have the feeling that you don't like it much."

"Théophile!" cried Mrs. Cormier, exasperated with her husband.

This time it was Elodie's turn to blush, for she had told her father this.

"Pardon, I didn't mean to pry," said Théophile, and he calmly resumed eating his soup. The girls looked at Daniel surreptitiously, who countered by refusing to look up from his soup plate. It was confusing to be in the same room with so many pretty girls.

"The problem with this parish is we have no miracles. If we had miracles, we would all be millionaires. I'm serious. Jeanine, if Sainte-Anne-de-Beaupré can have miracles, why can't Saint-Joseph-de-la-Mer? Sainte-Anne is just a little village in the middle of nowhere, and they have miracles by the ton. They have a great basilica, a hostel for pilgrims, if you don't believe me ask Marguerite à Medoc. She will tell you. She went there for a cure. And what do we have? A tiny little church and no one ever comes here who is not related. If I was the priest, the first thing I would do is have a few miracles, and then write to the Bishop to get them publicized in the *Diocesan News*. Then — bingo, we'd all be on easy street."

"What kind of miracles?" asked the boy cautiously.

"Oh, the regular kind, curing the lame, seeing the Virgin, that sort of thing."

"Théophile Michel Cormier, you are being blasphemous, blasphemous in front of the children."

"How am I being blasphemous? I'm saying we need a few miracles around this little parish. Why is that blasphemous? We have a priest who is supposed to be saintly, and what miracle has he ever done? Name me one! Brother André in Montreal does miracles by the thousands. People come from all over Canada to get themselves cured by Brother André. There's miracles galore at Sainte-Anne-de-Beaupré and what do we get? Sermons and piano lessons. I tell you in all honesty, Jeanine, if I was the priest, and I prayed as much as Father Aucoin, we would have miracles in Saint-Joseph-de-la-Mer as sure as we are all sitting here."

"I don't know if Father Aucoin believes in miracles," said the boy, thinking about this.

"See, what did I tell you? How can we have miracles in Saint-Joseph-de-la-Mer if our priest doesn't believe in them? He won't even pray to move the ice off the fishing grounds, which is a sin if you ask me," said Théophile, pouring gravy expertly onto his potatoes as he said this.

"He believes in some miracles," said Elodie, "doesn't he, Daniel?"

"Yes, he believes it is a miracle that your mother married your father."

Elodie rewarded Daniel with a grin.

Théophile hooted. "That wasn't a miracle, Elodie, that was just bad judgement on your mother's part. She could have married Albert à Didier and she'd be rich today."

Jeanine Cormier made a wry expression in her husband's direction, but said nothing.

"What is a miracle, then?" asked Elodie.

"A miracle is something that makes money," said her father firmly.

"That's not what Father Aucoin says," said the boy, stubbornly resisting the dominating tone of the older man.

"Oh yes, then what does he say?"

The boy shrugged. "He says miracles are little things like Elodie playing the piano."

"Then we have several miracles in this house because Bernadette and Mathilda can play the piano also, and we don't even own one. No, that's childish nonsense, miracles are described in the Bible and it doesn't say a word about playing the piano. A miracle is curing the lame, making the blind see, raising the dead, those kinds of things. If I woke up in the morning and found the stones in my front pasture had changed to potatoes that would be a miracle, a real miracle. And you know what, Daniel? Your priest is afraid of real miracles, because he's afraid he's not good enough for them. That's why he spends all his time with little miracles," he gestured towards Elodie, "because he's afraid of the big ones. If I was a priest, I'd let the little miracles take care of themselves and concentrate on the big ones, the ones that make money." By this time, Théophile was wagging his finger at the boy, lecturing him from his considerable height, and the boy kept his thoughts to himself.

"Ahh, Papa, how you talk," said Elodie sighing.

"Can we have the chocolate now?" asked Mathilda, who was the youngest.

"With the strawberries, you have chocolate with strawberries, not potatoes, Mathilda," said Madame Cormier smiling.

It was during the lecture from Théophile Cormier that the boy first thought of planting potatoes in the Cormiers' front field, and the more he thought about it, the more he liked the idea. He and Ulric Chiasson could make a miracle without any trouble at all.

On his way back to the Presbytery, he stopped at Ulric's and explained his idea for a potato miracle. Ulric's father had a big farm and more potatoes than he knew what to do with. He wouldn't miss a sack or two; that same night, Daniel harnessed the old mare to the cart, and took her over the grass so her shoes would not make a sound. Only when he was at some distance from the Presbytery did he go down the road to the Cormiers'.

He and Ulric worked like slaves picking stones and planting new potatoes. Then just before the sun came up, they went home. Daniel didn't even bother to go into the Presbytery. He just started milking the cow and then came in with the pails of milk. Mrs. Cross took one look at his dirty face and sent him upstairs for a bath.

He fell asleep in early morning mass and Father Aucoin gave him hell. He said he wasn't well. This was the best way of dealing with Father Aucoin. He understood sickness and Daniel went willingly to bed where he slept until the afternoon.

On Saturday, two of the Cormier girls were flying a brown paper kite in the front field and when one ran to pick it up, discovered new potatoes there where it had fallen and then they began to find more and more. There were whole rows of them and the stones seemed to have disappeared.

The news travelled up to the Cormiers' and around the parish like a thunder-clap. By the end of the day, everyone from Friar's Head to Chéticamp knew that stones had been turned to new potatoes in Théophile's front field.

"It was a miracle! A real miracle!" cried Théophile Cormier. "Imagine, my prayers have been answered." And like a man possessed, he harvested his potatoes, working away with a shovel and fork. No one had ever really seen Théophile work before and people watched his performance in amazement. He would let no one else near his potatoes, not even his wife and daughters.

No one really believed that they were miracle potatoes, but then no one really believed that they weren't either. If someone had planted them in the dead of night, it would not have been easy, because Théophile's front field was right beside the road in plain view of the Presbytery.

Théophile came cap in hand to the Presbytery to ask Father Aucoin to write to the Bishop in Antigonish to inform him of the great news. Stones had been changed to potatoes in Saint-Joseph-de-la-Mer! It needed to be published in the *Diocesan News*. A subscription should be taken up to build a Cathedral, just like in Sainte-Anne-de-Beaupré. It should be a huge Cathedral with stained glass and an enormous bell tower. The windows should look out onto the field and onto the sea. Théophile had it all planned out. He was ready. God had finally answered his prayers. A miracle had happened in Saint-Joseph-de-la-Mer.

But Father Aucoin would not write to the Bishop.

Théophile said Father Aucoin was jealous. God paid no attention to the priest, but he had answered his prayers. He had given him, Théophile Cormier, a miracle and nothing to the priest.

Father Aucoin did not argue with Théophile. There were no sermons from the pulpit on the nature of miracles. He said nothing for or against Théophile's miracle, but he would not write to the Bishop.

Théophile sent Philibert, the matchmaker, to speak with Father Aucoin. Philibert was the priest's first cousin and had influence with him. Nothing came of it.

Albert à Didier came cap in hand. If the miracle could be confirmed he predicted a great future for his hotel. He would be able to employ more people. He would need cooks and waitresses and chambermaids and on and on it went. Father Aucoin listened patiently to Albert à Didier who had influence with the Bishop in Antigonish and said, "Next year, let's wait until we see what happens next year." He said this so gently that Albert à Didier could not reproach him.

Théophile grew frantic. The Virgin didn't appear every year. "Why should stones be changed into potatoes every year?"

The Doucet boys opened a potato stand of their own just down the road from Théophile and immediately, a great argument erupted between Théo and the Doucets. Théophile complained the Doucets could not be selling genuine miracle potatoes. The Doucets said their potatoes weren't genuine miracle potatoes but merely souvenirs of the genuine miracle potatoes. Théophile said he didn't care what they were called, anything miraculous had to be sold from his stand.

The more frantic, the more greedy people became, the calmer the priest became. Then Théophile did something really extraordinary. He bought his girls a piano from the proceeds of his miracle potatoes. This news was almost as amazing as the appearance of the potatoes. Father Aucoin was invited to view this new piano at the Cormiers', and he accepted, dressed in his best soutane, with his shoes polished and his hair carefully combed. Mrs. Cross dressed the boy so that he too, would reflect well on the Presbytery, and the two of them walked off towards the Cormiers' as if prepared for a state occasion.

The gleaming new piano stood like a machine from Mars in the battered dining room of the Cormiers' little house. Father Aucoin was invited to play and he played for a long time, almost an hour. Whatever else one said about Father Aucoin, he could play the piano. He could make it sound like angels' wings.

Madame Cormier served tea and little cakes, and then Elodie Cormier played, not for long, but afterwards people said that she had played as well as Father Aucoin. Daniel Boudreau, the priest's boy, was asked to play also, but he refused and the piano, being thus blessed, passed onto others.

Towards the end of the evening, Father Aucoin announced that he would write a letter to the Bishop telling him about the potato field miracle. He said he would say only what he knew to be true, that Bernadette and Mathilda had found potatoes in their father's front field, and that no one would admit to planting them. He would show the letter to Albert à Didier before he sent it, so there would be no misunderstanding later about what he had said. He wanted to say only the truth, not consecrate anything, that was not for him to do.

Théophile was overjoyed. He could not say enough fine things about Simon Aucoin, RP. The priest blushed a little and said if Théophile Cormier could find it in his heart to buy his daughters a piano, he could find it in his heart to write a letter to the Bishop.

Théophile drank gallons of strong tea and made great plans. First, he must go to Sainte-Anne-de-Beaupré and see what they had built there. He would go as a simple pilgrim and have a real experience, and then he would talk to the Bishop of Québec. "Ahh, there was so much to do."

Elodie tried to persuade her friend Daniel to play, but the boy could not be persuaded even by Elodie. He ate very little. He and his friend, Ulric Chiasson were the only unhappy notes at the party. The two of them sat in a kind of droopy silence together, talking little, seeming pale and drawn. The priest said the boy had lately been sickly.

Around midnight, the party began to break up and people began to go their own way home. As usual the priest and the boy were the first to go because they had early morning mass to serve. On the way home, the priest drove the buggy and the boy rehearsed how he would say it. In the end, he just said as the priest turned off the main road towards the Presbytery, "Ulric and I planted the potatoes."

Father Aucoin pulled the mare up short and the buggy shuddered to a halt. "You what?"

"Ulric Chiasson and I planted the potatoes. We got the potatoes out of his father's barn and planted them at night."

"Why?"

"Théophile was talking about how a miracle had to make money. Ulric and I thought we would make a miracle for him. It was supposed to be a joke."

The priest sighed and loosened the reins on the mare who was anxious to go the last little distance to the barn.

"Whose idea was it?"

"Mine."

The priest said nothing more. Normally, it was the boy's chore to unhitch the mare, but this time the priest helped him. All the time, the boy became increasingly nervous until his head pounded and his stomach felt sick with a fever.

"Has Ulric told anyone?" the priest asked finally.

"No, he's afraid to."

"Not even his parents."

"No one, he was waiting for me to tell you."

"Can he keep a secret?"

"Yes."

"Then you should, for the moment, tell no one."

"Why?"

"Because," said the priest, pausing, "Théophile will lose his dream and some income. Both are important to him."

"But what about the basilica and the hostel for the pilgrims," said the boy, confused.

"They won't get built, that is all, that is all," said the priest without a trace of sadness in his voice. "And in the meantime, the Cormier girls will have a piano which is a miracle of sorts. I will write to a friend of mine in Boston and see if we can find a scholarship for Elodie."

The priest looked at his watch. "Time for bed, young man."

The boy went to bed without another word of reprimand. He slept fitfully. He had expected that the priest would fall on him like the wrath of God; instead, he had seemed almost amused. Daniel did not understand. He played his scales a fraction too fast and the priest bellowed at him like a gored bull. He turned the entire parish upside down with miracle potatoes and he said, "time for bed, young man."

In his study, the priest wrote a long letter to his friend in Boston explaining how he had two excellent students who deserved and needed a musical scholarship to continue their studies. Then he wrote a short letter to the Bishop explaining about the Miracle Potatoes and apologizing profusely. He blamed himself. He did not show the letter to Albert à Didier.

The Bishop replied immediately. He was not pleased. He asked his priest again to stay away from the Fisherman's Co-op and to concentrate on the spiritual life of the community. The spiritual life of the community did not include playing God with potatoes. He requested Father Aucoin to resign from the Board of the Credit Union and to include three novenas in his prayers as penance.

The young priest was grateful to have gotten off so lightly, resigned from the Board and said his novenas each evening with thankfulness.

Théophile visited Sainte-Anne-de-Beaupré. He took the train from Inverness all the way to Québec City and then a bus to Sainte-Anne. He came back with all kinds of great plans for Saint-Joseph. But the Bishop never came to the village and there never was a notice in the *Diocesan News* of the potato field miracle. Théophile blamed the priest. He said they could have all been rich if they had a real priest in Saint-Joseph. The priest said nothing.

Towards the end of Théophile's life when people had forgotten all about their own dreams of cathedrals and pilgrims and hotels, Théophile was thought of as a bit of a crank, and his grandchildren would be warned not to mention the subject of miracles.

Except after the potato field miracle, people in Saint-Joseph-de-la-Mer separated miracles into two types, *"un miracle à Théo,"* which came to mean something extraordinary like winning the Lotto, and *"un miracle Aucoin,"* which came to mean something ordinary like the birth of a baby; and this distinction endured long after Théo Cormier and Father Aucoin had passed on.

Deborah Joy Corey

Discovery

What's a girl without her dreams? Just a pumpkin head. Some are that. Nothing more than squash inside. Not my sister Sharon and me; we're big dreamers. Those girls downriver in Fredericton have heads full of lace and gossamer like in their pretty windows. No future to them at all. Sharon and me have time on our hands; that makes the future a real concern. No croquet set to make the afternoons go by, just the clouds passing over and us staring up. We've seen those city girls when Mama takes me to the doctor for my headaches. One yard all mowed pretty with a pitcher of lemonade on a little table. Girls standing round in colourful dresses. One girl looked at our old car and pointed. Them Fredericton girls always pointing, look at this, look at that, too busy to dream.

When Sharon and I are famous, we'll come back and be their friends. They could stand us then. We'll be honoured guests at their lawn party, magazine sherbet punch sticky on their lips, "I love you Sharon and Patty; you could make a rag look good. You were so pretty on the cover of *Chatelaine* magazine. Rags to riches," they'll say. "Imagine."

We got us this dream, Sharon and me, lingering like a sad movie in our heads. Fame. Just one minute of it, then we'll be back. River girls with city girlfriends. It's something we suffer, going off to make ourselves worthy. The river shore is what we like best. Sharon calls it the land of milk and honey. All day, we wander alongside it, picking cattails and marvelling at the swirling eddies. Mama taught us about the river and its ways. She's lived here all her life. Never once went off.

When we get to the big city, Sharon is going to be a fashion designer, and she says I'll make one fine model with my long legs. I can wear her fashions. Sharon gave me the idea. Before, I'd just say these chicken legs, why'd God give me these? Our big sister Ruthie says my nice legs will not save me. I ignore her. She says my ears are too big to make a pretty statement. I cover them up, all kinds of tricks for that. Anne of Green Gables braids are the best. Mama says I'll grow into my ears. She did. I've never really seen Mama's ears. She's a Pentecostal and wears long dark braids coiled around them like snakes sleeping. When we're not around, Mama takes her hair down and brushes it out on the porch. I find her broken hairs floating in the sun. Brushing, she tells me, is the secret to a good shine. No easy road.

I don't ignore everything Ruthie says, though. I watch her real close because she has a baby boy, even though she's not married and has had boyfriends galore. All that on one plate. She says with her, love is a fleeting matter. Just the same, Sharon and I take pointers, because that's what we're most interested in, love, even before our careers. Sharon says she wants most to be knowledgeable without giving anything up. I say that might be a tricky road to follow.

Right now, Ruthie has a new boyfriend, an explorer. He came here because there have been sightings of a strange long-necked bird flying over the river. So far, this is who has seen the strange bird: two boys named Hoss and Donald and a farmer, a housewife fishing, and a biology professor from the University of New Brunswick. No one paid it any mind until the professor saw it, then it was news. Sharon says the world loves an educated person.

Not long after the bird news, Ruthie found the explorer sitting on the river shore with a set of binoculars and more cameras than a photo shop. He and Ruthie got attached right off. Love, that is. Sharon and I think it is Ruthie's best boyfriend so far. Definitely better than the last one who fixed old cars and the one before that who worked at the new pulp mill downriver and smelled like rotten eggs.

The explorer says before he came here, he was over in Europe studying the bog people. Sharon and I roll down and laugh at that. Bog people, but he wants us to believe him. He says the bog people are perfectly preserved from hundreds of years ago. Even have hair. "What preserved them?" Sharon asks.

"The acid in the peat bog. They're absolutely beautiful," he says. "Shiny as bronze."

"Really," Sharon says, scratching her cheek. "A bird is going to be a letdown after those people."

"Oh no," Leonard smiles, "if the bird's neck is as long as the reports say, it will be a real discovery. A neck that long defies aerodynamics."

Sharon kicks at the dirt, then looks up. "Ever seen the Shroud of Turin, Leonard? We seen it in a movie at church. It's amazing."

Leonard runs his hand through his moist red hair. "That's a hoax," he says.

Sharon perks up. "You saw it?"

"No, and I don't want to. It's just some man's image burnt into a sheet."

"Oh no," Sharon says, "the movie said it was proof that Jesus was resurrected. That's why God left it. He raised him up without anyone seeing, you know. That's why he left that cloth behind. Proof."

Leonard smirks, shaking his head, and then looks down and fiddles with a camera lens.

"Where do you think the bird came from?" Sharon asks.

Leonard perks up. "Well, it could be something thought to be extinct or it could be a mutation."

"A mutation!" Sharon laughs. "Who cares about them?"

Leonard looks at her seriously, pinching his thin lips together.

Sharon fans herself with her hand. "They're nothing special, every kind has them."

A red squirrel runs in the tree over us. Sharon and I look up and chit-chit at it. We like to talk to the animals. In the land of milk and honey, everything is ours. Leonard stands up, his cameras rattling around his neck like chains. He grabs some rocks and starts throwing them up at the squirrel.

"Just a squirrel," I say.

"A red squirrel," Leonard says. "Do you know what red male squirrels do to grey male squirrels?"

I shake my head no.

"They bite their balls off."

Sharon and I look at each other and giggle.

Leonard keeps throwing the stones even though the squirrel is long gone. He's worked up a real sweat. "Someday, grey squirrels are going to be extinct," he huffs, "all because of those little bastards."

We look up at the tree. It's a beautiful maple with sunlight shining through it. "Those red squirrels are special," Sharon says, adjusting her new-sewed red sarong on her shoulder. "Mama says once they could go from here to the Mississippi without ever touching the ground. All that way on the treetops. Thousands of miles."

"They're common," Leonard says. Then for a bit, he turns quiet and sulks. He sits back down on his spot, squinting at the sky over the river.

For the most part, Leonard is real nice. We tell him our dreams and we value his opinions because he's educated. Leonard loves to tell us about advances in science. We eat it up. The topic of *biodeterminism* seems to be his favourite. He taught us that word. *Biodeterminism.* He said not long ago they made a goat from a human egg. I wondered what kind of advancement that would be. It made me think the whole world might be going backwards. Sharon smiled at the story, leaning against the big maple. "Is that goat thing true?"

A shadow came over Leonard's face, like something dark was flying over. "Truer than anything you know about." He said it almost sad, looking my way. "What do you think, Patty?"

I took a few steps back, watching Leonard. In the shade, his face was grey and still. I thought about the goat and wondered if it might be able to feel things the way we do. Sharon always says there's no heaven for the animals, that's why we have to be good to them. This is it.

"Patty?" Leonard said, stepping closer and squeezing my shoulder, "do you believe in the goat?"

"I'm not sure," I said.

"That's just it," he said, "that's the problem with you girls who get religion. It makes you afraid to see the world."

"That's not so," Sharon said, "everyone's got to look at the world. We can see Jesus anywhere, even in your goat."

Leonard shook his head.

"Would you know Him if you saw Him?" Sharon asked, but Leonard wouldn't talk anymore, so we shut up and looked at the river, too.

Sometimes, if Leonard thinks the bird is not going to show up and Ruthie is waitressing, he takes us swimming. He goes naked, so Sharon and I have seen his penis, which is a disappointment to us both. What did we expect? A bouquet of flowers? It just looks like a slug hanging from a burning bush. No passion to it. Sharon says it defies aerodynamics.

After Leonard gets over the red squirrel episode, he takes our picture together and then suggests we all take a dip. Sharon made me a red sarong for the river shore, too. We wear them in the water. Sharon's shiny black hair is pinned in a bun and mine is braided down past my tiny bosoms. All we're missing is that red jewel shot between our eyes. The red sarongs bleed and make the water red around us. We watch the red like it is our own blood circling out of us. Leonard says something as simple as dye in the river could throw off the ecological balance. "You should take those things off. Go naked." We hee-haw at that. He goes under water and skims our legs like a fish. This makes Sharon and me hold still. We sing low, *the river is deep and the river is wide, hallelujah*, then we laugh wild.

When Ruthie is finished work, she brings the baby down and we all fight to hold him. Mama has had him all day. No one is going near that baby when she's in charge. She loves him so. Leonard usually gets Ray the longest. He looks in his face and touches his chin, even his lips, which isn't really sanitary. You can't blame him though. Ray is roly-poly, all doughy and soft to touch. Blue eyes like the sky with the whole world reflecting in them.

Leonard gives Ray a jujube. He chews it watching Leonard, sweet pink spit dribbling down his chin. The baby is teething, so he loves to chew. He'll chew on a stick or rocks if you let him. Leonard studies the baby. Like always, he says he's never seen a baby up close before and Ruthie says, "I believe you're more interested in him than me." This is when Leonard gives Ray to me to take up the hill. The baby's smell is pure white and powdery and Sharon and I talk about it while we walk. We call it heaven scent.

Mama's at the door watching for the baby to come back. She comes out on the verandah when she sees us. She says you're never alone with a baby. They're the best company. I guess for that reason, we all love him.

Mama reaches out and takes Ray. He's asleep and the dye from my wet sarong has soaked into his head. That insults Mama. My care for him, that is. "Our only boy," she says, "stained."

Right away, I get a headache, lights flashing and pain like something driven through my head, right where the red jewel should be. The doctor tells me to go into a dark place when the pain comes, so I go and lift up the cellar hatch where the day lilies are growing.

Sharon follows along saying she'll wait in the sun for me to come up from the cellar. I say, "Good, but don't sit on the trap door like you did last time. I need to know I can get back up without knocking."

Sharon waves her hand like a fairy. "Free to come and go," she says, "everyone deserves that."

I step down the cellar steps and lower the door over my head. The cellar is practically a dungeon. Dark, cold and musty smelling. I feel my way along the rock wall and sit near the potato bin where I know old potatoes are sprouting little horns. They smell a thousand years old. Everything I touch is cold and gritty. I hang my head down and close my eyes. Sometimes I throw up sour, but today I try to concentrate on things over me. Mama's footsteps echoing on the kitchen floor and Ray making sounds like a mourning dove. After a bit, the flashing lights settle down and the pain is just a jab. Even though I'm cold, I tell myself to stay until nothing's left of my headache. I say, just leave it right here in the dark, Patty. Do what the doctor says.

When Ruthie comes up the hill, orange twilight is behind her. Sharon and I ask what she's been doing all this time. She says, "This and that." The back of her dress is dirty. "Where's Leonard?" we ask.

"Gone back to his motel," she says, waving her hand.

I picture Leonard driving downriver to Fredericton. I wonder if when he leaves the spot where he's been watching for the bird all day he stops watching.

Maybe he relaxes like he's in a dream. Maybe he stops looking, even if the orange sky is wild and pretty. Sharon twirls around the porch post. "Why doesn't he take you with him, Ruthie?"

Ruthie stops and blows a piece of wet hair from her mouth that she's been chewing on. "I have Ray," she says half hurt. "Besides, Leonard is busy at night."

Sharon looks off at the sky over the river, her face is peachy in its light. "Maybe you and him could go out driving sometime," she says dreamy, "look at all the pretty houses or get a frosty float from a takeout."

~❧

The next day is Ruthie's day off, so we take Ray down to the river shore. We pack sandwiches and invite Mama, but she always stays back if there's a stranger around. She tries to convince Ruthie to leave Ray at home, but Ruthie says it's her baby day.

The sun is bright and a breeze is blowing with the scent of sulphur from the mill. Ruthie carries Ray on her hip along with a bunch of orange lilies she picked for Leonard. The flowers are wrapped around Ray like he might have grown right out of one. Why not? If a goat can come from a human. I carry the brown bag of devilled ham sandwiches. Sharon is in a long black stretchy dress that she designed. She calls it *Easy-Wear*, because it's easy to get on and off. The armholes haven't been hemmed yet, but the rest is put together good. I'm in a dressy dress with lots of tiny buttons up the front. I was thinking of Fredericton girls when I got dressed. They look so happy in their colourful clothes.

Leonard is fiddling with a big camera on a tripod and there is a huge net strung in the tree over him. "What's the net for?" Ruthie asks.

Leonard turns and his eyes are lightning in his head. "I saw it," he says, holding his hands together like he's praying. He rushes towards us. "I saw the bird. Six o'clock this morning. Right up in this tree. It was glorious. Oh," he says, letting a big gush of air out, "a wingspan like you wouldn't believe. I've got to catch it. I've got to catch it and take it to the lab at UNB."

"What about the squirrel?" Sharon asks.

Leonard looks confused. "What about it?"

"That's his tree. What if he gets tangled in the net and strangles himself? That'd be worse than having his balls bit off. He won't be going to the Mississippi then."

Leonard looks up at the net, then out at the water and back at the net again. "That won't happen," he says like Sharon is stupid. That's the way Leonard acts if you get in the way of his curiosity.

"How do you know it won't?" Sharon asks. "A man can't know what a squirrel will do."

Sharon and I already had this discussion after Leonard taught us the word *biodeterminism*. Maybe scientists could plan the way something was going to look, but we didn't think they could shape its mind. That part is the wild kingdom. *Free to come and go.*

Leonard turns away and starts rummaging through one of his black bags. "I've got your photograph, Sharon and Patty," he says excited. "I developed it last night." He turns holding up a big black and white picture of us. "When you girls get to the big city, you can use this for your portfolio."

Sharon and I step closer and look at the picture. We're intertwined like Siamese twins. Our faces are bleached out white. No expression to them. If it wasn't for the red sarongs, we wouldn't even know it was us. Ruthie steps up and looks at the picture. Ray reaches his sweet hands out and coos. "Pitiful," Ruthie says. She says it in her jealous way, but I have to agree. With those washed-out faces, we could be anybody. I can't help but wonder if Leonard made the picture that way on purpose, like it's his wish not to recognize us. Sharon snatches the picture and steps back, and then looks up at the net. "That's still no way to catch a bird."

Leonard picks up one of his cameras and begins to polish the lens with his shirt. "What would you suggest then?"

Sharon fans her face with the photograph while she thinks. Mama always says a good hunter knows the area, that's the talent to hunting, but Sharon doesn't say that. She says, "You've got to prove yourself to it."

Ruthie laughs out.

Leonard gets a half-sneer on his face, then says in a fakey way, "Now Ruthie, don't laugh at Sharon. Let her explain what she means."

Sharon stops fanning the picture and looks down at it. "If you want to behold something, it's best to make friends with it."

Leonard starts howling with laughter. He bends over, grabbing his stomach.

"Make friends with a strange bird," he howls. "Almighty Christ, that is the best thing I ever heard."

Ruthie laughs with him. She passes him the lilies and he swats them at his knees, laughing.

"You can do it," Sharon says determined. She looks over at me and her eyes are frowning. "It just takes time."

For a long while, we've been bringing leftovers to the river shore. Potato peelings, old apples, peanuts shells, bread crusts. We never throw anything away. Everything comes to the river shore with us. We reckon that's why there are so many birds and animals here. It's their haven. One little rabbit eats right from our hands, and once, a hummingbird lit on Sharon's head and stayed there long enough for me to get a good look at it, its wings buzzing like two engines.

Leonard shakes his head. "Time," he says, "tick, tock, tick, tock," then he stops still and wide-eyed like a dead man. "I don't have time," he says mean. "That's for girls like you."

All day, we play along the river shore. We pick blackberries and dip our feet in the eddies. For the most part, Leonard is in a happy mood. He kisses Ruthie and Ray and he eats all of our sandwiches without asking. Ruthie tells him her dreams of getting married and having a nice house. She says she wants a big picture window in the living room, so the inside will always be bright. It's a dream Sharon and I have heard before. Leonard stares through his binoculars while Ruthie talks. Once in a while, he swats a bug away, but mostly he just watches.

When the sun gets high in the sky, it turns hot. We all start to complain in one way or another. "Hotter than a desert," someone says.

"Why don't you go for a swim," Leonard says, "cool yourselves off." He's got his shirt unbuttoned and is scratching his thin white belly.

"You come, too," Ruthie says, sliding her hand in under his shirt and touching him.

"Oh no. I'm staying right here. I'm waiting on that bird. But I'll watch Ray while you go."

Leonard takes the top off his canteen and guzzles down some water.

Ruthie looks up at Sharon and me. "You girls come, then. I don't want to go alone."

"Go on," Leonard says, smiling up at us and wiping drops of water from his lips. "Go back in the bushes and take your clothes off. The water feels good when you're naked. It's freedom gained."

Sharon looks at me worried.

"Don't worry," Leonard says as if reading our minds, "I'll close my eyes until you're in deep."

Ruthie hands the baby to Leonard. He sits Ray beside him and gives him a little treat. Ray chews it and smiles. Even if Leonard doesn't realize it, he's pretty well tamed Ray with those sweets.

We hang our clothes in the branches. It's hotter in the bushes. Almost breathless. Sharon and I stand with our privates covered, but Ruthie is brave. She said once that all modesty is gone after you give birth. "Cover your eyes," Ruthie yells out, "these girls are virgins."

That makes us blush, even though Ruthie doesn't say it in a teasing way. She says it more like a mother would.

"Covered," he yells back.

We take off running, dipping to one side when we step on a branch or a sharp rock. We hear the camera snapping and look over at Leonard who has the camera pointed at us. Sharon and I dive under water as fast as we can. When we come back up, Ruthie is standing waist-deep with her hands on her hips, her bosoms bare for all the world to see. "That's not respectful," she scolds.

"It's all in fun," Leonard says, snapping her picture.

"Taking pictures of me naked is one thing, but they are girls."

"Yeah," Sharon says. We're neck-deep holding hands. The current is strong and pulling us. Leonard opens the camera up and winds the film, then pops it in his shirt pocket and reloads. "They'll be proud as punch when they see their pictures tomorrow." He says this like we have exactly the same feelings as him, like there's no difference to us.

"Don't you dare develop those pictures," Ruthie says. "My sisters are nobody's business."

Leonard stares out beyond Ruthie. Nothing she says seems to affect him. He's acting like a dead person. Ruthie dives under and disappears. Ray picks up one of the lilies and swats it at the ground. The petals snap off and fly up like orange butterflies. He swats the lily until his mother comes back up. Sharon and I are still standing neck-deep. It doesn't feel good to be naked. It feels like freedom taken away, like something in the current could get us quick. I wish I was at that lawn party drinking lemonade. Things looked so simple there.

Leonard goads Sharon and me to race each other to the other side of the river, but we ignore him. Crossing the current is always dangerous and something we've been warned against. *You're better off floating downstream.* Besides, we're not interested in swimming anymore. The picture taking took away our desire. Ruthie goes under again, popping up beside us. Her hair is slicked back and her eyes as green as grass. She grabs our hands and lets her legs float out behind her. "Don't listen to him," she says squeezing our hands, her eyes sparkling like the water, "he's being a jerk."

A dark shadow glides over us. We let go of hands, then stand and look up, shading our eyes. The bird's long black neck is like a spear arching over us. Watching it, everything seems to stop and the air turns moist and lush. The back of the bird's body is bulbous like the weight of the world is there, but that doesn't seem to affect its grace. It circles the river over and over, never going near the tree with the net. I imagine telling Mama about the bird later. I'll make it out to be more than it is, even though what it is should be enough. Better than the Shroud of Turin, I'll say. Leonard snaps one picture after another. He doesn't once put the camera down and look at it with his real eyes. Proof is what he's after.

Ruthie gasps, "Leonard."

Without looking her way, Leonard hushes her.

"Leonard," she says louder, moving toward the shore, "where's Ray?"

Ruthie slaps her hand against the water and starts running. She looks like she's trying to fly. The bird is right over her and it makes a loud scratchy noise, a mutation of a caw. It dips down over her head and then flies low over the reeds. "The baby, Leonard," Ruthie's voice is pleading, "where is the baby?"

Leonard looks at Ruthie confused and then goes back to taking pictures like the baby is a common thing to him now. Sharon and I spread out in the water. A battered lily is floating in the middle of the river, downstream. "He's in the water," I say, picturing Ray as a bog person. Picturing his whole self shiny like bronzed baby shoes. Ruthie dives under water and so does Sharon, but I rush out past Leonard and into the bushes. I grab Sharon's *Easy-Wear* dress and pull it over my head, then run up the hill.

～ヒ

Mama is bent over the porch railing, brushing out her long hair. "Mama," I holler.

When she flips her head up, I see her ears for the first time. They're white and bigger than saucers. The sight of them tells me certain things about a person don't change no matter what they say. No way did she grow into her ears. "Patty, why have you got Sharon's dress on?" She knows I hate black. She knows the colour makes my head ache.

"It's Ray," I say, "we can't find him. We think he's in the water."

～ヒ

Ruthie and Sharon are still searching the river, but Leonard and his cameras and bags are gone. Mama walks into the water without taking her shoes off. She lets the hem of her dress soak through while she looks up and down the river. Ruthie and Sharon are swimming frantically, first diving in one spot, then another. I can't bring myself to step into the water. It's strange to me now. I look up at the sky for the bird, imagining for a moment that maybe it stole our baby, but all I see is the empty net, slung low.

Mama walks down along the shore with the current. She's walking slow, studying the shore. She looks like she's listening to a far off message, something on the breeze. I want to tell her to jump in and look for Ray, but I don't dare. Who am I to question her faith? Finally, she stops in a shallow eddy and smiles at the shore. I rush over and look. The baby is sitting in an old nest of reeds, chewing on a cattail and drooling. I've never seen the nest before, but it looks like it's been here forever. It looks like a relic from another time. Black feathers float in the water around it. Ray waves the cattail at Mama and then puts it back in his mouth and chews.

"You sweet thing," Mama says. She looks at me. "You girls weren't thinking," she says flatly. It sounds like something Leonard would say, but then I remember the night we watched the Shroud of Turin movie at the church. Mama was all smiles, thrilled with revelation. Driving home, she said, "You see girls, faith is a fine-tuned science. No hit and miss to it."

When Ruthie hears Mama cooing, she rushes in and grabs Ray from the nest. She's so happy that she starts to cry. She lifts him up and the nest sticks to him, then falls into the water and begins to float downriver. The bottom of the nest is missing, which makes it look like a crown of thorns.

Sharon stays neck-deep in the water, watching us. Her lower lip is trembling, but she won't come out.

Mama takes Ray from Ruthie and kisses his cheek. She holds him close, and then looks at Ruthie's naked body. "What went on here?"

Ruthie tries to take the baby back, but Mama won't let her.

"I said, what went on here?"

"Leonard was supposed to watch him, Mama. While we went swimming. We were hot. It was awful hot."

Mama shakes her head. "You sacrificed a baby's safety to cool off."

Ruthie looks down crossing her arms over her bosoms. "It wasn't like that."

"Oh?" Mama says.

Ruthie blinks, "I thought he was being watched."

Mama gets a sorry look on her face. A look that says the weight of that message is on her now. For a minute, I picture her back big and bulbous like the strange bird's. "You better get dressed, Ruthie," she says.

I don't put my colourful dress back on. I leave it for Sharon to wear and follow along after Mama. Her hair is long and dark down her back. In the sun, it's like silk. It amazes me that I've never seen it hung out beautiful like that before. That she kept its beauty hid all that time. Ray is looking at me waving his arms and smiling. He could have floated downriver so easy, he could have been lost forever. Lights start to flash in my head. Then a sharp pain starts between my eyes.

When we get near the house, the strange bird is sitting on the peak of our roof. It makes a sweet sound as if he's talking to the baby. Mama pays no attention to the bird. She keeps on walking like she's seen it a thousand times before, like maybe she's even chit-chatted with it. Ray turns and when he sees the bird, he coos with wonder. It's like a beautiful song. Listening,

I think how silly it is to want to leave this place even for a while, even for a dream. This place is what we know best. Besides, down by the river, things just come our way.

Ann-Marie MacDonald

Cave Paintings

When the attic door finally gave way, James saw this silent portrait: *Death and the Young Mother*. It's an overdone, tasteless, melodramatic painting. A folk painting from a hot culture. Naive. Grotesque. Authentic.

This is not a gauzy Victorian death scene. No fetishized feminine pallor, no agnostic slant of celestial light, no decorously distraught husband. This portrait is in livid colour. A crucified Christ hangs over a metal-framed single bed. On either side of the crucifix are two small pictures: one is of the Virgin Mary exposing her sacred heart aflame, the other is of her son Jesus, his heart likewise exposed and pierced to precious blood by a chain of thorns. They look utterly complaisant, Mother and Son. They have achieved a mutual plateau of exquisite suffering.

On the bed lies the Young Mother. Her eyes are closed. Her blonde-red hair is damp and ratty on the pillow. The sheets are black with blood. The centre of her body is ravaged. A plump dark woman who looks much older than thirty-three stands over her. This is the grandmother. She holds two dripping infants trussed by the ankles, one in each hand, like a canny shopper guesstimating the weight of a brace of chickens. The grandmother's face looks straight out from the picture at the viewer.

If this were really a painting, there would also be a demon peering out from under the lid of the hope chest at the foot of the bed, looking to steal the Young Mother's Soul. But he'd be pre-empted by her Guardian Angel waiting in the wings to guide her already departing Soul up to God. The

Soul, half in, half out of the tomb of her body, is in very good condition, the hair freshly combed, the nightgown spotless, the face expressionless — the first divine divestiture has taken place, she has sloughed off her personality like an old skin. She won't need it where she's going. Above the crucifix, the wall has dematerialized. Clouds hover. Somewhere within is God, waiting.

But since this is not really a painting but a moment freeze-framed by James's eye, the supernatural elements are, if present, invisible. There is the dead Young Mother, the Grandmother, the Infants, the Icons, the hope chest. What can you do with such a picture? You never want to see it again yet you can't bring yourself to burn it or slash it to dust. You have to keep it.

Put it in the hope chest, James. Yes. That's a good place for it. No one ever rummages in there. This is crazy, of course. You can't stuff a memory of a moment into a real-life hope chest as if it were a family heirloom. But for a second James feels as though that's what he's looking at — an old portrait that he hid in the hope chest many years ago and just stumbled upon again. This temporary confusion is a premonition; it tells him that he will never get over this sight. That it will be as fresh fourteen years from now, the colours not quite dry, just as it is today.

James goes out of the room, but not far. His legs give way and he collapses outside the fallen door, unconscious. He doesn't hear the first cries of the babies inside. The involuntary part of his mind does, though. It is just not conveying the message. It is keeping it on a crumpled piece of paper on the floor of its cave. It is taking a break, admiring its cave painting by the light of the dark.

A few moments later, James's hand shoots out and fastens on Materia's ankle, almost toppling her down the narrow staircase as she leaves the room. James's mouth opens a split second before his eyes. "Where the hell are you going?"

"I'm gonna get the priest."

"No you're not." He's awake now.

"They gonna be baptized."

"No they're not."

"They gotta be baptized."

"No!" James roars.

"You gonna kill them, you gonna kill their souls, you're the devil—"

She's hitting him. Closed fists in his face. If the scissors were handy she wouldn't bother to shut his eyes first — *"Ebn sharmoota, Kesemmak! Ya khereb bEytak, ya Hara' deenak!"* If the bayonet were near she would not hesitate. And God would understand. Why didn't she think of this before? Materia too is awake now, after a nineteen-year slumber. She will kill him if she can.

James gets her wrists in a vise grip. His other hand clamps across her mouth. Her eyes roll back. James tells her, "Who's the killer eh?! Who's the killer?! God damn you, God damn you, damn you—" He begins to punctuate the curses by slowly slamming her head into the wall. Her eyes are trying to reason with him, but without the help of words her eyes become a horses' eyes, as mute, as panicked. His tears are flowing now. His lips tripping on salt and snot, his nose bleeding, he's retching out the most agonizing man-sobs, the wall is starting to conform to her skull. This time, however, he hears the tiny cries from inside. Like kittens. He picks up Materia and carries her three flights down to the coal cellar and locks her in. Then he goes for a walk. And many fast drinks, of course. Some of us are just not equipped for suicide. When we're at the bottom, suicide is too creative an act to initiate.

Which leaves little Frances. At the bottom of the attic stairs. Based on her upbringing, and from what she has heard and seen tonight, one thing is clear: the babies up there must be baptized. But she has to be careful. She has to hurry. She mustn't get caught. She stands at the bottom looking up.

The attic room has been a place of absolute peace and quiet for the past many months. Until tonight. Her oldest sister has lain up there not saying anything. Frances and Mercedes have been allowed in to read to her and to bring her trays of food. They have read *Black Beauty, Treasure Island, Bleak House, Jane Eyre, What Katy Did, Little Women* and every story in *The Children's Treasury of Saints and Martyrs.* The two of them decided to look up the hard words next time around, rather than break up the reading aloud. They also got their mother to search out recipes for the invalid; food found in *What Katy Did* and *Little Women.* "Blancmange" seems to be the favourite of languishing girls. They never do find out what it is. "'White eat.'" What would that taste like?

Frances knew Kathleen must be very ill because of the huge lump in her stomach. Mercedes told her it was a tumour. "We must pray for her." Together Frances and Mercedes have prayed for Kathleen. They have made a little shrine and given up sweets for as long as it takes her to get well.

So here's Frances at the bottom of the narrow attic staircase. She is almost six. She is not afraid of the dark. Besides, there's a little light coming from that room. And she's not alone. Her big sister, Kathleen, is up there. And so are the babies. The babies, which sound exactly like kittens. Frances is very fond of kittens. She's in her bare feet. She's got her white nightgown on and her hair is in two long French braids. She gets to the landing. She's too small to be on eye level with the new depression in the wall; just as well. But what does it matter, she saw how it got here, and now the child is entering the room and she's going to see everything. She's stepping over the splintered caved-in door with her bare feet.

The difference between Frances and James is that, although she sees a version of the same horrible picture, Frances is young enough to be under the greater influence of the cave mind. It will never forget. But it steals the picture from her voluntary mind—grand theft art—and stows it, canvas side to the cave wall. It has decided, "If we are to continue functioning, we can't have this picture lying around." So Frances sees her sister and, unlike her father, will forget almost immediately, but, like her father, will not get over it.

What Frances sees: the gore. The pictures over the bed. The scissors. And the babies, squirming slightly and mewing between Kathleen's legs where they have been wedged for safekeeping until the priest can be dug up. So...the secret contents of Kathleen's tumour, revealed; this gets filed under "Normal" in Frances's mind.

Frances devises a way of carrying both babies: she spreads the front of her white nightie on the bed and places the slippery babies on it. She folds them into the fabric, making a cozy bundle. She cradles her bundle of babies and walks carefully all the way down two flights of stairs with her underpants showing, through the kitchen, out the back door, across the pitch-dark coal clinks in the backyard, until she comes to the bank of the creek. There is one scary thing: the scarecrow in the centre of the garden on the other side of the creek. If toys come alive at midnight, what happens to scarecrows? Frances avoids looking at it. "It's just a thing." But she doesn't want to offend it. She lovingly empties the tiny children onto the grass. It's a nice warm evening.

Frances regrets that she didn't think to rifle the hope chest for the white lace gown and bonnet—the outfit that she, Mercedes and Kathleen were all baptized in. Too late now, there's no time, *I have to get this done before Daddy comes home.*

Frances loves her little niece and nephew already. There is nothing she would not do to make sure their souls are safe. She knows that otherwise they die with Original Sin on them and go to the non-place, Limbo, and become no one for all eternity. Frances has never been up close at a baptism, but she's seen him dip the baby's head into the water. The priest is praying, that's for certain, so Frances must pray too. *Hurry Frances.* Frances makes the sign of the cross, *In nomine Patris.* . . . In the name of the Father, the Son and the Holy Ghost. She looks at the wee babies in the skimpy moonlight; "Ladies first." She picks up the girl baby, and shimmies on her bum down the embankment to the creek. She wades to the centre. The water is waist-deep. On wee Frances, that is. Her nightgown puffs and floats on the surface before taking on water and silting down around her legs. She makes the sign of the cross with her thumb on the baby's forehead.

Now's the part where you pray. Frances takes a stab at it: "Dear God, please baptize this baby." And then her favourite prayer from bedtime, "Angel of God, my guardian dear, to whom God's love commits me here, ever this day be at my side, to light, to guard, to rule and guide. Amen." Now's the part where you dip the head in the water. Frances tips the baby carefully towards the water. The little thing is still slick and slips through her hands and sinks. Oh no. Quick! *Hen, rooster, chicken, duck*! Frances plunges down, grabs the baby before it hits the bottom, then breaks the surface clutching it to her body. It's okay. Frances's little heart is beating like a bird in the jaws of a cat, she catches her breath, the baby lets out a tiny holler and the sweetest little sputtering coughs. It's okay, it just swallowed a bit of water, it's okay. It's okay. Frances rocks it gently and sings to it a small song composed then and there, "Baby, baby . . . baby, baby . . . baby baby." There. At least it's nice and clean now.

Frances crawls up the bank again, lays the girl baby down on the grass, kisses her little hands and head and picks up the boy. She knows that you have to be extra careful with new babies because their heads aren't closed yet. Like a ditch or something along the tip of their skulls. It's called a "soft spot" even though it's in the shape of a line. You can see it stretching along beneath the layer of bluish skin that's draped across it. Frances didn't see it on the girl baby's head because the girl baby has a weirdly dense thatch of black hair. But there it is on the boy baby's feathery pate: a shallow trench dividing his head in half. Frances enters once more the waters of the creek and lightly traces the pale blue fault line in the infant's skull. What if someone just came along and poked their fingers in there, what would happen? He would die. Frances squirms at the thought that just anyone could come along and do that. What if her fingers just went ahead and did that? *Oh no, hurry, you have to get him baptized before it's too late. Before Daddy comes home, or before anyone's fingers can press in his head.*

Frances drops the second baby. Oh no. Quick! *Hen, rooster, chicken—*

"What in God's name are you doing?"

Frances's head jerks up, arresting her plunge. It's Daddy. There's the great upside-down V of his legs towering at the top of the creek embankment. He's got the girl baby in one arm.

"Get the hell out of there!"

He's drunk, otherwise he would never curse in the presence of a child. He reaches down and gets Frances by one arm, easily swinging her up out of the water, her soaked nightgown hanging down past her toes, she could be the Little Mermaid invited at long last onto the good ship *Homo Sapiens*, ready to try out her new feet. Except for the bloodstains.

The water is dark. James doesn't see the child on the creek bed. "No!" Frances screams as he sets her down on the grass. She can't find the words. She can't tell him, telling is not an option, this is like a dream, she's forgotten how to say in waking English, "The other baby is in there, he's going to drown, we have to get him out!" James tosses her ahead, herding her in jerks back towards the house. Frances breaks and runs back. He lurches after her. She reaches the edge of the creek and leaps. Over the top. Splash and plunge. She scrabbles about on the bottom for the baby, her lungs are stinging, in this water she's as blind as the newborn she can't find, she finds him. She breaks the surface for the second time as James arrives back, swaying a little, at the creek's edge. She bundles the baby to her chest; it stirs once and is silent. She stares up at her father and the girl baby. She starts to shiver.

James either says or thinks, "Jesus Christ, Jesus Christ, Jesus Christ." He slides down the bank, takes the child and goes through the useless motions of resuscitation. But it's no use. The boy baby was in the water a good twenty seconds too long. Frances's teeth start to chatter, and she wonders if her black and white candy is still at the bottom of the creek or if it has been washed out to sea.

Michael Hennessey

The Priest
and the Pallbearer

The two middle-aged men in the black Buick waited restlessly, smoking, glancing out the rear window. The bells of Saint Dunstan's Basilica had already begun tolling, the strong southerly gusts ripping the sound from the steeples, flinging it over the roofs of the city. Dry leaves swirled around the car.

"I wish to God he'd hurry up," muttered Joe Cronin, his bony face scowling.

The driver, Tom Flynn, a light-haired man of average build, laughed shortly. "Are you planning to go to Confession on the way out, Joe?"

Cronin, who hadn't been a practising Catholic for thirty years, snorted in anger. Flynn reached into the back seat to tap Cronin's knee. "You always liked him, Joe, ever since we were in school."

"The son of a bitch!"

Flynn chuckled, adjusting the rear-view mirror. "Never mind, Joe," he said. "Here he comes. He can give you his blessing before we start."

The portly old priest, seventy if he was a day, came waddling along, giving his well-known imitation of a man in a hurry. His soutane blew around his still-sturdy legs. In the time it took him to puff and pant his way to the car their faces had settled into the neutrality generated by authority. A few leaves were swept into the car as the priest clambered in beside Flynn and slammed the door.

"All right," he said, nodding impatiently to the car ahead, knowing that the funeral director had been watching his approach. His tone implied that he hadn't all day for this nonsense.

A seagull up from the water two blocks south banked sharply, deposited its droppings on the shiny hood of the Buick, then, a flash of white, wheeled into the sky with a raucous cry. Flynn gave a short bark of a laugh. "Did you ever hear the story of the seagull that insulted the elephant?" he asked. No one spoke. Flynn gave a slight shrug and decided to drop the subject.

The funeral procession moved off, the men among the onlookers on the sidewalk removing their hats. The beefy priest strained forward, attempting to get his head below the level of the dash to light a cigarette. Cronin snorted. The priest inhaled deeply then exhaled with a heavy chesty cough. "First today," he muttered between wheezes, deciding to ignore Cronin and the common knowledge in the parish that he began his day with a cigarette between his lips. Cronin snorted again to inform him that he was not deceived.

The procession moved slowly at first, increasing speed as it moved north on Prince Street. "Poor old Kip won't be smoking any more cigarettes," Flynn said eventually into the silence. "Probably what killed him."

"It was his heart," Cronin said sourly, giving nothing.

The priest had been silent since his unsuccessful gambit about his first smoke of the day. He sat quietly, feeling the enmity of the man behind him. Flynn, now, although a grown man, was still something of an innocent. But Cronin—the intense and bitter Cronin who had always hated him—he was an enemy.

As they approached the railway crossing on Longworth Avenue, the priest said, "D'you mind when we used to walk out here to the jail crossing with some of these funerals?"

Flynn jumped in to do his part in the awkward silence. "Oh yes," he said. "I remember it well. The first time for me was Anthony Martin's funeral and it raining buckets—and afterwards I came down with pleurisy."

Cronin showed his first interest in the conversation. "Anthony Martin? That was a long time ago."

"Oh, a long time," Flynn said. "Nigh onto thirty years." He peered out the window. "TB," he said, adding softly, "we were all young pups then."

"Schoolboys. We were schoolboys," Cronin said, aiming his words like darts. "At Queen Square School—of fond memory."

His words floated there in the uneasy pause that followed. They drove past the Queens County Jail, the heads of the prisoners in the yard turning slowly to follow their progress. The men in the car studied them.

"There's Baldy O'Brien," Flynn said. "Again."

"Still," Cronin growled.

Flynn laughed, the priest adding an indulgent chuckle.

"Baldy's another one who'd have fond memories of Queen Square School," Cronin said. "That's probably where he learned to hate."

The priest stirred uneasily, his feelings finally forcing him to speak. "That's old times, Joe, long gone, long forgotten."

Cronin ran a strong hand through his bushy hair. "Forgotten by some maybe. Not by me. How about you, Tom? You remember your school days?"

Flynn disliked being invited to play the role of collaborator and was torn between loyalty to his friend and his desire not to give offence. He came down for his friend, but not strongly. "Oh yes," he said airily.

"Even poor old Kippy back there," Cronin said, indicating the hearse with a toss of his head, "he remembered his school days. The last two months we talked a lot about our school days—we ran out of everything else."

The priest finally forced himself all the way around in the seat until he could fix Cronin with his eyes. His left hand on the back of the seat was a soft white sleeping mouse. With his neck twisted to face Cronin, his jowls hung pink and smooth and heavy over his immaculate Roman collar. His grey hair was brushed back in two vain wings over his ears. His breathing was raspy, his lips tight, his eyes expressionless. He had handled a thousand rebellions in his day.

"What's all this talk about school days, Joe? Sure you'd think it was only yesterday. Those were bad times, best forgotten." His voice had hardened into command on the last sentence.

"Perhaps you're right," Cronin said, pausing, wanting to set him up. "I know *you'd* like to forget them because you helped cause them."

The priest's eyes became more shaded. He pursed his lips and nodded, being reasonable. "That could be," he admitted. "It was a tough job."

"That's what the Nazis claimed," Cronin snapped.

"Joe, Joe, take it easy," Flynn said.

"Take it easy be damned!" Cronin was almost shouting.

The priest drew back as if he had been slapped. "I will not be compared to the Nazis," he said, looking down his nose at Cronin. His voice held the imperious tone that had ruled the parish for years. "I took only the steps necessary to do the work of God."

Cronin sneered. "It seems to me God gets blamed for a lot. Was it God who sent you into the schools with your reign of terror?"

The priest's forehead wrinkled and he looked mystified, but his eyes were brittle and sharp, giving the lie to his bewilderment.

"Reign of terror?" he said grandly, at his oratorical best, implying that Cronin was a babbling idiot. "Reign of terror?" he repeated, his voice rising sharply on the last syllable. "How dare you imply such a thing. What do you know of it?"

"Know of it? You seem to forget I was there too. And I wasn't sitting up there in your grand Palace with His Excellency the Bishop eating four-course meals off Irish linen either. I was down there in the trenches of Hell Street where we often had to fight for our supper."

The tires hissed on the pavement. "Ah, the Thirties were a bad time," Flynn interjected soothingly. "Bad for everybody."

Cronin and the priest paid no attention to him. They had eyes and ears only for each other. The way he was twisted around in the seat caused the priest's face to grow ever more florid. He rolled an unlit cigarette between the fingers of his right hand, mangling it. Finally, he sighed.

"Let me tell you about the four-course meals," he said slowly. "We were all much younger then, and"—his mouth twisted for a moment—"slimmer, not used to our worldly comforts. Many's and many's a night my supper consisted of bread and tea. You forget, Joe, there was no money in the parish and we depended on the people for our subsistence. And even at that, when we did have it we often gave it away." He allowed himself a small smile. "There were hundreds of people not too proud to come to the Palace regularly looking for food. Anything. They literally had nothing to eat."

He was back in time. "Bishop O'Sullivan had laid down the rules: 'If anyone in the parish is to go hungry while there's food in this house, it will be you who are better sustained spiritually'." He paused. "I remember those words as if it were yesterday. So tell me, Joe, about fighting for your supper. I often had to pray for mine."

Flynn was filled with admiration for the old priest. Still a battler, he thought. But Cronin was tenacious and not about to let the priest score points that easily.

"Still and all," Cronin said, trying a wing shot, "that had nothing to do with the school. You came in there like the wrath of God, beating up kids and throwing them around. They were terrified of you. Hell, even the teachers were scared of you. They used your name to frighten the kids. And for what? What was it all about? Missing the eight o'clock Mass! It was crazy."

The priest dropped his eyes for a moment, looking inward. When he spoke his voice was gentle.

"Maybe it was crazy. It was the times. The eight o'clock Mass was the Children's Mass. I wanted them there together. I was trying to sow a spirit of unity in the young, a spirit of hope—trying to get them away from the despair of the older generation. You remember what it was like—it was terrible. They—the children—were our future."

He shrugged, back again in the present. "Maybe I didn't do much good, I don't know, but I was trying to do what I could for the young."

"With your fists?"

"It was all I had. I'm not a great theologian and in those times you weren't going to win anybody with reason. But I was a pretty fair scrapper in my day, so I coasted on that and tried to use it to advantage."

"Fear!"

"In some, yes, I'm afraid. Others I think liked me. I did some work I'm not ashamed of in the Holy Name Club."

"There were always a few sucking up to you."

The priest turned to stretch his aching neck and to light another cigarette, his hands trembling. He kept his voice down.

"And there were always a few who said just that." He drew the smoke greedily into his lungs, letting it dribble out. "Why is it so difficult for you to accept that there were a few boys and girls who appreciated a little guidance?"

"Because I don't believe it. They were no better than the rest of us."

The priest sighed. "That's it, don't you see? They were trying to be."

"And it was Fist City for the others?"

"Sometimes. I'm not proud of that, but—"

"I know. I know. It was necessary."

Flynn rolled down his window to let the smoke out, trying to act invisible, imagining that the hatred sizzling back and forth had arisen out of the bogs of Armagh or Monaghan or Cork. In some ancient Celtic battle, a forefather of one had slain a clansman of the other, and the bad blood had come down the centuries.

The priest declared a truce. "It was necessary," he said without emotion, his voice falling.

Cronin pounced, but there was anguish in his voice. "Why? Why was it necessary to terrorize young boys? I know one kid you beat so badly he quit school at grade seven and never returned." His eyes glistened. "He never had a chance for an education. Who were you to cut him off? He might have amounted to something."

The priest lowered his eyes. "He did, Joe. He became a man."

"A man!" cried Cronin, misunderstanding. "We all grow up. What the hell kind of an answer is that?"

The car pulled into the cemetery. "And what about poor Kippy back there?" Cronin said, jerking his thumb over his shoulder. "What about that poor bastard? I bet you don't even remember when you beat him so badly he curled up under his desk and pissed his pants. Do you? And he never had another day of schooling in his life. Did you know that? I wasn't the only one. You drove us out of school!"

The car stopped. The priest looked around, bewildered, as if trying to recall where he was. Then he sat still, facing the front, his head bowed.

"Joe," he said, "there's nothing I can do about that now except to say I'm sorry and ask you to forgive me."

"Forgive you? Never! It's the height of hypocrisy for you to be saying Mass for Kippy. He didn't forgive you either."

People were climbing out of the cars, stretching, heading towards the hearse. The grave was an open slash in the ground twenty yards away, the plastic greens bright over the mound of clay. Clouds raced overhead, driven by the now easterly wind. Rain before nightfall, Flynn thought, not moving, anxious to see how it would end.

When the priest spoke, his voice was soft.

"You're wrong about that, Joe. I was with Kippy when he died—remember? I asked him about it. 'D'you mind, Kip,' I said, 'the time I beat you up in school?' 'When was that, Father?' says he. 'Oh, a long time ago,' says I. 'No,' says he, 'I don't remember it at all.' So I told him about it—every detail was clear in my head—and says I, 'Even if you don't remember, Kip, you must forgive me.' He just laughed and said, 'What's to forgive if I don't remember?' And I had to beg him. Finally he put his hand on my head and said, 'I forgive you.' Then he gave that slow grin of his, and says he, 'Go in peace, my son, and may God bless you … I always wanted to say that.' And then he was gone …"

The priest's eyes wrinkled at the corners. He turned to Cronin. "Well, there it is." He paused and added simply, "Forgive me, Joe." He made no mention of Cronin's attempted deception.

Cronin studied the priest's face, shifting his gaze from one eye to the other, conquering the inclination to avert his own eyes. He pretended to be looking for sincerity and truth, but when his scurrying mind could find no escape, he faithfully donned the blinders of rage that had served him so well throughout his life.

"No!" he shouted. "No, I won't forgive you! I know you and your tricks. You're just as crafty as you ever were. You're not sorry. You just want your conscience to rest easy."

The priest turned slowly to the front and reached for the door handle, a flash of satisfaction coming and going in his eyes, indicating that he now considered the problem to be Cronin's alone. Flynn glanced into the mirror and his eyes dilated as he witnessed the buffeting of Cronin's frustrated hatred, and his soul shrivelled as he realized that if Cronin held a pistol he would put it to the priest's head and pull the trigger.

Alistair MacLeod

Vision

I don't remember when I first heard the story but I remember the first time that I heard it and remembered it. By that I mean the first time it made an impression on me and more or less became *mine*; sort of went into me the way such things do, went into me in such a way that I knew it would not leave again but would remain there forever. Something like when you cut your hand with a knife by accident, and even as you're trying to staunch the blood flowing out of the wound, you know the wound will never really heal totally and your hand will never look quite the same again. You can imagine the scar tissue that will form and be a different colour and texture from the rest of your skin. You know this even as you are trying to stop the blood and trying to squeeze the separated edges of skin together once more. Like trying to squeeze together the separated banks of a small and newly discovered river so that the stream will be subterranean once again. It is something like that, although you know in one case the future scar will be forever on the outside, while the memory will remain forever deep within.

Anyway, on this day we were about a mile and a half offshore but heading home on the last day of the lobster season. We could see the trucks of the New Brunswick buyers waiting for us on the wharf and because it was a sunny day, light reflected and glinted off the chrome trim and bumpers of the waiting trucks and off their gleaming rooftops as well. It was the last day of June and the time was early afternoon and I was seventeen.

My father was in good spirits because the season was over and we had done reasonably well and we were bringing in most of our gear intact. And there seemed no further need to rush.

The sea was almost calm, although there was a light breeze at our backs and we throttled down our engine because there really was no reason to hurry into the wharf for the last and final time. I was in the stern of the boat steadying the piled lobster traps that we had recently raised from the bottom of the sea. Some of them still gleamed with droplets of salt water and streamers of seaweed dangled from their laths. In the crates beside my feet the mottled blue-green lobsters moved and rustled quietly, snapping their tails as they slid over one another with that peculiar dry/wet sound of shell and claws over shell and claws. Their hammer claws had been pegged and fastened shut with rubber bands so they would not mutilate each other and so decrease their value.

"Put some of those in a sack for ourselves," said my father, turning his head back over his right shoulder as he spoke. He was standing ahead of me, facing the land and urinating over the side. His water fell into the sea and vanished into the rolling swell of the boat's slow passage.

"Put them in the back there," he said, "behind the bait bucket, and throw our oilers over them. They will want everything we've got, and what they won't see won't hurt them. Put in some markets too, not just canners."

I took a sack and began to pick some lobsters out of the crate, grasping them at the end of their body shells or by the ends of their tails and being careful not to get my fingers snapped. For even with their hammer claws banded shut there was still a certain danger.

"How many do you want?" I asked.

"Oh," he said, turning with a smile and running his hand along the front of his trousers to make sure his fly was closed, "as many as you want. Use your own good judgement."

We did not often take home lobsters for ourselves because they were so expensive and we needed the money they would bring. And the buyers wanted them with a desperation almost bordering on frenzy. Perhaps even now as I bent over the crate they were watching from the wharf with binoculars to see if any were being concealed. My father stood casually in front of me, once more facing the land and shielding my movements with his body. The boat followed its set course, its keel cutting the blue-green water and turning it temporarily into white.

There was a time long ago when the lobsters were not thought to be so valuable. Probably because the markets of the larger world had not yet been discovered or were so far away. People then ate all they wanted of them and even used them for fertilizer on their fields. And those who did eat them did not consider them to be a delicacy. There is a quoted story from the time which states that in the schools you could always identify the children of the poor because they were the ones with lobster in their sandwiches. The well-to-do were able to afford bologna.

With the establishment of the New England market, things changed. Lobster factories were set up along the coast for the canning of the lobsters at a time before good land transportation and refrigeration became common. In May and June and into July the girls in white caps and smocks packed the lobster meat into burnished cans before they were steam sealed. And the men in the smack boats brought the catches to the rickety piers which were built on piles and jutted out into the sea.

My father's mother was one of the girls, and her job was taking the black vein out of the meat of the lobster's tail before the tail was coiled around the inside of the can. At home they ate the black vein along with the rest of the meat, but the supervisors at the factory said it was unsightly. My father's father was one of the young men standing ready in the smack boat, wearing his cap at a jaunty angle and uttering witty sayings and singing little songs in Gaelic to the girls who stood above him on the wharf. All of this was, of course, a long time ago and I am just trying to recreate the scene.

On the day of the remembered story, though, the sea was almost serene as I placed the lobsters in the sack and prepared to hide them behind the bait bucket and under our oilers in the stern of the boat. Before we secreted the sack, we leaned over the side and scooped up water in the bailing bucket and soaked the sack to ensure the health and life of the lobsters kept within. The wet sack moved and cracked with the shape and sound of the lobsters and it reminded me vaguely of sacks of kittens which were being taken to be drowned. You could see the movement but not the individuals.

My father straightened from his last dip over the side and passed the dripping bucket carefully to me. He steadied himself with his left hand on the gunwale and then seated himself on the thwart and faced toward the north. I gave the lobsters another soaking and moved to place them behind the bait bucket. There was still some bait remaining but we would not have need of it anymore so I threw it over the side. The pieces of blue-grey mackerel turned and revolved before I lost sight of them within the water. The day before yesterday we had taken these same mackerel out of the same sea. We used nets for the spring mackerel because they were blind and could not see to take a baited hook; but in the fall, when they returned, the scales had fallen from their eyes and they would lunge at almost anything thrown before them. Even bits of other mackerel ground up and mixed with salt. Mackerel are a windward fish and always swim against the wind. If the wind is off the land, they swim toward the shore and perhaps the waiting nets; but if the wind blows in the opposite direction, they face out to sea and go so far out some years that we miss them altogether.

I put the empty bait bucket in front of the sack of lobsters and placed an empty crate upside down and at an angle over them so that their movements would not be noticeable. And I casually threw our oilers over them as well.

Ahead of us on the land and to the north of the wharf with its waiting trucks was the mile-long sandy beach cut by the river that acted as an erratic boundary between the fishing grounds of ourselves and our neighbours, the MacAllesters. We had traditionally fished to the right of the river and they to the left, and apparently for many years it was constant in its estuary. But in recent years the river mouth, because of the force of storms and tides and the buildup of sand, had become undependable as a visual guide. The shifting was especially affected by the ravages of the winter storms, and some springs the river might empty almost a mile to the north or the south of its previous point of entry. This had caused a tension between ourselves and the MacAllesters because, although we traditionally went to the same grounds, the boundary was no longer fixed and we had fallen into accusations and counter-accusations; sometimes using the actual river when it suited our purpose, and when it did not, using an earlier and imaginary river which we could no longer see.

The MacAllesters' boat was going in ahead of us now and I waved to Kenneth MacAllester, who had become a rather lukewarm friend because of the tension between our families. He was the same age as I, and he waved back, although the other two men in the boat did not.

At an earlier time when Kenneth MacAllester and I were friends and in about grade six he told me a story while we were walking home from school in the spring. He told me that his grandmother was descended from a man in Scotland who possessed *Da Shealladh*, two sights or the second sight, and that by looking through a hole in a magical white stone he could see distant contemporary events as well as those of the future. Nearly all of his visions came true. His name was either Munro or MacKenzie and his first name was Kenneth and the eye he placed to the stone for his visions was *cam* or blind in the sense of ordinary sight. He was a favourite of the powerful man for whom he worked, but he and the man's wife were jealous and disliked each other. Once when the powerful man was in Paris there was a big party on his estate. In one version "the prophet" commented rather unwisely on the paternity of some of the children present. In another version the man's wife asked him mockingly if he could "see" her husband in Paris but he refused. However, she insisted. Putting the stone to his eye he told her that her husband was enjoying himself rather too much with ladies in Paris and had little thought of her. Enraged and embarrassed, she ordered him to be burned in a barrel of tar into which spikes had been driven from the outside. In one version the execution took place right away, but in another it did not take place until some days later. In the second version the man was returning home when he heard the news and saw the black smoke rising. He spurred his horse at utmost speed toward the point where he saw the billowing smoke and called out in an attempt to stop the burning and save his friend, but his horse died beneath him, and though he ran the rest of the way, he arrived too late for any salvation.

Before the prophet died he hurled his white stone as far as he could out into the lake and told the lady that the family would come to an end years hence. And he told her that it would end when there was a deaf-and-dumb father who would outlive his four sons and then all their lands would pass into the hands of strangers. Generations later the deaf-and-dumb father was apparently a fine, good man who was helpless in the face of the prophecy he knew too much about and which he saw unfolding around him with the death of each of his four loved sons. Unable again to offer any salvation.

I thought it was a tremendous story at the time, and Kenneth picked up a white stone from the roadside and held it to his eye to see if "prophecy" would work for him.

"I guess I really wouldn't want it to work," he said with a laugh. "I wouldn't want to be blind," and he threw the stone away. At that time he planned on joining the Air Force and flying toward the sun and being able to see over the tops of mountains and across the sea.

When we got to his house we were still talking about the story and his mother cautioned us not to laugh at such things. She went and found a poem by Sir Walter Scott, which she read aloud to us. We did not pay much attention to it, but I remember the lines which referred to the father and his four doomed sons:

> *Thy sons rose around thee in light and in love*
> *All a father could hope, all a friend could approve;*
> *What 'vails it the tale of thy sorrows to tell?*
> *In the springtime of youth and of promise they fell!*

Now, as I said, the MacAllesters' boat was going in ahead of us, loaded down with its final catch and with its stern and washboard piled high with traps. We had no great wish to talk to the MacAllesters at the wharf and there were other boats ahead of us as well. They would unload their catches first and pile their traps upon the wharf and it would be some time before we would find a place to dock. My father cut our engine. There was no need to rush.

"Do you see Canna over there?" he asked, pointing to the north where he was facing. "Do you see the point of Canna?"

"Yes," I said, "I see it. There it is."

There was nothing very unusual about seeing the point of Canna. It was always visible except on the foggiest days or when there was rain or perhaps snow. It was twenty miles away by boat, and on the duller days it reached out low and blue like the foot of a giant's boot extended into the sea. On sunny days like this one it sparkled in a distant green. The clearings of the old farms were visible and above them the line of the encroaching trees, the spruce and fir of a darker green. Here and there the white houses stood out and even the grey and weather-beaten barns. It was called after the Hebridean island of Canna, "the green island" where most of its original settlers were born. It was the birthplace of my grandmother, who was one of the girls in the white smocks at the Canna lobster factory in that long-ago time.

"It was about this time of year," said my father, "that your Uncle Angus and I went by ourselves to visit our grandmother at the point of Canna. We were eleven at the time and had been asking our parents for weeks to let us go. They seemed reluctant to give us any answer and all they would say was 'We will see' or 'Wait and see.' We wanted to go on the smack boat when it was making its final run of the season. We wanted to go with the men on the smack who were buying lobsters and they would set us ashore at the wharf at Canna point and we would walk the mile to our grandmother's house. We had never gone there by ourselves before. We could hardly remember being there because if you went by land you had to travel by horse and buggy and it was a long way. First you had to go inland to the main road and drive about twenty miles and then come back down toward the shore. It was about twice as far by land as it was by sea and our parents went about once a year. Usually by themselves, as there was not enough room for others in the buggy. If we did not get to go on the smack, we were afraid that we would not get to go at all. 'Wait and see' was all they said."

It seemed strange to me, as my father spoke, to think of Canna as far away. By that time it took perhaps three-quarters of an hour by car, even though the final section of the road was often muddy and dangerous enough in the wet months of spring and fall and often blocked by snow in the winter. Still, it was not hard to get there if you really wanted to, and so the old letters from Canna which I discovered in the upstairs attic seemed quite strange and from another distant time. It seemed hard to believe that people only twenty miles away would write letters to one another and visit only once a year. But at that time the distance was hard to negotiate, and there were no telephones.

My father and his brother Angus were twins and they had been named after their grandfathers so their names were Angus and Alex. It was common for parents to name their first children after their own parents and it seemed that almost all of the men were called Angus or Alex. In the early years of the century the Syrian and Lebanese pedlars who walked the muddy country roads beneath their heavy backpacks sometimes called themselves Angus or Alex so that they would sound more familiar to their potential customers. The pedlars, like the Gaelic-speaking people in the houses which they visited, had very little English, so anything that aided communication was helpful. Sometimes they unfolded their bolts of cloth and displayed their shining needles before admirers who were unable to afford them, and sometimes, sensing the situation, they would leave the goods behind. Later, if money became available, the people would say, "Put aside what we owe Angus and Alex in the sugar bowl so that we can pay them when they come."

Sometimes the pedlars would carry letters from one community to the other, to and from the families of the different Anguses and Alexes strung out along the coast. Distinguishing the different families, although their names were much the same, and delivering letters which they could not read.

My father and his brother continued to pester their parents who continued to say "Wait and see," and then one day they went to visit their father's mother who lived in a house quite close to theirs. After they had finished the lunch she had given them, she offered to "read" their teacups and to tell them of the future events revealed in the tea leaves at the bottoms of their cups: "You are going on a journey," she said, peering into the cups as she turned them in her hands. "You are going to cross water. And to take food with you. You will meet a mysterious woman who has dark hair. She will be quite close to you. And..." she said, turning the cups in her hands to see the formation of the leaves better, "and...oh...oh...oh."

"What?" they asked. "What?"

"Oh, that's enough for today," she said. "You had better be getting home or they will be worrying about you."

They ran home and burst into their parents' kitchen. "We are going on a trip to Canna," they said. "Grandma told us. She saw it in the tea leaves. She read it in our cups. We are going to take a lunch. We are going across the water. She said we were going."

The morning they left they were dressed in their best clothes and waiting at the wharf long before the smack was due, clutching their lunches in their hands. It was sunny when the boat left the wharf but as they proceeded along the coast it became cloudy and then it began to rain. The trip seemed long in the rain and the men told them to go into the boat's cabin where they would be dry and where they could eat their lunch. The first part of the trip seemed to be spoiled by rain.

It was raining heavily when the boat approached the wharf at Canna point. It was almost impossible to see the figures on the wharf or to distinguish them as they moved about in their heavy oil slickers. The lobster buyers were in a hurry, as were the wet men impatiently waiting for them in the rain.

"Do you know where you're going?" said the men in the smack to their young passengers.

"Yes," they said, although they were not quite sure because the rain obscured the landmarks that they thought they would remember.

"Here," said the men in the smack, handing them two men's oil slickers from the boat's cabin. "Wear these to help keep you dry. You can give them back to us sometime."

They climbed up the iron ladder toward the wharf's cap and the busy men reached their hands down to help and pull them up.

The men were busy and because of the rain no one on the wharf asked them where they were going, and they were too shy and too proud to ask. So they turned the cuffs of the oil slickers back over their wrists and began to walk up the muddy road from the wharf. They were still trying to keep their best clothes clean and pick their spots carefully, placing their good shoes where there were fairly dry spots and avoiding the puddles and little rivulets which rolled the small stones along in their course. The oil slickers were so long that the bottoms of them dragged on the muddy road and sometimes they lifted them up in the way that older ladies might lift the hems of their skirts when stepping over a puddle or some other obstacle in the roadway. When they lifted them, the muddy bottoms rubbed against their good trousers so they let them fall again. Then their shoes were almost invisible and they could hear and feel the tails of the coats dragging behind them as they walked. They were wet and miserable inside the long coats, as well as indistinguishable to anyone who might see the small forms in the long coats walking along the road.

After they had walked for half a mile they were overtaken by an old man in a buggy who stopped and offered them a ride. He, too, was covered in an oil coat, and his cap was pulled down almost to his nose. When he stopped to pick them up, the steam rose from his horse as they clambered into the wagon beside him. He spoke to them in Gaelic and asked them their names and where they were from and where they were going.

"To see our grandmother," they said.

"Your grandmother?" he asked.

"Yes," they said. "Our grandmother."

"Oh," he said. "Your grandmother, are you sure?"

"Of course," they said, becoming a bit annoyed. For although they were more uncertain than they cared to admit, they did not want to appear so.

"Oh," he said, "all right then. Would you like some peppermints?" And he reached deeply into a pocket beneath his oil coat and brought out a brown paper bag full of peppermints. Even as he passed the bag to them, the raindrops pelted upon it and it became soggy and began to darken in deterioration.

"Oh," he said, "you may as well keep all of them. I got a whole lot more of them for the store. They just came in on the boat." He pointed to some metal containers in the back of the buggy.

"Are you going to spend the night with your grandmother?" he asked.

"Yes," they said.

"Oh," he answered, pulling on the reins and turning the horse into the laneway of a yard.

He drove them to the door of the house and helped them down from the buggy while his horse stomped its impatient hooves in the mud and tossed its head in the rain.

"Would you like me to go in with you?" he asked.

"No," they said, impatient for him to be gone and out of sight.

"All right," he said and spoke to his uneasy horse which began to trot down the laneway, the buggy wheels throwing hissing jets of mud and water behind them.

They hesitated for a while outside the doorway of the house, waiting for the man to go out of sight and feeling ridiculous for standing in the rain. But halfway down the lane he stopped and looked back. And then he stood up in the buggy and shouted to them and made a "go-forward" gesture with his hand toward the house. They opened the door then and went in because they felt embarrassed and did not want to admit that he had brought them to the wrong house.

When they went in, they found themselves in the middle of a combined porch and entranceway which was cluttered with an odd collection of household and farming utensils. Baking pans and jars and sealers and chamber pots and old milk pails and rakes and hoes and hay forks and bits of wire and lengths of chain. There was very little light, and in the gloom something started up from their feet and bounced against their legs and then into a collection of jars and pails, causing a crashing cacophony of sound. It was a half-grown lamb, and it bleated as it bounded toward the main door, dropping bits of manure behind it. In the same instant and in response to the sound, the main door opened and the lamb leaped through it and into the house.

Framed in the doorway was a tall old woman clad in layers of clothing, even though it was summer, and wearing wire-framed glasses. On either side of her were two black dogs. They were like collies, although they had no white markings. They growled softly but deep within their throats and the fur on the back of their necks rose and they raised their upper lips to reveal their gleaming teeth. They were poised on the tips of their paws and their eyes seemed to burn in the gloom. She lowered a hand to each of their heads but did not say anything. Everyone seemed to stare straight ahead. The boys would have run away but they were afraid that if they moved, the dogs would be upon them, so they stayed where they were as still as could be. The only sound was the tense growling of the dogs. "*Cò a th'ann?*" she said in Gaelic. "Who's there?"

The boys did not know what to say because all the possible answers seemed so complicated. They moved their feet uneasily, which caused the dogs to each take two steps forward as if they were part of some rehearsed choreography. "*Cò a th'ann?*" she said, repeating the question. "Who's there?"

"We're from Kintail," they said finally. "Our names are Alex and Angus. We're trying to find our grandmother's house. We came on the smack boat."

"Oh," she said. "How old are you?"

"Eleven," they said. "Both of us. We're twins."

"Oh," she said. "Both of you. I have relatives in Kintail. Come in."

They were still afraid, and the dogs remained poised, snarling softly, with their delicate, dangerous lips flickering above the whiteness of their teeth.

"All right," they said. "We'll come in, but just for a minute. We can't stay long."

Only then did she speak to the dogs. "Go and lie under the table and be quiet," she said. Immediately they relaxed and vanished behind her into the house.

"Did you know these dogs were twins?" she asked.

"No," they said. "We didn't."

"Well," she said. "They are."

Inside the house they sat on the first chairs that they could find and moved them as close to the door as possible. The room that they were in was a primitive kitchen and much of its floor was cluttered with objects not unlike the porch, except that the objects were smaller — knives and forks and spoons and the remains of broken cups and saucers. There was a half-completed partition between the kitchen and what might have been a living room or dining room. The upright studs of the partition were firmly in place and someone had nailed wainscotting on either side of them but it extended only halfway to the ceiling.

It was difficult to tell if the partition had been left incomplete or if it was gradually being lowered. The space between the walls of the partition was filled with cats. They pulled themselves up by their paws and looked curiously at the visitors and then jumped back down into the space. From the space between the uncompleted walls the visitors could hear the mewing of newborn kittens. Other cats were everywhere. They were on the table, licking what dishes there were, and on the backs of the chairs and in and out of a cavern beneath an old couch. Sometimes they leaped over the half-completed partition and vanished into the next room. Sometimes they snarled at one another and feinted with their paws. In one corner a large tiger-striped tomcat was energetically breeding a small grey female flattened out beneath him. Other tentative males circled the breeding pair, growling deeply within their throats. The tiger cat would interrupt his movements from time to time to snarl at them and keep them at bay. The female's nose was pressed against the floor and her ears flattened down against her head. Sometimes he held the fur at the back of her neck within his teeth.

The two black dogs lay under the table and seemed oblivious to the cats. The lamb stood watchfully behind the stove. Everything in the house was extremely dirty—spilled milk and cat hair and unwashed and broken dishes. The old woman wore men's rubber boots upon her feet and her clothing seemed to consist of layers of petticoats and skirts and dresses and sweaters upon sweaters. All of it was very dirty and covered with stains of spilled tea and food remnants and spattered grease. Her hands seemed brown, and her fingernails were long, and there was a half inch of black grime under each of them. She raised her hands to touch her glasses and they noticed that the outside lenses were smeared and filthy as well. It was then that they realized that she was blind and that the glasses served no useful purpose. They became even more uncertain and frightened than they were before.

"Which one of you is Alex?" she asked, and he raised his hand as if answering a question at school before realizing that she could not see him.

"I am," he answered then, and she turned her face in his direction.

"I have a long association with that name," she said, and they were surprised at her use of a word like "association."

Because of the rain the day seemed to darken early and they could see the fading light through the grimy windows. They wondered for a moment why she did not light a lamp until they realized that there was none and that to her it made no difference.

"I will make you a lunch," she said. "Don't move."

She went to the partial partition and ripped the top board off with her strong brown hands and then she leaned it against the partition and stomped on it with her rubber-booted foot. It splintered and she repeated the action, feeling about the floor for the lengths of splintered wood. She gathered them up and went to the stove and, after removing the lids, began to feed them into the fire. She moved the kettle over the crackling flame.

She began to feel about the cupboards for food, brushing away the insistent cats which crowded about her hands. She found two biscuits in a tin and placed them on plates which she put into the cupboard so the cats would not devour them. She put her hand into a tea tin and took a handful of tea which she placed in the teapot and then she poured the hot water in as well. She found some milk in a dirty pitcher and, feeling for the cups, she splashed some of it into each.

Then she took the teapot and began to pour the tea. She turned her back to them but as she poured they could see her quickly dip her long brown finger with the half inch of grimy fingernail quickly into each cup. They realized she was doing it because she had no other way of knowing when the cups were full but their stomachs revolved and they feared they might throw up.

She brought them a cup of tea each and retrieved the biscuits from the cupboard and passed the plates to them. They sat holding the offerings on their laps while she faced them. Although they realized she could not see them, they still felt that she was watching them. They looked at the tea and the biscuits with the cat hair and did not know what to do. After a while they began to make slurping sounds with their lips.

"Well, we will have to be on our way," they said. Carefully they bent forward and placed the still-full teacups under their chairs and the biscuits in their pockets.

"Do you know where you are going?" she asked.

"Yes," they said with determination.

"Can you see your way in the dark?"

"Yes," they said again with equal determination.

"We will meet again?" she said, raising her voice to form a question.

"Yes," they said.

"Some are more loyal than others," she said. "Remember that."

They hurried down the laneway, surprised to find that it was not so dark outside as it seemed within the blind woman's house. When they got to the main road, they followed it in the direction that led away from the wharf and it seemed that in a short time they could make out the buildings of their original destination.

It was still raining as they entered the laneway to the buildings, and by this time it was indeed quite dark. The laneway ended at the door of the barn and the house was some yards farther. The barn door was open and they stepped inside for a moment to compose themselves. It was very quiet within the barn, for all of the animals were away in their summer pastures. They hesitated for a moment in the first stall and then they were aware of a rhythm of sound coming from the next area, the threshing floor. They opened the small connecting door and stepped inside and waited for their eyes to adjust to the gloom. And then in the farthest corner they noticed a lantern turned to its lowest and hanging on a nail. And beyond it they could make out the shape of a man. He was tall and wore rubber boots and bib overalls and had a tweed cap pulled down upon his head. He was facing the south wall of the barn but was sideways to them and presented a profile. He was rhythmically rocking from his heels to the balls of his feet and thrusting his hips back and forth and moaning and talking to himself in Gaelic. But it did not seem that he was talking to himself but to someone of the opposite sex who was not there. The front of his overalls was open and he had a hold of himself in his right hand which he moved to the rhythm of his rocking body.

They did not know what to do. They did not recognize the man, and they were terrified that he might turn and see them, and they were afraid that if they tried to make a retreat they might cause a sound which would betray their presence. At home they slept upstairs while their parents slept below in a private room ("to keep an eye on the fire," their parents said); and although they were becoming curious about sex, they did not know a great deal about it. They had seen the mating of animals, such as the cats earlier, but they had never seen a fully aroused grown man before, although they recognized some of the words he was moaning to himself and his imaginary partner. Suddenly, with a groan, he slumped forward as the grey jets of seed spurted onto the south wall of the barn and down to the dry and dusty hay before his feet. He placed his left arm against the wall and rested his forehead against it. They stepped back quietly through the little door and then out of the barn and then they walked rapidly but on their tiptoes through the rain toward the house.

When they entered the porch and the screen door slammed behind them, they heard a voice from within the kitchen. It was harsh and angry and seemed to be cursing, and then the door flew open and they were face to face with their grandmother. At first she did not recognize them in their long coats, and her face remained suspicious and angry, but then her expression changed and she came forward to hug them.

"Angus and Alex," she said. "What a surprise!" Looking over their shoulders, she said, "Are you alone? Did you come by yourselves?" And then, "Why didn't you tell us you were coming? We would have gone to meet you."

It had never entered their minds that their arrival would be such a surprise. They had been thinking of the trip with such intensity that in spite of the day's happenings they still somehow assumed that everyone knew they were coming.

"Well, come in, come in," she said, "and take those wet clothes off. How did you say you came again? And are you just arriving now?"

They told her they had come on the smack and of their walk and the ride with the man who had the peppermints and of their visit to the blind woman, but they omitted the part about the man in the barn. She listened intently as she moved about the kitchen, hanging up their coats and setting the teapot on the stove. She asked for a description of the man with the peppermints and they told her he said he owned a store, and then she asked them how the blind woman was. They told her of the tea she had served them which they had left and she said, "Poor soul!"

And then the screen door banged again and a heavy foot was heard in the porch, and in through the kitchen door walked the man they had seen in the barn.

"Your grandchildren are here to see you," she said with an icy edge to her voice. "They came on the smack from Kintail."

He stood blinking and swaying in the light, trying to focus his eyes upon them. They realized then that he was quite drunk and having difficulty comprehending. His eyes were red-rimmed and bloodshot and a white stubble speckled with black indicated that he had not shaved for a number of days.

He swayed back and forth, looking at them carefully and trying to see who they really were. They could not help looking at the front of his overalls to see if there were flecks of semen, but he had been out in the rain and all of his clothing was splattered with moisture.

"Oh," he said, as if a veil had been lifted from his eyes. "Oh," he said. "I love you. I love you." And he came forward and hugged each of them and kissed them on the cheek. They could smell the sourness of his breath and feel the rasping scratch of his stubble on their faces.

"Well," he said, turning on his heel, "I am going upstairs to rest for a while. I have been out in the barn and have been busier than you might think. But I will be back down later." And then he kicked off his boots, steadying himself with one hand on a kitchen chair, and swayed upstairs.

The visitors were shocked that they had not recognized their grandfather. When he came to visit them perhaps once a year, he was always splendid and handsome in his blue serge suit, with a gold watch chain linked across the expansiveness of his vest, and with his pockets filled with peppermints. And when they visited in the company of their parents, he had always been gracious and clear-headed and well attired.

When they could no longer hear his footsteps, their grandmother again began to talk to them, asking them questions, inquiring of their parents and of their school work as she busied herself about the stove and began to set the table.

Later he came back downstairs and they all sat around the table. He had changed his clothes, and his face was covered with bleeding nicks because he had tried to shave. The meal was uncomfortable as he knocked over his water glass and dropped his food on his lap. The visitors were as exhausted as he was, and only their grandmother seemed in control. He went back upstairs as soon as the meal was finished, saying, "Tomorrow will be a better day," and their grandmother suggested that they go to bed soon after.

"We are all tired," she said. "He will be all right tomorrow. He tried to shave in honour of your coming. I will talk to him myself. We are glad that you have come."

They slept together under a mountain of quilts and in a room next to their grandparents'. Before they went to sleep they could hear them talking in Gaelic, and the next thing they remembered was waking in the morning. Their grandparents were standing near their bed and the sun was shining through the window. Each of their grandparents held a tray containing porridge and sugar and milk and tea and butter. They were both rather formally dressed and like the grandparents they thought they knew. The drunk moaning man in the barn was like a dream they wished they had not had.

When they got up to put on their clothes they discovered bits of the blind woman's biscuits still in their pockets, and when they went outside they threw them behind the barn.

They stayed a week at Canna and all during that time the sun shone and the days were golden. They went visiting with their grandfather in his buggy—visiting women in houses and sometimes standing in barns with men. One day they visited the store and had trouble identifying the man behind the counter with the one who had offered them the ride and the peppermints. He seemed equally surprised when he recognized them and said to their grandfather, "I'm sorry if I made a mistake."

During their week in Canna they noticed small differences in the way of doing things. The people of Canna tied their horses with ropes around their necks instead of with halters. They laid out their gardens in beds instead of in rows and they grew a particular type of strawberry whose fruit grew far from the original root. When they drew water from their wells they threw away the first dipperful and the water itself had a slightly different taste. They set their tables for breakfast before retiring for the night. They bowed or curtsied to the new moon, and in the Church of St. Columba the women sat on one side of the aisle and the men on the other.

The Church of St. Columba, said their grandfather, was called after the original chapel on the island of Canna. St. Columba of Colum Cille was a brilliant, dedicated missionary in Ireland and he possessed *Da Shealladh*, the second sight, and used a stone to "see" his visions. He was also a lover of beauty and very strong-willed. Once, continued their grandfather, he copied a religious manuscript without permission but believed the copy was rightfully his. The High King of Ireland who was asked to judge the dispute ruled against Colum Cille, saying, "To every cow its calf and to every book its copy." Later the High King of Ireland also executed a young man who had sought sanctuary under the protection of Colum Cille. Enraged at what he perceived as injustice and bad judgement, Colum Cille told the High King he would lead his relations and clansmen against him in battle. On the eve of the battle, as they prayed and fasted, the archangel Michael appeared to Colum Cille in a vision. The angel told him that God would answer his prayers and allow him to win the battle but that He was not pleased with him for praying for such a worldly request and that he should exile himself from Ireland and never see the country anymore, or its people, or partake of its food and drink except on his outward journey. The forces of Colum Cille won the battle and inflicted losses of three thousand men, and perhaps he could have been the King of Ireland, but he obeyed the vision. Some said he left also to do penance for the three thousand lives he had cost. In a small boat and with a few followers who were his relatives, he crossed the sea to the small islands of Scotland and spent the last thirty-four years of his life establishing monasteries and chapels and travelling among the people. Working as a missionary, making predictions, seeing visions and changing forever that region of the world. Leaving Ireland, he said:

> *There is a grey eye*
> *Looking back on Ireland,*
> *That will never see again*
> *Her men or her women.*
>
> *Early and late my lamentation,*
> *Alas, the journey I am making;*
> *This will be my secret bye-name*
> *"Back turned on Ireland."*

"Did he ever go back?" they asked.

"Once," said their grandfather, "the poets of Ireland were in danger of being banned and he crossed the sea from Scotland to speak on their behalf. But when he came, he came blindfolded so that he could not see the country or its people."

"Did you know him?" they asked. "Did you ever see him?"

"That was a very long time ago," he laughed. "Over thirteen hundred years ago. But, yes, sometimes I feel I know him and I think I see him as well. This church, as I said, is called after the chapel he established on Canna. That chapel is fallen a long time ago, too, and all of the people gone, and the well beside the chapel filled up with rocks and the Celtic crosses of their graveyards smashed down and used for the building of roads. But sometimes I imagine I still see them," he said, looking toward the ocean and across it as if he could see the "green island" and its people. "I see them going about their rituals: riding their horses on Michaelmas and carrying the bodies of their dead round toward the sun. And courting and getting married. Almost all of the people on Canna got married before they were twenty. They considered it unlucky to be either a single man or woman so there were very few single people among them. Perhaps they also found it difficult to wait," he added with a smile, "and that is why their population rose so rapidly. Anyway, all gone."

"You mean dead?" they asked.

"Well, some of them, yes," he said, "but I mean gone from there, scattered all over the world. But some of us are here. That is why this place is called Canna and we carry certain things within us. Sometimes there are things within us which we do not know or fully understand and sometimes it is hard to stamp out what you can't see. It is good that you are here for this while."

Toward the end of the week they learned that there was a government boat checking lighthouses along the coast. It would stop at the point of Canna and later, on its southern journey, also at Kintail. It was an excellent chance for them to get home, and it was decided that they should take it. The night before they left, their grandparents served them a splendid dinner with a white tablecloth and candles.

As they prepared to leave on the following morning, the rain began to fall. Their grandmother gave them some packages to deliver to their mother, and also a letter, and packed a lunch with lobster sandwiches for them. She hugged and kissed them as they were leaving and said, "Thank you for coming. It was good to have you here and it made us feel better about ourselves." She looked at her husband and he nodded.

They climbed into their grandfather's buggy as the rain fell upon them, and carefully placed their packages beneath the seat. On the road down to the wharf they passed the lane to the blind woman's house. She was near the roadway with the two black dogs. She was wearing her men's rubber boots and a large kerchief and a heavy rubber raincoat. When she heard the buggy approaching, she called out, "*Cò a th'ann? Cò a th'ann?* Who's there? Who's there?"

But their grandfather said nothing.

"Who's there?" she called. "Who's there? Who's there?"

The rain fell upon her streaked and empty glasses and down her face and along her coat and her strong protruding hands with their grimy fingernails.

"Don't say anything," said their grandfather under his breath. "I don't want her to know you're here."

As the horse approached, she continued to call, but none of them said anything. Above the regular hoofbeats of the horse her voice seemed to rise through the falling rain, causing a tension within all of them as they tried to pretend they could not hear her.

"*Cò a th'ann?*" she called. "Who's there? Who's there?"

They lowered their heads as if she could see them. But when they were exactly opposite her, their grandfather could not stand it any longer and suddenly reined in the horse.

"*Cò a th'ann?*" she called. "Who's there?"

"*'Se mi-fhìn,*" he answered quietly. "It's myself!"

She began to curse him in Gaelic and he became embarrassed.

"Do you understand what she's saying?" he said to them.

They were uncertain. "Some of it," they said.

"Here," he said, "hold the horse," and he passed the reins to them. He took the buggy whip out of its socket as he descended from the buggy, and they were uncertain about that, too, until they realized he was taking it to protect himself from the dogs who came snarling towards him, but kept their distance because of the whip. He began to talk to the blind woman in Gaelic and they both walked away from the buggy along the laneway to her house until they were out of earshot. The dogs lay down on the wet roadway and watched and listened carefully.

The visitors could not hear the conversation, only the rising and falling of the two voices through the descending rain. When their grandfather returned, he seemed upset and took the reins from them and spoke to the horse immediately.

"God help me," he said softly and almost to himself, "but I could not pass her by."

There was water running down his face and they thought for a moment he might be crying; but just as when they had looked for the semen on his overalls a week earlier, they could not tell because of the rain.

The blind woman stood in the laneway facing them as they moved off along the road. It was one of those situations which almost automatically calls for waving but even as they began to raise their hands they remembered her blindness and realized it was no use. She stood as if watching them for a long time and then, perhaps when she could no longer hear the sound of the horse and buggy, she turned and walked with the two dogs back toward her house.

"Do you know her well?" they asked.

"Oh," said their grandfather, as if being called back from another time and place, "yes, I do know her quite well and since a long, long time."

Their grandfather waited with them on the wharf for the coming of the government boat, but it was late. When it finally arrived, the men said they would not be long checking the lighthouse and told them to go into the boat to wait. They said their goodbyes then, and their grandfather turned his wet and impatient horse towards home.

Although the wait was not supposed to be long, it was longer than expected and it was afternoon before the boat left the protection of the wharf and ventured out into the ocean. The rain was still falling and a wind had come up and the sea was choppy. The wind was off the land, so they stood with their backs toward Canna and to the wind and the rain. When they were far enough out to sea to have perspective, one of the men said, "It looks like there is a fire back there." And when they looked back they could see the billowing smoke, somehow seeming ironic in the rain. It rose in the distance and was carried by the wind but it was difficult to see its source not only because of the smoke but also because of the driving rain. And because the perspective from the water was different from what it was on the land. The government men did not know any of the local people and they were behind schedule and already well out to sea, so there was no thought of turning back. They were mildly concerned, too, about the rising wind, and wanted to make as much headway as possible before conditions worsened.

It was that period of the day when the afternoon blends into evening before the boat reached the Kintail wharf. During the last miles the ocean had roughened and within the rocking boat the passengers had become green and seasick and vomited their lobster sandwiches over the side. Canna seemed very far away and the golden week seemed temporarily lost within the reality of the swaying boat and the pelting rain. When the boat docked, they ran to their house as quickly as they could. Their mother gave them soup and dry clothes and they went to bed earlier than usual.

They slept late the next day, and when they awoke and went downstairs it was still raining and blowing. And then the Syrian pedlars, Angus and Alex, knocked on the door. They put their heavy wet leather packs upon the kitchen floor and told the boys' mother that there had been a death in Canna. The Canna people were sending word but they had heard the news earlier in the day from another pedlar arriving from that direction and he had asked them to carry the message. The pedlars and the boys' parents talked for a while and the boys were told to "go outside and play" even though it was raining. They went out to the barn.

Almost immediately the boys' parents began to get ready for the journey. The ocean was by this time too rough for a boat, and they had already hauled their boat up at the end of the lobster season. They readied their horse and buggy, and later in the afternoon they were gone. They were away for five days, and when they returned they were drawn and tired.

Through bits and pieces of conversation, the boys learned that it was the blind woman's house that had burned and she within it.

Later, and they were not sure just when, they gathered other details and bits of information. She had been at the stove, it was thought, and her clothes had caught fire. The animals had burned with her. Most of their bones were found before the door to which they had gone to seek escape but she had been unable to open it for them or, it seemed, for herself.

Over the weeks the details blended in with their own experience. They imagined her strong hands pulling down the wainscotting of her own house and placing it in the fire, consuming her own house somehow from within as it was later to consume her. And they could see the fire going up the front of her layers of dirty clothing. Consuming the dirt which she herself had been unable to see. Rising up the front of her clothing, rising up above her shoulders toward her hair, the imaginary orange flames flickering and framing her face and being reflected in the staring lenses of her glasses.

And they imagined the animals, too. The savage faithful dogs which were twins snarling at the doorway with their fur in flames, and the lusty cats engaged in their growling copulation in the corner, somehow keeping on, driven by their own heat while the other heat surrounded them, and the bleating lamb with its wool on fire. And in the space between the walls the mewing unseen kittens, dying with their eyes still closed.

And sometimes they imagined her, too, in her porch or in her house or standing by the roadside in the rain. *Cò a th'ann?* they heard her call in their imagination and in their dreams. *Cò a th'ann? Cò a th'ann?* Who's there? Who's there? And one night they dreamed they heard themselves answer. *"'Se mi-fhìn* they heard themselves say as with one voice. It is myself.'"

My father and his brother never again spent a week on the green hills of Canna. Perhaps their lives went by too fast or circumstances changed or there were reasons that they did not fully understand themselves.

And one Sunday six years later when they were in church the clergyman gave a rousing sermon on why young men should enlist in World War I. They were very enthusiastic about the idea and told their parents that they were going to Halifax to enlist although they were too young. Their parents were very upset and went to the clergyman in an attempt to convince him it was a mistake. The clergyman was their friend and came to their house and told them it was a general sermon for the day. "I didn't mean *you*," he added, but his first success was better than his second.

They left the next day for Halifax, getting a ride to the nearest railroad station. They had never been on a train before and when they arrived, the city of Halifax was large and awesome. At the induction centre their age was easily overlooked but the medical examination was more serious. Although they were young and strong, the routine tests seemed strange and provoked a tension within them. They were unable to urinate in a bottle on request and were asked to wait awhile and then try again. But sitting on two chairs wishing for urine did little good. They drank more and more water and waited and tried but it did not work. On their final attempt, they were discussing their problem in Gaelic while standing in a tiny cubicle with their legs spread apart and their trousers opened. Unexpectedly a voice from the next cubicle responded to them in Gaelic.

The voice belonged to a young man from Canna who had come to enlist as well but who did not have their problem. "Can we 'borrow' some of that?" they asked, looking at his full bottle of urine.

"Sure," he said, "no need to give it back," and he splashed some of his urine into each of their waiting bottles. All of them "passed" the test; and later in the alleyway behind the induction centre, standing in the steam of their own urine, they began to talk to the young man from Canna. His grandfather owned the store in Canna, he said, and was opposed to his coming to enlist.

"Do you know Alex?" they asked and mentioned their grandfather's formal name.

He seemed puzzled for a moment and then brightened. "Oh," he said, "*Mac an Amharuis*, sure, everyone knows him. He's my grandfather's friend."

And then, perhaps because they were far from home and more lonely and frightened than they cared to admit, they began to talk in Gaelic. They began with the subject of *Mac an Amharuis*, and the young man told them everything he knew. Surprised perhaps at his own knowledge and at having such attentive listeners. *Mac an Amharuis* translates as "Son of Uncertainty," which meant that he was illegitimate or uncertain as to who his father was. He was supposed to be tremendously talented and clever as a young man but also restless and reluctant to join the other young men of Canna in their fishing boats. Instead he saved his money and purchased a splendid stallion and travelled the country offering the stallion's services. He rode on the stallion's back with only a loose rope around its neck for guidance.

He was also thought to be handsome and to possess a "strong nature" or "too much nature," which meant that he was highly sexed. "Some say," said the young man, "that he sowed almost as much seed as the stallion and who knows who might be descended from him. If we only knew, eh?" he added with a laugh.

Then he became involved with a woman from Canna. She was thought to be "odd" by some because she was given to rages and uncertainty and sometimes she would scream and shout at him in public. At times he would bring back books and sometimes moonshine from wherever he went with the stallion. And sometimes they would read quietly together and talk and at other times they would curse and shout and become physically violent.

And then he became possessed of *Da Shealladh*, the second sight. It seemed he did not want it and some said it came about because of too much reading of the books or perhaps it was inherited from his unknown father. Once he "saw" a storm on the evening of a day which was so calm that no one would believe him. When it came in the evening the boats could not get back and all the men were drowned. And once when he was away with the stallion, he "saw" his mother's house burn down, and when he returned he found that it had happened on the very night he saw it, and his mother was burned to death.

It became a weight upon him and he could not stop the visions or do anything to interfere with the events. One day after he and the woman had had too much to drink they went to visit a well-known clergyman. He told the clergyman he wanted the visions to stop but it did not seem within his power. He and the woman were sitting on two chairs beside each other. The clergyman went for the Bible and prayed over it and then he came and flicked the pages of the Bible before their eyes. He told them the visions would stop but that they would have to give up one another because they were causing a scandal in the community. The woman became enraged and leaped at the clergyman and tried to scratch out his eyes with her long nails. She accused *Mac an Amharuis* of deceiving her and said that he was willing to exchange their stormy relationship for his lack of vision. She spat in his face and cursed him and stormed out the door. *Mac an Amharuis* rose to follow her but the clergyman put his arms around him and wrestled him to the floor. He was far gone in drink and within the clergyman's power.

They stopped appearing with one another and *Mac an Amharuis* stopped travelling with the stallion and bought himself a boat. He began to visit the woman's younger sister, who was patient and kind. The woman moved out of her parents' house and into an older house nearer the shore. Some thought she moved because she could not stand *Mac an Amharuis* visiting her sister, and others thought that it was planned to allow him to visit her at night without anyone seeing.

Within two months *Mac an Amharuis* and the woman's sister were married. At the wedding the woman cursed the clergyman until he warned her to be careful and told her to leave the building. She cursed her sister, too, and said, "You will never be able to give him what I can." And as she was going out the door, she said to *Mac an Amharuis* either "I will never forgive you" or "I will never forget you." Her voice was charged with emotion but her back was turned to them and the people were uncertain whether it was a curse or a cry.

The woman did not come near anyone for a long time and people saw her only from a distance, moving about the house and the dilapidated barn, caring for the few animals which her father had given her, and muffled in clothes as autumn turned to winter. At night people watched for a light in her window. Sometimes they saw it and sometimes they did not.

And then one day her father came to the house of his daughter and *Mac an Amharuis* and said that he had not seen a light for three nights and he was worried. The three of them went to the house but it was cold. There was no heat when they put their hands on the stove and the glass of the windowpanes was covered with frost. There was nobody in any of the rooms.

They went out into the barn and found her lying in a heap. Most of the top part of her body was still covered by layers of clothes, although the lower part was not. She was unconscious or in something like a frozen coma and her eyes were inflamed, with beads of pus at their corners. She had given birth to twin girls and one of them was dead but the other somehow still alive, lying on her breast amidst her layers of clothing. Her father and *Mac an Amharuis* and her sister carried the living into the house and started a fire in the stove, and sent for the nearest medical attention, which was some miles away. Later they also carried in the body of the dead baby and placed it in a lobster crate, which was all that they could find. When the doctor came, he said he could not be certain of the baby's exact time of birth but he felt that it would live. He said that the mother had lost a great deal of blood and he thought she might have lacerated her eyes during the birth with her long fingernails and that infection had set in, caused perhaps by the unsanitary conditions within the barn. He was not sure if she would live and, if she did, he feared her sight would never be restored.

Mac an Amharuis and his wife cared for the baby throughout the days that the woman was unconscious, and the baby thrived. The woman herself began to rally and the first time she heard the baby cry she reached out instinctively for it but could not find it in the dark. Gradually, as she recognized by sound the people around her, she began to curse them and accused them of having sex when she could not see them. As she grew stronger, she became more resentful of their presence and finally asked them to leave. She began to rise from her bed and walk with her hands before her, sometimes during the day and sometimes during the night because it made no difference to her. And once they saw her with a knife in her hand. They left her then, as she had requested them to do and perhaps because they were afraid. And because there seemed no other choice, they took the baby with them.

They continued to bring her food and to leave it at the door of her porch. Sometimes she cursed at them but at other times she was quieter. One day while they were talking she extended her hand with the long fingernails to the face of *Mac an Amharuis*. She ran the balls of her fingers and the palm of her hand from his hair down over his eyes and nose and his lips and his chin and down along the buttons of his shirt and below his belt to between his legs; and then her hand closed for an instant and she grasped what she had held before but would never see again.

Mac an Amharuis and his wife had no children of their own. It was thought that it caused a great sadness within her and perhaps a tension because, as people said, "It's sure as hell not *his* fault." Their childlessness was thought also to prey on him and to lead to periodic drinking binges, although he never mentioned it to anyone. For the most part, they were helpful and supportive of each other and no one knew what they talked about when they were alone and together in their bed at night.

This, I guess, is my retelling of the story told by the young man of Canna to my father and his brother at a time when they were all young and on the verge of war. All of the information that spilled out of him came because it was there to be released and he was revealing more than he realized to his attentive listeners. The story was told in Gaelic, and as the people say, "It is not the same in English," although the images are true.

When the war was over, the generous young man from Canna was dead; and my father's brother had lost his leg.

My father returned to Kintail and the life that he had left, the boat and the nets and the lobster traps. All of them in the cycle of the seasons. He married before World War II; and when he was asked to go again, he went with the other Highlanders from Cape Breton, leaving his wife pregnant, perhaps without realizing it.

On the beach at Normandy they were emptied into ten feet of water as the rockets and shells exploded around them. And in the mud they fell face-down, leaving the imprints of their faces temporarily in the soil, before clawing their way some few feet forward. At the command they rose, as would a wave trying to break farther forward on the shore. And then all of it seemed to happen at once. Before my father's eyes there rose a wall of orange flame and a billowing wave of black smoke. It rose before him even as he felt the power of the strong hand upon his left shoulder. The grip was so powerful that he felt the imprint of the fingers almost as a bruise; and even as he turned his searing eyes, he fell back into his own language. "*Cò a th'ann?*" he said. "*Cò a th'ann?* Who's there?" And in the instant before his blindness, he recognized the long brown fingers on his shoulder with their pointed fingernails caked in dirt. "'*Se mi-fhìn,*" she said quietly. "It is myself."

All of the soldiers in front of my father were killed and in the spot where he stood there was a crater, but this was told to him because he was unable ever to see it for himself.

Later he was told that on the day of his blinding, his grandfather, the man known to some as *Mac an Amharuis*, died. *Mac an Amharuis* was a man of over a hundred years at the time of his death and his eyes had become covered with the cataracts of age. He did not recognize, either by sight or sound, any of the people around him, and much of his talk was of youth and sex and of the splendid young stallion with the loose rope around its neck. And much of it was of the green island of Canna which he had never literally seen and of the people riding their horses at Michaelmas and carrying the bodies of their dead round toward the sun. And of the strong-willed St. Columba determined to be ascetic with his "back turned on Ireland" and the region of his early love. And of walls of flame and billowing smoke.

When I began this story I was recounting the story which my father told to me as he faced the green hills of Canna on the last day of the lobster season a long time ago. But when I look on it now I realize that all of it did not come from him, exactly as I have told it, on that day. The part about seeing his grandfather in the barn and much of the story of the young man from Canna came instead from his twin brother who participated in most of the events. Perhaps because of the loss of his leg, my father's brother became one of those veterans from World War I who spent a lot of their time in the Legion Hall. When he spoke to me he had none of the embarrassment which my father sometimes showed when discussing certain subjects. Perhaps my father, by omitting certain parts of his story, was merely repeating the custom of his parents who did not reveal to him at once everything there was to be shown.

But perhaps the story also went into me because of other events which happened on that day. After my father had finished, we started our engine and went into the wharf. By the time we arrived, the MacAllesters had gone and many of the other men as well. We hoisted the lobsters to the wharf's cap and I looked at the weight that the scales showed.

Whether the buyers noticed the concealed lobsters behind the crate we were never to know, but they said nothing. We unloaded our traps on the wharf and then climbed up the iron ladder and talked casually to the buyers and received our money. We planned to come back later for the lobsters behind the crate.

There were still other fishermen about and most of them shared my father's good mood because they were glad that the season had ended and pleased to have the money which was their final payment. Someone offered us a ride in a truck to the Legion and we went.

The Legion Hall was filled with men, most of them fishermen, and the noise was loud and the conversation boisterous. Toward the back of the hall I noticed Kenneth MacAllester with a number of his relatives. Both of us were underage but it did not matter a great deal. If you looked as if you were old enough, no one asked any questions. My father's brother and a number of our own relatives were at a table in the middle. They waved to us and I moved toward them. Behind me, my father followed, touching my belt from time to time for guidance. Most of the men pulled in their feet as we approached so that my father would not stumble. The crutch my uncle used in place of his missing leg was propped up across a chair and he removed it as we approached and leaned it against the table so that he could offer the chair to my father. We sat down and my uncle gave me some money to go to the bar for beer. Coming back, I passed another table of MacAllesters. They were relatives of our neighbours and although I recognized them I did not know them very well. One of them said something as I passed but I did not hear what he said and it seemed best not to stop. The afternoon grew more boisterous and bottles and glasses began to shatter on the cement floor. And then there was a shower of droplets over our head.

"What's that?" said my father.

Two of the MacAllesters from the table I had passed were throwing quarts of beer to their relatives at the back of the hall. They were standing up like quarterbacks and spiralling the open quarts off the palms of their hands and I saw Kenneth reach up and catch one as if he were a wide receiver. The quarts, for the most part, stayed upright; but as they revolved and spun, their foaming contents sprinkled or drenched those seated beneath them.

"Those bastards," said my uncle.

The two of them came over to the table. They were about thirty, and strong and heavily muscled.

"Who are you talking to?" one of them said.

"Never mind," said my uncle. "Go and sit down."

"I asked you a question," he said. And then turning to me he added, "I asked you a question before, too. What's the matter, can't some of you hear? I just thought that some of you couldn't see."

There was a silence then that began to spread to the neighbouring tables and the conversations slowed and the men took their hands off their bottles and their glasses.

"I asked you your age," he said, still looking at me. "Are you the oldest or the youngest?"

"He's the only one," said the other man. "Since the war, his father is so blind he can't find his way into his wife's cunt to make any more."

I remember my uncle reaching for the bottom of his crutch, and he swung it like a baseball bat from his sitting position. And I remember the way he planted his one leg onto the floor even as he swung. And I remember the crutch exploding into the nose and mouth of the man and his blood splashing down upon us and then the overturning of tables and chairs and the crashing of broken glass. And I remember also two of the MacAllesters who were our neighbours reaching our table with amazing speed. Each of them went to a side of my father's chair, and they lifted it up with him still sitting upon it. And they carried him as carefully as if he were eggs or perhaps an object of religious veneration, and the men who were smashing their fists into one another's mouths moved out of their way when they saw them coming. They deposited him with great gentleness against the far wall where they felt no harm could come to him, bending their knees in unison as they lowered his chair to the floor. And then each of them placed a hand upon his shoulder as one might comfort a frightened child. And then one of them picked up a chair and smashed it over the head of my cousin, who had his brother by the throat.

Someone grabbed me and spun me around but I could see by his eyes that he was intent on someone across the hall and that I was merely in his way. And then I saw Kenneth coming toward me, as I half expected him to. It was like the bench-clearing brawls at the hockey games when the goalies seek each other out because they have the most in common.

I saw him coming with his eyes intent upon me and because I knew him well I believed that he would leap from a spot about three strides ahead of him and that the force of his momentum would carry us backward and I would be on the bottom with my head on the cement floor. It all took perhaps a fraction of a second, his leap and my bending and moving forward and sideways, either to go toward him or to get out of the way, and my shoulder grazing his hip as he was airborne with his hands stretched out before him and his body parallel to the floor. He came crashing down on top of the table, knocking it over and forward and beneath him to the cement.

He lay face-down and still for a moment and I thought he was unconscious, and then I saw the blood spreading from beneath his face and reddening the shards of different-coloured glass.

"Are you all right?" I said, placing my hand upon his shoulder.

"It's okay," he said. "It's just my eye."

He sat up then with his hands over his face and the blood streaming down between his fingers. I was aware of a pair of rubber boots beside us, and then a man's voice. "Stop," he shouted to the brawling hall. "For Christ's sake, stop, someone's been hurt."

In retrospect, and even then, it seemed like a strange thing to say because when one looked at the bloodied men it seemed that almost everyone had been hurt in some way, although not to the same degree. But given the circumstances, he said exactly the right thing, and everyone stopped and unclenched his fist and released his grip on his opponent's throat.

In the rush to the doctor and to the hospital, everyone's original plans went awry. No one thought of the lobsters we had hidden and saved for our end-of-the-season feast; and when we discovered them days later, it was with something like surprise. They were dead and had to be thrown back into the sea, perhaps to serve as food for the spring mackerel with the scales upon their eyes.

That night two cars of MacAllesters came to our house. They told us that Kenneth's eye was lost; and Mr. MacAllester, who was about my father's age, began to cry. The two young men who were throwing the beer held their caps in their hands, and their knuckles were still raw and bleeding. Both of them apologized to my father. "We didn't see it getting that out of hand," one of them said. My uncle came in from another room and said that he shouldn't have swung the crutch.

Mr. MacAllester said that if my father would agree, all of us should stop using the fickle river as the boundary between our fishing grounds and take our sightings instead from the two rocky promontories on either side of the beach. One family would fish off the beach one year and the other the next. My father agreed. "I can't see the boundary anyway," he said with a smile. It all seemed so simple in hindsight.

This has been the telling of a story about a story but like most stories it has spun off into others and relied on others and perhaps no story every really stands alone. This began as the story of two children who long ago went to visit their grandparents but who, because of circumstances, did not recognize them when they saw them. As their grandparents did not see them. And this is a story related by a man who is a descendant of those people. The son of a father who never saw his son but knew him only through sound or by the running of his fingers across the features of his face.

As I write this, my own small daughter comes in from kindergarten. She is at the age where each day she asks a riddle and I am not supposed to know the answer. Today's question is, "What has eyes but cannot see?" Under the circumstances, the question seems overwhelmingly profound. "I don't know," I say and I feel I really mean it.

"A potato," she shouts and flings herself into my arms, elated and impressed by her own cleverness and by my lack of understanding.

She is the great-great-granddaughter of the blind woman who died in flames and of the man called *Mac an Amharuis*; and both of us, in spite of our age and comprehension, are indeed the children of uncertainty.

Most of the major characters in this story are, as the man called *Mac an Amharuis* once said of others, "all gone" in the literal sense. There remains only Kenneth MacAllester, who works as a janitor for a soap company in Toronto. Unable ever to join the Air Force and fly toward the sun and see over the tops of mountains and across the ocean because of what happened to his eye on that afternoon so long ago. Now he has an artificial eye and, as he says, "Only a few people know the difference."

When we were boys we would try to catch the slippery spring mackerel in our hands and look into the blindness of their eyes, hoping to see our own reflections. And when the wet ropes of the lobster traps came out of the sea, we would pick out a single strand and then try to identify it some few feet farther on. It was difficult to do because of the twisting and turning of the different strands within the rope. Difficult ever to be certain in our judgements or to fully see or understand. Difficult then to see and understand the twisted strands within the rope. And forever difficult to see and understand the tangled twisted strands of love.

Lynn Coady

Batter My Heart

You see it there, every time on the way back to the old man's. Put up by Baptists or the like, about twenty miles or so from the tollbooths. What always happens is that you go away and you forget that it's there until the next time. Just when the fog and eternal drizzle have seeped deep enough inside your head and sufficiently dampened your thinking, it leaps out from the grey and yellow landscape — the same landscape that has been unravelling in front of your eyes for the last three hours. Lurid, oversized letters painted with green and red and black:

PREPARE
TO MEET
THY GOD

Then the bus zips past almost before you can be startled. And it makes you smile for a moment, just like it always has, and then you forget about it, until, presumably, the next time you've gone away and then come back again.

By the time it gets dark, you are driving through Monastery, so called because there is a monastery. You know when you're passing it because there is a large cross lit up by spotlights positioned on either side of the turnoff. Earlier in the day, the driver slowed down and the people oohed and pointed because a small (it looked small, in the distance) brown bear was scampering towards the woods. Just before disappearing, it turned around to glare. These are all the signs.

The monastery you remember from twice in your life. Once, a pious little kid with your family. You saw the crosses marking the graves of dead monks, you saw the building but didn't go inside that day. It hadn't looked like a monastery. Industrial, like a hospital or a prison. It had been built sometime in the fifties. You drank water from a blessed stream.

Now they run some kind of detox program there, the drunks living with the monks. The second time, you were a less-than-pious teenager there to visit both your boyfriend and your history teacher. The two of them were actually related somehow—same last name. He had told you it was a disease that runs in his family. The history teacher, far worse than him, older, having had more time to perfect his craft. The monastery like a second home. Word was, this time it was because he had showed up at an end-of-the-year staff party at the principal's house and walked directly through a sliding-glass door. He had a PhD and spoke fluent Russian. You walked into the common room with your boyfriend and the history teacher was sitting at a table playing gin rummy (ha, ha, ha,) with the other drunks. You and he chatted a moment, he condescending, as usual. But not nearly so much as when he was drunk. You can't remember why, but the last thing he said was that you would never make it in the big world. You could only agree, pliant. You still agree. What did that mean, though, *make it*? Did he think you would shrivel up like an unwatered plant? But at the time, you didn't care, you didn't care to defend yourself, you didn't care about any of it. It was liberating, that. It was almost fun. All of a sudden you didn't have to be nice to the boyfriend who used to seem so sad and fragile, who used to get drunk and then go and take a dirty steak knife from out of the dishpan and look at it.

Now about Daddy, different people have said different things. He is the kindest man you could ever know. Well—he's got his own way. He's got his own opinions and, goddamnit, he's not afraid to express them. With his fists if it comes down to that. Quite the temper. Quite the mouth, if you get him going. A good man. The only honest man in town. A visionary. A saint. Would do anything for you, but if you disappoint him, I guess he'll let you know it. Stark raving mad. One mean son of a bitch.

You get home, and Daddy's throwing a man off the step.

"Mr. Leary, I implore you." The man is filthy, flabby, pale.

"Get offa my step, you goddamn drunk."

"Mr. Leary, I've changed. I've turned over a new Jesus leaf."

"And what d'ya know, there's a bottle of Hermit underneath it!" (a sometime wit, Dad.) "You're more full of shit than my own arse. I'm through wasting time with you, Martin. Offa my step."

"Another chance, Mr. Leary, that's all I ask." The bum straightens himself with boozy dignity.

The old fella has caught sight of you. "Hello, Katey! Martin, I'm telling you for the last time to fuck off. I won't have my little girl gazing on the likes of you."

Martin turns, he seems to bow, but may have just lost his balance. "Hello, dear. I'm sorry not to have a hat to tip at you."

Daddy steps forward with a no-nonsense air. His fists are clenched, his jaw is clenched. It should be laughable in a man this side of sixty, but here is the truth: he is terrifying.

"I'm not gonna tell you again," his voice breaks a little, as though any minute he's going to lose control. Again, it seems so put on that it should be ridiculous. You would think that, anyway. Martin is no fool. He retreats into the driveway.

"Mr. Leary," the bum says, actually resting his hand on his heart. "You were my last hope. I went around tellin' everybody who would listen, Jane at the hospital and them, I ain't worried, no matter how down I get, I know I can count on Mr. Leary to come through for me."

"Don't you try to make me feel guilty, you sick bastard!" Daddy shouts. "I broke my ass for you, Martin, I put my ass on the line!" But Martin is stumbling down the driveway. He has his pride.

"Jesus bum." Dad looks like he wants to hit something. He always looks like that. "Come in and have a bite of tea, now, Katherine."

Daddy had done all he could for Martin. This is what you hear over tea and bannock and Cheddar. Put his ass on the line. Tried to get him straightened up. On his Jesus feet again. Martin lived in an old pulp-cutter's shack out in the woods with no water or electricity. His wife dead of a ruined liver. Both boys in jail for the drunk driving. His girl off living with someone. Dad spits, sickened.

Dad normally wouldn't have done a blessed thing for the drunken idiot, but there had been something rather enchanting about him when they had met over the summer. "Lyrical," Daddy says around a mouthful of bannock, surprising you with the word. Daddy had been on the river helping out a friend with his gaspereaux catch. This was etiquette—everyone who had a fish trap helped everyone else load their vats. Daddy didn't begrudge his friend this, particularly because his own catch, brought in last week, had been larger.

Dad had been sitting on the edge of the trap once the last vat was filled, wiping sweat from his pink, hairless forehead, when Martin Carlyle appeared from out of nowhere and greeted him. The two men had never actually come face to face before, but as both had attained a kind of notoriety within the community, they recognized one another, and each knew the other's name. Now Daddy puts on a show, acting out the two parts:

"Good day, Mr. Leary, sir!"

"Hullo, Martin."

"By the Lord Jesus, it's a beautiful day!"

"Yes."

"Did you catch a lot of fish today?"

"One or two, Martin, one or two," Dad says, squinting up at the man, who had a terrible matted beard and pee stains on the front of his pants.

Now Martin stands in silence, weaving just a little bit, and appears to be thinking very deeply about something.

"Mr. Leary," he says at last, "I put it to you. Would this not be the perfect day to be bobbing along down the river in one of those vats with a big blonde in one hand and a bottle of Captain Morgan in the other and a pink ribbon tied around your pinocchio?"

Daddy concludes the performance, sputtering bannock crumbs from his laughter. "Lyrical," he says. "That's what you would call lyrical, isn't it, Katey?"

There you were in the monastery, once upon a time, a walking sin.

Defiling the floor tile upon which you tread. A sin taking life in your gut. No one can see it, which is good. Being a girl is bad enough, in a monastery. The drunks turn and stare.

Martin Carlyle among them at the time. A pink ribbon tied around his pinocchio. Sitting on the bridge that crosses the blessed stream as you and the boyfriend traipse by along the muddy path. Spring. Grimy, miserable season. You irreverently spit your gum out into an oncoming mud puddle, and he shoots you a dirty look. Impiety. He's religious now, after two weeks among them. Martin is on the bridge with a fishing pole between his legs. He calls:

"Hey-ho, Stephen, boy!"

"Martin!" Raises his hand.

"Whee-hoo! You got a little friend!"

"How are you, Martin?"

"Ready to break into the vestry, that's how. Get meself a little taste of wine!"

"Don't do that, Martin, don't do that now."

"No—"

Together, you walk up the hill to look at the stations of the cross. He is insistent that you pause at every station. The women clamour at the feet of the suffering Christ. He keeps telling you about how different he is. He keeps saying things like: "I pray now. I honestly pray," and, "Everything seems right. Like all my problems were meaningless."

And you say, "Of course it does," and he says, "What?" and you say, "You get to be in a monastery."

He tells you, "The monastery doesn't have anything to do with it. You just have to learn to pray. I mean really pray. What that means is accepting God."

Well, you are certainly too much of a hardened and worldly wise seventeen-year-old to go for that. "No way," you say.

"Why?" He gives you a gentle look, and you see that he thinks he is a monk. Wise, wizened. Sleeping in a narrow bed, in a little cell, humble. But when you spit your gum out onto the path, and were impolite to Brother Mike, he wanted to hit you. You could see that. Any fool could see that.

"Nothing to accept," you say.

"You can't believe that," Misguided woman. Is there no one left to condemn you? No one, Lord. Then I will condemn you.

"Belief," you say, "doesn't come into it."

He attempts to look at peace with himself yet disappointed with you all at once. Then: "Do you want to go see the shrine to the Virgin?"

Why not? Very nice, very pretty. Easily the prettiest thing here in man-land, white stones and plastic flowers all about. He tries to hold your hand, to create some kind of moment, sinner and saviour. He looks over: "Do you want to kneel?"

"No, I don't want to kneel!"

He smiles when you leave, all benevolence, alongside of his favourite monk, Brother Mike. He had wanted you to talk to Brother Mike for some reason, but you said no. He was disappointed, but he said he understood. He thinks that you're making the wrong decision, going away, but he understands that too. He understands everything. He and the monk stand side by side waving goodbye.

When you first arrived, it was Brother Mike who intercepted you. You had gone into the chapel instead of the main entrance, and stood overwhelmed by the height of the ceiling, the lit candles, the looming statues of saints looking down from every corner, the darkness. For want of something to do while you waited for someone to come and find you, you went over and lit a candle for your dead Gramma.

Brother Mike had been kneeling up front, but you didn't even see him, it was so dark. He was standing right beside you before you noticed him. He spoke in a natural speaking voice, not a whisper, which in a church seemed abnormal. "Are you Katherine?"

He led you to the common room, and that was when, watching your feet hit the grey industrial floor tile, it occurred to you what a desecration your presence constituted. Every heartbeat, every snoutful of sanctified oxygen you took went blasphemously down into your bellyful of sin to give it strength. Brother Mike looks around to see if you are still following and gives you a kindly smile.

"Well, the boy had a lot of anger when he came here. A good deal of anger with himself and the world. I think you'll see a big difference."

Now, a few years gone by, the phone will ring late at night. Not often, but every now and again. Bitch. Heartless, stupid. . . . Just like old times!

The day after you arrive is Sunday, and it is clear that he expects you to accompany your mother to church. No argument. *My, hasn't Katey changed.* Because then it used to seem like there was some kind of moral imperative to jump up and down on the backs of their sacred cows. Isn't it, you used to argue into Daddy's pulsating face, more of a sin to be sitting there thinking the whole proceeding is a pile of shit than to just stay at home? And now you don't care if it is or not, sins and moral imperatives alike being figments of the past.

But when the choir isn't present, ruining the peace, church can be nice, the sun coming in through the fragmented window. You can sit alone among everybody, enjoying your mild hangover. Everybody murmuring responses to the priest in unison. You do it too and are not even aware. That's nice. The powdery smell of clean old men and old ladies all around. The feel of their dry hands when it comes time to extend the blessing to one another. You love the sight of old men in glasses, kneeling, fingering their beads.

But one of the last times you were to mass, also sixteen, Mommy insisted for some reason on going to the early one and there you are with the worst hangover in the world. Ever, in the world. Mother, God love her, with no idea. You say in the car: Hm, Mom, I'm not feeling so good this morning. She says, Yes, Margaret-Ann's kids are all coming down with the flu.

Inside, everything makes you nauseous. You remember that your Gramma had this bottle of perfume that she only wore on Sundays, for mass. She said that she had been using the same bottle for thirty years, and only on Sundays and for weddings and for funerals. You remember that because it smells like the old women sitting on all sides of you must do that too — don thirty-year-old scent for mass. Everything smells putrid. You think that the old man in the pew ahead must have pissed himself a little, as old men will. The priest waves around incense. You stand up, you sit down, you stand up, you sit down, you mutter the response to the priest. You turn to tell your mother that you need to go outside for air — dang flu bug. Halfway down the aisle, bile fills your cheeks.

Outside, you run around to the back of the church where no one will see you because it faces the water. It's February, the puddle steams. Your breath steams. You eat some snow and gaze out at the frozen strait, mist hanging above it. Hm, you think.

Today, it's not like that. You feel pleasant, dozy, as soon as you take a seat beside your mother in the pew. You pick up the Catholic Book of Worship and read the words to the songs. You've always done that, every since you were small.

Sadly, the choir will be singing today. The well-to-do matrons with sprayed, silver hair and chunky gold jewellery. Most of them are members of the Ladies Auxiliary. You don't know what that is. Mrs. Tamara Cameron approaches the microphone and tells everybody that the opening hymn will be "Seek Ye First." This is the one where they all try to harmonize one long, high-pitched "ALLLLL-LEEEEE-LOOOOO-YAAAAA" with a whole verse. They think it sounds ethereal. The organist is a stiff, skinny fifteen-year-old outcast who appears to be scared out of her mind. You lean over to ask Mommy where the real organist is, Mrs. Fougere, who has been there for as long as you can remember, and your mother whispers that she is dead, as of only two weeks ago.

The first chord that the fifteen-year-old hits is off-key, causing Mrs. Cameron to glower. The girl is going to cry, maybe. No—the song begins.

The congregation has always liked the choir because it means they don't have to sing. They are content to stand there, holding their books open in front of them. But Mommy always sings, choir or no, and she holds her book at an angle so that you can see the words and sing too.

A wonderful thing happens now. You notice Martin Carlyle, shuffling unobtrusively into the back row of the choir box. He is wearing the same clothes as you saw him in yesterday. He blows his nose quietly, with deference, into a repulsive piece of cloth and then tucks it back into his sleeve, where he got it. He picks up a hymn book, flips it open to the correct page after peeking at someone else's, and decides to join in on the high-pitched "Alleluia" rather than the regular verse. Except that his voice isn't high-pitched, like the ladies'.

> Seek ye first the Kingdom of God
> And his righteousness
> And all these things will be offered unto you
> Allelu, alleluia.

Mommy says into your ear, "There's Martin," unsurprised, which must mean he shows up for this every Sunday. That is why Mrs. Cameron has failed to glower, and only looks a little put out. What can she say? They are all God's children.

After you've been around for a while, Martin seems to turn up everywhere. He's the town drunk, is why, and the town is small. Every Sunday, you see him at church, singing in the choir, his voice even more off-note than the ladies'. Half the time he doesn't even know the words and sort of yah-yahs his way through. One day you do an experiment and go to the nine o'clock mass instead of the later one. There Martin is, singing away.

He never recognizes you, even after the time on the step. One time you see him at the bar bumming for drinks and you are so pissed that you say to the assholes you are with: "Look! It's my soulmate," and you go over and fling your arm around him and call for two scotch and sodas. You remember him blinking at you with reservation and saying, "Thank you, dear. Thank you, Miss."

Another day you go to the bar — even though you have been saying to yourself all along: I probably shouldn't go to the bar — and of course on that day you see him there and he comes and sits down at the table you're at. So then you go and sit down at a different one but then he comes and sits down there too. All he does is look at you and smoke. It is the first time you've been face to face in two years. At a third table, he sits down right beside you and tells you, in a number of ways, that you are a terrible person and why. The assholes you are with examine their drinks. If one of them would at least move, you could get up from the table.

For a long time, nothing much happens.

Then, word comes around that Martin has shot himself in the head. Doctor Bernie, a second cousin, calls from the hospital and informs Daddy that the patient has been asking for him.

"Holy shit!" says Dad.

"Yes," the doctor replies. He has an implacable, singsong voice which has always annoyed you and your father equally.

"He's been asking for you ever since they brought him in here, Alec."

"Well, holy shit, Bernie, is he going to live or what?"

"Oh yes, he's sitting up having a cup of tea."

Dad has to get you to drive him to the hospital because he is "so Jesus pissed off I can't see straight."

"Holy shit," he keeps muttering, and, "Stupid bugger."

In the hospital, you hang around the reception desk listening to his voice resound in the corridor. It is a small hospital. Nurses rush past to silence him, not understanding that their pasty, wrinkled faces and harsh, hushed voices and fingers pressed against their lipless mouths are just going to make him angrier. You remember this from all your life. Shrinking down in the front seat of the car while Daddy yells at a careless driver. Shrinking down in the wooden desk while Daddy yells at your math teacher. Shrinking down into the chesterfield while Daddy yells at the television. Everything making him angrier and angrier and nobody getting it right.

But when Daddy emerges, trailing flustered and ignored nurses, he is laughing.

"Leave it to Martin," he says. "Shoots himself through the head and even that doesn't do him a bit of good."

"So are you going to help him again, Daddy?"

"Well, Jesus Christ, Katey, what are you gonna do, you know?"

He doesn't really know what to do anymore, he's done so much already. He used to drive Martin to AA meetings (much as he had hated them himself in the old days) but was soon informed by such-and-such that Martin took advantage of the trips into town to visit the liquor store and drop in at Buddy's Tavern. And everything ended up like that. Daddy had badgered social services into boosting Martin's allowance so that he could buy some soap and deodorant and Aqua Velva and clothes to get himself cleaned up for the job Dad had managed to get him sweeping up at the mill. Then, when Dad heard about the new public housing units that were going up, social services found themselves duly annoyed into putting one aside for Martin, even though they were being clamoured for by single mothers and the like.

So Daddy drove out to Martin's shack in the woods, which had no water or electricity, and laid all of this at his feet.

"By God, Martin," he said, "you'll get the new place all snugged up nice and pretty soon you'll be having your daughter over for Sunday dinner."

"No, Mr. Leary, my daughter wouldn't come over so she could spit on me."

"Well, goddamnit, you can have me over to dinner!"

"Proud to, Mr. Leary."

Daddy handed him the keys and, looking around at the differing piles of junk that served as Martin's furniture, told him to just give social services a call once he got everything packed away and ready to go. They'd come and get him moved in. "By the Jesus, I'll come and help too," he added.

"God bless you, Mr. Leary."

"Aw, well, what the fuck."

Dad left, feeling good, stepping over Martin's sick, emaciated dog, King.

But months went by and social services called up: "Mr. Leary, there is a list of people as long as my arm who are waiting to get into that unit, and it just sitting there..." Dad barks something that shuts the sarcastic little bastard right up, and then hangs up so he can phone his buddy at the mill. How has Martin been getting along? Martin Carlyle? He didn't show up, Alec, and I wasn't expecting him to.

Outside the shack with no water or electricity, Daddy found Martin asleep on the ground while King sniffed daintily at the surrounding vomit. Martin's drinking friend, Alistair, was leaning against the side of the house, taking in the sunshine. A beautiful spring day. He was not passed out, but cradled a near-empty bottle of White Shark against his crotch, serene and Buddha-like. He squinted up at Daddy and said that himself and Martin had been having "a regular ceilidh" all month long with the extra welfare that Martin was now getting. Daddy kicked the dog into the woods and threw the bottle of White Shark in after it. This having been the incident that preceded the throwing of Martin Carlyle from Alec Leary's step, where you came in.

֍

Daddy has a sore knee. It makes him hobble when he walks, and it makes him angry. You have to go out and help him bring the wood in because none of your brothers are about. If you were one of them, it would be a bonding moment between you and he. It might be anyway. He likes you when you work. Here is one thing you know: men love work. You might not know anything about what women love, but men love work.

You can always tell when it's Martin phoning, because Daddy's tone will become reserved. You hear him say things like: Well, I'll do what I can, Martin, but I'm not making any promises, you hear me? I can't just give give give. Then Dad will hang up and turn to you.

"If that Martin Carlyle ever comes around when I'm not here, don't you let him in."

"No."

"Do you know what he looks like?"

"Yes, I've seen him a million—"

"A big fat hairy ugly bastard and he's got a hole in his head"—Daddy points to a spot above one of his eyebrows—"where the bullet went in."

Daddy is busy these days with Little League. The head of the recreation department called him up and asked him to coach. "Nobody else wanted to do it, I suppose," he grunted into the phone. "Selfish whores."

And your mother, observing that you never seem to go out anymore and have absolutely nothing to occupy your time, ever so delicately suggests that it would be nice and he would like it if you attended the games. So you do, even though you have no understanding of baseball and don't know when to cheer or when to boo and are the only woman there who isn't somebody's mother and almost get hit on the head with a foul ball twice. You watch him hobbling back and forth in front of the dugout, hollering at both teams and causing the little guy at bat's knees to knock together. At the end of every game, win or lose, he takes them to the Dairy Queen and buys them all sundaes. You get to come along too. You have coffee. The little boys look at you and ask you questions about yourself. Are you married? What grade are you in? They can't quite figure out where you fit. You answer every question as honestly as you can, but it doesn't help them any.

Soon, you're attending the practices. Maybe you are the unofficial mascot. Dad gets frustrated with them one day and steps up to the plate to show them how it's done. He can't throw anymore because his arm cramps up when he raises it above his shoulder, and he can't run because of his knee, but he gets the best pitcher on the team to throw him one so they can see how to hit. The clenched fists and clenched jaw all over again—overweight, balding man clutching a child's tool in his large, pink hands. When he swings the bat, it makes a sound that frightens you and you look up from picking at your nails and see that all the little round faces are turned upward in awe.

Carol Bruneau

Doves

It is a long way from Lagos to Greystone, and God's will that brings me here. His hand steers the car into the frozen, bumpy parking lot. Helping Hand, says the sign. Put your hand in the hand: music stirs in my head, clapping too. The sound of clapping hands, marching feet; of people on the move, dancing in the Spirit. But on this most bitter of days, Mission Monday, there is no time for singing. There is work to be done.

The woman inside greets me, smiles as if seeing the Holy Mother. I swing my bag up onto the counter, mittens collected by the diocese. "Any large ones?" She mouths the words wide as if that will aid my understanding. My face is so cold I do not speak, emptying out the contents. A mother with a small boy comes up and rummages.

"You givin' these away? Or do we gotta buy 'em?" The mother looks past me, past my hands, which are starting to thaw. She has a blue rucksack tucked under her arm. The boy clutches an orange plastic gun. There are rules regarding such donations, rules too often broken. His eyes are milky brown, like a river. There is mud—chocolate—around his mouth. He grabs a mitten; his mother slaps his hand.

"Don't touch, I said. How many times I gotta tell you?" The mother's voice is a nail splitting wood. She jerks the boy's arm—"Wha'd I say?"—and the boy drops the mitts in the puddle at our feet.

My veil sweeps my cheek as I retrieve them. Wiping them off, I hold them out. The boy slaps them away, and the mother swats his head. I retrieve them again and pass them to her. But her eyes move past me and fix on the woman behind the counter, who blinks and says, "Take them."

We see so many mothers like this, Sister Marcetta and I: pale white girls pushing strollers, with their thin white boyfriends wearing ball caps. They choose clothes that don't look warm enough and they smoke, looking at us in a way that makes me want to cover my face. The look is cold and shameless. God forgive me for throwing stones. It is the children in the strollers whom Jesus gathers to Himself, for whom Marcetta and I most gratefully labour.

"The peace of the Lord be with you," I say softly. The boy aims his weapon, lets it fall to his side.

"Put that down, I toldja. I'm not buyin' nothing."

Clothing is free to those who cannot pay, though the sale of donations funds our mission. I pray for patience and to not grow weary, and that the love of Jesus will spill from my heart into the hearts of others.

The woman behind the counter says, "Sister, if you wouldn't mind—"

There is sorting to be done, and I am in charge of it. Pots and pans, children's books, baby clothes and women's dresses such as Jezebel, wife of Ahab, might wear. Everything comes in large green garbage bags stuffed to overflowing. The donations are so plentiful they could be things collected after a famine perhaps, or a massacre—but they are clean, of course, if threadbare. Today there is a girl to help me, a volunteer named Tina.

"Tina," I say. "What is that short for?"

"Christina," she says, not looking up. The thing most noticeable in this mission is the way the helpers and the helped look past you, as if talking to a bystander. As if they see your guardian angel, and it is she, not you, who is speaking.

"What should I do with this?" Tina asks. It looks like a man's belt, studded dangerously with chrome. "My boyfriend wants one just like it," she hints, and smiles, and tucks it inside her coat. She isn't dressed for the cold either, the skin above her slacks so very white, white as milk watered to nourish a multitude.

"Sister Berthe?" The girl's voice is flat, and I think of the doulas whom Sister Marcetta enlists to attend mothers giving birth to babies without fathers. I can't help but look at this girl's stomach, the way she has no stomach at all, but doesn't look hungry. No one here looks hungry for anything but guidance. The light of Christ, who came into the world so that we might see.

"Yes, my child," I say, a pair of trousers folded over my arm and many pairs more to sort and hang.

"Shit—oh, shoot. Someone needs help."

The woman from behind the counter appears. Her grin confuses me; her eyes are hard and grey as the roadway. Before I can step into the big room full of clothing, broken toys, mugs, plates, ashtrays and plastic flowers, there's a shout, a cry that sends needles up my spine. Buses and cars spit, shooting past just outside.

"What is it, my child?"

The man before me has wild hair, as though he has stood for days on a mountain in the freezing wind. His eyes spin and dart. He's wearing a torn quilted coat, gold in colour, gold as threshed wheat. His hands are bare and chapped and he wrings them—to warm them, perhaps. But then he waves them, his hands a burning bush of activity, a firestorm, and he curtsies the way people curtsy for Queen Elizabeth, a trip-step then up again, and pushes himself past my outstretched arms. Briefly I feel his breath on my face and catch his smell; it is the smell of spiritual hunger: too much wine at the wedding feast.

Tina and the woman from the counter shy behind a rack of coats—worn, thick woolen coats that make me think of sheep, sacrifices made to God before our washing in the Blood of the Lamb. The woman, whose name escapes me, clears her throat and gasps. As if spotting a body swinging past in a current. Parting the sea of rags, I peer through. The man with wild eyes is urinating on the furniture, a plaid sofa that would have gone free to whomever asked. Seek and ye shall find; ask and it shall be given.

"Get out. Get out now," the woman orders. "You are not welcome in this place." Her voice is as stony as the soil of our mission, as cold as the dawn when, on Fridays, I rise to prepare the small white loaves for Holy Communion. Just in case, as Sister Marcetta says.

The man zips his pants, wipes his nose. His gaze is cast downwards. There is a roll of Lifesaver candies beside the cash box, and I peel one away and offer it. He puts his tongue out as if to receive the Host. It calms him and, thank the Lord, the community of saints and all the archangels, he turns, shrugging his shoulders, and leaves.

When all the garbage bags have been emptied and their contents sorted, I take the volunteers' hands and we pray in a small circle. Their hands are pale as fish, and I think of the miracle of the loaves and fishes, the feeding of the five thousand. Such a numbering of the hungry challenges me: I see multitudes of the living coursing down dusty streets. I see rivers running red.

"See ya next week," Tina shouts, following me to the car, carrying the large white mittens I have almost forgotten. Sister Marcetta was kind enough to provide them, along with a gift of a lock de-icer. It's a very long way from Lagos, Satan's voice cajoles as I scrape frost from the car.

"God be with you," I call out. "Bless you, dear. Bless you."

At the convent Sister Marcetta is mashing potatoes for the hungry at the Hot Meal held near the mall. I think of the man in the quilted coat, and of mothers and dark-skinned babies, and pray silently for new ways to serve the Lord. Marcetta mixes in an egg, margarine and bluish milk for extra nutrition, and sets aside a dishful for us. Putting on boots she calls mukluks, she carries the pot to her car. Just the tip of the cross in our front yard shows above the snow; it's as plain as a grave marker when there aren't the means for something permanent. The blue security sign is buried, too. I vaguely recall the presence of grass.

"Don't forget the wash," Sister calls. "Man the fort. Good luck!"

Waving, I think of the Juju market where people purchase wares for voodoo: shrivelled heads of animals, paws and teeth. "You're not to think of luck," we counsel the sorrowful, who appear at odd hours seeking our prayers. It has nothing to do with luck: it is grace, we tell them. God's will, I remind myself, reeling our habits from the line. Dancing stiffly in the bitter gusts, they resemble pieces of sky, the lavender blue of forget-me-nots, Sister says, the flowers she hopes to plant by the cross. To me it is the Virgin's blue: the blue of sorrows, abandonment.

This is my afternoon for contemplation, but first there are chores: mending, the basement pews to be polished. With its red candle burning day and night like the Sacred Heart, our chapel is Golgotha, a place of bones bleached as white as this landscape. But we have no stations of the cross, nor do we have a regular priest, which grieves us when the faithful come to say confession. "You are marching in the light of Christ," an inner voice promised when I departed Nigeria. With gunshots echoing through the heat, I was glad to board the plane. But the rosy light of the sanctuary brings back the sound of soldiers, and I trudge upstairs.

Sister Marcetta has collected the clothing from the supermarket bin, a mountain of it serviceable with repair. I contemplate her machine in the kitchen, on which she plays her CDs, inspirational ones like "Eternal Light: Music of Inner Peace," my favourite. But it's all too easy to get lost in it, and one must be ready, always ready, not just for the faithful, but for all seeking respite from woe. Since the priest stopped coming, Sister and I have been forced to break rules, our duty being to listen and lighten burdens.

"I'm addicted, Sister," a woman confessed once, "to that stuff on the Internet." Her hands flapped like helpless doves. "Every Wednesday Satan tells me to play the slots. He's there, Sister. Honest to God, right there in my bathroom, under the sink." What does one say? Go forth, my child; gamble your life away? It is meet and right to take chances?

The bell rings as I thread the needle, a small pair of trousers over my knee. The sound jars the stillness. I descend the stairs. The caller's shape looms through the entry's pebbled glass. Blurred, he appears agitated, his hair a bush in a fierce gale. Hesitating but a moment, I quickly open the door, hear a gasp — my own. I recognize his coat; it is gold and puffy, with stains on the front.

"How may we be of service, brother?" It takes extra breath to push this out.

He holds a shoebox in his gloveless hands. My eyes flit to the label: Airwalk. The man snarls like a wild dog. Before I can speak again, he lifts the lid. What I see surprises me, shocks me a little but not very much. Not when you have seen people in rivers and roadways. It is a pigeon, its feathers layered grey like billowing smoke. There's a greenish pink shine around its staring eye. Its wing sticks up like that of a chicken about to be roasted.

"Service," the man mutters. "Please ma'am. Help me out. I have to bury him." It takes me a moment to comprehend. He tugs at my sleeve, tugs so sharply I fear it will rip. I explain, rather quickly, that the priest no longer makes regular calls, the need being insufficiently great. "All things bright and beauteeeful," the man says. "Don't you think he deserves a decent burial?"

But I am thinking of the priest's final visit, to hear the confessions of a grandmother and her daughter. The faithful are seldom men; of course, it was women who found Jesus risen from the tomb. Women like the gambling lady who came to me, asking, "Life is about taking risks — am I right, Sister? God spoke to me in a dream," she said. "There's this man, see? He's gonna meet me in Kissimmee."

"What is this Kissimmee?"

"Sister, you don't want to know: it's warm there."

"You must listen to what your heart tells you."

"Like, I met this guy on the Net."

"Listen to the Spirit. He's there to guide you."

"Now Sister, the heart and the Spirit — ain't they the same?"

After a time their faces — those of the faithful and the afflicted — are faces in a river.

The man replaces the lid and shakes the box. Its contents thud against cardboard. "Sister!" His voice relocates me, the look in his eyes angry, indignant. He clutches the shoebox to his chest. I think rather idly of the security system — the sign on its post beneath the snow. A buzzer meant to deter intruders will sound unless you disable it. The buzzer makes Marcetta nervous. Once it went off accidentally, the police came and the convent was billed — an amount that could have provided food for many. His will be done on earth as it is in heaven.

The man gazes at the front of my habit. Someone — the gambler making her confession — called us bluebirds, Marcetta and me. She seemed a decent person, put five dollars in the donations box, on her way out to her car. She has not returned, and I wonder how things are in Kissimmee, whether she and the Internet man have tied the knot, been blessed in Holy Matrimony.

My brother with the pigeon slackens, his shoulders droop. I no longer see the man who spoiled the sofa, and whom the volunteer cast out. He isn't much more than a boy, really. Below his wild hair his face is flat, white, swollen, with a spray of pimples on his jaw. His mouth resembles a fish's. "Help me, Miss," he begs. The look in his eyes is one I have seen before, in the eyes of men running with knives through the streets.

"You got a church here," he says, and his gaze climbs the small flight of stairs to the kitchen, to the clean white curtains, the sink, the table, walls spotless and bare but for a crucifix. Cold, cold air blows in past him, filling the stairwell.

"There's no priest, I'm sorry. No one to conduct a funeral, I'm afraid."

I keep my voice gentle, imagining Sister Marcetta at the soup kitchen, her nervousness if she returned now. "You are not welcome in this building," she too has told undesirables.

"We must open our hearts to the stranger," I've reminded her, but Marcetta can be set in her ways.

The man-boy begins to weep, a gruff coughing.

"Come with me," I say softly. "Are you hungry?" Sister Marcetta would not approve, but I lead him to the kitchen, take a sandwich from the refrigerator. The bread is very white; everything about this place is so. He looks like he is eating snow, devouring it—a jackal that has not eaten in some time. The food soothes him. The dominion of God is suddenly vast and in the man's calm I am a refugee, nation-less before God's will. My life exists without borders. Sometimes it seems I will never comprehend the ways of this frozen place, but as Marcetta says, it is up to us to cast the seeds. Only the Lord can make them grow.

I boil water, stir the powdered coffee in. His dirty hands reach for the cup.

"Will you take care of it for me, Sister?" he says meekly, and I remember the box on the stairs. "Can you gimme a lift somewheres, Sister?"

I think of my car, how it will need to be scraped again, and Sister Marcetta's instructions as she loaded the pot into the back of hers.

"Sister. I need a drive to my girlfriend's." Once more the man looks around like a hungry animal.

Allow me, Lord, to open my heart, to open my life to you. The stranger.

"I know you got the keys to your car here someplace," he says.

I take them from the hook beneath the cupboard, and put on my coat. He ignores the shoebox by the mat. "Leave it," he says, when I go to pick it up.

The car does not want to start at first. "Don't flood it," he says, and I think of the river full of rags. His breathing makes an ocean sound in my ears. "I shore appreciate this."

My hands on the wheel tremble, not from the engine's vibration so much as the pulse of fear, as he directs me through a zigzag of streets. Oh Holy Spirit, Counsellor: what wilderness have you led me into?

Outside a small house he orders me to stop. The tires skid on the icy road and my chest contracts. Holding my breath, I pray for the guidance of the Counsellor, the blameless, ever-present Comforter.

"Wait here." His coat rides up as he gets out. The motor tick-tick-ticks as he slouches to the door and lets himself in. I think of Marcetta finding the shoebox but no sign of me.

"Cherished and Holy Infant," I pray aloud.

The man reappears, with a paper bag under his arm, and gets in, telling me to drive again. I hear the slosh as he uncaps the bottle inside and drinks, a long slurp, as I try to keep my gaze on the road.

The Spirit led the Saviour into the wilderness, not *in* the wilderness. Thou shalt worship the Lord thy God, He said, and Him only shalt thou serve. I want to cross myself but my hand won't leave the wheel.

"Got some thirst, boy," the man apologizes. "Just a little errand, Sister." But his voice grows sharp again. "Right here. Left there. Right, now! At these lights," he directs. "Now drive. That's right. Now. See them lights?"

Deliver me, Lord.

Obeying, I turn onto a road that climbs a hill higher than the one on which our convent sits. Children slog over the snowbanks. A few look slightly familiar; perhaps they have visited the Helping Hand. We pass rows and rows of buildings, their homes perhaps. Many have boarded-up windows.

Thou shalt not tempt the Lord thy God.

"A ghost town," I observe, my voice quaking, and he smirks.

"Shut up!"

Quietly I pray, "Our Father, who art —"

"Shut up that God stuff!" He pushes the bottle at me, its neck nudging my coat.

Oh Lord, forgive me all my transgressions.

Up and up the hill we drive, miles and miles it seems, past more of these houses. Some have Christmas ornaments flapping in the wind. Big sheets of foil in the windows, big metal doors, barricades. I think of the faithful and all their confessions, of the woman in Kissimmee.

"Welcome to Greystone, Sister." He laughs.

"When" — I swallow — "did your bird die, sir?"

He scowls, and the liquor slides back down the neck of the bottle. "Bird?" he says, and barks something unrepeatable. Before us the top of the hill shines, the snow's brilliance reflecting the afternoon sun. In front of the last row of houses the man shouts, "Right here, Sister. This is where my girlfriend lives. You better wait, though, till I see if she's home."

The tires bite into ice. I'm perspiring. In the name of the Father, and of the Son...Against my heart's advice I park. The heater has finally come on, emitting a dry burst of heat. Perspiration twists under my clothing, a clammy wetness. Still I am grateful for the heater and for my heavy coat, and give thanks—for it and for Sister Marcetta and even her catalogue, the one she brought before the snow arrived, filled with every imaginable good. Choose a good warm coat and boots, she said and placed the order; such was her welcome.

In the name of—I imagine her juggling the empty pot, wrestling it and the shoebox upstairs.

A child answers the door and the man pushes inside. Through the strips of tinsel in the window he waves to me, like a priest passing benediction. Lord have mercy. Tears of gratitude blur my vision. Wiping my eyes, I bow my head and breathe. Next door someone appears with a large black dog on a chain. Neither looks as I pull away. By now Sister will be warming our supper, dividing the bowl of potato, mixing it with leftover meat.

My stomach races with hunger; this climate feeds the body's appetite where heat would stifle it. The sun is a low orange glare shining off every surface now, and carefully I proceed downhill, wondering about the man's girlfriend and the child—his child? Perhaps I should have stopped, knocked, made sure the child was all right, that there was food. Something other than the brown paper bag under his arm.

The same children are climbing the snowbanks uphill. They look like small, bright-coated animals squirming towards me.

Please, Lord Jesus, forgive my selfishness and sins of omission.

A car comes racing up behind, passing, its tires making a hissing sound.

I see the boy, the one from this morning, from the Helping Hand, the one with the plastic gun. He is walking the top of the snowbank like an astronaut exploring the moon. His face is wide and pale, so pale, like all the faces in our mission. Even his hair is pale as he turns and shouts to his friends. He has the blue rucksack strapped to his back, and takes big floppy steps in his boots.

As the snow breaks and spills, he slips and the car ahead of me skids and spins.

The thud is like the Lord's fist coming down. All I see are the boots flying up, one a little higher than the other, then falling like heavy, flapping birds.

I don't even feel the slip of the seat belt as I jump out. The rusty blue car sits across the road. Its driver takes a long moment to appear. A white man with a dirty growth of beard and a ball cap, he could be the boyfriend of any of the mothers we minister to, Sister Marcetta and I. Perhaps he is coming home from the supper Marcetta has helped serve.

He sucks a cigarette, sucks it as if it were a mother's nipple, as the two of us kneel over the boy.

My heart turns hollow, my soul like the hot-cold roar inside a seashell plucked from the scorching sand of a beach.

Children, rosy-cheeked and smelling of school and damp clothing, press around us, the driver and me, and the boy who lies limp and cold on the icy pavement.

Only my soul hears. An anguished noise, hysterical. If there are words, voices, they float far above us, like a hurricane wind threshing the palms.

Already the boy's face is turning grey as the slush. A sliver of orange plastic sticks out from his jacket, but there is no blood. His eyes are closed. His mouth is serene, peaceful, without a hint of astonishment or surprise. I put my hand over his heart. Someone folds a scarf, places it under his head.

Tenderly, trembling with the love of Jesus in my throat, I make the sign of the cross.

The driver waits in his car, the engine running. Glancing back, I glimpse the pigeon man's face in the window, but he does not come outside. I take off my coat and cover the boy with it. It covers him from head to toe, his body is so small. It surprises me, how small.

The air freezes my breath. I don't want to leave the boy, I will not leave him. The wind pulls and tugs at my habit. It is a cold that scorches, but I no longer feel it. The sting is in the wait for the authorities—the ambulance and the police, who eventually arrive and take our statements.

I do not even know the boy's name. His mother is merely a voice scratching in my head, a pair of hands holding mittens.

"Sister Berthe Uledi Adumi," I offer my identity, "Order of the Eucharistic Heart—."No one blinks, or bats an eye. It was an accident: God knows this, I tell the authorities and everyone who will listen. No one contests my statement.

The driver, whose name becomes a single sound, smokes and kicks the snow, smokes and scratches beneath his cap, keeping his lips drawn tight.

It is dusk when we are free to go, the orange sky aflame and the streetlights blazing as I drive slowly through the blackened streets. The traffic lights remind me of Lifesaver candies and the colours of Kwanzaa. In this wilderness everything is black now, red and yellow and green.

At the convent Sister Marcetta has placed the shoebox under the back step, and taken up the mending that I have neglected.

She lays her hands on me as we kneel before each other to pray. It is a special prayer, which we offer before the tiny altar, with the light of Christ's sacred gift burning brightly. Through my tears I promise to do one thing: I will bury the bird in the backyard, as soon as the ground thaws enough to work. With this promise made, we pray deep into the night for the rocks and the trees, the grass and the soil; for the good of all children, the seeds of our mission, whether or not they take root.

Jessica Grant

My Husband's Jump

My husband was an Olympic ski jumper. (*Is* an Olympic ski jumper?) But in the last Olympics, he never landed.

It began like any other jump. His speed was exactly what it should be. His height was impressive, as always. Up, up he went, into a perfect sky that held its breath for him. He soared. Past the ninety- and hundred-metre marks, past every mark, past the marks that weren't really marks at all, just marks for decoration, impossible reference points, marks nobody ever expected to hit. Up. Over the crowd, slicing the sky. Every cheer in every language stopped; every flag in every colour dropped.

It was a wondrous sight.

Then he was gone, and they came after me. Desperate to make sense of it. And what could I tell them? He'd always warned me ski jumping was his life. I'd assumed he meant metaphorically. I didn't know he meant to spend (*sus*pend) his life mid-jump.

How did I feel? Honestly, and I swear this is true, at first I felt only wonder. It was pure, even as I watched him disappear. I wasn't worried about him, not then. I didn't begrudge him, not then. I didn't feel jealous, suspicious, forsaken.

I was pure as that sky.

But through a crack in the blue, in slithered Iago and Cassius and every troublemaker, doubt-planter and doomsayer there ever was. In slithered the faithless.

Family, friends, teammates, the bloody IOC—they had "thoughts" they wanted to share with me.

The first, from the IOC, was drugs. What did I think about drugs? Of course he must have been taking something, they said. Something their tests had overlooked? They were charming, disarming.

It was not a proud moment for me, shaking my head in public, saying no, no, no in my heart, and secretly checking every pocket, shoe, ski boot, cabinet, canister and drawer in the house. I found nothing. Neither did the IOC. They tested and retested his blood, his urine, his hair. (They still had these *pieces* of him? Could I have them, I wondered, when they were done?)

The drug theory fizzled, for lack of evidence. Besides, the experts said (and why had they not spoken earlier?) such a drug did not, *could not*, exist. Yet. Though no doubt somebody somewhere was working on it.

A Swiss ski jumper, exhausted and slippery-looking, a rival of my husband's, took me to dinner.

He told me the story of a French man whose hang-glider had caught a bizarre air current. An insidious Alpine wind, he said, one wind in a billion (what were the chances?) had scooped up his wings and lifted him to a cold, airless altitude that could not support life.

Ah. So my husband's skis had caught a similarly rare and determined air current? He had been carried off, against his will, into the stratosphere?

The Swiss ski jumper nodded enthusiastically.

You believe, then, that my husband is dead?

He nodded again, but with less gusto. He was not heartless—just nervous and desperate to persuade me of something he didn't quite believe himself. I watched him fumble helplessly with his fork.

Have you slept recently? I asked. You seem jumpy—excuse the pun.

He frowned. You don't believe it was the wind?

I shook my head. I'd been doing that a lot lately.

His fist hit the table. Then how? He looked around, as if he expected my husband to step out from behind the coat rack. *Ta da*!

I invited him to check under the table.

Was it jealousy? Had my husband achieved what every ski jumper ultimately longs for, but dares not articulate? A dream that lies dormant, the sleeping back of a ski hill, beneath every jump. A silent, monstrous wish.

Yes, it was jealousy—and I pitied the Swiss ski jumper. I pitied them all. For any jump to follow my husband's, any jump *with a landing*, was now pointless. A hundred metres, a hundred and ten, twenty, thirty metres. Who cared? I had heard the IOC was planning to scrap ski jumping from the next Olympics. How could they hold a new event when the last one had never officially ended?

They needed closure, they said. Until they had it, they couldn't move on.

Neither, apparently, could my Swiss friend. He continued to take me to dinner, to lecture me about winds and aerodynamics. He produced weather maps. He insisted, he impressed upon me... couldn't I see the veracity, the validity of... look here... put your finger here on this line and follow it to its logical end. Don't you see how it might have happened?

I shook my head—no. But I did. After the fifth dinner, how could I help but see, even if I couldn't believe?

I caught sleeplessness like an air current. It coiled and uncoiled beneath my blankets, a tiny tornado of worry, fraying the edges of sleep. I would wake, gasping—the *enormity* of what had happened: my husband had never landed. Where was he, *now*, at this instant? Was he dead? Pinned to the side of some unskiable mountain? Had he been carried out to sea and dropped like Icarus, with no witnesses, no one to congratulate him, no one to grieve?

I had an undersea image of him: a slow-motion landing through a fish-suspended world—his skis still in perfect V formation.

Meanwhile the media were attributing my husband's incredible jump to an extramarital affair. They failed to elaborate, or offer proof, or to draw any logical connection between the affair and the feat itself. But this, I understand, is what the media do: they attribute the inexplicable to extramarital affairs. So I tried not to take it personally.

I did, however, tell one reporter that while adultery may break the law of *marriage*, it has never been known to break the law of *gravity*. I was quite pleased with my quip, but they never published it.

My husband's family adopted a more distressing theory. While they didn't believe he was having an affair, they believed he was trying to escape *me*. To jump ship, so to speak. Evidently the marriage was bad. Look at the lengths he'd gone to. Literally, the *lengths*.

In my heart of hearts I knew it wasn't true. I had only to remember the way he proposed, spontaneously, on a chair lift in New Mexico. Or the way he littered our bed with Hershey's Kisses every Valentine's Day. Or the way he taught me to snowplow with my beginner's skis, making an upside-down V in the snow, the reverse of his in the air.

But their suspicions hurt nonetheless and, I confess, sometimes they were my suspicions too. Sometimes my life was a country-and-western song: had he really loved me? How could he just fly away? Not a word, no goodbye. Couldn't he have shared his sky…with me?

But these were surface doubts. They came, they went. Like I said, where it counted, in my heart of hearts, I never faltered.

The world was not interested in *my* theory, however. When I mentioned God, eyes glazed or were quickly averted, the subject politely changed. I tried to explain that my husband's jump had made a believer out of me. Out of *me*. That in itself was a miracle.

So where were the religious zealots, now that I'd joined their ranks? I'd spent my life feeling outnumbered by them—how dare they all defect? Now they screamed *Stunt*, or *Affair*, or *Air Current*, or *Fraud*. Only I screamed *God*. Mine was the lone voice, howling *God* at the moon, night after night, half expecting to see my husband's silhouette pass before it like Santa Claus.

God was mine. He belonged to me now. I felt the weight of responsibility. Lost a husband, gained a deity. What did it mean? It was like inheriting a pet, unexpectedly. A very large St. Bernard. What would I feed him? Where would he sleep? Could he cure me of loneliness, bring me a hot beverage when I was sick?

ও

I went to see Sister Perpetua, my old high school principal. She coughed frequently—and her coughs were bigger than she was. Vast, hungry coughs.

Her room was spare: a bed, a table, a chair. Through a gabled window I could see the overpass linking the convent to the school. Tall black triangles drifted to and fro behind the glass.

You've found your faith, Sister Perpetua said.

I couldn't help it.

And then she said what I most dreaded to hear: that she had lost hers.

I left the window and went to her. The bed groaned beneath my weight. Beside me, Sister Perpetua scarcely dented the blanket.

She had lost her faith the night she saw my husband jump. She and the other sisters had been gathered around the television in the common room. When he failed to land, she said, they felt something yanked from them, something sucked from the room, from the world entire — something irrevocably lost.

God?

She shrugged. What we had *thought* was God.

His failure to land, she continued, but I didn't hear the rest. His failure to land. *His failure to land.*

Why not miracle of flight? Why not leap of faith?

I told her I was sure of God's existence now, as sure as if he were tied up in my backyard. I could smell him on my hands. That's how close he was. How real, how tangible, how furry.

She lifted her hands to her face, inhaled deeply, and coughed. For a good three minutes she coughed, and I crouched beneath the swirling air in the room, afraid.

It was a warm night in July. A plaintive wind sang under my sleep. I woke, went to the window, lifted the screen. In the yard below, the dog was softly whining. It was not the wind after all. When he saw me, he was quiet. He had such great sad eyes — they broke the heart, they really did.

I sank to my knees beside the window.

I was content, I told him, when everyone else believed and I did not. Why is that?

He shook his great floppy head. Spittle flew like stars around him.

And now all I'm left with is a dog — forgive me, but you are a very silent partner.

I knelt there for a long time, watching him, watching the sky. I thought about the word *jump*. My husband's word.

I considered it first as a noun, the lesser of its forms. As a noun, it was already over. A completed thing. *A* jump. A half-circle you could trace with your finger, follow on the screen, measure against lines on the ground. Here is where you took off, here is where you landed.

But my husband's *jump* was a verb, not a noun. Forever unfinished. What must it be like, I wondered, to hang your life on a single word? To *jump*. A verb ridden into the sunset. One verb to end all others.

To *jump*. Not to doubt, to pity, to worry, to prove or disprove. Not to remember, to howl, to ask, to answer. Not to love. Not even to *be*.

And not to *land*. Never, ever to land.

Samuel Thomas Martin

Running the
Whale's Back

The weatherman's hand sweeps from Labrador down Newfoundland's fanged north coast to St. John's, his finger squiggling from there down to Renews: the sea white against green land. He's talking about winds *rifling* in from the north. The pack ice circling the island on the TV map feels like a tight collar to Patrick, choking him. This is the first time he has felt this hemmed in, this claustrophobic, in his own home.

It was a heart attack is what Gerta said over the phone, and that was enough for Anne to call Porter Airlines and book her ticket back to Ontario. Her whirling about the house Patrick took as worry for her father Gurney, but since Hab showed him Anne's Facebook file he knows she had other reasons to get out of the house that was once *their* house.

Patrick is alone, and a shot of the pack ice jammed into Middle Cove on the TV makes him feel that much more isolated from the world. Funny, because as a kid he would hop the ice pans and copy quick-like from one to the next. But he's spent enough time away from the sea that the idea of venturing out onto the slob ice now is terrifying. Almost as much as admitting to his new congregation that his wife has left him.

He has long since sewn up his tongue to keep from swearing and save face as the new Pentecostal pastor in town, but *fuck*, he thinks. How did he not know his wife was having an Internet affair after months of listless sex, silent dinners, her pillow damp some mornings to his touch, even though she always flipped it before heading to the shower before him?

He had thought she was just missing home and would eventually come around, once things were more settled.

But no, more was going on than that. *Obviously.*

And Hab knew about the affair. Knew for months, and said *nothing* to him, not until the day they came back from the airport.

Dad, I think you need to see something.

He said it gently, like Patrick was talking to him and he was seven with a scraped knee, sitting on his dad's lap on the concrete step outside their red brick house back in Peterborough, before they moved to St. John's.

Patrick had kept the Promised Land clichés to himself when speaking of the move, but the thought of partridgeberry jam in late fall, showing Hab his old home in Fawkes Cove along the Killick Coast and driving the Irish Loop in summer—brushing his fingers over those fossils at Mistaken Point—these thoughts married like milk and honey in him.

But that dream of coming home seems like a farce now: treacherous, slick as black ice underfoot. *Home.* Thinking of it is as painful as the time he slipped on the slob ice and broke his front teeth. He was thirteen: strings of blood blowing across the ice like splashed ink on one of those weird paintings Hab likes so much.

Patrick has no idea why.

But when he thinks now of his hope for happiness then, he remembers his broken teeth—the briny taste of blood, Anne's betrayal like a sucker punch. He imagines a headline for this week's church bulletin: *Today's message is on the wiles of Jezebel.* It's a weak mental jab. And he keeps imagining her plane going down and her screaming and wishing she'd never left. He imagines dipping his finger in her blood and with eyes closed painting her name on the oval of an airplane window, longingly, his hand conducting emptiness before his eyes as he sits on the couch here in the dark. Motionless. The room silent. Stern. Because there was writing on the wall: all that time she spent in the computer room.

Why didn't Hab say anything?

Patrick feels like David betrayed by Absalom, but he also feels like Absalom, hanging from his long hair tangled up in that tree. Clumps of knotted hair ripping from his skull as he swings, feeling ungrounded in his thoughts, helpless against grief: that stabbing pain, like a sword between his ribs. But

Absalom was the traitor, the backstabber. *My companion*, David had raged in one of his psalms, *my companion stretched out his hand against me*. Anne is the one Patrick would like to see swinging from that tree. *She has broken her covenant*. She is the one who ran away—the one who pierced him—not Hab. But why, he keeps asking himself, why didn't his son say anything?

And why didn't I see?

Hab had said nothing. Even after the hike that he and Patrick had taken out at Flatrock when Sheilagh's Brush, the last big snowstorm of the season, hit them hard while they were out on the point and had to take shelter in an old army bunker—holed up with some punk kid from around the bay who was already huddled in the bunker before he and Hab had staggered in, snow-covered and half-frozen. They all sat in silence for hours, waiting for the storm to die down enough to make it back to the car—the kid in jackshirt, jeans and ice-coated workboots. Patrick had wondered, as he sat there watching the kid spin a silver skull ring on his bruised knuckles, if the young lad had been out on the sea ice before the storm struck. Thinking back on that day, Patrick remembers longing to be out on the ice himself, leaping from pan to pan.

When he thinks of the bunker he feels trapped, like David huddled in his cave, hiding from Saul who wanted him dead. He knows this is a silly comparison. No one is hurling spears at his head. But he feels hunted, betrayed, deserted.

He had offered the young lad in the bunker a ride after the storm died down, but the kid had *hmphed* and walked off into the dark, hands deep in his pockets—didn't say a simple thank you for the shell of Patrick's coat thrown over him while he slept in the cold.

As thankless as Saul after David spared his life, Patrick thinks, though he knows he's being self-righteous in comparing himself to the Hebrew king. But he can't help it. He can't make sense of his life without seeing it enmeshed in the biblical story. The problem is that he'll slip into David's skin, see himself as a man after God's own heart. But then he'll remember how much of a bastard David was at times, and he finds himself more convicted than comforted. He'll picture what Anne has done as Michal's betrayal of David, when the shepherd king danced before the Ark of the Covenant. He has preached on the passage many times: David stripping down to his linen ephod—what Patrick liked to call his priestly Fruit-of-the-Looms—and dancing furiously before the Lord.

Laughing, singing, sweating, foaming at the mouth, praising God and doing what he felt in his heart he should do—just as Patrick had done in moving here and starting the church. He had danced, preached, worked long hours, sacrificed...and Anne had left him. He thinks of Michal's barrenness after she ridiculed her husband for dancing half-naked before the servant girls. Patrick had always told his congregations that this was not a curse from God but occurred because David had never slept with her again. And Patrick wants to punish Anne in this way, deprive her of his love, but it was *she* who left him. Yet he feels as if *he* is being judged, like David for lusting after Bathsheba: his child, his church, stillborn. What was it that he wanted so badly? Was it souls, converts, miracles? *Is it wrong to want these things?* Was it the church itself that was his Bathsheba? He smirks at this because when he thinks of the church he thinks of old Mildred Hallett, his first member, and the idea of lusting after Mildred's wrinkly, eighty-seven-year-old body sets him laughing until he can barely breathe.

But his laughter is nervous and joyless. His thoughts choke him: like thick mud around his limbs, his neck—he is Jeremiah in the cistern, Absalom tangled up in the tree, David hiding in his cave, Saul alone in his tower. He is Peter drowning, waiting for the hand of Christ. He is all of them and none of them. He's confused and alone—as alone as he felt the day Hab had showed him the traces of Anne's affair.

And after showing Patrick her Facebook file, Hab had gone upstairs to his room, leaving his dad transfixed in the monitor's cold blue glow.

What stung most is that Hab had said that Anne's password was *Patrick*.

How'd you figure that out? he'd asked his son.

I just guessed.

You knew?

I thought she'd tell you. I wanted her to tell you herself. It shouldn't have been me.

Clicking her message box, Patrick had begun scrolling through, reading and trying to picture *Dave*. Had he seen him before? Had he ever met him? Did this Dave guy find Anne online, or did she find him? Pictures: he needed to see a picture of the bastard.

So he'd clicked on Dave's icon and brought up his page, opened his album but there was only a fuzzy yearbook picture from high school and his profile pic. He noticed that Dave was broader in the shoulders than he was. But he was going bald. Hair shaved close to hide it. *Anne, for frig's sake, he's going bald! And he's . . . pasty.*

Patrick had been flipping out in his head when Hab came down with a large duffel bag, packed. He handed his dad a folded piece of paper. Said he could call him *there*, indicating a number scrawled in red ink. *Natalie's number*, it said. And there was an address for Merrymeeting Road below.

Get some sleep, Dad.

And he was gone before Patrick could resent his son for sounding like his father.

Dear Patrick,

I hope this finds you well. (And I hope you can read the writing.) Gerta tells me she phoned you and Anne shortly after I was taken into the hospital. It wasn't a full heart attack but I am still interned here until they can perform an angiogram on me. That is to get things cleared up.

I'm writing (actually it is me, Gerta, writing for Gurney) because I don't feel well enough to talk long on the phone and you know I've always hated talking to disembodied voices. I know, funny for a man who has spent a lifetime talking to God. But the thing I've always loved about being an evangelist was talking to people, seeing their faces. And reading someone's handwriting is in a way like seeing his face. This is how it is when I read the Bible, though I haven't the strength to read it now. And Gerta hates reading aloud. (He thinks I won't put that in the letter but I've told him I'll write whatever he wants said.)

My reason for writing is to see how you and Anne are doing. Gerta tells me Anne came to see me but I was asleep and she didn't want to wake me. I wished she had. She came all that way. This question may be answered before you get this, but is she staying with friends or family here or in St. Lola? I would like to see her before she flies back to Newfoundland. But maybe she is visiting. I only ask because it's been a week and no sign of her yet. But I'm sure she is fine and tells you each night on the phone not to worry. That is Anne for you.

Tell me how the church is going and how many have been saved. Newfoundland was once the Pentecostal capital of Canada, you know. And I preached there many times in the early seventies. Once I prayed for a man missing three fingers and two of them grew back. I always thought it was strange of God to only do half a miracle. (Actually it was two-thirds of a miracle.) But the man said God kept a finger to make sure he'd come collect it some bright morning. That memory is still clear as a photo now, almost forty years later.

When you get this, send us word of where Anne is staying.

She told Gerta she had come to stay for a while. But Gerta hasn't seen her since and I haven't seen her at all. Also, tell us how Hab is doing in his new home. That's all for now. I'm tired and should sleep. (The doctors say he's doing better but he looks grey as a sheet.)

Affectionately,
Gurney (and Gerta too!)

Patrick sees a letter from Gurney in the mix of mail but he doesn't open it, only tosses the whole wad in the recycling bin with all the rest of the mail for the past week. He keeps telling himself that he will go back through it all and pull out the bills and the church-related letters. But for now the fact that the latest letter from the Pentecostal Assemblies of Newfoundland is wrapped in a McDonald's flyer eases something in him: a guttural groan, almost a growl.

Deep down.

Official church business taken so lightly, treated with such disrespect, is a small, affordable rebellion. He can always repent, pull the envelope marked PAON out of the trash, and re-enter the world.

Or can he? Sometimes he is not so sure.

He assumes Gurney and Gerta know now of their daughter's *choice*. The letter probably says as much. Maybe some words of comfort for him. That thought is almost enough to get him off this couch where he's been sleeping for the past week.

There were mornings this past winter when he would get up late—with Hab gone to school and Anne in the basement on the computer—and he'd come out to the couch to watch some morning news. The couch would be warm as if a body had been curled there for hours. He always thought it was Hab who'd slept out in front of the TV all night, watching God knows what. But now he wonders—if he could go back to one of those mornings and feel Anne's side of the bed when he woke—he wonders if he would find it cold, sheets crisp. Was it her warmth he settled into on those winter mornings while she sat in the basement, typing with numb fingers to that man?

He sleeps with the phone on his chest. It shocks him awake each time it rings. But the call display never says *Anne cell*, it never comes up as the number Hab scrawled for him in red ink before his son left. So he lets it ring, lets it go to the answering service, which he doesn't check because the recording is Anne's voice.

He wants to hear her and he doesn't. He wants her to miss him and come back. He wants her to be hit by a car or assaulted. But he doesn't really want that to happen. Or does he? He feels guilty for thinking such things, wishing such things on her. He prays for her to come back, and in the same breath he prays for God to punish her—to make her feel guilty, plague her with insomnia, night terrors, voices in her head. Call her to repentance in a dream, like he called so many in the Bible. But more often than not he asks himself why in hell he is even talking to God. He knows the answer: because there is no one else. But this doesn't stop him from wondering if God even hears him.

Father, he whispers, lying on the couch, the phone on his chest, *if that's you—if you're here, in this room—tell me to come to you.*

The phone rings and his heart jumps. The number looks familiar for some reason, so he answers it and hears Hab's voice asking him how he is, telling him he should come for a visit—get out of the house.

I will, he says, I will soon. I wasn't expecting to hear your voice just now. But I'm glad you called. I'm really glad you called.

Dear Patrick,

I've just received a letter from Anne. In it she says she has left you. She says she is not going back to Newfoundland. She says she is going to London, Ontario, to be with a man she calls Dave. (Who is this Dave, Patrick? Do you know him?)

She gave a phone number for us to call her at but I won't call her if what she says is true. (He won't call but I want so badly to. To hear it from my own daughter's lips why it is she is doing what she is doing.) Patrick, you are like a son to me. You always have been, ever since you travelled with me that summer after you were done Bible College at Eastern and we went to the Arctic together — to Iqaluit and Rankin Inlet and Frobisher Bay. You saw so much that summer. People healed, set free from addictions, baptized by the native pastors there in the frigid rivers, the air swarming with flies and blood running down our faces because there were so many. And we didn't care, didn't feel it. Because of God's glory and joy.

To me that memory is more real than the memory of my daughter's birth. (He can say that because he wasn't there. He was out getting a sandwich while I gave birth! Foolish man. But I will write what he says.) You are the son of my choice, and the bottle of olive oil I poured over your head to anoint you on the shores of Lemming's Lake on that summer evening long ago stands out in my mind more clearly than your wedding day. (He is shaking now and crying. I ask him if he wants me to stop but he says no. Patrick, he is trying to touch you now. Feel that in his words.)

Patrick, I don't know why she has gone. I don't know where she has gone. If she was here I would not raise a hand to her either for comfort or rebuke. (I would slap her, stupid girl.) She has done you a grievous wrong and my prayers are that she will see this and that God will help you forgive and that Hab will not be without his mother.

But she is strong-willed, Patrick. She's the only one I know who can stand against the force of my prayers. (This has always troubled him, since she was a girl.) Talk to me, my son (our son).

I need to hear from you now. (You can phone our home number or the Bancroft hospital and ask for Gurney Gunther's room. Please call, Patrick.)

Yours,
Gurney (and Gerta)

It's the third Sunday since Anne left. Patrick cancelled the service on the first Sunday and sent everyone to Elim Tabernacle on the second. He has no idea how he could possibly stand up and preach. He remembers Gurney's words to him when he was to preach in Rankin Inlet, when he confessed that sometimes he felt there was nothing to say, that he had no deep spiritual vision to impart. *That's when you feel the cross*, Gurney had said, placing his two heavy hands on Patrick's shoulders. And he feels them now, their same weight—like a rough-cut cedar beam—but he can hardly bring himself to get up off the couch. How could he possibly stand up and say anything? But he knows he cannot cancel a month of services without questions.

So this Sunday he called in a favour and asked Fred Archer, a youth pastor from Mount Pearl who he knows from his Eastern days, to preach at New Life. The name seems like a joke now to him, only nobody is laughing. Or they would be, if they knew that Pastor Wiseman's wife was off on some cyber fling, using her dad's heart attack as an excuse to get off the island.

Patrick knows he romanced the ocean in his descriptions of it to Anne. But he wanted her to want to come here. Once here, however, she must have seen through his stories: seen the truth—that the North Atlantic is terrifying, frothing where it gnaws at the jagged shoreline. Patrick came face to face with the beast the day he went on that strange trek with Hab in March, out onto the barren point at Flatrock—after seeing the grotto by the Catholic Church and telling Hab about his grandfather's obsession with the Virgin. The sea was a heaving grey Leviathan that day, and the snow drove them into that old bunker there for shelter, with that strange boy.

Sheilagh's Brush, Patrick's dad called it when Dale and he were kids and the March winds would spatter salt on their windows, all the way up Noseworthy Drive at the top of the hill overlooking the harbour. He remembers the taste of salt on the wind when he was a boy: the same as when Hab and he huddled together in that memory — that kid not saying a word but watching them until he fell asleep. It seems to Patrick like another world now: a brine-flavoured recollection. And he thinks of himself in that bunker as Jonah in the belly of the whale, rank with longing for Mildred Hallett's pease pudding and boiled potatoes — a big slab of stringy salt beef and that same saltiness the first time he kissed his way from Anne's toes to her centre, her long fingers tangled in his hair, drawing him down and him wondering if this was okay and half not caring.

When they first got to Newfoundland, all Anne wanted to do was get out on an iceberg tour and see puffins and whales and smell the salt air Patrick had talked so much about. It was so foggy they saw nothing and Anne puked all over the deck, her stomach no match for the swells, especially with no steady landmark to concentrate on in the distance. Patrick fared better only because he insisted on taking a Gravol before boarding the boat, knowing his sea legs wouldn't hold. They never had.

He wore his good Sunday shoes on the boat. He thought he was silly for doing so, until he saw that a lady across from him was wearing flip-flops, and it cold enough he could see her breath. *Mainlander.* That was his last time on the water, though he remembers as a kid how they would dare each other to jump from ice pan to ice pan — *running the whale's back*, they called it. Criss-crossing the bay before their mums would yell and tell them to get the hell off the slobby ice.

But that was a long time ago. Before Patrick started wearing Sunday shoes everywhere. And before he began punctuating his sentences with Mainland-erisms like *eh*.

How are you doing, eh?

Yeah, eh?

Crazy cold weather, eh?

You've heard the one about the Newfie and the plane crash, eh?

He successfully left Newfoundland behind him when he went to Bible college — quirky relatives like his great-uncle Gil and his father's unquestioned Roman religion — but returning he found it different. As if the whole place had moved on and left him behind, in a past he remembered fondly but was unable to share with Anne or Hab—a past it seemed only he recalled.

He knows this out-of-joint feeling should not surprise him. He chose to leave the Catholic Church his parents had raised him in to go to a Pentecostal Bible college away on the mainland. The defiance, the righteous choice, being cast out—all that was once salt to him was now bland, a heap of white mineral no good for anything but being scattered over icy roads. That's why they moved to Paradise rather than nearby Fawkes Cove. His parents can smile at him at family dinners but being neighbours would be too much, he thinks. Even with Dale living there now, since his divorce. Patrick hasn't talked to his brother in years. He doesn't even know Dale's son's name, only that he's been put in foster care temporarily since Dale and Rhiana's split. *Crazy arse.* Maybe that was extreme, but then again Hab had never tried blow up *his* shed. Patrick knows Rhiana hates his dad as much as she despises Dale, but he has no idea why. These are bits of news that have gotten to him like Yahoo updates in his inbox. Family spam. Delete delete delete. And now he wonders what all he's been told and has ignored, forgotten. All that has rushed by floods in on him now—all that he doesn't know. *They've gone on with their lives*, he thinks, *and left me to mine and mine has gone on without me. Whoosh.*

And here he is: left behind again, staring into the bathroom mirror, watching his hands tie a full Windsor around his neck as if the hands are somebody else's. He pulls the tie up taut with the top button of his shirt. But he has no idea why he is wearing a shirt and tie when he is simply going to see his son at his apartment. So he undoes the tie and casts it aside. Looks in the mirror. Undoes the top button. *There.* Dressed but not too dressy. Comfortable casual. *Anne's choice.* He places a hand on each collar, yanks outward suddenly, and pops a button off the shirt.

So much for that, he thinks.

Patrick untucks the shirt and pulls it over his head, leaving it on the bathroom floor as he goes to the bedroom to find another. He wants something he can wear untucked.

No, tucked is better.

More comfortable.

He needs the proper outfit to show he's coping—no messy hair hidden in a hoodie, no ripped jeans or T-shirts.

No camel skins, he tells himself. *You're no prophet and you're not homeless.*

He finds a green-and-beige checked shirt and cargo pants that are almost white. Then he fills the bathroom sink with water and carefully shaves his patchy beard, washing away the shaving cream and splashing on Old Spice.

He thinks, finally, he is ready. *At last.* He is just about to leave when he remembers that he hasn't brushed his teeth in sixteen days.

As he is leaving the house he notices another wad of paper in the mailbox: bills from Newfoundland Power, MasterCard, Rogers, Sears — and another letter from Gurney. He throws the bills on the desk and pockets his father-in-law's letter along with the last one Gurney sent that had remained unopened in the recycling bin with all the junk mail and church business since they had arrived.

Patrick thinks that today he may read the two letters. He also thinks he might burn them. So he goes to the kitchen drawer, grabs the barbeque lighter and pockets it. When he steps outside he feels for a second like Moses leaving Egypt — excited and terrified. He drives slowly to the address on Merrymeeting Road, the one that was scribbled beneath Hab's contact number on that crumpled shred of paper. There is no driveway so he parks on the street. Every drive on the road is shovelled except the neighbour's house, leading to the basement entrance. Patrick thinks the place looks abandoned.

Trashy.

He stamps the snow off his Sunday shoes before knocking, his fists gloved in leather that creaks in the cold. He smoothes out his coat, and knocks again.

A girl with her boots on answers the door. She's holding her jacket in one hand and a cigarette in the other. Can I help you? she asks, stepping out onto the stoop.

I came to see Hab, he says with less emotion than he's feeling.

He's in the tub now but you can sit on the couch and wait, if you want.

That would be great. Thanks.

You don't have a light, do you?

She's a little weirded-out when Patrick draws the barbeque lighter from his pocket. But she lets him awkwardly click and cup the flame, and hold it steady as she leans in and puffs. Nice, she says, and steps off the porch, looking down the street toward the Coleman's Grocery Store. Thanks for the light.

No problem, Patrick says as he watches her stroll away, wondering if she knows he's a pastor — or if that matters.

He goes in, slips off his shoes and sets them neatly beside the random pile of other shoes, and then meanders over to the green couch. There is a three-wick candle on the coffee table and a stack of novels on the lampstand by authors he doesn't know. The novel on the top of the stack looks to be about alligators, judging by the cover. The room smells of coffee and oranges. He couldn't drink a coffee now if he wanted to. His hands are shaking too much. He grips them tightly on his lap and tries to look at ease, sitting there surrounded by student messiness.

He hears the shower stop. A little while later the door opens down the hall and he hears Hab go into a bedroom. There is a girl's voice with his son's, and it is all he can do not to jump up and run down the hall to see what they're doing. But he reminds himself that Hab no longer lives in his house and perhaps no longer follows his rules. He wonders if he still goes to church. And if so, which one?

He hears the girl shriek and laugh.

Hab?

He starts but stops himself: *I have no control over him now.* He knows that his son has chosen to move out, to get away from their house, from him. And the shock of this hits him again like that belligerent gust of wind on Flatrock — that slap of cold air that nearly toppled him over the cliff and into the sea.

It was Hab's hand that stopped him.

He remembers his own hands shaking for an hour after, like they are shaking now.

Patrick fingers the lighter in his pocket: grips it to keep his hand from vibrating, pulls it out, looks at it, pushes the safety with his thumb and clicks. The flame is the size of his pinky finger, which he passes through it twice before leaning over and lighting the candle in the centre of the coffee table, thinking of his duties as an altar boy during mass as a kid and of the lack of candles of any kind in the Pentecostal church — no votive, Advent or Christ candles at all.

He watches the three little wicks gutter, almost go out, and then begin to burn steadily. *A smouldering wick I will not extinguish. Pray for us now, and at the hour of our death.*

Wax pools as he puts his shoes back on and heads out the front entrance, hearing a door down the hall open.

Footsteps.

His son's voice: Dad?

But he is running to his car now, flinging the door open and climbing in, turning it over and dropping it into gear. He pulls away from the curb without signalling and almost gets hits by a snowplow. The angry trucker blasts his horn all the way to the light. But Patrick doesn't hear him. All he's thinking about, as he turns down Aldershot, is the quickest route to the boat launch in Fawkes Cove.

Dear Patrick,

I had a dream last night. The type of dreams I've told you about: when I walk in the spirit and not in the flesh. (He woke up crying, Patrick.) You were in the dream and I saw a great seething gulf before you. It was dark. And there was smoke and snowflakes scattering like ash.

In the dream you were running, Patrick: running over the water with hail pouring down on you as you crossed the gulf.

I can't get you out of my head, son. (He speaks of you daily and when I come into his room while he is praying your name is on his lips.) Anne called Gerta and they spoke but I couldn't speak to her. I couldn't bring myself to say a word to my own daughter. She is strange to me now. (Anne told me she went to this Dave character and said she had left her husband and he panicked and turned her out. It appears he was married as well and he had never told her. She is living with friends in Hamilton, temporarily. Ruth and Christopher Rhynes, do you remember them? I mentioned her going home but she hung up.)

Patrick, be wary of this gulf ahead of you. Keep your footing. Trust in the Lord and not in yourself. The Psalmist says

that God scatters his hoarfrost like ash, that he tosses hail like
breadcrumbs. Who can stand against his cold?

I don't know why this storm has come to you but I see you
running. Finish, Patrick. Finish what you must. But please write.

(Why haven't you answered the other two letters?)

Sincerely,
Gurney (and Gerta)

Patrick can hear the pack ice grinding against the cliffs encompassing the
bay, creaking and groaning against other ice pans. The seething white mass
stretches almost out to the grey horizon. There is an iceberg out there — probably the size of the church down the street, but it looks no bigger than a
fingernail from where he stands at the top of the boat launch on the south
side of the bay, looking north to the other steeper launch.

In warmer weather boats dangle below where he stands on the ramp,
ropes stretched from their bows to anchors by his feet, each vessel fastened
tight against the fierce wind. An icy gale rips through his pea coat suddenly,
freezing his ankles in thin socks.

The boat ramp is bare and ice slicked below him.

He reaches inside his coat and pulls out Gurney's two letters. He thinks
for a second of opening them but he feels he needs to fall out of contact for
a while: to think of something other than Anne's father, or mother, or Anne
herself with that other man.

He rolls the two letters together into a tube and sticks the end of the barbeque
lighter inside and clicks, his back to the wind, holding both the paper and the
fire to his chest. It takes three tries for the letters to catch, but when they do
he holds them flaming in a gloved hand, smelling the leather beginning to
smoulder but knowing the paper will flame out before he gets burned. A few
seconds in that wind and all the words are gone to ash, which blows away even
as it begins to snow.

Anyone watching the bay from a darkened window would see a man in
Sunday clothes taking hold of a ratty rope and lowering himself down toward
the heaving pans of ice crashing against each other, salt water sluicing over
them, spewing between them.

Patrick is out of sight now, out of sight of everyone.

On the edge of the world.

No, Anne, I'll not be careful. If I can jump the pack ice from one side of the seething bay to the other, then it's not me who's sinned. But if I slip and drown, then so be it. You will have got what you wanted.

He lets out a *whoop* and leaps from the shore onto the slob ice, slips, scrambles, gets splashed by frigid salt water, finds his footing and begins to run. The pan he's on jars and rises, like a whale cresting, and he claws up it, toes the edge and leaps to the next pan that tips till he's up to his crotch in slushy sea water — the cold sharking as he lunges forward and uses the tilt to propel himself to the next pan. And the next. The sea heaving slob ice all around him. Eon-old ice is cracking like bones on rock. One slip and he's dead. But he's running, running like he's fourteen and devil-may-care. *My God!* he thinks, *this is it!*

Wooo!

Michelle Butler Hallett

The Shadow Side of Grace

Despite the vomitus spattering his scrubs, Keefer Breen dreamt of hot fries, a ham and Swiss and a few minutes' peace. He hadn't eaten for over twelve hours. John Crimm, a tube-fed cancer patient in his mid-forties, hadn't eaten for over a month, but thanks to his chemo he could still throw up. John shook his head, flushed deep red and gasped. Keefer rubbed John's shoulders, his strong hands gentle. — S'all right, b'y. Just breathe. Just breathe, and we'll get you back into bed.

The nurse, readying a shot of morphine, winced at Keefer in sympathy. John tried again. — S-sorry.

Keefer grinned. — Bit of bile, that's all. Had worse than that thrown at me.

John laughed. It was quiet, and it might have been mistaken for a whispered prayer.

The nurse injected morphine into John's IV plug. — Fresh laundry cart in the hall, Keefer. Dart out and get fresh scrubs. Change in Mr. Crimm's bathroom. Mr. Crimm won't mind, will you?

John's head lolled towards Keefer, deadeyed. Then a blink, recognition and sweet courtesy. — Yes. No. Please.

Rain beat the windows. Keefer changed quickly, startled and annoyed by his reflection in the little mirror. Normally the mirror was utilitarian: check the shave, comb the cowlick. Tonight it showed a tired man scowling as if he'd just been struck. *Come on, b'y.* Keefer broke gaze with the taller, younger version of his father and washed his hands. *Patients don't need to see that.*

When Keefer came out, the nurse was gone and John was asleep, eyes not quite closed. Keefer quietly released the brake on the wheelchair.

John woke up. — Some rain.

— Tail-end of that storm. Not as bad as they were saying on the radio this morning. You want one of them swabs for your mouth?

John's voice rustled in weak solitude, like a page turning. — Yes.

The lights flicked. John accepted the swab and nearly dropped it. Anger lined his face, anger and bitter weakness. He fought it down.

Keefer held out his hand. — May I?

John shut his eyes and nodded; Keefer swabbed John's lips.

John took a shaky breath. — You been working here long?

Keefer laid the swab back in its wrapper. — Eight or nine years now.

— They don't call you orderlies anymore.

Keefer took the wheelchair handles. — Big old fancy job title these days. Personal Care Attendant.

— It must be hard on you.

— The title?

John looked at him steadily. — This floor. Patients keep dying on you.

Mercy, some days. — S'pose. But you crowd are a joke compared to the kids down to the Janeway.

John looked at the rain. Keefer looked at the bed. The smells of sickness, stubborn over the gall of disinfectant: sweet rot, sulphur, ketones, feces, hard blackblood corrupted growth. Keefer didn't mind that. What bothered him was the fragility of John Crimm's body in a suddenly large bed. Keefer sighed.

John nodded. — Yes. If this had happened to one of my sons...

The fire alarm sounded.

Fuck. — Excuse me, Mr. Crimm.

Keefer went into the hallway: IV poles, empty wheelchairs, blood pressure monitors and then nurses coming out of patients' rooms and closing the doors. Fire alarms rarely came to patient evacuations; more often they were the annoying results of power bumps. The supervising nurse, harassed beyond politeness and past any memory of Keefer's name, waved at him. — You. Stick around.

Over the intercom, a woman informed everyone that smoke had been

detected near the cardiac cath lab. Keefer rolled his eyes. *Someone sneaking a*
cigarette now, that's all that is.

Wind blew rain. Keefer went back into John's room.

John spoke as if there'd been no interruption. — If this had happened to
one of my sons, I...I couldn't handle it.

Keefer knew the signs of a patient who needed to talk. He sat down in
the wheelchair and nodded as though he and John Crimm were in the smoke
room on the *Kyle*. Keefer half expected John to offer him a turn with his swab.

John shifted, frowned. — But I guess you don't see much stomach cancer
in kids.

— Head and neck. Fair bit of leukemia.

— Do you have children?

— No. Not even married.

John smiled gently. — Strapping young man like you?

— Thirty-six. Not that young anymore.

— Young enough. I married my second wife when I was thirty-eight. Nearly
went into the priesthood. Father Crimm, can you see that? Redemption after
a messy divorce. Ready to take my vows, teaching Bible study, I looked up,
and there she was.

Long teeth in smile; even John's gums were surrendering.

Keefer leaned back. — So you gave up on God?

— No! No, not God. Just...I'm sorry.

Breen, you stunned fucker. — No b'y, it's me who should be sorry. I just say
stupid things. Got as much class as a crocodile most days. Really, I'm sorry.

Some form of contentment rolled beneath the morphine dulling John's
eyes. — I feel like I'm already underwater.

— You want your glasses?

— Please.

Keefer passed John the delicate rimless frames, and John put them on
crooked. He read Keefer's ID badge. — Breen. Breen. Where have I heard
that name? The radio.

Keefer glanced out the window, hating the rain. On a roof below, a puddle
was wrinkled with waves.

The intercom came on; the cardiac cath lab was clear.

John's thoughts roamed. — Gerald Breen. Poor man. Trafficking what, crystal meth? No, the other one.

— OxyContin.

— I worked with a woman who used it. Legally. Prescribed. She had terrible pain. She said she could function with pills, but then, pain, the thing with pain...

— You should get some rest, Mr. Crimm.

— No.

It was like a child's cry, defiance and fear.

— I've been resting. Rest does nothing. I wake up rested and still sick. I wake up. Please. Can...

Keefer sat down. — I can stay.

John shut his eyes. Nearly twenty minutes passed. Rain and IV pump, snatched and shallow breaths. Then, words. — He died in custody.

— Who?

— Gerald Breen. People were talking about him on *Open Line*. A shame. Be a big inquiry into that.

— Yeah.

— People say it was a screwdriver.

Keefer said nothing.

John smiled. — You're good.

— Me?

— Your patience. You've done this before. A vigil. A friend, maybe?

— Not really.

— Not really?

— Friend of mine died of cancer about a year and a half ago now.

— But you were with her.

— Not when it mattered.

— My tissues are on the wheeled tray, Keefer. Could you get them for me?

Keefer did this, taking some for himself and turning away. — How old are your children?

— Five, three and six months.

— I'm sorry.

— Don't be. They were gifts.

Keefer looked back at John, shaking his head. — That morphine should have knocked you out long ago.

John seemed not to hear him. — Three sons on a second marriage for a novice who'd had a vasectomy. Everyone laughed when I went to get it reversed. My turn to laugh when it worked.

— That them in the picture?

— Yes. Taken before the youngest could sit up.

Keefer grinned. — Fine looking boys. They don't resemble you at all.

John's laugh whispered again. — You look anything like your father?

— Spittin' image.

— Do you know where that comes from? The woman at work told me, the one taking OxyContin. Corruption of the phrase *spirit and image*. What does your father do?

— He's dead.

— Oh.

First it was courteous sympathy; then it was heavy with knowledge.

— Oh. Him. Yes. An inquiry.

Keefer realized he was breathing hard. — How can you just lie there?

John smiled. — I am dying.

— We got patients in here who don't stop raving against God the whole time, don't stop crying...

— There's a reason for this.

— A reason for what? You starving to death in pain, leaving your kids behind?

— There are reasons we can't see, let alone understand.

— And you're cool with that, are you?

John said nothing.

— You'll just lie there and wait for God to come pick you up in a Citywide cab? Or is God driving Bugden's these days?

— Do you always talk to patients this way?

— No. I'm just...

— I'm sorry I upset you about your father.

— Will you just stop apologizing? Please?

Neither man spoke. Neither man noticed the window leaking.

Then John cleared his throat. — I haven't apologized to God yet.

Keefer's anger fell away. — For what?

— Doubting.

Keefer waited.

—Doubting. That there was a reason for this. That I was some thread in a plan, that maybe, I don't know, my sons would become doctors because they'd miss me, or even...who the hell am I to presume I'm a thread in God's plan? One cell mutates, then another. Reproduce, lump together, eat out its host. Life cycle of the parasite. Am I the mutation or the parasite? Or am I even smaller than that, like some star we can't even see. Distant light. I want to see. That's where it comes down. I'm nothing to God. I believe that now. No more than bones and water and air. Dropped. A hair on the floor. So far away, Keefer. So far away. And it hurts.

—May I?

—Hurts like hell.

Keefer took a tissue and dabbed John's face. John shut his eyes awhile.

Keefer's pager vibrated. The emergency room needed him.

—I got to go, Mr. Crimm. But I'll come back. You get some rest.

John seemed finally to be asleep.

Turning his hand so he couldn't see the scars, Keefer reached to switch off the bright fluorescent over John's head.

John sighed. —Leave it on. Please.

Keefer did.

Michael Winter

Stay the
Way You Are

So Sam asked God. He was climbing the stairs in the dark, asking for a sign. Sam said, in his head, God, I need to know if Martha is the one.

He opened the bedroom door. Flicked on the light. He looked at his bed and there she was — on her back, her little feet pressed out of the blankets. Her gold hair flung on the pillow. She lifts her neck, scrunches her eyes at the brightness. She is here. It hadn't occurred to Sam that she could be here, but she is and he knows it is the sign that he is looking for. But the sharpness fades and he thinks, Well, it's not that remarkable that she's here. And soon he has the sign twisted into a normal event.

He couldn't really believe in God, anyway.

Martha knew all of this.

She stared at the floor, at the walls, the table, the mattress on the floor and even the clay vase with dried flowers, searching, not for some addition, a stain or a ruffled signature of their being together, but an absence in the objects of their former selves. She wanted to see the physical appearance of things diminished since she had lain in his bed.

Why this diminished appearance?

Because she knew Sam thought she was stealing from him. She robbed him of his self. Or, taking the blame for his own fate, she helped him disintegrate. He was not in control, his direction uncharted.

That was after three months. Then Martha moved in and three years passed. One night they were pulling out of the mall parking lot, about to enter the traffic steaming down Kenmount Road, when Martha said, Look.

Over to the side, in the corner of the parking lot, was a high canvas trailer. There were doors on the side of the trailer, swung open, and a man in a black suit stood at a podium bathed in a cone of light. Behind him glowed a tall gold cross. A couple dozen cars had pulled up around the trailer. The man leaned into a microphone. A slight rain fell. Sam pulled over.

When they stopped a boy trotted up, tapped on the window. Sam rolled it down. The boy placed a speaker on the window. He adjusted the volume, the knob crackling, nodded in at Sam and Martha. God and you, the boy said.

It was a drive-in evangelical service. The preacher's name was Jimmy Boland. Jimmy thanked those who joined in late and asked them to wink their high beam to let him know they were there with God's spirit. Sam went for the lights, but stopped. The mirror flashed. He turned down the volume and stared at the woman sitting next to him.

Sam and Martha are nearing thirty. They are surprised at their own intimacy, that they are, in fact, very childish. They have pet names, they use baby talk. But they've known each other, or have known of each other, since junior high. They have heard stories through mutual friends. Each living in the peripheral sphere of the other, never enough to consume or to be consumed by the other. They even grew up in the same small town, went to school together, a grade apart. They both moved to St. John's to study at Memorial. And this is a comfort. They have a common store of memory, although their impressions of the past differ greatly.

When people ask, Oh how did you meet? they are slightly embarrassed. They have no story to tell, nothing dramatic. No flash of knowing. No fast link. They have been gradual friends. Now they are confronted with, not a new lover, but a partner in the shell of someone else. They have to figure out the truth. Peel off the lacquer. Get to what it is that is them.

Jimmy Boland's voice reaches them indirectly, from other car speakers. I don't want to listen, Sam says. Tell me a story.

Martha relieves her seatbelt.

My family never talked, she says. We were pleasant to each other. We didn't fight. But there was little communication. I found love through experiences.

They let us do what we wanted. I never had to wash dishes. I mean I did, but I didn't have to. We never fought over TV shows. I was never told when to come home. I'd just say where I was going. That's why I don't think about cooking or cleaning up, or telling you I'll be late, because I never had to. It doesn't occur to me.

Do you like the wood stove?

I love the wood stove. I'm just not cracked about every weekend cutting wood. Operating a Ski-Doo, how much gas do we burn getting out to the woods? How much is a wood stove? Cleaning the chimney of creosote. How much is your back worth, Sam? How much your time? Running a chainsaw. Sharpening the teeth. Mixing the oil and gas. God, the racket of a chainsaw, all day long. And the fury in getting the wood. The rush, the absolute drive to get as much wood in a day. Sometimes I think all this expense can't be less than the cost of oil.

But you love the thermos at break time. Sitting on the Ski-Doo seat, or on the load of birch chained to the sled. Cracking the plastic cup off the thermos. Unscrewing the plug. Vapour rising. Eating our corned beef sandwiches and hearing the trace buzz of chainsaw left hanging in the trees.

You know I love that, Sam.

Sam notices that the cars have been parked in rows. There is a corridor leading from Jimmy Boland down to where they have parked. Sam sees the preacher pointing, pointing at them.

My father, Sam says, we called him Rogie. Rogie would mark the label of the 7-Up bottle. He came home once and some was gone. No one owned up to it. We were sent to our rooms. I said Frank, why don't you tell him. Tell Rogie you drank it, and he yelled I didn't, that's why, I didn't!

Mom and Rogie got into it. A fight about other things, food-related. It's feast or famine around here. There's no butter or margarine. My mother would spread shortening on the bread. She called it white butter and I preferred it. We drank powdered milk.

I thought of that when you were in the bathroom, dabbing your eyes and I said, Martha, you know what you are? You're a first-class bitch, that's what. And I walked to the porch, shoved my arms down the sleeves of my coat. The jingle of keys. I thought, Sam, that is exactly what Rogie would do.

You went to the bedroom. I heard you in the closet. I wanted to warm up the car but you were crying. You said I can't take this anymore, this is too much. Over and over.

Martha, to hear you out of control. I crept in to you and saw you kneeling in the closet. The light showing the sleeves of my shirts. The peg with my belt. You had pulled the suitcase out of the closet. You were unpacking blue and white bags of sugar. There was a shortage in Cuba and you were stocking up. There were seven 2-kilo bags. All our sweetness lying there in seven bags. Then you opened the third drawer in the chest. Your drawer. I said Martha, you can't go, and you said Sam I love you but I can't take the pressure. I wasn't made for it. I'll have you killed.

You couldn't leave the house without me holding you. I held your hand and led you back to the seven bags of sugar. That made things right again.

Sam turns up the preacher. Jimmy Boland is pointing out over the vehicles, to some distant point past the shopping mall, some place west of where they are, as if a destination is always a little further west, a little further. His voice scratches over the monitor. Wait for the change, he says. Don't be rigid. Don't build love on a vision.

I have a scar, Martha says over Jimmy. On my finger from a spark when I was five.

She loops the steering wheel with her ring finger. Sam has never given her a ring.

A family bonfire. The spark twirled quick in the air, darted in the wind as if it was looking where to go, landed on my finger and dug in. I stared at it. My mother had to brush it off. The scar, look, it's four times larger now.

You're four times bigger.

I've had big burns that have disappeared. With some there's no reminder.

What multiplies the cells in a scar, or a mole? My moles are moving, Sam thinks. Growing. They erupt with a hard surface and then subside. The surface of my body is changing. I am no longer growing into a better body. I'm disintegrating.

Can you stay the way you are?

As they pull out of the parking lot Sam is longing for something more. He knows this is his problem. Longing is nothing but the candle flicker of thought, of an absence, a faith that cannot be sustained, which will erode into the gravel of any relationship. Love is not ignition of gasoline, but the slow turn of bone to oil. He knows this and yet he longs with a desire as large as any conversion.

D.R. MacDonald

The Flowers
of Bermuda

Bilkie Sutherland took the postcard from behind his rubber bib and slowly read the message one more time: "I'm going here soon. I hope your lobsters are plentiful. My best to Bella. God bless you. Yours, Gordon MacLean." Bilkie flipped it over: a washed-out photograph in black and white. *The Holy Isle. Iona. Inner Hebrides.* On the land stood stone ruins, no man or woman anywhere, and grim fences of cloud shadowed a dark sea. So this was Iona.

"You want that engine looked at?" Angus Carmichael, in his deepwater boots, was standing on the wharf above Bilkie's boat.

"Not now. I heard from the minister."

"MacLean?"

"He's almost to Iona now."

Angus laughed, working a toothpick around in his teeth. "Man dear, *I've* been to Iona, was there last Sunday." Angus meant where his wife was from, a Cape Breton village with a Highland museum open in the summer, and a St. Columba Church.

"It's a very religious place," Bilkie said, ignoring him. "Very ancient, in that way."

"Like you, Bilkie."

"I'm the same as the rest of you."

"No, Bilkie. Sometimes you're not. And neither is your Reverend MacLean."

Angus's discarded toothpick fluttered down to the deck. Bilkie picked it up and dropped it over the side. Angus never cared whether his own deck was flecked with gurry and flies. Nor was he keen on Gordon MacLean. Said the man was after putting in a good word for the Catholics. But that wasn't the minister's point at all. "We're all one faith, if we go back to Iona," is what he'd said. And nothing much more than that.

As Bilkie laid out his gear for the next day's work, he heard singing. No one sang around here anymore. Radios took care of that. He stood up to listen. Ah! It was Johnny, Angus's only boy, home from Dalhousie for the summer. He had a good strong voice, that boy, one they could use over at the church. But you didn't see him there, not since college. No singer himself, Bilkie could appreciate a good tune. His grandfather had worked the schooners in the West Indies trade, and Johnny's song had the flavour of that, of those rolling vessels... "'He could smell the flowers of Bermuda in the gale, when he died on the North Rock Shoal...'" Bilkie stared into the wet darkness underneath the wharf where pilings were studded with snails. Algae hung like slicked hair on the rocks. He had saved Gordon MacLean under that wharf, when the man was just a tyke. While hunting for eels, Gordon had slipped and fallen, and Bilkie heard his cries and came down along the rocks on the other side to pull him out, a desperate boy clutching for his hand.

Bilkie's car, a big salt-eaten Ford, was parked at the end of the wharf, and whenever he saw it he wished again for horses who could shuck salt like rain. At home the well pump had quit this morning and made him grumpy. He'd had to use the woods, squat out there under a fir, the birds barely stirring overhead, him staring at shoots of Indian pipe wondering what in hell they lived on, leafless, white as wax, hardly a flower at all. Up by the roadside blue lupines were a little past their prime. What flowers, he wondered, grew on Iona?

The car swayed through rain ruts, past clumps of St. John's wort (*allas Colmcille* his grandfather had called them) that gave a wild yellow border to the driveway. His house appeared slowly behind a corridor of tall maples. In their long shade, red cows rested. Sometimes everything seemed fixed, for good. His animals, his life. But God had taken away his only boy, and Bilkie could not fathom that even yet. For a time he had kept sheep, but quit because killing the lambs bothered him.

Bella was waiting at the front door, not the back, her palm pressed to her face. He stopped shy of the porch, hoping it wasn't a new well pump they needed.

"What's wrong?"

"Reverend MacLean's been stabbed in Oban," his wife said, her voice thin.

Bilkie repeated the words to himself. There was a swallow's nest above the door. The birds swooped and clamoured. "Not there?" he said. "Not in Scotland?" A mist of respect, almost of reverence, hovered over the old country. You didn't get stabbed there.

"Jessie told me on the phone, not a minute ago. Oh, he'll live all right. He's living."

Over supper Bella related what she knew. Gordon MacLean had been walking in Oban, in the evening it was, a woman friend with him. Two young thugs up from Glasgow went for her handbag, right rough about it too. Gordon collared one but the other shoved a knife in his back.

"He's not a big man either," Bilkie said, returning a forkful of boiled potato to his plate. He had known Gordon as a child around the wharf, a little boy who asked hard questions. He had pulled him from the water. He'd seen him go off to seminary, thinking he would never come back to Cape Breton, not to this corner of it, but after a while he did. To think of him lying in blood, on a sidewalk in Oban. "Did they catch the devils?"

"They did. He'll have to testify."

"What, go back there?"

"When he's able. Be a long time until the trial."

Bilkie felt betrayed. A big stone had slipped somehow out of place. Certain things did not go wrong there, not in the Islands where his people came from. Here, crime was up, too few caring about a day's work, kids scorning church. Greedier now, more for themselves, people were. But knives, what the hell. There in the Hebrides they'd worked things out, hadn't they, over a long span of time? It had seemed to him a place of hard wisdom, hard won. Not a definite place, for he had never been there, but something like stone about it: sea-washed, nicely worn, and high cliffs where waves whitened against the rocks. He knew about the Clearances, yes, about the bad laws that drove his grandfather out of Lewis where he'd lived in a turf house. But even then they weren't knifing people. Gordon MacLean, a minister of God, couldn't return there and come to no harm? To Mull first he'd been headed, to MacLean country. And then to Iona, across a strait not much wider than this one. But a knife stopped him in Oban, a nice sort of town by the sea.

From his parlour window Bilkie could see a bit of the church in the east, the dull white shingles of its steeple above the dark spruce. *We all have Iona inside us*, the man had said. *Our faith was lighted there.* Why then did this happen?

Bilkie had asked such a question before and found no answer. They'd had a son, he and Bella, so he knew about shock, and about grief. Even now, thinking of his son and the schoolhouse could suck the wind right out of him. The boy was born late in their lives anyway, and maybe Bilkie's hopes had come too much to rest in him. Was that the sin? Torquil they called him, an old name out of the Hebrides, after Bella's dad. But one October afternoon when the boy was nine, he left the schoolhouse and forgot his coat, a pea coat, new, with a big collar turned up like a sailor's. So he went back to get it, back to the old white schoolhouse where he was learning about the world. It was just a summer house now, owned by strangers. But that day it was locked tight, and the teacher gone home. A young woman. No blame to her. His boy jimmied open the window with his knife. They were big, double-hung windows, and you could see them open yet on a warm weekend, hear people drunk behind the screens. But Torquil had tried to hoist himself over the sill, and the upper half of the window unjammed then and came down on his neck. Late in the day it was they found him, searching last the grounds of the school. A time of day about now. The sash lay along his small shoulders like a yoke, that cruel piece of wood, blood in his nose like someone had punched him...

Bilkie barely slept. He was chased by a misty street, black and wet, and harrowing cries that seemed one moment a man's, the next a beast's. He was not given to getting up in the night but he dressed and went outside to walk off the dreariness he'd woke to. A cold and brilliant moon brightened the ground fog which layered the pasture like a fallen cloud. The high ridge of hill behind his fields was ragged with wormshot spruce, wicks of branch against the sky. As a boy he'd walked those high woods with his grandfather who offered him the Gaelic names of things, most of them forgotten now, gone with the good trees. One day he'd told Bilkie about the words for heaven and hell, how they, Druid words, went far back before the time of Christ. *Ifrinn*, the Isle of the Cold Clime, was a dark and frigid region of venomous reptiles and savage wolves. There the wicked were doomed to wander, chilled to their very bones and bereft even of the company of their fellow sinners. And the old heaven, though the Christians kept that name too, was also different: *Flath-innis*, the Isle of the Brave, a paradise full of light which lay far distant, somewhere in the Western Ocean. "I like that some better," his grandfather had said, "just the going there would be good. As for hell, nothing's worse than cold and loneliness."

As he moved through the fog, it thinned like steam, but gathered again and closed in behind him. Suddenly he heard hoofbeats. Faintly at first, then louder. He turned in a circle, listening. Not a cow of his. They were well-fenced. Maybe the Dunlop's next door. But cow or horse it was coming toward him at a good clip and yet he couldn't make it out, strain as he might. Soon his heart picked up the quick, even thud of the hooves, and when in the pale fog a shape grew and darkened and then burst forth, a head shaggy as seaweed and cruelly horned, he raised his arms wildly in a shout of fear and confusion as the bull shied past him, a dark rush of heat and breath, staggering him like a blow. Aw, that goddamn Highland bull, that ugly bugger. Trembling with anger and surprise, he listened to it crash through thickets off up the hill, the fog eddying in its wake, until Bella called him and he turned back to the house.

On the porch of the manse Bilkie waited for Mrs. MacQueen to answer the door. The porch Reverend MacLean had built, but the white paint and black trim were Bilkie's work, donated last summer when his lobstering was done. He'd enjoyed those few days around the minister. One afternoon when Bilkie was on the ladder he thought he heard Gordon talking to himself, but no, he was looking up, shading his eyes. "It's only a mile from Mull, Iona," Gordon said to him. "Just across the Sound. So it's part of going home, really." Bilkie had said yes, he could see that. But he wasn't sure, even now, that he and the minister meant home in the same way. "Monks lived there, Bilkie. For a long, long time. They had a different view of the world, a different feel for it altogether. God was still *new* there, you see. Their faith was...robust."

Mrs. MacQueen, the housekeeper, filled the doorway and Bilkie told her what he would like.

"A book about Iona?" She was looking him up and down. She smelled of Joy, lemon-scented, the same stuff he used on his decks. "I don't read the man's books, dear, I dust them."

"He wouldn't mind me looking. Me and himself are friends." He rapped the trim of the door. "My paint."

"Well, he could have used some friends in Oban."

Mrs. MacQueen showed him into the minister's study, making it clear she would not leave. She turned the television on low, as if this were a sickroom, and sat down on a hassock, craning her ear to the screen.

Wine-coloured drapes, half-drawn, gave the room a warm light. Bookshelves lined one wall, floor to ceiling, and Bilkie touched their bindings as he passed. He hadn't a clue where to begin or how to search in this hush: he only wanted to know more about that place, and maybe when the man returned they could talk about what went wrong there. But he felt shy with Mrs. MacQueen in the room. A map of Scotland was thumbtacked to the wall. The old clan territories were done in bright colours. Lewis he spotted easily, and Mull. And tiny Iona. On the desktop, under sprigs of lilac in a small vase, he saw a slim red book. In it were notes in Gordon's hand. With a quick glance at the housekeeper, he took it to the leather chair close by the north window, a good bright spot where Gordon must have sat many a time, binoculars propped on the sill. Bilkie put them to his eyes instinctively. Behind the manse a long meadow ran down to the shore. Across the half mile of water his boat rocked gently in the light swells. Strange to see his yellow slicker hanging by the wheel, emptied of him. Moving the glasses slightly he made out Angus standing over his boy, Johnny hunched down into some work or other. Good with engines, was Johnny. Suddenly Angus looked toward Bilkie. Of course his eyes would take in only the white manse on the hill, and the church beside it. Yet Bilkie felt seen in a peculiar way and he put down the binoculars.

Aware of the time, he turned pages, reading what he could grasp. That Iona's founder, St. Columba, had sailed there from Ireland to serve his kinsmen, the Scots of Dalriada. That he and his monks laboured with their own hands, tilling and building, and that in their tiny boats they spread the faith into the remote and lesser isles, converting even the heathen Picts. That even before he was born, Columba's glory had been foretold to his mother in a dream: "An angel of the Lord appeared to her, and brought her a beautiful robe—a robe which had all the colours of all the flowers of the world. Immediately it was rapt away from her, and she saw it spread across the heavens, stretched out over plains and woods and mountains...." He read testaments to St. Columba's powers and example, how once in a great storm his ship met swelling waves that rose like mountains, but at his prayer they were stilled. He was a poet and loved singing, and songs praising Columba could keep you from harm. His bed was bare rock and his pillow a stone. During the three days and three nights of his funeral, a great wind blew, without rain, and no boat could reach or leave the island.

Bilkie was deep in the book when Mrs. MacQueen, exclaiming, "That's desperate, just desperate!" turned off the soap opera and came over to him.

"You'll have to go now," she said. "This isn't the public library, dear, and I have cleaning to do."

He would never talk himself past her again, not with Gordon away. He returned the book to the desk and followed her to the front door.

"Did you ever pray to a saint, Mrs. MacQueen?"

She crossed her arms. "I'm no R.C., Mr. Sutherland."

"I don't think that matters, Mrs. MacQueen. The minister has a terrible wound. Say a word to St. Columba."

"He's healing. He's getting better and soon might be coming home, is what I heard."

The next morning the sun glared up from a smooth sea as Bilkie hauled his traps, moving from one swing to another over the grounds his grandfather had claimed. By the time Bilkie was old enough to fish, there was a little money in it. But you had to work. Nobody ever gave it to you, and the season was short. He had started out young hauling by hand, setting out his swings in the old method, the backlines anchored with kellicks, and when he wasn't hauling he was rowing, and damned hard if a wind was on or the tide against you. He had always worked alone, rowed alone. Except when his boy was with him, and that seemed as brief now as a passing bird. He preferred it out here by himself, free of the land for a while, the ocean at his back.

This season the water was so clear he could see ten fathoms, see the yellow backline snaking down, the traps rising. His grandfather told him about the waters of the West Indies, the clear blue seas with the sun so far down in them it wouldn't seem like drowning at all, for the light there.

He gaffed a buoy and passed the line over the hauler, drawing the trap up to the washboard where he quickly culled the dripping, scurrying collection. He measured the lobsters, threw a berried one back. But after he dropped the trap and moved on, he knew he'd forgotten, for the second time that morning, to put in fresh bait. To hell with it. On the bleak rocks of the Bird Islands shags spread their dark wings to dry. A school of mackerel shimmered near the boat, an expanding and contracting disturbance just beneath the surface as they fed. He cut the engine, letting the boat drift like his mind. He hummed the song of Johnny Carmichael but stopped. Couldn't get the damn tune out of his head. Sick of it. He picked a mackerel out of the bait box and turned it over in his hands, stroking the luminous flow of stripes a kind of sky was named for: a beautiful fish, if you looked at it — the smooth skin, dark yet silvery. Gordon MacLean said from the pulpit that a man should find beauty in what's around him, for that too was God. But for Bilkie everything had been so familiar, everything he knew and saw and felt, until Torquil died. He took out his knife and slid it slowly into the dead fish: now, what might that be like, a piece of steel like that inside you? A feeling you'd carry a long while, there, under the scar.

Astern, the head of the cape rose behind buff-coloured cliffs, up into the deep green nap of the mountain. He had no fears here, never in weather like this when the sea was barely breathing. Still, he missed the man, the sound of his voice on Sunday. The last service before he left for Iona, the minister had read Psalm 44, the one, he said, that St. Columba sang to win the Picts away from their magi, the Druids... *O God, our fathers have told us, what work thou didst in their days, in the times of old...*

After Bilkie lost his son, he'd stayed away from church, from the mournful looks and explanations, why he should accept God's taking an innocent boy in such a way. His heart was sore, he told Bella, and had to heal up, and nothing in the church then could help it. But a few weeks after Reverend MacLean arrived, Bilkie went to hear him. Damn it, the man could preach. Not like those TV preachers who couldn't put out anything much but their palms and a phone number. A slender string it was that Gordon MacLean couldn't take a tune from. And only once had he mentioned Torquil in a roundabout way, to show he was aware there'd been a boy, that he knew what a son could mean.

As Bilkie turned in toward the wharf that afternoon he saw three boats in ahead of him. Above Angus's blue and white Cape Islander the men had gathered in a close circle, talking and nodding. Only Johnny Carmichael was still down below, sitting on the gunnels with his guitar. Bilkie approached the wharf in a wide arc, trying to discern what he saw in the huddled men and the boy off alone bent into his instrument. He brought his boat up into the lee and flung a line to Angus who was waving for it.

"Bilkie, you're late, boy!" he shouted.

"Aw, I was feeling slow today!"

When the lines were secured, Angus called down to him. "Did you hear about it?"

"About what?"

"The minister, Bilkie, for God's sake! He's passed away! It was sudden, you know. Complications. Not expected at all."

Bilkie's hands were pressed against a crate he'd been about to shift. He could feel the lobsters stirring under the wood. He looked up at Angus. "I knew that already," he said.

Instead of going home, Bilkie drove to a tavern fifteen miles away. He sat near a window at one of the many small tables. Complications. Lord. The sun felt warm on his hands and he watched bubbles rise in his glass of beer. The tavern was quiet but tonight it would be roaring. Peering into the dim interior he made out Jimmy Carey alone at a table. Jimmy was Irish and had acted cranky here more than once. But he seemed old and mild now, back there in the afternoon dark, not the hellraiser he used to be. And wasn't St. Columba an Irishman, after all? Bilkie raised his glass and held it there until Jimmy, who looked as if he'd been hailed from across the world, noticed it and raised his own in return. Bilkie beckoned him over. They drank until well past supper, leaning over the little table and knocking glasses from time to time. Bilkie told him about St. Columba, about the monks in their frail vessels.

"You know about St. Brendan, of course," Jimmy said, his eyes fixing on

Bilkie but looking nowhere. "They say he got as far as here even, and clear to Bermuda before he was done."

"Bermuda I know about." Bilkie tried to sing what he remembered. "'Oh there be flowers in Bermuda, beauty lies on every hand...and there be laughter, ease and drink for every man...'" He leaned close to Jimmy's face: "'...but there not be joy for *me*.'"

On the highway Bilkie focused hard on the centre line, thinking that Jimmy Carey might have bought one round at least, St. Brendan be damned. To the west the strait ran deep and dark, the sun just gone from it as he turned away toward home. Bad time to meet the Mounties. He lurched to a stop by the roadside where a small waterfall lay hidden. He plunged through a line of alders into air immediately cool. The falls stepped gently through mossed granite, down to a wide, clear pool, and he remembered Bella bending her head into it years ago, her hair fanning out red there as she washed the salt away after swimming. He knelt and cupped the water, so cold he groaned, over his face again and again.

As he drove the curves the white church appeared and disappeared above the trees. When he came upon it, it seemed aloof, unattended. Cars were parked carelessly along the driveway to the manse, and Bilkie slowed down long enough to see a man and woman climbing the front steps, Mrs. MacQueen, in her flowered apron, waiting at the door. Oh, there'd be some coming and going today, the sharing of the hard news. When he felt the schoolhouse approaching, he vowed again not to look, not to bother what went on there. But he couldn't miss the blue tent in the front yard, and the life raft filled with water for a wading pool. This time he did not slow down. Too often he had wondered about the blow on the neck, about what his son had felt and who, in that instant, he had blamed...something so simple as a window coming down on his bones. There. In a schoolhouse.

Bella had not seen Bilkie drunk like this in years, but she knew why and said nothing, not even about Reverend MacLean. She could not get him to come inside for supper. He reeled around angrily in the lower pasture, hieing cows away when they trotted toward the fence for handouts of fresh hay. He shouted up at the ridge. Finally he stalked to the back door.

"Gordon was going to Iona," he said to his wife. "He could check the fury of wild animals, that saint they had there. Did Gordon no damn good, eh?"

"You've had some drink, Bilkie, and I've had none. I'm tired now."

He stepped up close to her and took her face in his hands. "Ah, Bella. Your hair was so pretty."

She made him go to bed, but after dark he woke. He smelled of the boat and wanted to wash. Hearing a car, he went over to the window. Near his neighbour's upper pasture headlights bounced and staggered over the rough ground. They halted, backed up, then swept suddenly in another direction until the shaggy bull galloped across the beams. Loose again. A smallish, wild-looking beast they'd imported from Scotland. Could live out on its own in the dead of winter, that animal. You might see it way off in a clearing, quiet, shouldering snow like a monument. The headlights, off again in pursuit, captured the bull briefly but it careened away into the darkness, and the car—a Dunlop boy at the wheel no doubt—raked the field blindly. Complications. A stone for a pillow. His own boy would be a man now. Passed away, like a wave.

It was difficult for Bilkie to get up that day. He had always opened his eyes on the dark side of four a.m. but now Bella had to push and coax him. He sat on the edge of the bed for a long time staring at the half-model of a schooner mounted on the wall. His grandfather had worked her, the *Ocean Rose*, lost on Hogsty Reef in the Bahamas with his Uncle Bill aboard.

"You don't get up anymore. What's the matter with you?" Bella said. He took the cup of coffee she held out to him, nodding vaguely. Squalls had lashed the house all night and now a thick drizzle whispered over the roof. "You know Reverend MacLean is coming home this day, and tonight they'll wake him."

"I can't go," Bilkie said.

"What would he think, you not there at his wake with the others who loved him?"

"He's not thinking at all anymore. That's just a body there, coming back."

"Don't be terrible. Don't be the way you were after Torquil."

"They could have buried him over there. Couldn't they have? Near where he wanted to go?"

"He was born *here*, Bilkie. Nobody asked, I don't suppose, one way or the other."

He could see that she'd been crying. He put the coffee down carefully on the windowsill and took her hands in his, still warm from the cup. "Bella, dear," he said. "You washed your hair in that water. It must have hurt, eh? Water so cold as that?"

Gusts rocked the car as Bilkie crossed the bridge that joined the other island. He was determined to take himself out of the fuss, some of it from people who would never bestir themselves were Gordon MacLean here and breathing. Above him the weather moved fast. The sky would whiten in patches but all the while churn with clouds black as the cliffs by the lighthouse. There was a good lop on the water, looking east from the bridge, and when the strait opened out a few miles away the Atlantic flashed white against an ebbing tide.

In the lee of the wharf the lobster boats were surging like tethered horses. No one was around. The waves broke among the pilings beneath him and the timbers creaked. He walked to the seaward end where Angus had stacked his broken traps. Across the roughening water the manse looked small, the cars tiny around it. Every morning his grandfather would say, old as he was, *Dh'iarr am muir a thadhal.* The sea wants to be visited.

He threw off his lines and headed out into the strait, rounding up into the wind, battering the waves until he checked back on the throttle. In the turns of wind he smelled the mackerel in the bait box, the fumes of the engine. But as he drew abreast of Campbell Point, a gust of fragrance came off the land and he strained to see its source in the long, blowing grass of the point. It was quickly gone and there was nothing to account for it but what had been there all along—the thin line of beach, the grass thick as hay all the way back to the woods. To the west, on the New Skye Road, he glimpsed St. David's Church, a small white building behind a veil of rain, set in the dense spruce, no one there now but Bible Camp kids in the summer.

The sea was lively at the mouth of the strait where wind and tide met head to head. He bucked into the whitecaps, slashes of spray cracking over the bow. The waves deepened as the sea widened out but he'd ride better when he reached the deeper water where the breaking crests would cease. He had a notion of the West Indies, of his grandfather under sails, out there over the curve of the world and rolling along in worse weather than this. Hadn't the Irish monks set out in their currachs of wickerwork and hide, just for the love of God? They had survived. They reached those islands they sailed for, only dimly sure where they were. But maybe you could come by miracles easier then, when all of life was harder, and God closer to the sea than he was now. Now with no saints around, saints who could sow a field and sail a boat, you had to find your own miracles. You couldn't travel to them, could you, Gordon, boy?

He would have to go back. He would have to stand at the wake holding his hat like the rest of them, looking at Gordon who'd come dead such a distance. Bilkie watched the rhythm of the waves. He needed a break in them to bring his boat around and run with the sea. But then he wasn't hearing the engine anymore, and the boat was falling away, coming around slowly with no more sound than a sail would make. Columba. A dove. Strange name for a man. *Colmcille. Caoir gheal,* his grandfather called waves like these. A bright flaming of white. The sea had turned darker than the sky, and over the land the boat was swinging toward, clouds lay heavy and thick, eased along like stones, dark as dolmens. "Ah!" was all Bilkie said when the wave rose under him, lifting the boat high like an offering.

Kathleen Winter

French Doors

The taste of partridgeberry has bogs and marshes in it behind the sharp taste of fruit. It has the same taste as Newfoundland air that has collected scents from its travels; caribou moss, red blueberry leaves, black ponds, trout and peat moss. Moose and ducks, boulders and juniper. You get that taste in the fall.

There were meadows and thick trees near the shore in Aspel Harbour, but close behind the trees lay the wild barren land where sticks cracked underfoot and fireweed petals lay fallen in the rock crevices, their perfume smelled by no one. Marianne had to wear her red lumber shirt if she wanted to walk to Spur Cove Pond, because all the men were in the woods hunting partridge and moose. The decaying leaves smelled sweet and thick, and the red maple leaves battled the blue sky, the scarlet and yellow-blue grating against each other. Marianne loved the wild smell of the woods and marshes, but she hated it as well, especially the marshes. Once the trees thinned you were in an unfriendly place. You had to know how to be at home there, and Marianne did not. A desire in her soul rebelled against the barrens. She could understand the desert better than this. Here the dry, grey sticks scraped her ankles. White scrapes with blood showing through some of them. The sky blared down a merciless blue with smug puffballs of white cloud in it, and the Indian tea plant with its clothy white blooms and its evil orange furze on the leaves' pointy undersides gave off a sharp, medicinal odour that shrouded every pond.

Women didn't go in the barrens, except to pick a few berries. Mrs. Halloran had told her that at one time the women would be in to the ponds every evening with their bamboos for trout. She said all one summer she had gone in with Mary and Martha and they'd been pregnant, and Mrs. Halloran had had to keep climbing up in the trees to untangle their hooks. But the women of Marianne's generation did not go outdoors. They stayed in, looking after their babies and watching the soap operas, or some of them got in their cars and went to work in the Fox Cove drugstore, the fish plant or the new communications centre that took signals from aircraft and big vessels far offshore.

Only men went in the wild places now, and they were no company for Marianne. They had no interest in a woman from town who walked in the woods, looking at reflections in the ponds and picking bunches of leaves. They went in with their guns and rabbit dogs, their packs of Export A and their half-dozens of Dominion. They never directed the slightest sexual energy at her either, so she figured they thought she was good for nothing, or crazy. Marianne thought something had dulled their fire. They should have been full of that fire you could taste in the partridgeberries because they came from the same earth. But they weren't. She didn't know why, unless it was the beer, and the cigarettes, the ten months of unemployment insurance every year, and the fish getting smaller and scarcer the other two months as the years passed. Then there was *Three's Company* and *The Price is Right* and the soaps. She knew that big unmarried men watched the soaps in their mothers' houses. TV was always on in every saltbox house, eroding the big soul in each inhabitant of the shore. All the days long the soul of the earth called out through the voices of the trees speaking in the hills, while the peat-and-needles-scented breath of the earth stole through the woods. The sea, with the islands in it and the stars over it in the night, was more of the soul that the people had lost. Everyone was timid under the majesty of creation here, Marianne thought. It was as if they had been created by a wizened, meaner god than the god of whom the psalmist had proclaimed, "in his hand are all the corners of the earth: and the strength of the hills is his also. The sea is his, and he made it: and his hands prepared the dry land."

That the wizened god was mean, Marianne could tell by the way he had instilled in everyone the malady of bondage to caution. There was a connection that nobody was making, she thought, and that was the connection between their own souls and the big soul of creation. There should have been an artery through which the same blood could pass between the islands and the

people; between the people and the stars; between the people and the stars'
creator—who should have been their creator, but apparently was not.

But there was one man in the cove who had star-blood in him, and he was called Larry. He looked like the other men, but he had different thoughts. Everyone said his trouble was that that was all he did: think. He hunted and fished and all the rest of it, but there was no sign of him buying any lumber and getting out of his mother's house to build a place of his own, and he was thirty-seven. He was a real philosopher, they said, and they laughed behind mugs of tea.

Larry was pretty quiet, except when he went on the beer, and then he would cruise along the shore in his truck and torment girls who were walking in twos to the store for a tin of baking powder or a pack of Export A. He would roll his window down and talk to them and tease them until they'd be ready to cry; he didn't know when to stop when he was drunk, just like any of the men. He would keep his headlights on low beam so the girls were always in the spotlight, and he would inch along after them, keeping up a continual banter of good will and innocent intention mixed with an evil persistence, cigarette smoke and the yeasty smell of his breath. He wore a Greek fisherman's cap, and he always swore he was innocent of everything.

On these fall nights Marianne used to walk south along the road, away from Mrs. Ruby's house and Spur Cove, towards South Bight. The road ended in South Bight; from it ran a trail up into the woods and towards La Manche, which had been abandoned during resettlement after a tidal wave had damaged half the dwellings. Years ago the women of Aspel Harbour had ridden every Sunday from the church in Fox Cove to La Manche on white horses, through the woods and across the swinging bridge. La Manche had been their home. Now all that was left was part of the bridge strung across the ravine, dilapidated but still graceful and lacy.

But South Bight was as far as Marianne usually walked at night. She passed South Bight Pond that lay alongside the road, and she passed a droke of blue trees that spoke to a dark mountain on the road's seaward side. She turned where the road ended and walked down through the white fish shed and onto the South Bight wharf. The wharf was covered by a wooden canopy and had twelve fishing boats tied by green and yellow ropes to its posts. At South Bight you could still see the islands. There were shoals between the islands and shore there, so on a day of heavy seas big geysers would spout up from the ocean. If there was moonlight they were lit up like fireworks.

Now Marianne stood at the wharf's end looking at the Pleiades and the Dog Star. She was searching for Orion, whom she had not yet seen after his summer dissolved in the day skies. A big moon hung. Near her feet on the wharf planks lay seven silver codfish, moonlit, their gills open black, each eye like an olive slice. A fisherman had thrown them down and they had landed in the shape of a sun wheel, heads pointing towards a centre and tails fanning out in a shining circle of rays. She could imagine the slapping noises they had made as they had hit the planks.

Near the fish rested a collection of hot-pink buoys, glowing from within under the moon's influence. Marianne beat them like drums; they had a musical "ping" sound within their other hollow sound. As the water moved under the boats, the taut ropes creaked around their tying-posts. Marianne could smell the dead fish, and she could smell the sea, and the turpentine in the trees on the dark mountain. In the black water that slapped the wharf-head swam spirals of fluorescence, fiery as neon. Mysterious, they appeared and disappeared, silently. Along the horizon moved a ship, harmonious as a bar of Mozart, her soft lights fizzing like drizzle on Marianne's eyes. When she had finished gazing she turned back along the wharf to go home. A truck with its headlights off loomed at the other end. Closer, she could see Larry's lit cigarette end and Larry's elbow resting out the driver's window.

"'Lo Marian." All the men shortened the anne. "What are you at?" He had a beer in the other hand but he wasn't drunk.

She told him the truth. "Looking at the night-sparkles."

"I can understand that. I can well understand that." He took a swig of his beer. "Listen Mar, would you go to a wedding with me on the eighth of October?"

"No."

"Why?" He was laughing.

"Because you're always drunk."

"Get away girl I'm not drunk now. Come and sit in here and look at the moon on the water. Get out of the cold. Then I'll drive you home. Get in, it's cold."

It was. She got in the truck and they sat and watched the moon sparkling on the water, the dark islands, the stars and the creaking tied-on boats, in silence. Larry smoked. She took one of his beers. He turned the heater on. The moon poured gold oil on the ocean. Fir and spruce tree points rose up the hillside against the gold and black water, then against the indigo and rhinestone sky. Larry pointed his beer bottle at the moon-path.

"Do you see that?"

"Yes." She thought he meant the light on the water generally. But he meant something more specific.

"No but do you see that...not the main part of the path of light but the edges of it! Good god, look at the edges...do you see that?"

When you looked at the edges of the moon-path you saw that there were sparks flying off the main path — they clung like drops of condensation to the path's edge as long as they could, travelling, sliding up, and then they clung no longer but shot out like great sparks and flung themselves halfway across the ocean.

"Yes, I see it."

"Do you really?"

"The sparks."

"Yes. You can see it then." He smoked and watched. They were silent together for a long time. Their communion thrilled her. The silence of it. He had to turn the heater off and on to save the batteries. The warm blasts were luxurious. Finally he turned on the ignition. It was past one o'clock. He drove past her house and around the wharf down at Spur Cove, just so they could see the moon-path from there, but then he drove her home. He had to get up at six o'clock. He had a temporary construction job on the road outside Witless Bay.

Marianne had never seen much of Larry's mother. Once she had met her coming out of the woods with a pan of blueberries. She was small, with soft, powdery wrinkles that smelled good. She was stuffed up with the flu, and her hands were stained with berry juice, the cracks in the skin purply black. "The berries are soft," she said. "The frost got into them last night. Are they ever sweet now." Her lips and tongue were blue. Another time Marianne had gone over to her house with Mrs. Halloran. She had made seventeen kinds of cookies and arranged them on a Royal Albert plate. Her wood stove top was rubbed bright silver, and inset in the kitchen wall was a statuette of the

Virgin Mary wreathed in plastic foliage and strung with soft pink lights. Her tablecloth had been embroidered and hemmed in hand-worked lace. Her own name was Mary. There had been no sign of Larry in the house whatsoever.

A few days after the moonlit night Marianne heard that Larry had moved out of his mother's house. He was fixing up the shed in the back meadow and was living in that. He came over to her place on a Friday evening to ask her if he could have the broken kitchen chair that was lying in the long grass by the side of her house.

"I could haul the legs off it and set it on a crate." He was snuffling with the flu.

"I'll walk over with you," she said.

The shed was made of pressboard.

"Where did you get the doors?" They were a pale, shell-pink and they opened from the centre with two cut glass handles, like French doors.

"I got them at the dump." He twisted the cap off a bottle of Dominion and stood in the middle of the floor until she sat down.

"They're nice." She chose a torn leatherette seat that had been ripped out of a truck and set on a couple of old tires. He sat on an upturned crate. There was a normal kitchen chair beside the window. The chairs formed a semicircle. In front of them stood an ornate black stove whose doors reached out in an open embrace. The stove had leaves, moons and flowers scrolled in the corners, and from its top front corners two iron gargoyles glared magnificently at Marianne. The stove was empty. They sat in front of it, their hands in their laps, swinging their crossed legs as meditatively as if slow-pulsed embers were cracking and glowing and loving them with warmth. Through the cracked window Marianne could see pink fingers soaking through the pale blue above Great Island. A star soaked through and hung glittering. The island had lit emerald mounds and shaded hollows like a velvet garment on the floor.

"You have a beautiful view."

"Yeah."

"How come you moved out here Larry?"

He drank some beer. "My mother boy. She was driving me crazy." A red bird landed on an alder outside the window. On his head perched a flat speckled cap like a liquorice allsort, the kind coated in tiny blue beads. He let out a vengeful trill of rolled Rs, then shook out his wing-ends like a crone settling down to her tea and sweet bun at a church bazaar. Up came the fat moon like a pound of butter.

Larry hunched forward, clutching his beer, elbows on his knees, gazing into the empty stove. The stove was no good, he told her. It smoked. He'd got it out of Tom Silver's shed. Whoever had dumped it there had done the right thing. Nevertheless, he remained enthusiastic about his shed. There was a current moving through his body even when he was sitting. He sat with his shoulders forward, his feet tapping. Every now and then he adjusted his cap. The shed was his project, and it excited him like an eighty-thousand-dollar pale blue bungalow in the Pinehaven Meadows Estates outside town would have excited Mrs. Halloran. When the sky darkened around the moon he stood and pulled a chain on the ceiling, and a bulb came on. He had connected his shed to an outlet in his mother's house. The bulb was screwed into a lampstand made out of fancy red glass which Larry had hung upside down from the ceiling. Marianne laughed. He said it was a ruby chandelier.

The window darkened and the silence of the night roared in their throats and ears like air in winkle shells. Marianne thought of all the pursuits in which people involved themselves; all the things they wanted, and the beauty they wanted to attract to themselves. Here was beauty all around Larry, in the stillness, in the simplicity here.

That was true, she thought, if he was satisfied. She wondered if he was.

"I'm going home now."

"All right. Don't talk to any bears."

Wisdom, thought Marianne. Wisdom kept eluding her. Foolishness seemed like wisdom to her in so many places. She had closed the French doors and was taking the path that lay under Larry's mother's kitchen window. The light was shining through frilled cotton curtains patterned with tiny brown salt shakers, salad forks, cookie jars and daisies. Larry's mother must be behind them, she thought, rocking in her chair by the stove where she has laid a covered plate of fresh meat stew and a partridgeberry tart for Larry, knitting him a pair of grey socks, thinking of him out there in the woodshed that everyone is talking about and feeling ashamed.

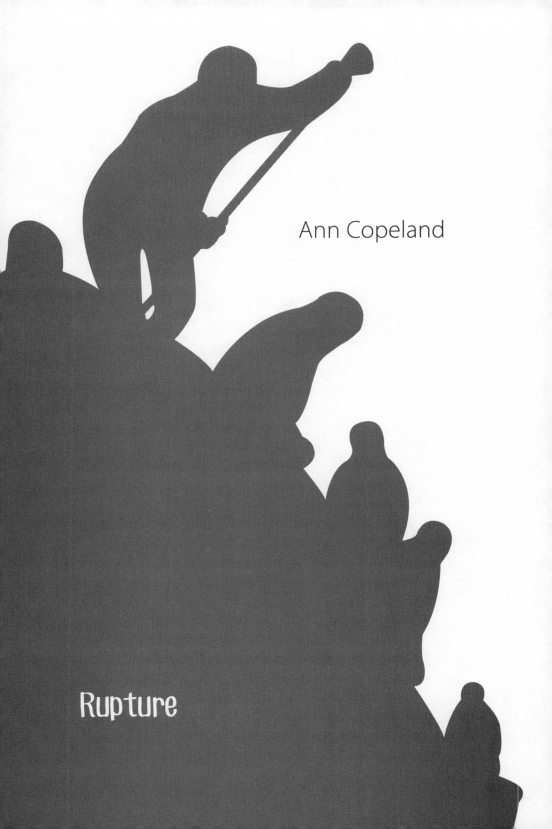

Ann Copeland

Rupture

He smells of hair tonic or shaving cream, something faintly sweet and sickening. She looks out the window, trying to see down, but today there's cloud cover and nothing to be seen.

"Going far?"

He's determined to be friendly.

"Toronto."

"You're from the Maritimes?"

"I'm from the other world," she murmurs and, squeezing her elbow close to her side, tries to cut into the hunk of mystery meat Air Canada has served up for this flight.

He begins also to chew.

Claire Richardson is on her way to a TV show.

She is fifty-eight years old, in good health, reasonably good-natured, a bit flabby, going grey. She's decided not to touch up her hair. She has a husband, Jim, fifty-five, three children: Peter, twenty, away at university; Anna, sixteen, aggressively adolescent and recently tattooed; and Jerry, about to turn fifteen, a budding couch potato with a quirky imagination. She is resolved to accept wrinkles. She has been looking forward to this trip, a break from home routine where she teaches high school French and does occasional freelance editing.

She has left behind an angry daughter. It tugs at her now, Anna's anger, as she, escaping mother, sits high in the clouds, heading toward a guest appearance on Laura LeMonde's talk show. She thinks she's nuts to have said yes. Especially, given the topic.

The call from Toronto came several weeks ago, injecting excitement (fake, she thinks now) into a particularly grey November afternoon. She'd just come in from a brisk walk and was in the kitchen, near the phone, watching the vegetables and warming up the leftover stew for supper.

"Mrs. Richardson?" said the voice.

"Yes."

"We're putting together a program. Perhaps you've heard of the *Laura LeMonde Show*?"

"To tell the truth, no. I haven't."

Proof again of how thoroughly out of it she is. Anna was right. But she has better things to do with her time.

Like read her daughter's mail, she thinks now, staring out at cloudy heavens. It gnaws at her, this violation. She's particularly sensitive to the intimacy of letters, having resented for years the fact that hers were routinely read by censoring eyes. *Why* did she have to give in to that momentary impulse? She rarely invaded Anna's room. Privacy matters. How well she knew! We all need to feel some things are our own. Letters, certainly. But that day she needed the hair dryer. It wasn't in the bathroom. It could be in only one other place, so with dripping hair she'd threaded her way through the labyrinth and in so doing found not only the hair dryer but the unfinished letter her daughter was writing to a friend from summer camp. Open on the unmade bed. Asking to be read.

It was the very same day the phone call came from Toronto.

"Your name has been suggested," said the high girlish voice of the assistant producer that day. "I understand you spent some time, when you were younger, in... religious life? The convent?"

She seemed to have difficulty wrapping her tongue around the words.

"Yes." Stretching the phone cord so she could reach the stove, Claire speared a carrot and eyed a crumbling potato. "But that was ages ago."

"You've written some articles on that experience?"

"Well, yes. But again... that was a couple of years ago. Largely an editing job of other people's views."

She tried to gather her wits. The carrots were still hard.

"We're putting together a show on women who have been in the convent and have left," said the voice. "The statistics are interesting and we thought it might fascinate our viewers."

Our viewers.

"Why do you want to do this?" she asked. Through the kitchen window she could see Hal Jones, their next door neighbour, pulling into his drive. Jim would be home soon. Jerry had basketball after supper.

Late afternoon was always the worst time. Leaden. "I'm not interested in participating if this is simply church-bashing," she said, surprising herself. She harboured major gripes about the church. "If you intend to treat the subject seriously, I think you should have a theologian on the panel, and someone who's chosen to remain in religious life."

"What a good idea."

The response sounded genuine.

"I could give you some suggestions for names," she said. "Not people I know personally but whose articles I've read. Articulate women do exist."

Snide. She'd have to watch it. It was too easy for her to slip over into gratuitous irony. Already she was seeing herself on TV. What would she wear? What was she getting herself in for? TV was a medium for selling, as she was forever telling the children. Period. Boob Tube.

"We'll get back to you, Mrs. Richardson. Thank you for your suggestions. Before the show airs, we'll have a substantial telephone conversation with you to fill in background."

What, Claire wondered, stirring the stew, did they consider "substantial."

The people at *Laura LeMonde* took her suggestions, contacted the women whose names she offered, then phoned her back a few days later with a panel of four all arranged.

"We're calling the show 'Hanging Up the Habit,'" said that voice.

O God.

"You're participating in idiocy," her husband said when she told him.

"I think it's cool," Anna said. "What are you gonna wear?"

Should I tell her about the letter now? thought Claire. *Clear the air before I leave? Would she forgive?* One never knew with Anna.

Her son, glued to *Star Trek* reruns, eyed her coolly. "Watch it, Mom. Don't get too fresh. You can come on pretty strong without meaning to."

In her heart she hoped something could be said that was serious. She didn't want the panel to be talk-show dumb.

Now, weeks later, floating on puff, hemmed in by male smell, masticating Air Canada meat, she regrets it. Is a talk show ever serious? Shouldn't she be at home trying to deal with her daughter? Does anyone ever really hang up the habit? Misplaced moral earnestness has been known to complicate her life before. It's a dead issue. Why try to drum up interest?

Face it. They ran out of topics. Reached in the grab bag and pulled out this one. Quick fix for the three-minute attention span: today, ex-nuns; tomorrow, prostitutes; next day, lesbian marriages; next day, adoptions; next day, the new female condom. Ho-hum.

What made her, or them, think religious life was such a special topic?

So here you are again, she thinks, as her ears explode and the plane hits ground, taking an absurdity seriously.

At the airport a stretch limo displaying a large LAURA LEMONDE SHOW sign in the window meets her. And to think she'd never heard of Laura!

Toronto is even greyer than the Maritimes. She rests against dark blue upholstery and lets herself be driven through this drab Vanity Fair to the Delta Chelsea Inn where, on the twelfth floor, next to a window overlooking concrete canyons crawling with fashionable ants, she discovers a china dish with four chocolate cherries and a large fresh strawberry beneath a glass dome. Beside the dish lies a note. WE HOPE YOU WILL ENJOY YOUR STAY WITH US. Signed, so to speak, by the president of the corporation.

Later that night, when she has returned from a sumptuous meal at a gay restaurant run by the brother of her good friend Millie, she will find her bed turned down and a chocolate peppermint lying on her pillow. Beneath it, a deckle-edged napkin with a message on it in gold script: *Sleep Well*.

‿

But she cannot sleep — despite the king-size bed, the satin sheets, the extravagant puff, the full liquor closet in which, a couple of hours ago, she discovered a hermetically sealed bottle of cashews and, with the glee of a ten-year-old, pried off the sealing tape, popped the lid and pigged out as she watched the late news.

Now she cannot sleep.

One scene will not leave her.

‿

Midsummer sun beating down on them, they stand out back of the house. This is a comfortable sprawling summer home in Delaware, on the Elk River. She is standing there, beneath the clothesline. She has just hung up her wet bathing suit. They've spent the afternoon on the beach, stripped at last of their black serge, these ten nuns on holiday at the edge of the Elk. The year is 1963. Almost thirty years ago.

She wears sneakers, protection against the tall grasses wisping her bare legs. They are on a week's vacation from the rigours of teaching, studying, praying and surviving life in community. During this week their routine is more relaxed. Once they've finished chores and prayers in the morning, except for prayer time and dinner, they are allowed to wear the students' blue gym suits. A few of the older nuns opt to stay in habits all day, but the younger ones shed cloth readily and head for the beach in mid-morning. This is living.

The scratch of grass against her calves, her knees, as she stands by the clothesline should perhaps annoy her. Instead, it holds something fresh and electric for skin too long covered.

"How come you didn't go swimming?" she asks Sister Dolores, a nun two years ahead of her in religion.

Sister Dolores is taking in some things from the line. Two white T-shirts, a long black undershirt. She is in her habit, minus veil. She has put on her night veil. Curly blonde hair sticks out around the edges of white seersucker.

"I can't. I've got my period."

They speak quietly. Even out here by the line, there's the possibility that someone nearby may be trying to pray or doing her spiritual reading.

Sister Claire pauses. It's always risky to tamper with another's conscience, especially in a world dedicated to formation of conscience. She decides to take the risk.

"Look," she says. "That's no reason to stay out of the water. We only get here once a year and you're missing the chance to swim."

She sees the perspiration streaming down Sister Dolores's pale face — a young nun with skin the colour of worn piano keys, and soft brown eyes that carry in their depths a hint of something haunted. What that is, Sister Claire does not know. She's noticed it before — as far back as the novitiate. When Claire came to the novitiate, Sister Dolores already knew the ropes. Now, nine years later, they are both back teaching at the same college they had attended years before.

They've been at the Elk for three days. Only two more days of vacation left. It's ninety-eight degrees Fahrenheit in the shade and there's no relief from heat except the luscious soothing touch of ole man river himself as they swim around in gym suits. The full split skirts swirl and cling annoyingly against their thighs, but it's better than nothing. Better that sitting on the beach lusting for immersion. That's for sure.

They are a sight on the beach and they know it. They don't care. Yesterday a motorboat with three tanned young men wielding field glasses zoomed in close to shore and ogled them. One of them called out, "Having fun, Sisters?"

The sisters waved back, laughing.

"But I can't go down to the beach," says Sister Dolores. She drops the clothespins into a cloth bag attached to the end of the line.

"I'd...well...it'd be messy."

"No problem. Use a tampon."

Sister Dolores looks puzzled. "What's that?"

"It's…" Sister Claire stops. "Look, I have my period, too. But I was darned if I was going to miss this chance. So I went to Mother Josefa and asked her to get me some tampons."

The sisters must ask for all their supplies, which are distributed by the nun in charge from a source called Common Good.

"She didn't even know what they were, but when I explained, she said she'd send out to the store. Don't ask me how she did it."

Sister Claire feels again the embarrassed flush on her face as she dared to ask Mother Josefa, a small, kind-eyed, simple nun of about seventy who was sent to take charge of these vacationing teachers at the Elk.

"What do you do with it?" Sister Dolores wiped her streaming face with a large white handkerchief.

"I'd have to give you the instructions. I kept them from the packet I got," says Sister Claire, remembering where she put them under her T-shirts in the underwear drawer in the dormitory upstairs where five of them sleep in an orderly row. "Can you meet me in a few minutes?"

Sister Dolores agrees. They'll meet in ten minutes out behind the garage where surely no one will be trying to pray.

Now, almost thirty years later, lying alone in the extravagant suite of the Delta Chelsea, Claire thinks of that moment, feels again the heat, the prickles, the puzzle of just how to deal with a nun she'd suspected might be given to scruples.

She hasn't thought of that word in years: *scruples*.

It comes back to her in a flash, straight from *The Spiritual Exercises of St. Ignatius*, as she lies there swimming in a king-size bed, her head on a satin pillow. *Scruples*—the tendency to judge something a sin which is not a sin. She even remembers his example. How odd, when she forgets exactly how many years she's been married, or what her husband gave her last Christmas. How deeply she absorbed it all! What an apt student!

Ignatius offered the religious neophyte the example of someone who steps, by accident, on a cross formed by two straws and judges that he has sinned thereby. A trivial example, he said, but not in a class with a bona fide case of Scruples. Real, full-blown Scruples was a disease of the soul, pervasive, exhausting, perhaps even terminal. The person so afflicted lost all sense of judgement, all sense of proportion. Felt everything she was doing might be a sin. Couldn't tell the trivial from the serious.

Claire remembers, too, the old Ignatian solution, one often told them. The only solution for Scruples, he claimed, was total obedience to an enlightened superior or spiritual director. The soul must confide in someone wiser and holier, someone who would direct the soul back to the path of right thinking. It was a matter of total trust. Total surrender to someone who had that ever-to-be-desired grace called *discernment of spirits*.

Ah, there's the rub, she thinks now. *Someone wiser. Someone holier. Someone capable of discerning spirits. Laura LeMonde, here I come.*

As arranged, she and Sister Dolores met a few minutes later out behind the garage, the sun reflecting off the bright white rear of the building, a massive clump of tiger lilies preening beside them. She'd brought the instructions.

"Look..." She showed the illustration, a clinically exact drawing of the relevant parts of the anatomy, isolated from the rest of the body.

Sister Dolores took the small set of directions and studied it in silence, frowning.

"It's a little tricky the first time. You sit on the john, at least that's what I finally did, you may have to search around a bit."

Claire smiles now, her head against the soft pillow, remembering. She could have said, "We're not exactly used to searching for the right place."

These are the things you think of later, too late, when you realize you missed a chance. At that time, she could neither have thought it nor said it. Instead, she just went on explaining. "You just insert it with this," illustrating with the round cardboard tube. "You remove the tube and leave in the tampon and a string hangs down."

Sister Dolores studied the mysterious object. She held it, turning it over in her hot hand. They were both in their habits now, veils and all. The bell for supper was due to ring in about ten minutes.

"And it works?"

"It works fine. When you can, just pull on the string and it comes out. It expands inside you. It's highly absorbent."

Like Christian indoctrination, she thinks now, lying there. What a thought! This is what it is to be raised Catholic—or what it was in the old days. It's a question these days just how much of any doctrine can be absorbed. In those days, you absorbed it, it penetrated the most intimate crevices of mind, heart, soul. Yes, even body. As you grew, it expanded inside you. Not so easily removed, though. Even major surgery couldn't do that. Psychoanalysis has its limits, though she's never tried it herself. Why suppose an expensive shrink is holy or wise? Where, these days, can one hope to find a discerner of spirits?

Such thoughts were not hers that day as she stood in the hot July sun by the Elk River in Delaware.

Sister Dolores glanced behind her friend as if she saw someone approaching. She started to say something, seemed to think better of it. Then she handed the tube and the instructions back to Sister Claire.

"Thanks, but I…I just don't think I could do it."

"You're afraid it'll hurt?"

"Not so much that." Sister Claire didn't think it would be that. Sister Dolores was nothing if not mortified. "It's just that I'm afraid…" Sister Dolores blushed, bit her lip, then finally spit it out. "Well, will it break the hymen?"

GOOD GOD.

The question had never once occurred to her! This was simply a way to secure time in the water, defeat the heat, float free of routine, minimize the discomfort of menstruation. And even Mother Josefa, dear simple nun that she was, hadn't demurred.

This was a case where the end definitely justified the means.

"Heavens, I don't know."

"Well…" Sister Dolores was getting ready to leave. She looked sad, almost rueful. "I just can't do it…I just can't."

They never spoke of it again.

For the next two days, while Claire splashed around and chased small fish, welcomed the sting of salt to her eyes and the tantalizing itch of dried salt on her flesh, she'd catch sight of Sister Dolores up on the lawn, sitting in a chair, habit on, reading or just looking out to sea.

Will it break the hymen?

Rupture. Rapture...So slight a change, so great a difference. She sees Anna in the kitchen two nights ago, angry, stamping her foot, turning like a ten-year-old to leave and walk around the block. With that toss of her long snarled black hair over her insulted shoulder. "This is how you always treat me," she shouted. "Like a baby. As if I didn't have a mind of my own! As if I didn't know what I was doing."

All this outburst, this stamping, this genuine distress and tension, from a little butterfly drilled forever into pubescent flesh beneath her fragile sixteen-year-old collarbone.

She came in half an hour later, calmer.

Claire was at the dishpan, her back to the door.

"I know it's permanent," said Anna to that back as she slammed the door behind her. The deadly calm of her tone was frightening. "I *wanted* it permanent. I've always been fascinated by tattoos. Chelsea's mother has one on her thigh. A Christmas tree. With decorations! At least I didn't go that far! I *do* have some judgement, you know! Even though *you* don't seem to think so!"

Claire tries now to shut out the thought of Anna, of the kitchen that night—the lingering smell of onion, the steamed-up kitchen window over the dishpan, the soft lather of suds on her hands as her daughter threw words of challenge and hurt against her back.

Someone is running up and down the hall outside the room. A door nearby slams.

She must prepare herself for tomorrow's inane probing, the secular mind in the form of Laura LeMonde, taking on one nun and three former nuns to question them, play out their stories before an audience gathered in the studio to listen, participate and gawk. But she cannot erase the vision of Sister Dolores behind the garage that sweltering day—rueful, determined, regretfully declining. *Will it break the hymen*? The pain in her eyes as she asked the question.

Nor can she quell the sense of Anna's recent anger. Their parting had been cool. "So long, Mom. Break a leg." Then, no hug or kiss goodbye, just slamming out the door with her jacket open and her backpack slung over one still-insulted shoulder. She'd always been one to hold a grudge.

The day of the butterfly upset—was it really just two days ago?—Anna had come home after school and gone immediately to her room. Unusual. As a rule, she'd rummage for a snack, flick on the TV. Later, she sat quietly at the supper table, saying little until Jerry left for his basketball practice. Jim was still out, delayed with a client.

Suddenly, as Claire sat there nursing her coffee, Anna said, "I want to show you something." The statement held no defensiveness, she didn't seem nervous. She pulled at the loose neck of her T-shirt until it stretched toward her shoulder. The fragility of the pale, flesh-covered collarbone smote Claire's heart as she watched her daughter and waited. What was coming?

There, nestled in the soft flesh beneath the bone, in exquisite colours of green, yellow, blue and purple, sat a small butterfly tattoo.

"Why?" was all the mother could think to ask.

"I just wanted to," was all the daughter could think to say, stricken by the pain in her mother's eye. It had been a lark. A thought-out lark. Six of them had made the appointment weeks ago, gone after school, made sure it was a clean establishment. They were savvy. They knew about unclean needles.

"Was it—was it very painful?" Claire tried to keep her voice calm.

"A little. Not bad."

Anna released the neck of her shirt.

Then, Claire's control broke down. She saw her daughter on the table, someone leaning over her with a needle. Anything could have happened.

"But—but why would you want to?"

She hadn't intended to sound accusatory. She did.

"This is the way it always is!" Anna said, like a ten-year-old, wanting to stamp her foot but knowing better. "I just wanted to do it. That's all. So I did."

She'd looked her mother square in the eye, turned on her heel, left.

Claire found herself unable to separate her own feelings, the confusing rush of them, the sense of that flesh broken, the flesh that had once been part of her, yet she squelched that thought because she wasn't sentimental, she did love her daughter, though there was a certain distance between them she couldn't seem to penetrate. At times the air between them seemed to grow clotted with unexpressed emotion in a way it never did between Anna and her father. (Or maybe, thought Claire, I imagine this. How can I tell?) Other times, the same air stretched out thin and vaporous, acquired a strange emptying power, as if it could change the substance of whatever Claire wanted to say to her daughter into pointless drivel.

What she couldn't confess to Anna, or at least wouldn't, was that she'd read that letter. Had violated that trust. Now, such a confession seemed ruled out forever.

She was paying for it. The discomfort would fade. It always does. But for the moment she felt bad and unable to repair.

The lines she'd read in that letter haunted her: *I don't mind lying to my mother*, wrote Anna, *I'm just sorry I can't share. She never tells me the stories like your mom. All my friends know stories about their mother's growing up, about their sexual experiences... about, well anything.*

She'd dropped the letter, forever sorry she'd weakened, sorry she'd snooped. Her face burned. She felt caught in a lump of sadness. Nothing could really help. Nothing at all. So her trespass became her burden and that was that. No way to exorcise it.

She left the house, walked out into cleansing wind, a bitter salty wind off the bay, and walked and walked, wondering what stories she had to tell her daughter. She recognized the truth of Anna's complaint. No, she didn't tell her daughter stories. She'd never thought of it quite that way. The problem is this, she argued with Anna mentally as she fed her face to the stinging wind: what would hold resonance? No point in telling a story that holds no meaning. There has to be some way to make it connect.

She thought of her daughter's friends: Isobel with her green hair, her sad frightened dark eyes, her evasive responses, her nose ring that so perfectly matched the flesh tones of her face. Isobel always looked hungry but wouldn't touch a morsel in their house. Moody Caroline, whose parents claimed she was a genius, who had no curfew and made it tough for other parents because Caroline, already an alcoholic, had her parents fooled. Jessie, already through one abortion and now involved with another sleazebag from grade twelve. Chelsea—what kind of a name was that?—always wearing calculated tatters with designer labels, who came to the house now and then, browsed through the kitchen, draped herself over the chesterfield, picked up magazines and books lying around and made comments like, "Your parents actually read this stuff?"

What stories did she have to tell?

Plenty.

She knew another reason she couldn't seem to tell them. Because they'd sound like high comedy, and looked at from a certain angle they were just that, but she wanted them to be more than that when she told them. She wanted her daughter to hear them against an echo of recognition in her own head, her own life, that would give them meaning. And that seemed strangely absent in the 1990s.

So she never found words to tell the stories she might have. Weren't they better simply forgotten, anyway? She'd thought so.

Though one couldn't really forget.

And now Anna's words: *I don't mind lying to my mother. I mind that I can't share. She never tells me stories...*

Anna was right. The loneliness of her comment reached deep inside Claire, touched a nerve she couldn't name.

She returned from that brisk, sad walk at five o'clock, chilled to the bone, ready to prepare a supper of leftover stew.

❧

Laura LeMonde is tiny—five feet, perhaps. This morning she wears a black leather miniskirt, black heels and stockings (over excellent legs), a blazing green sweater, black beads. She has large dark eyes, short curly red hair, and wears shining red lipstick. Energetic, focused, she is all business with her four guests in the ten minutes they have together before the show starts. She has rushed in to meet them after taping another show. She holds a sheaf of papers in one hand, notes on her guests furnished by her assistant producer, and sips coffee from a YOU'RE THE GREATEST mug as she talks to them in a firm business-like voice.

"In segment one," she says, "we'll talk about why you left the convent. What made you reach that decision—after so many years."

They are crowded into a small space outside the makeup room next to the studio. The four guests have just had their faces improved for the camera. Their hostess's makeup is already perfect.

"You" — Laura eyes a small slim woman in a flowered split skirt sitting to her left — "it is Rachel Beaubassin, isn't it? Am I right? You were in the convent how many years?"

"Thirty-five," says Rachel quietly, "I just left last year."

"My. What an adjustment," breathes Laura. She shifts forward to the edge of her chair, crosses her legs, and swings one black leg as she talks.

"And you?" to Claire.

"Thirteen."

"And of course I know about *you*," she says with a wicked grin to the younger woman on Claire's right. "But tell me again, Judith."

Judith Frank, a slim well-tailored woman of about forty, carries herself with composed confidence. Obviously she knows how to dress for TV. Cool colours. A specialist in child management, she has visited the LeMonde show several times, offering seasoned advice on how to manage difficult children. "I was in only three years," says Judith, in a husky voice. "I went in at sixteen."

Doesn't qualify, thinks Claire. *Too young to know what she was doing. Adolescent.* She remembers well her own adolescent yearnings. The crushes on nuns.

"They took you at sixteen?"

"I had to fight for it," says Judith. She holds her coffee mug with both hands as if to heat them, though this windowless room is very close. "I had an aunt who was a nun in the same community. That helped."

"Ah, fascinating. You can tell us all later." Laura eyes each guest in turn. "Now then, I have all your names straight, I think: Rachel, Claire, Judith..."

She turns to the fourth woman, a nun wearing a brilliant blue suit. She is attractive, fortyish, with a gentle voice, a radiant smile.

"And your name is — Sister Clothilde deAngelis? Right? I'll have to practice that. *Clothilde deAngelis*? *WOW*!" Laura says it with italics, then swallows and laughs lightly. "Right?" She eyes Sister Clothilde, who nods. "Okay. After we've dealt with that question, how and why and when, there will be a commercial break."

The audience is already waiting in the small studio next door.

"Then, in the next segment of the show, I'll ask you *why* you entered? What made you make that decision."

"I—" starts Sister Clothilde.

"Four minutes, Laura," says a voice from the doorway. The assistant producer.

"Okay. Okay, thanks. We'll make it."

"I—" starts Sister Clothilde again.

"Sorry, Sister. You'll have to hold it for the show. Now then, for the third segment I'll get into what everyone wonders, of course. Why is this life a life of celibacy? Why does the church require...I mean, it's not natural, is it? This is everyone's question. How do you live without sex?"

Claire imagines her with a different lover every night. The assistant producer has told Claire Laura has an eighteen-year-old son. She too has a hidden life. It's hard to believe.

"I mean the church is really down on women, isn't it? Can you talk about that? You can't be priests, can you?" She laughs. "Not, of course, that any of you might want to. But just the same....And I understand that there are many...aberrations in religious life," Laura sets down her emptied mug on the small black table beside her, "and I'm sure it would interest our audience to hear something about that. Wasn't there a book a few years ago about lesbianism in the convent?" She addresses her question to Claire.

Ah, on to something juicy.

"I never experienced it," Claire comments. "Though yes, there was a book on it. And no doubt it existed. But I don't think that's the real issue here—"

"Now just relax," says Laura. "Everyone is eager to hear what you all have to say. It's going to be an exciting show. I can feel it. And then, for the final fifteen minutes, the audience can question you about anything they want to." She stands, shakes her small red curls a bit and pulls down her green sweater. "All clear? Any questions?"

The assembled guests eye one another.

What are we doing here?

The nun by the clothesline was named Dolores. It fit. She would have her share of dolour. But oddly enough the memory Claire has of her from the novitiate is of a relentlessly smiling face. That was encouraged in those days: compulsory joy. The children of God should be joyous. What does it mean if one who lives a life of faith is dour?

Sister Dolores as a postulant and novice, in the days when they were all learning how to be religious, set the example of joy. Upbeat. Bright, no doubt about that. She had memorable brown eyes, a round face, a wide generous mouth, a complexion of peaches and cream and gorgeous blonde curly hair. That of course was covered now. She spoke in a slightly breathless voice and sang like an angel. The sound of that sweet pure soprano singing "Hark, the Herald Angels Sing" to awaken the postulants for their first Christmas was etched forever in Claire's memory. When Sister Dolores was assigned to teach the novices Latin, she greeted them daily with a Latin motto for them to translate. *Amor vincit omnia. Per aspera ad astra. Ad maiorem dei gloriam. Miserere mei Deus. Nisi Dominus aedivicavit domum.* Offering her Latin thought for the day, her eyes lighted up as if she were offering them a bonbon from heaven.

Sister Claire found it off-putting. Yet fascinating. She saw the tremendous effort of will. Even then, there was something strung very tight inside Sister Dolores, something that never relaxed.

Yet she was exquisitely, unobtrusively kind. She watched the younger sisters struggle to learn the ways of poverty, chastity and obedience, tried to help them through days that could grow bleak that long first winter. No task was too small for her. She was quick to kiss the floor when she'd broken silence, a penance Claire detested. She jumped to anticipate the smallest wish of their superior. In mid-winter she volunteered to carry garbage to the pigs, half a mile up the snow-covered road, a task everyone avoided. Always, she took the dirtiest jobs. This beautiful young novice bent her considerable intelligence to mining possibilities for humility in a life that offered a bottomless lode.

She was bent on becoming a saint.

The audience this morning is composed of about fifty women, all ages, shapes, sizes, sitting on a graduated platform. The visiting guests sit in a row on a small stage facing their audience. Laura LeMonde, holding a microphone in one hand and her notes in the other, fairly leaps among the audience. She seems to have had an enormous surge of adrenalin now that the camera's eye is focused on her. It's hard to believe she just finished another hour of this with the same audience.

She waves her notes as she talks. Her guests had a few seconds before the show after Laura left the room. Three married women, one nun, all familiar with the patriarchy, one way or another. They've seen the pitch she plans to make and resolved, quietly, to deflate it. Maybe something serious will emerge. It's clear they're all intelligent women who have grown past some forms of bitterness. They are wary.

Laura works them quickly through the factual part. How long were they in? Why did they leave? Rachel: "I ceased believing in the structures of the life." Claire: "A tragic fire was the ultimate catalyst. It brought home to me that I had only one life." Judith: "I was too young. I was impressionable and infatuated. My idea had little to do with the reality." Laura doesn't linger over Sister Clothilde.

Now she's on to the juicier question. "I want to ask you what we all wonder. How could you...I mean..."—here she waves her sheaf of papers and turns to the audience for confirmation—"I'm sure many in the audience have this same question. It just isn't NATURAL to live without...sex. Is it? I mean why would you choose that? What's the point? You can teach, you can help the poor, you can do all sorts of things, but you don't have to go without..."

Ah, THE question.

For a fleeting instant Claire wishes she dared address the audience directly: *How many of you are married? How many of you long for a man? How many of you have tried it and found it wanting? How many of you really hunger for intimacy? Are you lonely? Do you feel valued? Are these real questions for you? Is there anyone you really trust?*

It isn't until later, on the flight back home, that she thinks she should have said, "Is it natural to live without God? Or without belief in something larger than oneself?"

But under the glare of blinding lights, faced by a hungry audience, prodded by a canny hostess and flanked by other guests, limited by the time allotted for commercials, one can't find these thoughts. The audience watches, the camera swivels and the hostess paces herself and you, aims to finish each segment on a tantalizing question that will keep that larger audience out there glued to the tube.

What on earth *is* natural?

Sister Dolores taught in high school. An excellent teacher. Her major as an undergraduate had been English literature, her minor Latin. After the novitiate and her first profession, she was sent on to graduate school at Catholic University. It so happened that the septuagenarian classics teacher at the college would soon have to leave teaching. It was decreed, therefore, that Sister Dolores would undertake the study of Greek and Latin. Perhaps the reasoning went that she already had a start with the Latin.

Claire remembers seeing her bent over her Greek grammar, propping it up by the ironing board when she had work in the laundry, silently mouthing vocabulary as they walked back and forth to campus, straining always to look happy. It was a burden, no doubt about it. Languages did not come easy to her. But it would be hard to assess the weight of her burden in those days. They were all straining.

Even then, Claire knew that the assignment to learn Greek and Latin would have done her in. It would have meant the booby hatch or out the nearest window. Which would have won? She was never put to that test. Evidently her superiors had sized up the limits of her potential for virtue.

Sister Dolores, however, persevered and conquered. She went on to teach Latin for a year or two at one of the Order's academies. This was the late fifties, before questions of relevance and social usefulness became an issue for high school students. Her students liked her, even though she taught Latin. She was perhaps a trifle too bright, just a bit too resolute in her joyousness. Still,

she was better than some of the lemons they'd experienced in their earlier
years of Catholic education.

Eventually, she was sent to teach at the college. She brought to her classes there the same competence and enthusiasm. The years were passing. She was thirty-four. She'd been a professed Agnetine for almost ten years.

At the college, she and Sister Claire met again, now as teachers. During the school year following that summer of the hymen fiasco, Sister Claire began to suspect that all was not right with Sister Dolores.

Scruples. A loss of a sense of proportion. A tendency to see sin or fault in the most infinitesimal slip. A need to be constantly reassured.

She scrupled to use a tampon.

She scrupled to rupture the hymen.

She wanted to remain intact.

That, perhaps, was the first clue. There is no remaining intact. Broken is the norm, healing the wonder.

Such thoughts would come only years later to Claire Richardson.

The *Laura LeMonde Show* is still on segment three. Laura LeMonde has pranced up the steps in the midst of the audience. She turns to face her guests, camera swinging with her. "Can one of you explain this to me?" she asks, a challenge in her voice. She has not been satisfied with their explanations. "I mean, I can see wanting to do social work. I can see helping the poor. I can see teaching. But…I just can't see why you'd have to be living like that. Celibate! Explain!"

One by one they take her on.

"You completely overlook one part of this life," says Rachel quietly. "We lived in community. We had sisters."

"The point was," says Claire, suppressing her own sense of irony, "that as well as teaching, or social work, or nursing, or whatever the work of the Order was, our life together was to bear witness to Christian charity. To represent the reality of Christ in this world."

Laura looks puzzled and a bit anxious.

"Why," says Sister Clothilde, "would you insist it's unnatural? How can we decide for anyone else what that is? And by the way, I'd just like to say that you keep ignoring me. As if I'm the one who's unnatural on this platform. I resent that."

Laura is taken aback. Or appears to be.

"But, but," she insists, looking to her audience for agreement, "I still say it just isn't natural. I mean you were all normal women. That's clear. Why then...why no men?"

Later, as the family sat together watching the video, Claire's husband would say drily, "You should have said to her *what makes you think life with a man is normal?*"

"I mean, didn't you ever want to be married?" Laura goes on. "Or at least —at least share your life with someone? Now you, Sister...uh...Clothilde," Laura glances at her notes, "it says here that you regret never having married."

"No! I never said that! I don't know where you got it but your information is wrong!" Sister Clothilde is outraged. Her tone is convincing, winning. She leans forward, addresses not Laura but the audience. "I don't believe lacking a husband is the greatest loss," she says. "There are loads of miserable marriages. We all know that. I don't deny religious life has its loneliness. Of course there have been times when I might have liked a partner with whom to share things. But I have my community. They are my family. And I've taught hundreds of children over the years. They are my family. My life is given to God."

Laura tears her prompt papers in half, tosses them in the air.

"Well," she says, looking at the audience with a laugh, "I've been misinformed!"

Four years ago, Claire got a phone call. It broke into her universe of marriage, wifehood, motherhood. A voice from the past.

She had no French classes that day. She was ironing, an occupation she found meditative, as she listened to Bob Kerr's early afternoon music show on CBC radio.

"Is this Claire Richardson?"

She knew the voice instantly. Sister Dolores.

"Where ARE you?"

"In Toronto. I'm on my honeymoon. I wondered if we could come and see you. Just overnight. We have to be in the Maritimes for a couple of days."

Anna at that time was twelve. She'd just had her first period and they'd shopped for a bra a few months before. She was feeling grown up, shy and evasive about it. They'd had fun over the bra shopping and Claire was pleased at her daughter's matter-of-fact acceptance of her menses. Some things, at least, were no longer such a Big Deal.

"Come," she said to former Sister Dolores, delighted. "Stay as long as you want."

It had been over twenty-two years since she'd seen or heard from Sister Dolores.

~

So it was that Fran Cullinan, formerly Fran O'Neill, formerly Sister Dolores, arrived at the Richardson home on an early December evening. Fortunately, the predicted snow had held off. She and her husband Mike landed in Moncton, rented a car and planned to drive on the next day to Halifax. As luck would have it, since Jim was in Ottawa, there was no one to share the impact of the visit with afterward. Except Anna, and somehow she seemed too young.

They arrived shortly before eleven o'clock. The children were already in bed. Mike was a tall, extraordinarily thin man with a pockmarked face and a scraggly sandy-coloured moustache. His handshake was limp. *Dead fish*, thought Claire, as she tried to make him feel at home. She wanted to like him.

They accepted one drink, a Scotch, chatted for a few minutes in the living room.

"You're just here for a couple of days?"

"Getting some information on software markets in Canada," said Mike. "I have a little company in New Hampshire. We're looking to expand our markets."

"Mike knows everything about computers," said Fran, eyeing him with pride.

"You should talk to my older son," said Claire.

He didn't pick her up on it.

"What're you doing?" she asked Fran.

"For now, I'm going to help Mike with his company."

"She'll be a big help," said Mike. "She's a technological whiz." Fran had a strange puffy look. Before, as Claire remembered well, she'd been slim, almost skinny. Her cheeks looked bloated now, stretched and shiny. She smiled less. When Claire hugged her at the door, Fran's body had felt stiff, reserved. Still, her eyes were bright, she had the same breathless intensity to her voice, and she seemed capable of enthusiasm. She wore a stunning suede suit and a deep green coat with a high stand-up fur collar.

After half an hour of small talk, Mike yawned meaningfully and looked at Fran. "Well, I guess…"

His bride stood up instantly.

"I've put you in our room," said Claire, leading them down the hall together. "If you need anything, just yell."

She longed to corner Fran, ask her directly: *How are you? What happened?* There was no opportunity. Nor had there been any indication that Fran wanted that. Besides, why push it? Maybe the last thing wanted, needed, was a question, the regurgitation of a story, a part of a story. Some things were better left buried.

Next morning, Claire took Anna and Jerry to school. She came home, made blueberry muffins, and waited.

Ten o'clock.

No sound.

Eleven o'clock.

No sound.

She ate a muffin and drank a cup of coffee.

Twelve o'clock.

No sound.

She cooked herself an egg.

Twelve thirty.

At last, the shower was running.

Her last view of Sister Dolores had been at midnight from a third-floor window in the girls' residence at the college. Sister Claire watched, on that early spring night, as two white-coated attendants carried a body out of the main convent across the street, wrapped in a blanket and strapped to a board. The face was exposed, but she could barely make it out as she leaned on the windowsill in Sister Dolores's room. Just a few moments before, she'd climbed the stairs in the dormitory to talk to Sister Dolores, who was always in her room at midnight. She found the door unlocked, the room empty. No sign of her. Sister Claire opened the closet: Sunday habit, shoes, nightgown, bathrobe all hanging neatly, side by side. The headdress and everyday habit were gone. She looked at the desk: *Dear Reverend Mother*...A letter started, unfinished, left lying there.

Disturbed, she had gone over to the window, looked out. An ambulance was parked in front of the main convent, where Reverend Mother and the older nuns lived. Claire jerked open the window. The sweet smell of lilacs hung in the night air. Above the convent a full moon shone, tingeing the slate roof with silver light. The air against her cheeks as she stood there watching felt gently warm, like a loving hand.

The ambulance moved down the street. No siren sounded.

This was the climax. There had been a narrative, but Claire knew only bits and pieces, not enough to make a satisfying story. This last piece—the ambulance, the darkness, the body on the stretcher, the white-coated attendants, the figure of Sister Marianne, community infirmarian, standing in the doorway of the convent with another nun (Reverend Mother?) and finally, the ambulance taking off down the street—had an ominous feel to it. Claire went back downstairs to her own room with a shadow on her heart. She wouldn't know for sure what had happened until the next morning, when she read the note on the refectory bulletin board: *Please pray for Sister Dolores. She is in the hospital.*

In the hospital. One never knew what that meant. What *kind* of hospital?

They had taught at the same college for three years. They had studied together in graduate school for one year. They had shared time in the novitiate. There were gaps, years unshared. Yet crucial times in the cauldron of formation they had gone through, survived, together. They were not intimate friends. They were sisters. And Sister Dolores had always been kind and generous, sensitive to the needs of others. She was a person who kept a promise, came through.

After that first summer at Elk River, her problem had become more and more evident, though no one in the community spoke of it.

Day after day, in most of the free hours of the day, she was to be found sitting outside the superior's office, waiting. This was a busy community of eighty nuns, many engaged in teaching at the college. No one had time to sit by the hour outside the superior's office. Only Sister Dolores. She was there before class in the morning. At midday she could be seen there, sometimes with a book on her lap. After school hours, if she was not busy advising a student activity, she sat there. Sometimes she was saying her rosary, other times simply sitting. And in the evening, after night prayer, before she returned to the girls' dormitory, she could be found there.

Obviously, she was troubled.

"Now," says Laura LeMonde, "I understand that in many convents there were aberrations... lesbianism, alcoholism, whatever..."

WHY is she calling lesbianism an aberration? thinks Claire.

"Would you care to comment on that, Judith? Was that your experience?"

Judith is smart. "I would say," she begins, "that there were proportionately no more aberrations inside the convent than outside. There will always be cases where one seeks compensation... through drink, whatever. It could be a lonely life." She adds, "Even though it was a community, or was supposed to be a community."

Claire feels disinclined to comment. The camera facing them has taken on strange, ominous weight. If she speaks, she'll say too much.

Let me tell you about a nun who stood by the clothesline and wouldn't dare use a tampon, she'll say. She watches Laura LeMonde prance about the audience. *Let me tell you how she was carried out one night to the mental hospital, how they put her through shock treatments, how she returned hollowed out, how I never saw her afterward until she appeared at my house one December evening twenty-two years later... Let me tell you what I felt, what I saw.*

You want aberrations? I'll give you aberrations.

Frances and her new husband never came to breakfast. Around two o'clock that afternoon they arrived in the kitchen, a bit sheepish. Hungry. Ready for whatever Claire could concoct for them.

They were in a hurry. Fran was, perhaps, embarrassed. It was hard to tell. She still carried traces of the old resolute smile. Still the same shell—protectiveness? self-doubt? virtue? scrupulosity?—that one could never really break through. And perhaps, anyway, that wouldn't have been a good thing. There had been enough breaking. That was clear.

Claire offered them grilled cheese sandwiches, a salad, fancy cookies from a tin. She asked no questions. If Fran wanted to talk, she'd find a way.

Tell me, she wanted to ask. *How is it? Are you okay? How is marriage? Are you afraid? Does he treat you well? Is he a boor? A bore? Were you a fool?*

She said none of this.

She was a perfect hostess.

There are stories we never tell.

I don't mind lying to her, said Anna's note to her friend. *I only mind that I can't share. That she never tells me any stories like other mothers do.*

Why don't we tell them? What keeps us back, makes us hold them in? Is it the fear that there's no one to hear?

Laura LeMonde is untroubled by such a scruple.

Look at her now as, into the last segment of her show, she cruises through the audience with her microphone, looking for raised hands. "Come now," she says. "Some of you must have questions. I want a question, a comment, Ah, here's one!"

A thin woman in a yellow coat. Loose mousey hair falls about her thin face. She brushes it out of her eyes as she speaks into the mike Laura holds before her like a chalice to catch the golden question.

"I'd just like to say to you all," says the woman, her voice shaking, "that I'm in awe of you. I think we all are. You've done something with your lives. You took a risk, made a commitment. And most of us, in the rush of everyday, don't ever do that—"

Claire feels like vomiting. She leans forward to interrupt.

"I want to answer you," she says loudly, distinctly. "Why do you insist on making us *different*? Can't you see there's more that joins us than separates us?" The woman is listening, shaking her head. "We've put ourselves together today to be on TV, we're up here separated from you, but really, underneath it all, we have the same problems as you. We just had a certain chance and a certain kind of conditioning. Three of us chose to leave that life. One of us remained in. But we're still women, all of us, we're still more like you than different. We're still human beings."

The woman is stubborn in her point of view.

"No," she says. "You've done something."

"My younger sister," says Rachel quietly, "has two small children. When I visit her, I see what an opportunity I had, in one sense. I had the time to reflect, to consider my life, to *look* at it. That's a real luxury. Most women, especially those who have a family and are also working at a job outside their homes, simply don't have time."

The woman is nodding. "That's it," she agrees. "But you took the opportunity. You *did something*."

One afternoon in the February before Sister Dolores was taken away, a few months before Claire left the Order forever, they met in one of the classroom buildings. Sister Dolores was coming out of class. She looked haggard. She stopped Sister Claire, muttered something to her.

"Pardon?"

Even here, away from the convent, Sister Dolores was using the silence tone, a tone usually reserved for after Great Silence or within the convent walls. Sister Claire was struck by a look of desperation in her sister's eyes.

"I said, could—could I see you for a few moments?"

"Sure. Where?"

They looked about.

"Maybe down the hall in the faculty office room?"

This was a large room for the use of younger faculty, with ten desks spaced equidistant from each other. It was Friday afternoon. No one would be there.

They went down the corridor, pushed open the heavy door. Empty.

They went to a far corner and sat down. Or Sister Claire did. Sister Dolores remained standing.

"What's up?"

"It's just that...well, she's refusing to see me."

Sister Dolores looked around nervously, anxious that she might be overheard. "She?"

"Reverend Mother."

Sister Claire saw Sister Dolores's left eye begin to quiver. Would she start to cry?

"Sit down," she said, pointing to the chair beside the desk. "She can't refuse to see you. Superiors are required to see any subject who asks to see them. How do you know she refuses?"

She was, of course, well aware of the hourly vigils Sister Dolores kept by Reverend Mother's closed doors. One could only guess what went on between the two of them. This was a matter too intimate, too private, to probe. Superiors were bound to hold their subjects' confidences as sacred.

"I write her a note and she doesn't answer," said Sister Dolores, finally relenting and placing herself on the edge of the chair by the desk. "I knock on the door and she doesn't answer. I waited for four hours yesterday. She never opened her door. I just don't know what to do." Her hands rested on her black lap. The cuticle was bitten raw.

Claire could think of nothing to say, nothing to do. Blank. She did not trust this superior. She couldn't say that. First of all, it would not be comprehended. Second of all, why inflict her own doubts on another? Pain and bafflement were writ too large on Sister Dolores's fair features.

"Maybe she's just busy."

Lame. They both knew it.

"But...but...you don't understand," sobbed Sister Dolores. "I have to see her. The voices tell me—"

"Voices?" asked Sister Claire quietly. This was definitely out of her depth.

Sister Dolores nodded. Tears were running down her cheeks, falling onto her plastic guimpe. Sister Claire fished in her deep pocket for a handkerchief as she listened. "Yes. Voices. They tell me when I'm doing wrong. They tell me to see Reverend Mother. That she is the only one who can guide me. She is my superior. She is the voice of God in my life. This is the only way I'll grow perfect in obedience."

Sister Claire looked at her watch. Matins would begin in five minutes. She handed the handkerchief to Sister Dolores.

"Look," she said. "We've got to go to chapel. Clean up. You're a mess."

Sister Dolores tried a brave smile and began to wipe her face.

Sister Claire felt inadequate. A betrayer. No friend at all. Here was a need she could never meet. If she said what she really thought it would be destructive. There was no way she could make a genuinely helpful remark. The only thing to do, it seemed to her, was nothing.

"We've got to go," she said. "But listen, if I can ever *do* anything, even just listen, I will," she added, as the two of them stood.

The door swung open. A small bearded man in jeans and a sweatshirt entered. Mr. Stenson, the art teacher. "Oops, sorry."

"That's okay," said Sister Claire quickly. "We're just leaving."

"Seen Harry around?" asked Mr. Stenson.

"No, we haven't."

"Thanks. Sorry to disturb." With a quick last look, Mr. Stenson was gone. And so were they — over to chapel for Matins, supper, recreation.

A few days later the midnight meetings began.

Incredible as it now seems, the dormitory had a nightly curfew then. Lights were to go out by eleven o'clock. Sister Claire could remember when, back in her days as a college student, curfew had been even earlier. A master switch was pulled at ten o'clock. Gone the days of those extremes, thank God. Time marches on. In these days, the early sixties, students would be roaming around until midnight or after, disdaining curfew. They did try to be quiet, however.

Sister Claire and Sister Dolores were both "Corridor Mothers," nuns who lived in the dorms with the girls as advisors, overseers, surrogate mothers. They stayed up late preparing classes every night. The desperate plea of Sister Dolores, her reference to "voices," her hour-long vigils, her evident distress of spirit, haunted Sister Claire. After midnight, impelled by a sense of impending disaster she couldn't name, she'd often climb the stairs to Sister Dolores's third-floor room.

In her black bathrobe, ready for bed, her head covered with her night veil, Sister Claire crept up the worn stone steps quietly, hoping not to meet students. Her slippers made no sound and she wore no rosary beads, so she travelled stealthily. A gentle knock on the door.

Sister Dolores would be at her small desk studying, perhaps, or writing a long note to Reverend Mother. Sometimes she was already in bed.

"How'd it go today?"

Sister Claire knew her coming might pose a conscience problem for Sister Dolores. Technically, in Great Silence time, one was to speak only necessary words. What was "necessary"? Clearly, Sister Dolores, whose whole being these days projected a certain hopelessness, needed help. Someone to hear her. That, at least. Week by week she grew thinner. She was visibly nervous. A few girls had questioned Sister Claire about her, wondering if Sister Dolores were sick. Her face had grown so thin her headdress hung loose against her cheeks.

Yes, having a visitor at midnight might trouble her conscience. What wouldn't? Clearly, Sister Dolores was past the power to choose her own poison.

"I'm okay," she might say. Or, as on one night Claire particularly remembers, she might burst out crying. More and more, she was given to crying late at night. "She still won't see me," she'd sob. "She says she has no time to see me. She's ordered me to stay away. How can I stay away if she is to tell me what is obedience? How can I know the right thing to do?"

The situation seemed crazy to Sister Claire. Yet, looked at from one angle, quite understandable. Sister Dolores had never been one to compromise. She took things to extremes, even in the novitiate. Always, though, to her own pain. She had absorbed to the finest jot and tittle the lessons of humility and obedience. She was ruined. No doubt a secular analyst would have a fancy name, perhaps even a cure for her condition. The term scruples, however, seemed accurate enough. A deadly disease of the spirit.

The stakes were high. Sister Claire sensed that. That's why she climbed the stairs at midnight so often. Yet she couldn't see just what to do. It seemed impossible to say: "This obsession is nuts. You need to free yourself of it."

Because she couldn't. That was clear.

So Sister Claire would stay with her, hear her out for half an hour, an hour, and wonder just where it would end.

Until the midnight of the ambulance, the body strapped to a board, the white-coated attendants, the shining silvering moon...

That was all Claire knew.

"You've done something with your life," said the woman in the audience. Admiration filled her voice. "You've *done something*."

There came one more scene—brief, troubling, electrifying—a week after Sister Dolores disappeared.

After dinner at noon the nuns would file through the long parlour into chapel to recite their *Miserere* before recreation. Not all of them could stay for recreation, of course. During the week many had duties elsewhere on campus. Most, however, could manage time for the brief chapel visit.

Sister Claire, as one of the younger nuns, was near the end of the line that day as they were filing toward chapel.

As she entered the long parlour, a sedately appointed room where, on reunion weekend, alumnae were treated to high tea by the nuns, she felt a tap on her arm and heard a whisper: "Sister Claire."

She looked up.

And stepped out of the line to face her superior.

Reverend Mother's face was almost purple. Her eyes—a bright penetrating blue—burned with anger. She didn't touch Sister Claire. She stood there with her hands hidden in her black sleeves, almost hissing as she spoke.

"Sister," she said in a low voice, struggling for control, "I want the truth."

Ah, the implication of it.

Sister Claire flinched inwardly. "Yes, Reverend Mother."

"When did you call Sister Dolores's mother?"

Blank. Utter blank.

"I didn't, Reverend Mother. I don't know what you're talking about."

"Don't lie to me, Sister. I want to know when you called Mrs. O'Neill."

"I did not call Sister Dolores's mother, Reverend Mother."

If she stood there another instant she'd say too much. What was the point? Clearly she wouldn't be believed. Sister Claire turned on her heel, away from that contorted face, started to leave, then wheeled back for a moment to face her superior. "I'm only sorry, Reverend Mother, that I never even thought of doing it."

As Reverend Mother opened her mouth to reply, Sister Claire wheeled away again and headed through the long parlour toward chapel.

She was furious.

Furious with Reverend Mother. Furious with Sister Dolores. Furious with herself. Because it had never once occurred to her to do that. Because obviously someone else had had the wits, the good sense. Thank God! Someone else had found a way to bring to light the hidden condition Sister Claire had seen and felt for months, but found no way to deal with. Someone else had taken action. Such a simple action. So obvious, if you thought about it.

And so necessary. No doubt about that.

But she, Sister Claire, for all her well-intended listening and praying, for all her supposed smarts, for all her wariness and calculation, had never once thought of calling Sister Dolores's mother.

Oh, there were stories afterward: how Mrs. O'Neill was enraged that the family had never been notified until Sister Dolores was hospitalized, diagnosed, already under treatment — but what did they expect? She'd left their life, put that world behind her. How the family made trouble for Reverend Mother — but how much trouble could they really make? Sister Dolores had merely sought a way to obey. Someone to obey. How Sister Dolores, returned from the hospital some eight months later, a shell of her former self (what exactly did that mean?), had been sent to do bookkeeping in an academy far away from the college.

By that time, Claire herself had terminated her connection with that life, that place, that set of questions.

Four weeks later, the promised video of the *Laura LeMonde Show* arrives. They're all in the living room viewing it: Jim, Anna, Jerry, Claire. Jim has made a fire in the fireplace and the room feels cozy as the logs crackle and he fiddles with the TV to get a perfect picture. Anna is on the chesterfield beside Claire, nestled in beneath an afghan. Jerry, sitting cross-legged on the floor in front of them, is stuffing his face with fresh popcorn. "Gotta have stuff to eat for the show," he said. Chomp chomp.

"Laura LeMonde is a pretty ditsy specimen," says Jim, adjusting the light on the picture. She's already into segment three. "Think she could tolerate a serious thought?"

"Anyone with her legs," says Anna, "wouldn't need a serious thought."

Anna wears a T-shirt tonight that should be in the ragbag. The Eighties look. When she appeared at breakfast with it on, having silently rescued it from the Sally Ann bag, Claire concentrated on swallowing her coffee. All things are passing.

Anna leans forward, takes a handful of popcorn, crams it into her mouth.

Tonight Claire sees, more clearly than ever, that the whole Laura LeMonde thing was a mistake. Her idealism run amok again. As if this dumb show could reveal anything. Accomplish anything. But it's over. On tape forever. And little damage done. Certainly no good.

She feels her daughter's body, warm and solid, beside her on the chesterfield. They haven't said much to each other since her return from Toronto. Anna appears to be in a pretty good mood tonight. Maybe the popcorn, maybe just being here, in the warm room, with them, no pressures on her. Who knows?

Her T-shirt has a jagged gash near the right shoulder.

As she slips out from under the afghan again to lean forward, stretch her arm over Jerry's shoulder and scoop up another handful of popcorn, Claire catches a glimpse of purple and yellow through the gash.

It all comes back: Sister Dolores, the tampon, the hot day, the refusal to break the hymen. The board, the attendants, the desperation, the surrender of self.

Suddenly she thinks, *I'll tell her. Tomorrow. I'll tell Anna about Sister Dolores and the hymen. The whole damn story. Surely something of it can be communicated. I'll tell her how absurd I thought it was. I'll tell her about Dolores being carried out to an ambulance in the dead of night. I'll even tell her about the voices. . . . I'll tell her about the young men with the binoculars. About trying to figure out how to use a tampon. About the innocence of Mother Josefa. I'll tell her everything.*

Maybe she won't understand a word of it. Maybe she'll even laugh.

But I'll tell her. I'll give it a try. Take my time and spread it all out before her.

If she laughs, what of it?

Something may sink in.

Who am I to know?

Acknowledgements

The editors would like to thank Peter S. Hawkins and Paula J. Carlson. It was reading *Listening for God: Contemporary Literature and the Life of Faith* some fifteen years ago that sowed the seed of this book. The early advice of experienced anthologistsWanda Campbell and Priscila Uppal spared us from making any number of mistakes, though we did manage to be quite inventive in making many on our own. To Bethany Gibson at Goose Lane Editions, huge thanks for plying those secret editorial arts with such patience and wisdom.

Mark would like to thank Loren Wilkinson and Maxine Hancock for their inspiration, and friends Trevor Tucker, Andrew Steeves, Mike Janz, Dan Steeves, Dave Langille, Heather Price, Tom Balke, Dave Harris and Mat Cupido for each finding their unique ways to connect the arts and spirituality. Thanks, too, to Emily Pond, Adrienne Hope and Laura Harris for their careful reading of manuscripts.

Andrew would like to thank Peter Erb and Benjamin Lefebvre for their encouragement, and his English students at Laurier Brantford for keeping him on his toes.

The editors and publisher are grateful for kind permission to reprint the following stories in *Running the Whale's Back: Stories of Faith and Doubt from Atlantic Canada*.

"Miracles" excerpted from *Flesh and Blood* by Michael Crummey copyright © 2003 by Michael Crummey Ink, reprinted by permission of Doubleday Canada, Anne McDermid & Associates and Michael Crummey; "The Accident" from *The Story So Far...* by Sheldon Currie copyright © 1997 by Sheldon Currie, reprinted by permission of Breton Books; "Salvation" from *From a High Thin Wire* by Joan Clark copyright © 1982, 2004 by Joan Clark, reprinted by arrangement of the Cooke Agency; "We, Who Have Never Suffered" from *Dancers at Night* by David Adams

Richards copyright © 1978 by David Adams Richards, reprinted by permission of Oberon Press; "Two Crosses" from *The Flesh So Close* by Kenneth J. Harvey copyright © 1998 by Kenneth J. Harvey, reprinted by permission of Kenneth J. Harvey; "Miracle Potatoes" from *The Priest's Boy* by Clive Doucet copyright © 1992 by Clive Doucet, reprinted by permission of Black Moss Press; "Discovery" by Deborah Joy Corey copyright © 1999 by Deborah Joy Corey, reprinted by permission of Deborah Joy Corey; "Cave Paintings" excerpted from *Fall On Your Knees* by Ann-Marie MacDonald copyright © 1996 by Ann-Marie MacDonald, reprinted by permission of Knopf Canada, and Jonathan Cape Ltd.; "The Priest and the Pallbearer" from *An Arch for the King* by Michael Hennessey copyright © 1984 by Michael Hennessey, reprinted by permission of Michael Hennessey; "Vision" excerpted from *Island: The Collected Stories of Alistair MacLeod* by Alistair MacLeod copyright © 2000 by Alistair MacLeod, reprinted by permission of McClelland & Stewart and Jonathan Cape Ltd.; "Batter My Heart" excerpted from *Play the Monster Blind* by Lynn Coady copyright © 2000 by Lynn Coady, reprinted by permission of Doubleday Canada and Lynn Coady; "Doves" by Carol Bruneau copyright © 2005 by Carol Bruneau, reprinted by permission of Carol Bruneau; "My Husband's Jump" from *Making Light of Tragedy* by Jessica Grant copyright © 2004 by Jessica Grant, reprinted by permission of Porcupine's Quill; "Running the Whale's Back" from *A Blessed Snarl* by Samuel Thomas Martin copyright © 2012 by Samuel Thomas Martin, reprinted by permission of Breakwater Books; "The Shadow Side of Grace" from *The Shadow Side of Grace* by Michelle Butler Hallett copyright © 2006 by Michelle Butler Hallett, reprinted by permission of Creative Book Publishing, St. John's, NL; "Stay the Way You Are" from *Creaking in Their Skins* by Michael Winter copyright © 1994 by Michael Winter, reprinted by permission of Anne McDermid & Associates; "The Flowers of Bermuda" by D.R. MacDonald copyright © 1988 by D.R. MacDonald, reprinted by permission of D.R. MacDonald; "French Doors" from *boYs* by Kathleen Winter copyright © 2007 by Kathleen Winter, reprinted by permission of Biblioasis; and "Rupture" from *Strange Bodies on a Stranger Shore* by Ann Copeland copyright © 1994 by Ann Copeland, reprinted by permission of Ann Copeland.

The Authors

Carol Bruneau hails from Halifax. The author of two short story collections and three novels, her first novel, *Purple for Sky*, won the Dartmouth Book Award for Fiction and the Thomas H. Raddall Atlantic Fiction Award in 2001, while her most recent novel, *Glass Voices*, was a *Globe and Mail* Best Book of 2007.

Joan Clark was born in Liverpool, Nova Scotia, and currently resides in Newfoundland. She is the author of five novels including *The Victory of Geraldine Gull*, which won the 1998 Canadian Authors Association Award. She has also written award-winning books for children and two short story collections including *From a High Thin Wire*.

Lynn Coady now lives in Edmonton, though she was born and raised in Cape Breton. She has published a collection of short stories, *Play the Monster Blind*, and four novels. Her first novel, *Strange Heaven*, was nominated for the 1998 Governor General's Award for Fiction, while her latest novel, *The Antagonist*, was shortlisted for the 2011 Scotiabank Giller Prize.

Ann Copeland currently lives in Oregon. For twenty-six years a resident of New Brunswick, Copeland's short stories have appeared in *Best Canadian Short Stories* and *The Best American Short Stories*. She has written six collections of short stories, including two linked story collections that feature Claire Delaney: *The Golden Thread*, a finalist for the 1990 Governor General's Award for Fiction, and *Strange Bodies on a Stranger Shore*.

Deborah Joy Corey has lived much of her life in New Brunswick and in neighbouring Maine. Her first novel, *Losing Eddie*, won the W.H. Smith/*Books in Canada* First Novel Award. She is also the author of the novel *The Skating Pond,* and she was recently awarded the Stella Kupferberg Memorial Short Story Prize by the radio program *Selected Shorts*.

Michael Crummey is a native of Newfoundland, a poet, short story writer and novelist. His short story collection is titled *Flesh and Blood*. The most recent of his three novels, *Galore*, was a finalist for the Governor General's Award for Fiction and the winner of the 2010 Commonwealth Writers' Prize for Best Novel.

Sheldon Currie was a professor of English at St. Francis Xavier University. He is the author of two short story collections and four novels. The film *Margaret's Museum* was based on one of his short stories. His short fiction has appeared in *Best Canadian Short Stories*. His most recent novel, *Two More Solitudes*, was a finalist for the 2011 Dartmouth Book Award for Fiction.

Clive Doucet is a well-known city councillor in Ottawa. His first novel, *Disneyland Please*, was shortlisted for the W.H. Smith/*Books in Canada* First Novel Award. He is the author of three other novels and the linked short story collection *The Priest's Boy*. His non-fiction works include *Lost and Found in Acadie* and *My Grandfather's Cape Breton*.

Jessica Grant is a native of St. John's. She is the author of the novel *Come, Thou Tortoise*, which won the 2009 Winterset Award and the Amazon.ca/*Books in Canada* First Novel Award. Her short story collection, *Making Light of Tragedy*, includes a story which won the McClelland & Stewart Journey Prize for 2003.

Michelle Butler Hallett calls St. John's home. She has published one short story collection, *The Shadow Side of Grace*, and three novels, *Double-blind, Sky Waves* and *Deluded Your Sailors*.

Kenneth J. Harvey lives in the outport of Burnt Head, Cupids, in Newfoundland. In addition to being a filmmaker and poet, he is the author of many novels, including *Inside*, winner of the 2006 Winterset Award and the Rogers Writers' Trust Fiction Prize, and numerous short story collections, including *The Flesh So Close*.

Michael Hennessey calls Charlottetown his home. He is the author of two short story collections, *An Arch for the King* and *My Broken Hero*. His novel, *The Betrayer*, is featured in Trevor Adams and Stephen Cole's *Atlantic Canada's 100 Greatest Books*.

Ann-Marie MacDonald is a playwright, novelist and actor who lives in Toronto. Her first novel, *Fall on Your Knees,* became an international bestseller, while her second novel, *The Way the Crow Flies,* was a finalist for the 2003 Scotiabank Giller Prize.

D.R. MacDonald was born in Cape Breton but mostly grew up in the United States. He has received two Pushcart Prizes and an O. Henry Award for his short fiction. The author of three novels, his most recent novel, *Anna from Away,* won the 2013 Dartmouth Book Award for Fiction.

Alistair MacLeod was born in Saskatchewan but was raised in Cape Breton. He has published three short story collections: *The Lost Salt Gift of Blood, As Birds Bring Forth the Sun,* and *Island: The Collected Stories.* His novel, *No Great Mischief,* won many honours including the Trillium Award for Fiction, the Thomas H. Raddall Atlantic Fiction Award and the International IMPAC Dublin Literary Award.

Samuel Thomas Martin lives in Orange City, Iowa, where he is a Professor of Creative Writing at Northwestern College. His short story collection, *This Ramshackle Tabernacle,* was nominated for the 2010 Winterset Award. He published his first novel, *A Blessed Snarl,* in 2012.

David Adams Richards is a resident of Fredericton and is one of only three Canadian writers who have won Governor General's Awards for Fiction and Non-Fiction. His novel *Mercy Among the Children* won the 2000 Scotiabank Giller Prize, while his most recent novel, *Incidents in the Life of Marcus Paul,* won the 2012 Thomas H. Raddall Atlantic Fiction Award.

Kathleen Winter is a long-time resident of St. John's who currently lives in Montreal. Her first novel, *Annabel,* achieved the distinction of being a finalist for all three of Canada's major literary awards for fiction: the Scotiabank Giller Prize, the Governor General's Award and the Rogers Writers' Trust Fiction Prize. She is also the author of the short story collection *boYs,* which won the 2007 Winterset Award.

Michael Winter divides his time between Toronto and St. John's. His first novel, *This All Happened,* won the inaugural Winterset Award in 2000. His latest novel, *The Life and Death of Donna Whalen,* was shortlisted for the 2010 Rogers Writers' Trust Fiction Prize. He is also the author of two short story collections, including *Creaking in Their Skins.*